P9-DIJ-950

More Praise for *Dancing With Werewolves*

"[T]his fantastic first of a new paranormal series might not be a shocker for urban fantasy fans . . . Douglas handles the premise with such spectacular style, it feels fresh . . . Douglas spices the action with fabulous characters: Quicksilver, Delilah's protective dog; CinSims (Cinema Simulacrums), dead celebrities recreated via science and magic; the oldest living vampire in Vegas, once a famous aviator; and Cocaine (aka Snow), a devilish albino rocker. Readers will eagerly await the sequel." **(Starred Review)**

—*Publishers Weekly*

"With a brilliant eye for detail, Ms. Nelson Douglas demonstrates her creative talents with a captivating storyline and some of the most unique supporting characters around. This is truly a fantastic start to a series that paranormal romance readers are sure to enjoy."

—*Darque Reviews*

"This is a smartly written, plot-driven, original novel that deftly combines the elements of fantasy, mystery, and romance to the well sated delight of the reader. *Dancing With Werewolves* is enthusiastically recommended."

—*Midwest Review of Books*

"Carole Nelson Douglas's writing is crisp and edgy. Delilah's voice came through loud and clear, a perfect mix of hard-nosed reporter and small town girl. She's a likable character, the kind you would quickly become a best friends with. *Dancing With Werewolves* is a wonderful addition to the paranormal genre and I can only hope that we'll be seeing Delilah again."

—*BlogCritics*

"[M]ystery meets paranormal with a touch of romance and intrigue added."

—*Scooper*

More Praise for *Dancing With Werewolves*

"What a thrill ride! . . . *Dancing With Werewolves* is a fascinating combination of romance, mystery, fantasy, and paranormal. . . . Douglas has definitely created a character and a setting that will keep readers coming back for more."

—The Romance Reader

"Award-winning Douglas turns her hand to the urban fantasy genre, creating a savvy and highly inquisitive new heroine. This first-person narrative follows Delilah Street's journey into a creepy and dangerous new world, where telling friend from foe is not so easy. A wild new ride!"

—Romantic Times Book Reviews

"In a genre that's quickly filling with authors left and right, Nelson brings a fresh and sassy voice to Delilah Street . . . Vegas has always been considered a bit strange, but in this alternative world, werewolves are literally running the town. Besides the werewolves, there are a few witches and other not quite humans that keep the plot moving and full of surprises. . . . an odd blend of urban fantasy and film noir that is brought to life under the talented pen . . . hum . . . keyboard of Ms. Douglas."

—ParaNormalRomance.org

". . . one of the smoothest and most satisfying of the current flood of contemporary paranormal romances or whatever the category is calling itself these days. A second adventure is already in the works and I'm sure it will be a good one."

—Don D'Ammassa

"A great read."

—Curled Up With a Good Book

By Carole Nelson Douglas

FANTASY

Delilah Street, Paranormal Investigator
Dancing with Werewolves
Brimstone Kiss
Vampire Sunrise (forthcoming)

Sword and Circlet: Irissa and Kendric
Six of Swords
Exiles of the Rynth
and other titles

MYSTERY SERIES

Midnight Louie, Feline PI
Catnap
Cat in a Sapphire Slipper
and other titles

Irene Adler Sherlockian Suspense
Good Night, Mr. Holmes
and other titles

Delilah Street, Paranormal Investigator
Book Two

BRIMSTONE KISS

Carole Nelson Douglas

JUNO

BRIMSTONE KISS

ISBN: 978-0-8095-7304-2

Juno Books
Rockville, MD
www.juno-books.com

For the wonderful writers who welcomed Delilah to the paranormal fold with generous cover quotes: Heather Graham, Sherrilyn Kenyon, Nancy Pickard and Rebecca York

Meet Me, Delilah Street

Everyone has family issues but I have only one: that I don't have any family. My fresh new business card reads *Delilah Street, Paranormal Investigator*, but my old personal card could read *Delilah Street, Unadoptable Orphan*.

I was supposedly named after the street where I was found abandoned as an infant in Wichita, Kansas. (I guess I should just thank God and DC Comics it wasn't Lois Lane.) Of course, I've Googled and Groggled (the drinking person's search engine) the World Wide Web for Delilah Streets and not a single bloody one of them is to be found in Kansas.

Whoever my forebears, they gave me the Black Irish, Snow White coloring that is catnip to vampires: corpse-pale skin and dead-of-night-black hair. By the time I turned twelve I was fighting off aspiring juvie rapists with retractable fangs and body odor that mixed blood, sweat and semen. Really made me enjoy being a girl.

My growing-up years of group homes in Wichita are history now that I'm twenty-four and on my own. I had a good job as a reporter covering the paranormal beat for WTCH-TV in Kansas—until a jealous weather witch forecaster forced me out. Now I freelance as an investigator in wicked, mysterious post-Millennium Revelation Las Vegas. Vegas was wicked, of course, long before the turn of the twenty-first century brought all the bogeymen and women of myth and legends out of the closet and into human lives and society. Now it is 2013 and Vegas is crawling with half-vamps and half-weres and all-werewolf mobs and celebrity zombies and who-knows-what-else *un*human.

My ambitions are simple:

One: Staying alive. (Being turned into an immortal vampire doesn't count.)

Two: Being able to make love in the missionary position without having panic attacks. (Whoever thought someone would *aim* for the missionary position?) Position hadn't been an issue until recently and neither had sex, but now I've finally found a man I *want* to make love with. Ex-FBI guy Ricardo Montoya—a.k.a. the Cadaver Kid—is tall, dark, handsome, Hispanic and my brand-new horizontal ambition. He has my back—and my front—at every opportunity.

And, three: Tracking down "Lilith Quince"—my spitting image—to find out if she is a twin, double, clone or whatever. Or even if she is alive. Seeing her/me being autopsied on *Crime Scene Instincts V: Las Vegas* one rerun TV night in Wichita brought me to Sin City in the first place.

Lucky me, Lilith turned out to be the most desirable corpse ever featured on the internationally franchised show. She had an early-exit contract to kill herself, so her star turn as a *CSI* corpse was supposedly a "Reality TV" dissection. (I knew Millennium Revelation pop culture and taste tended towards the dark—now I know *how* dark.) When the *CSI* cameras showed a discreet maggot camping out in a nostril that held a tiny blue topaz stud like my very own, Lilith's corpse was dubbed "Maggie" and a fantasy franchise was born. Maggie is the It Girl of 2013: Maggie dolls and merchandise are hot and so are bootleg Maggie films, out-takes and my hide, if anyone could snag it—dead or alive. One werewolf mobster almost did already.

Then comes ambition number four: Identifying the embracing skeletons Ric and I discovered in Vegas's Sunset Park just after I hit town and just before town hit me back, hard.

I have allies other than Ric helping me achieve my ambitions. One has heavenly blue eyes and is seriously gray and hairy. That's my dog, Quicksilver. He's a wolfhound-wolf cross I saved from death at the pound. He returns the favor with fang, claw and warm, paranormally talented tongue.

(I have a soft spot for dogs—especially since Achilles, my valiant little white Lhasa apso in Wichita, died from blood poisoning after biting a vampire. Achilles' ashes rest in a dragon-decorated urn on my mantel, but I haven't given up the ghost on him.)

That mantel is located in an Enchanted Cottage on the Hector Nightwine estate. Hector rents it to me cheap because, as producer of the many worldwide *CSI* franchises, he's presumably guilty of offing my possible twin on national TV.

When Hector's *CSI* show made Lilith Quince into a macabre international sex symbol, he inadvertently made me, Delilah Street—her twin, double, clone, simulacrum, whatever—a wanted woman. Not for myself alone, mind you, but for the naked and dead image of another woman, who may be dead, or not.

Hector has a profit motive rather than a conscience. He's banking on my finding Lilith or becoming her for his enduring financial benefit.

The only thing Hector and I have in common is loving vintage black-and-white films. The Enchanted Cottage is based on a setting from a 1945 movie. A shy-to-the-point-of-invisible staff of who-knows-what supernaturals run the place and I suspect it's supplied with the mirror from *Snow White*. Maybe it talks like the wicked step-mom's gabby glass but, so far, it's been mum with me. I just see dead people in it.

The most complicated beings in my brave new world are the CinSims. Cinema Simulacrums are created when fresh zombie bodies illegally imported from Mexico are blended with black-and-white film characters. The resulting "live" personas are wholly owned entertainment entities leased to various Vegas hotels.

Hector and Ric are sure the Immortality Mob is behind the brisk business in zombie CinSims, but can't prove it. Hector wants to wrest the CinSims from the mob's control into his. Ric aches to stop the traffic in illegally imported zombies. It's personal—he was forced to work in the trade as a child.

I'd like to help them both out—and not just because I'm a former investigative reporter crusading against human and inhuman exploitation. My own freedom is on the line from several merciless and downright repellent factions trying to make life after the Millennium Revelation literal Hell.

Luckily, I seem to have some off-the-chart abilities simmering myself, most of them having to do with the silver from the silver nitrate in mirror backings, black-and-white films and reflective surfaces.

Which reminds me—I have one more sorta sidekick: a freaky little shape-changing lock of hair from the albino rock star who owns the Inferno Hotel. The guy goes by at least three names: *Christophe,* for business; *Cocaine,* when fronting his Seven Deadly Sins rock band; and *Snow* to his intimates. I seem to be considered an intimate, but don't want to be.

The long white lock of hair became a sterling silver familiar that transforms itself into various pieces of often-protective (and always attractive) jewelry. It's handy at times, but I also consider it a variety of talisman-cum-leech.

I've been called a "silver medium," but I don't aim to be medium at anything. I won't do things halfway. I intend to succeed at finding out who I really am, and who's been bad and who's been good in my new Millennium Revelation neighborhood.

Chapter One

NOT EVERY modern career girl can have her rented house blown away by a jealous weather witch in Kansas one week and end up in the post-Millennium Las Vegas sleeping in an Enchanted Cottage the next.

But, as Disney says: *fairy tales can come true, it can happen to you*, and it had happened to me, Delilah Street, forever orphan and ex-WTCH-TV reporter.

The Enchanted Cottage is a charming little place from the 1945 film of that name. Robert Young played a pilot disfigured in World War II and Dorothy McGuire portrayed a plain shy spinster. They find sanctuary and happily-ever-after love in a cottage just like mine.

But this is not the 1940s and films are no longer made in black and white—unless the director is trying to be retro or pretentious or both. And nobody knows who Robert Young and Dorothy McGuire were except film buffs like me and my new boss, Hector Nightwine, producer of the internationally franchised *CSI V* forensic TV shows.

For a number of reasons, my life in the Las Vegas of 2013 isn't worth a five-dollar chip from Cesar Cicereau's Gehenna Hotel and Casino. Fortunately, though, I'm worth a lot to Hector. So, here I am in a pseudo-quaint cottage on the grounds of Nightwine's Fort-Knox-secure Sunset Road estate, surrounded by Hobbity English charm mixed with high-tech convenience. I am tucked under an eiderdown comforter in a high four-poster bed with gargoyles carved onto the posts while a Jacuzzi tub in the adjoining bathroom softly gurgles me to sleep.

Surely none of my half-vampire bullyboy nightmares will come home to roost in this place. It's as safe as fairy tales and Nightwine's state-of-the-art security technology can make it.

Even so, I was not quite sleeping, just snuggling into the thousand-thread-count sheets, when I heard a scratching at my second-story casement windows.

Fruit trees and blossom-bearing vines grow around my Enchanted Cottage as thick as Sleeping Beauty's thorny forest. A stray vine was probably blowing against the window glass. I opened my eyes to stare up at the peaked white-plaster ceiling. A small shifting shadow danced there in rhythm with the exterior scratching.

Had a cat climbed the vines and was now trying to get in?

I was warmer than a toasted English muffin from my formerly cold feet to the top of my brunet head. This may be Las Vegas, but I'm cold-natured. My feet and hands never seem to get warm enough at night. Now, though, they finally were.

So I didn't want to get up.

From the stairs came the faint whiff of dinner's garlic chicken. I seldom saw the kitchen witch who came with the property, along with the yard troll and the garden pixies and who knew what else, but she could bake fragrant loaves of crusty bread in the wood stove as readily as she could nuke a frozen Weight Watchers entrée in the microwave.

I wasn't crazy about the garlic odor from that night's homemade dish, but I was comforted to hear my awesomely large wolfhound-wolf-cross dog wheezing in sleep from one of the downstairs rooms. This was not one of Quicksilver's frequent solo nights out on the town that never shuts down. I figure adopting him doesn't give me a lock on his nocturnal need to patrol and rock and roll with his kind.

I wriggled deeper into the warm covers, but the insinuating snare-drum rhythm of that exterior scratching kept me from sliding into sleep. It could be a kitten caught up a tree, clinging there, helpless . . .

Forcing myself to sit up, I shivered at an inrush of air-conditioned air and put my bare feet to the icy wooden floor. My sleep-T hem snarled in the covers as I got out of bed, almost tripping me. I moved toward the pair of windows.

A Rorschach blot of black was indeed pressed to the window glass. It was as big as my spread hand, with four clinging limbs and a bigger head. It looked like a starfish shadow.

I stumbled nearer and squinted to make it out in the dark. Surely, a young kitten—but why wasn't it mewing up a storm as cats do when trapped up so high? Only when a squeal revealed rows of tiny fangs did I realize that my visitor was a bat.

Naturally, I squealed a bit too.

Mind you, I'm a former TV news reporter, an intrepid investigator of rural phenomena like cattle mutilations. One midsummer night's window-clinging bat shouldn't set me screeching.

I reminded myself that bats were enormously useful consumers of insects and other pests and returned to bed, shuddering as my floor-cooled feet found the sheets already chilly. Even the slim silver chain on my wrist felt icy.

I snuggled stomach-down, curled up, and waited for sleep to find me.

Then I heard the rustling. *And the silken sad uncertain rustling of each purple curtain thrilled me, filled me with fantastic terrors never felt before . . .*

Damn! Why was my subconscious quoting Edgar Allan- Poe's "The Raven?"

Maybe because the rustling sounded like curtains and there weren't any curtains on my dormer windows. Or maybe because the rustling sounded like a big bird's wings . . .

'Tis the wind and nothing more!

If that mantra had worked for Poe's uneasy scholar it would work for me. I pulled the covers farther over my head.

The raven-size wing rustling increased to a California condor-size *woosh,* with a wingspread of, say, ten freaking feet. Only an idiot would ignore that kind of indoor tempest. This was no little lost bat or even a misplaced sparrow.

I sat up, turning the covers half down, and faced the windows. "All right!" I challenged the night.

Not all right, baby girl, whispered my internal invisible friend since childhood, Irma. *We are getting called on by more than Big Bird. We're not on Sesame Street anymore, Delilah.*

No. The room's temperature had dropped to meat-freezer cold and I was instantly afraid I was the meat. Post-Millennium Las Vegas teemed with things that went bump, stump, hump and slurp in the night.

I was appalled to see that the small shadow from the windowpane had moved inside to become a pillar of darkness draped in black, severe and funereal. I was almost getting used to seeing apparitions in the tall hall mirror, but not in thin air. Slowly, the head of the entity moved, lifted and the cloaked sides spread their wings.

Awe mated with my fear, and both held me frozen. A pale white face came into partial focus. Only cruel, slanting dark eyebrows and a gray grinning mouth were fully visible.

The black fell back, revealing an ash-gray satin lining framing a man's black evening suit of elegant antique cut. The vintage clothing collector in me couldn't help but admire the tailoring even as goose bumps ran races up and down my arms. The figure had no color at all, not even red around the eye whites.

Then I recognized my visitor from his many collectible photographs and posters.

I was beholding the most commercially potent incarnation of Dracula of all time: 1932's Bela Lugosi, slithering onscreen with Eastern Euro-trash swagger and Art Deco decadence. I recalled a few pre-adolescent longings to someday meet a classic vampire: suave, smooth and deliciously sinister. I hankered for any one of a dozen pop culture reinventions of the father of all vampires as a sex symbol. Bela Lugosi had a certain predatory hunger, but he wasn't the hunky anti-hero women would willingly welcome, swooning for his seductive suction action.

Lugosi was nasty. Not as nasty as the ancient devouring vamp in Bram Stoker's novel, but far from the lounge lizard, oral-sex fiend Frank Langella's portrayal had made women go crazy over a few decades back. Why do women always go for the bad boys? I sure hadn't liked the variety I fought off in the group homes.

I could think clearly, but sat paralyzed—just like all those passive silver-screen victims—my fingers curled into the sheets. At least this wasn't a debased half-vamp from the group homes. He was the *reel* thing, although not a Gollum-gaunt creature of the night like Nosferatu from the days of silent films. That scrawny, long-clawed leech and lech was all too reminiscent of the real-life crackpot Howard Hughes in his current undead state to conjure.

No, Bela Lugosi's slo-mo sinister diction may seem hokey today, but in person, gliding to your bedside, he was mesmerizing. He leaned in and down, showed only the tips of his pointed canine teeth, and lowered his gaze to drink in the sight of my bare neck.

By now my silver chain bracelet had subtly shimmied up my arm. Even as he ogled my throat, it looped itself into a solid wide dog collar around my neck, blocking all ports of entry.

"Bah," Dracula said, recoiling. "Cheesy silver trinket! I only wanted to take a tiny symbolic taste."

"Bad taste is never symbolic," I said, my fingers tracing the smooth, defensive form my silver familiar had taken. It never failed to surprise—and defend—me.

"My master wants you."

"Isn't that Renfield's line?" I didn't mean to be a smart-mouth; I was just surprised that Dracula would admit to a master. He *was* "the Master."

"Renfield's words may, regrettably, live on, but the bug-eater ended with that blasted film. The message I bear remains: You must come with me."

"Now?" I couldn't believe I was asking that question, like I might consider it some other day.

"No. Never," I corrected myself. "We know all about you these days. You can't reverse your surname and pretend to be some Transylvanian nobleman, 'Count Alucard'! This is not sleepy old England between the World Wars of the last century. This is post-Millennium Revelation America. We're all on to you."

"Perhaps, Miss Street, but you have tried to trick my master. He's had time to discover your name and profession. He could choose to crush you like one of that pathetic Renfield's bugs. Instead, he is magnanimous. He wishes to employ you. You call yourself a paranormal investigator, do you not?"

"Barely. I just phoned the Yellow Pages today to order the ad. It'll take ages to show up. How would your master, whoever he is, know that?"

"We . . . he knows many things through many means."

"And how'd you know where to find me?"

"All my kind know Hector Nightwine and his Sunset Road estate. You are becoming known as his creature," Dracula announced with loathing.

"His part-time private investigator! I'm nobody's creature. What have you got against Hector?" I was puzzled, because Nightwine was a known admirer of CinSims.

"He has leased all three of my brides." Dracula positively hissed the last word through his fangs. "I am denied all . . . access."

"Oh."

I had to admit that the trio of willowy train-dragging thirties femmes fatales made a pretty good girl back-up group for Drac. They were the only vampire chick role models I aspired to. I made the height requirement, being five-eight flat-footed, but not the weight one. Lean and hungry (i.e., anorexic) is definitely not my look. I'm a substantial girl, more hourglass than swizzle stick. Still, it'd be fun to slink around in fangs and furbelows.

"Enough chitchat. Come with me." He extended a graceful gray hand.

Well, adolescent me had wanted to meet a gentleman vampire of the old school and now here I had one.

Don't go, Irma urged. *You don't know where that walking corpse has been.*

"Do not be afraid," Dracula said in slow formal tones, noting my hesitancy. "These days I only drink from those who pay for the privilege. I am *the* resident attraction at the Love in Vein Social Club."

"Then what are you doing here tonight?"

"My master occasionally needs me mobile. The night has always been mine. Sometimes what he wants from me is what I also want for myself . . . a beautiful but shaken young woman, a midnight mission, an opportunity to stretch my wings and my reach, as of old. To be powerful. To be irresistible. You will come with me, Miss Delilah Street, because you must."

He leaned nearer. I inhaled the stale scent of cigar smoke and raw meat and old blood. Then he withdrew. I wondered if the chicken garlic on my breath was slapping him in the undead kisser. Good! But I had a feeling this was an offer I shouldn't refuse.

"Not so fast," I told him. "Not in this outfit do I go anywhere. Turn your back while I change clothes if you want me to go with you."

No! Irma was kicking up an internal storm. *You don't know where and you don't know who. You can't go.*

Irma was my alter ego, the psychological crutch of a lonely kid, I figured, but she could get bossy. I didn't feel the need to heed her at the moment. The King Vampire in this town had called on me for help, no matter how rudely he had put it or how seedy his operation. I had to live up to my new business card: Delilah Street, P.I.

What kind of paranormal investigator would flinch from a CinSim vampire? Underneath all the props and persona, even Dracula was just an animated zombie these days. A lot of classic horror film creatures had been resurrected by the Immortality Mob to entertain the tourists. At least Mothra hadn't been sent to pick me up.

I thought about Quicksilver asleep below as I pulled a black knit turtleneck down over my black yoga pants. Old Drac must have some spell to put animals asleep, even big supernaturally strong wolfhound-wolf crossbreeds. Otherwise, he'd be at the vampire's throat.

I thrust my feet into a pair of black cowboy boot mules and grabbed the slim Baggalini uptown messenger bag I'd found so handy during my incarnation as a TV reporter. I slung it across my body and stuffed my cell phone, ID and some cash inside so my hands would be free in an emergency. Unfortunately, it had no space for wooden stakes or garlic garlands. But if someone found my body, I'd at least have a chance to be properly identified.

Of course, if I wound up dead, I hoped somebody would make sure I wasn't resurrected—even if my future as a Lilith stand-in was worth a fortune.

Couldn't count on Hector Nightwine for the job; he had an addictive profit motive. I'd need my new beau, Ric Montoya, to make sure I was dead and buried and kept that way. Ric had his unusual ways with the dead, but our relationship is anything but lifeless.

Bela was waiting, polite, his caped back to me, bare gray hand still extended. The other wore a white glove.

I put my own pale hand into that dead, ashen flesh. Icy. Icky.

Dracula turned slowly to face me, his arms lifting his cloak into black wings again. With those "wings," he clasped me to the formal front of his evening dress, the starched white shirt. His cloak curled around me, enclosing me in the scent of mothballs, must and cold decay.

With a swoop and a *whoosh,* I felt us break the "ground barrier" and fly through the window to soar into the warm night air. His arms remained around me, but the cloak folds unfurled, fanning out like giant wings as we sped through the night sky. I eyed the gorgeous glitter of Las Vegas a hundred and fifty stories below.

Being in Dracula's arms felt like waltzing with a marble pillar; his skin and bones formed one hardened, heartless surface. It was odd to fly vertically, as if we stood on an invisible floor, but it certainly eased my horizontal phobia, if not the acrophobia any human being with a brain would feel in this situation.

The wind chilled my ears. I curled my toes to keep my mules from falling off and braining some unlucky tourist below.

I distracted myself during the terrifying flight by wondering who could send Dracula as an errand boy. Certainly not mobster Cesar Cicereau of the Gehenna Hotel-Casino and werewolf syndicate. I wasn't sure from our last encounter whether he now preferred to forget me instead of tearing my throat out, but I was pretty sure he'd never want to hire me.

The Strip lights below had dimmed. We were dropping toward a square black blot in the lightscape. I squinched my eyes shut, sure we would smack hard into that rectilinear bull's-eye.

Instead my soles touched roof, the dangling heels first, then the toes. Note to self: Never wear mules for night flights with the dead. Nun-like lace-up oxfords would have been better. At least Drac and I were once more on solid ground.

But whose solid ground?

Dracula slowly loosened his custody, but kept his hands on me, now both gloved—how did he do that?—in a waltz position. Did every supernatural in Vegas want to cha-cha-cha with me?

Listen, pal, Irma tried to tell him, *these Irish gams only do jigs, not waltzes with weirdoes.* She was wrong about that; I'd waltzed with Snow, weird only in the ancient demonic definition of word. He was the sexy long-haired rock-star owner of the Inferno Hotel and purveyor of the "Brimstone Kiss," an after-show perk he bestowed on groupies who became enslaved at one touch of his ice-white lips. Rumor had it he was an albino vampire, the obverse of my current partner. Both of them were deeply unwanted on my dance card, even though Snow's lock of white hair-turned-silver-familiar was still guarding my throat.

Dracula swept me into a stately gliding circle. "A little movement warms the blood after a chilling night flight."

That line was almost worse than his classic "I do not drrrink . . . vine."

"I'm not dressed for the Creature Feature Cotillion," I told him. "Let's go see the Master."

"He is not so civil . . . and dashing as Dracula."

"But he *is* the Master, right? You don't want to cut him out."

Dracula's face gleamed with anticipation. Then the calculated look faded. "I live only to serve. For now."

Master, whoever he was, had better watch his front, especially the carotid arteries.

Despite the probable danger, this outing was fascinating to an investigator. I considered CinSims as animated movie posters, in a way, able to walk and talk, but that was it. If I'd thought about it, they could do a lot more or they'd never be in demand at brothels. Although I'd heard that some human sex partners could be pretty lifeless. . . .

Luckily, I'd lost my virginity right here in Sin City, with a guy who could tease an orgasm out of a corpse. I was only slightly harder to win over. During those literally magical minutes, Ric and I had accidentally tapped the borrowed emotions of the Sunset Park lovers killed during their most ecstatic moments. A little paranormal passion by proxy had not hurt one bit.

But I didn't know that CinSims could freaking fly! And with me along. Apparently, if the CinSim was gifted with paranormal skills in the originating film, those abilities carried over to the zombie reincarnation. That made the rumors of a brewing CinSim insurrection pretty scary. I mean, think: Godzilla loose on the Strip.

"I must leave you," Dracula announced dramatically, bowing to kiss my hand. "My task is done."

With that he walked to the end of the flat roof and jumped off.

"Wait!" I ran to the edge, seeing mostly dead black below, with a smattering of streetlights and signs.

Then I spotted the large humped figure rushing straight down like a beetle, just as Jonathan Harker described his host's creepy manner of egress from his Transylvanian castle in Bram Stoker's classic novel. I watched Dracula's form become one with the dark street below. And where, pray, was I to go?

The usual answer to that in an uncaring world was, "To Hell!"

And in post-Millennium Revelation Las Vegas, it was all too often the literal truth.

Chapter Two

I EXPLORED THE ROOF on foot, vertical and a slave of gravity again, thank God.

The surface tar was overlaid with gravel. Occasional air-conditioning units poked up in knee-high hummocks just the right height to trip me in the dark. They were humming away, so the building was in use and occupied.

I circled until I found a larger hummock, the sort of inset entry you find to a storm cellar in Kansas. What it was in post-Millennium Revelation Las Vegas, I hadn't a clue. It could have been the low road to a crypt.

Okay. What does the alert investigator do? She walks down into the dark and finds out.

Mules, do your duty! Irma offered a small cry of encouragement to my footwear. *I am so glad we are not wearing your Wicked Witch of the West spike heels for this outing.*

Listen to the born spike freak, I sassed her back. *You'd wear heels to a golf course.*

The steps were steep and I hadn't thought to bring along a high-beam flashlight. What woman would expect Dracula to dump her off in the dark like undelivered mail, without even one courtly swipe at her circulatory system?

But once on level flooring, my humble mules were able to shuffle me into a vaguely lit area. The metal door to the service stairs was chained shut with a sign reading BUILDING CONDEMNED: DO NOT USE affixed with rusted screws. A search revealed no other access but an air conditioning shaft grille. Spotlighted by a distant neon sign, I could see it was enameled white, but now grimed a dusky gray. I was able to shake it free after further loosening the screws with my fingernails. What shoddy maintenance work! Probably hadn't been inspected in decades.

I set the grille aside and crawled in headfirst. The shaft ran straight, turned, then dropped what felt like four feet and ran straight again.

There was no use cursing the darkness. The only way to enter or leave this building was via down.

I gulped, cheered by the absence of cobwebs pushing over my features like an unwanted, unseen veil. Then I stopped. And wondered *why* there were no cobwebs. Oh. Maybe I wasn't the only intruder to use this route.

Investigation work was already losing its glamour.

Then I heard voices.

No, I am not Joan of Arc. I am a simple Kansas girl turned loose in the big bad city. And I am a PI. So, onward toward the voices. Another ten feet and I could hear giggles echoing off the hollow aluminum shafts. Giggles?

Definitely female voices, those cloying, phony tones I hated from the girls at Our Lady of the Lake Convent School. Girls who had power and tried to pretend they didn't. Voices I'd heard, once out of high school, directed almost exclusively at men. At powerful men they aimed to seduce.

Seduction had been against my religion . . . until I'd met Ric here in Vegas. And he'd been the seducer. No, we'd both been seduced, by love and death and lust and dust six feet under in the desert.

I paused, wishing I had my dowsing partner with me, only Ric dowsed for the dead. I was afraid he'd find some where I was headed now. Those voices echoed as if in a vault. A burial chamber. Great. I wished Quicksilver was with me. I almost wished Dracula was with me, but he, wisely, had split.

When in doubt, advance.

At last, some light leaked into my square metal tunnel. I crawled right into another grille, my nose flat against the metal.

I could look down. A little. I saw a lot of white and began to recognize the location.

Oh, no! The 1001 Knights Hotel. Not here! Not *him* again! What had I done to deserve this?

At that moment a tremor ran through the shaft, like a boiler deep below going postal. Probably the periodic hiccough of the condemned building. The grille gyrated off its loose screws. I was shaken into it, past it and down the rabbit hole into the white light.

Luckily, unlike Alice, I landed on a bed. Unluckily, there was someone repellent in it. Several someones.

Scarlet-painted worm-lipped women in white scattered at my descent.

The desiccated scrawny figure of an old man in cerise satin pajamas stayed put to aim his lecherous death's head grin at me.

"Howard Hughes," I said, scrambling off the high hospital bed and its stiff white linens. "What an unexpected . . . meeting."

"*Hmm*," he said, "I liked you better in white."

His "nurses" regrouped around the hospital bed, licking their lips at me.

I had nowhere to go. Howard's mandarin-long fingernails scratched his sparsely haired chest, drawing blood. The vampire nurses sighed in unison and, with fangs descended, came uncomfortably closer.

He waved a cadaverous hand. "Back! You had your share during the turning. Now if Miss Street cares for a friendly lick from me—"

Ick. The sanitary issues alone were stomach-turning. Historically, he'd been famously vermin phobic. You'd think he'd still have serious inner conflicts about germs in his new state.

"I'm here on your business this time," I said.

We'd first met a couple of weeks ago, when I'd finagled myself in disguised as a nurse—the sexy fantasy sort found in *Playboy* magazine. Howard Hughes and Hugh

Hefner had more in common than initials. Hughes was
supposedly the most powerful vampire still left in town,
which doesn't say much for Vegas vamps.

"Too bad." Howard's watery dark eyes studied my
face. "I could have made you a star."

When he'd been a playboy movie mogul, star-making
had been the name of his game. His single success was
busty Jane Russell, for whom the engineer-aviator had
designed the world's first pushup bra. Come to think,
maybe the old coot had earned a crack at immortality. He
certainly was a Renaissance man. Pilot, inventor, unreal
real estate tycoon, lech . . . .

"A star?" I hooted. "Hector Nightwine's already
taking a shot at it. I'll be doing featured cameos on his
next TV series."

"Nightwine!" he snorted. "A minor, a very minor
player. Still, my condition has certain limitations and I
require agents to act on my behalf. I would like you to
become one of them, Delilah Street."

"How do you know my name?" The last time I had
been here, I had ducked out without any introductions.

His smile revealed teeth so ancient they all looked like
fangs. "You are already gaining a reputation in this town.
I assume anyone the Cicereau mob wants to assassinate is
someone worth knowing. Or at least using."

"Ever the straight-talking billionaire," I said. "How do
you know about my near-death experience at Cicereau's
mountain lodge?"

"Cesar Cicereau thinks he's a rival, but I'm merely
giving him the space to screw up. I have sources inside
his organization. You look lovely in that python unitard
with a Rome Beauty apple in your mouth. Delicious!
Cicereau was a fool to let you escape him."

Holy Hugh Hefner, Catwoman! Irma whispered,
*this undead lech knows about your secret birthday-suit
command performance at the Gehenna. He must have
better intelligence and organization than you'd think.*

"If you have Cicereau's operation wired then why do you need me on your payroll?"

His scraggly-haired head nodded regally. "This may take more legwork than my in-place operatives can handle. I want to know who shared that Sunset Park unmarked grave with Cicereau's daughter."

"You know who the dead woman was?"

"Yes, my tasty little runaway winesap. In today's Vegas, even the spider webs have ears. The creatures of the night's hearing can outdo the most advanced electronic bugs. Better, they can return to me with information."

Bats and wolves were associated with Old World vampires, but spiders? *Wolves.* Did Quicksilver have a gene susceptible to vamps? He was at least as much wolf as wolfhound. That might explain why he'd slept while I was being airlifted up, up and away by Dracula.

Then there was that spider-fey familiar of Madrigal, the house magician at Cicereau's Gehenna Hotel and Casino, Sylphia . . .

Thinking of creepy-crawlies made my pale Irish skin break out in gooseflesh.

"Nice." Howard ran a yellowed nail down my arm. I was undecided: did spooked women most titillate his inner mogul, playboy, or vampire?

Time to stop being terrified and deal.

"Okay, Hughes. You know that Cicereau's own daughter was in that grave, but you don't know who the guy was. We're assuming he was a vampire. Is that why you're so interested?"

"I wasn't a vampire myself at that time. No one believed in vampires then. But I did believe in the future of Las Vegas, although I didn't openly invest until thirty years later—in the seventies. Obviously, a lot was going on here in Vegas in the 1940s and 1950s that no one had a clue about until after the Millennium Revelation. I want to know who that slain vampire was. I want to know who put thirty silver dollars in the grave and why. The answers are worth a nice sum to me, Delilah Street, and I will keep my creatures' fangs off you if you achieve my objectives."

"Off me *and* mine."

"Not including Nightwine."

I shrugged. Hector was my boss, but something of a voyeur and an epicurean ghoul. He'd done quite well here since the Millennium Revelation and I suspected he could protect himself equally well.

"I don't know what you have against Nightwine, but he's not on my personal five fave call list."

"Nor anyone's. So, who is?" Hughes eyed me slyly. "I suppose that big bad doggie of yours."

I nodded. "How do you know about him?"

"He trashed the Lunatics. They're still whining about it. You think a domestic dog taking out a motorcycle gang of half-weres in a parking lot doesn't get on the weird-news Internet? And I suppose you'd want me to spare that big bad ex-FBI man."

How the hell did he know about Ric? I wasn't going to satisfy him by asking.

Meanwhile, the nurses had crowded closer, sighing while sucking air through their fangs. "Fox Mulder," they wailed hungrily.

Honestly, women in all forms are just too inclined to be groupies!

"Forget *The X-Files*," I told them. "That was fiction and is now only reruns and DVDs. Ric is real life." I eyed them all and then Hughes. "And I want him to stay that way."

"That certainly is something to bear in mind," Hughes noted.

"So . . . do you have any clues who the dead vamp might be, or who he might have been allied with?"

Hughes folded his age-spotted, blue-veined scrawny claws on the immaculate white bed sheet. It was like viewing leprous orchids in the snow. "I didn't come here to buy up the Strip until the seventies. So I have no clues. Not a one. That's your job, Delish Delilah. And keep in mind, if you fail to find out anything useful, all those no-fang concessions are off. Including on you."

He loomed up from the bed like a striking cobra, the IV stand at his side crashing over to spray both the nurses and sheets with watery pink blood.

I jumped back and off, streaking away through the outer chambers containing germicidal lights and sprays. The startled human-for-now attendants jumped out of my way. I banged through doors until I was in the truly deserted run-down part of the derelict hotel building.

Just what I needed: a notorious, undercover vampire as my first client.

Chapter Three

From my previous fact-finding mission here, I knew I had to get down ten floors and through a ring of decadent vampire druggie-guards to reach the main floor and exit the building.

My silver familiar, which had remained dormant around my throat all through my adventure with Hughes Tool and Vampire Company, crept down my right arm to curl around the bases of my fingers. The silver metal thickened into rings and then grew two-inch diamond-dusted spikes on each finger: the glitzy Vegas version of brass knuckles.

Well! How had Snow's unwanted gift known to produce the glittering knuckle spikes? They echoed the diamond-dust-embedded nail file points I'd used to hold off group-home, half-vamp bullies years ago. Eerie.

Snow had sent me the lock of his albino hair as a play on my name and his enigmatic powers. I couldn't resist petting it in memory of my lost white Lhasa apso's flowing coat. Like a striking serpent, the soft tendril of hair had morphed into a hard silver bangle on my arm with a permanent lock on me, unable to be sawn or burned off. Whether or not the silver familiar taunted me by migrating to various body parts and becoming simply decorative jewelry, changed into protective adornment or transformed into instant weaponry, I resented being protected at the cost of being invaded.

Once again the mobile parasite had worked its bizarre mind-reading magic. Silver knuckles were even better than brass for punching my way through the house vampires at the 1001 Knights Hotel.

It was just like a heartless businessman of Howard Hughes's ilk to have me dropped into his lair, then force me to fight my way out of it. Cesar Cicereau, the werewolf mob alpha boss, wasn't very likeable, but he had a heart as big as the Tin Man's compared to Howard Hughes.

I decided to take the stairs. I'd have the advantage of height when I ran into the vamp patrol. The cowboy heels on my mules were good and thick—great for kicks and full-body shoves. I knew from my last visit that, to conceal his presence, Hughes employed deliberately lame, tame vampires as derelict as the building. Still, even debased vampires were unhumanly powerful.

Of course there was no way to avoid announcing my descent as my shoes clattered down the dozens of concrete steps. The 1001 Knights Hotel, Howard Hughes's hidden headquarters, was supposedly abandoned and ripe for razing. I wondered if it was just Hughes's economic clout or some eerie supernatural mojo that kept this prime property at the south end of the Strip off the rebuilding market and looking deceptively empty.

A savage cry announced a vamp in a burned leather coat charging up the stairs. I grabbed a railing with my left hand, kicked out my right foot, aiming at his throat, and flashed my spiked silver brass knuckles across his brow bone.

The blood ran down in sheets, blinding him as he tumbled backward . . .

. . . into a second vamp, who pushed him aside and down like deadwood.

I hadn't expected the blinding flood of blood, but I suppose well-fed vamps are like ticks, gorged and ready to burst.

This new guy's fangs were already rusted by an evening meal too. He seized my kicking foot and tried to twist my leg. I grabbed the railing with both hands and pushed out that leg with all my strength. That knocked him back, but I was going to land supine on the concrete steps, the edges slamming my spine in a couple places, both blows likely to hurt like hell, not to mention paralyze.

I pedaled my legs to give my feet some sort of traction on the stairs. A mule went flying off and upward, right into the snarling vampire mouth. I saw teeth fly, maybe even fangs. The vamp howled and covered his bleeding mouth, backing up too far and falling. The stair edges wouldn't wound his immortal body.

But I was upright again and ran down after the tumbling defanged vampire. It would have been a smooth descent, except something hit me hard in the back. I was stumbling down the stairs faster and faster, out of control, my hands ripped from any grasp I got on the railing as soon as I found it.

I heard a disgusting slurping sound behind me and realized the pursuing vamp was licking my blood off the metal railing. I wished this was happening in the middle of a Kansas blizzard and his blood-sucking tongue would stick to the icy metal . . .

No, this was a warm spring Vegas night. And blood would be hot too. . . .

At the bottom of the stairs, the blood-blinded vamp was waiting for the others to catch me as I tumbled into them.

I got both feet—one bare—on the same step, bent my aching knees and jumped as high and far as I could. I almost cleared the rapacious welcoming committee, feeling their filthy, clawed hands clutching at my legs as I sailed over. Then something incredibly fast and hard slammed me back. . . oh, no!

Back *into* my attackers!

I landed on them hard, sinking into their bones and muscles, their clawed hands closing on my arms and scratching my throat.

But before the lifting hands could capture me, something bit them off at the wrist. Blood, who knows whose, that filled those undead veins spewed over me like warm syrup on a buttered pancake.

White fangs snapped as I heard bones breaking.

Not my own.

That realization got my body going, arms and legs flailing to gain balance, struggle upright and get running again. A last bolt of energy sprang me forward, away from the building's covered driveway toward the street.

I finally collapsed at the curb, panting like a winded marathon runner, too exhausted to move.

Something was coming up behind me. I could barely manage to move, but I did not want to become a half-vamp—something, according to rumor, a single bite would accomplish. Two more and a reciprocal sip from my killer's immortal veins, and I'd be turned. Or so they said. I figured that three vamps were still ambulatory and fanged enough for the job.

I reared up as best I could, teeth gritted, fist extended. Wait! Where were my silver "brass" knuckles? The damned familiar had run out on me! My wrist sported a wimpy charm bracelet now. *Damn Snow to Hell!*

My redundant curse forgotten, I gazed into two burning blue eyes and a jaw full of grinning white fangs.

The jagged teeth were clamped on some disgusting amputation, black and burnt and dead as . . . as shoe leather.

I pulled farther back, took a deep breath.

Oh.

Quicksilver was sitting there, panting hotly and smiling that wolfish grin, my lost leather mule firmly in his teeth. Cinderella had never had a handier Prince Charming.

Good doggie, Irma said.

Quicksilver dropped the shoe when my right hand reached for it, and began laving my bleeding hand with his huge pink tongue. Dog saliva heals doggie wounds over time. Quicksilver saliva heals human wounds instantly, as Ric and I had found out.

In seconds, we were both on our feet, me fully shod, my hand on Quick's wide leather collar. I realized the bracelet familiar now boasted canine figures and that a matching silver-studded dog collar had been coiled protectively around my neck for some time. This was the first occasion that my silver familiar had revealed a split protective personality.

Dracula's sleep spell on the wolf part of Quicksilver had probably evaporated the moment Drac dropped me on Howard Hughes's roof. We were a paranormal K-9 team. My dog could track me through a swamp or a thunderstorm and probably thin air. He was an awesome animal. I'd seen him lick Ric's barbed-wire-shredded hands whole in a couple minutes. Now my once-scraped palm was flexible and smooth. Nice trick.

"Good dog! Good boy." That was hardly sufficient praise, but we humans have talked down to animals for so long it's a hard habit to break.

Meanwhile, I jumped with my two shod feet into the roadway, tried to grin as innocently as Quicksilver, wiped the blood off my pants and looked for a cab to hail.

No way was I walking all the way back to Hector's estate.

Chapter Four

I ENDED UP having to call a cab from the office of the Araby Motel, a cheesy place opposite the 1001 Knights Hotel.

The driver was snotty about giving a dog a ride, so Quicksilver had a good run home. Luckily, we'd been on the south end of the Strip and Hector Nightwine's estate wasn't that far away for Quicksilver.

In fifteen minutes the four charging bronze horsemen of the Apocalypse that guarded the gates loomed into the headlights.

The cab driver was happier cruising along to my more modest entry area down Sunset Drive to let me out. Quicksilver was waiting there for me to disengage the security system and open the gate. He was just being polite. He could scale the eight-foot wall, but didn't like to alarm the main house.

After our unexpected nocturnal adventure, I made sure he had fresh water and some doggie treats and left him with a puppy biscuit sticking out of his awesome muzzle like a small green tongue-tip.

Upstairs, on my way to my interrupted beauty sleep in my bedroom, the meager light caught my image in the long mirror at the hall's end.

I nodded at myself and moved on, absorbed.

Wait!

The self I'd nodded at was nude!

I ducked back into the hall.

Yup, the nude "me" in the mirror was as whitewashed as my pale Black Irish skin was in the light of day. The tangle of black on my head repeated at the crux of my legs. Sure, I'd seen myself nude in a mirror before, but always

critically: pale skin that would burn but not tan, the fairly tall
frame with too much breast and hip. I was an unfashionable
hourglass. That's why vintage clothing looked cool on me.
I'd always loved the looks of female Silver Screen stars. To
paraphrase Norma Desmond in *Sunset Boulevard*, "They
had faces then." They also had busts and hips, S curves and
sensuous thighs. But this image wasn't me. It was me in
a separate semblance. This was Lilith. Maybe I could tell
by her faint blue aura. Or the tiny blue topaz stud in her
nostril. Look at her and see me, once removed.

I blushed to view my body objectively. I was used to
seeing myself as deficient: lacking relatives, lacking a
home, an identity, a positive body image, a Blue Fairy
with a star to wish upon . . .

I forced myself to confront what usually made me
cringe.

"Are you me?" I asked.

My mirror image didn't answer, but her mouth moved
as if she was interrogating me.

"Lilith?" I hadn't meant to sound either tentative or
desperate. But I did, both.

Seeing this double of me on network TV is what
brought me to Las Vegas to put up with such things as
Count Dracula as an alarm clock.

Her mouth mimicked my word. *Lil-ith*.

"Are you dead?"

She winked at me. Assumed a fashion model pose.

"You'll never make it in the rag trade, Lil," I told her.
"Too busty."

She stuck her tongue out at me.

Nothing in the magic mirror had ever interacted so
boldly with me before.

"Why don't you speak?"

She shrugged, lifted her dark eyebrows. Eloquently,
she asked without words. *Why speak?*

"I need to know I'm not alone." I sounded needy, even
to myself.

Honesty seemed too much for her. She looked aside, flashed her profile, which duplicated mine, and vanished.

"Wait! Lilith!"

I rushed the mirror, pressed against it. My fingertips retreated. The surface was not only warm, but there was no distance between my splayed, groping fingers and their reflection.

The Enchanted Cottage mirror used front-surface glass, like Madrigal's magic-act mirrors! Although I'd learned that any mirror bowed to my presence, front-surface mirror seemed more powerful. That was a fact I could use and build on. Madrigal, the magician at the Gehenna, would know more. Besides, he hadn't been surprised by my Alice-through-the-looking-glass antics in his stage mirror. I wanted to know more about how and why.

"Mirror, mirror, on the wall," I murmured, my hot cheek pressed to the cooler glass, thinking of Lilith. "Who's the fairest of them all?"

It didn't answer, which was a relief.

WHAT WERE THE ODDS that the bad old dreams from my orphan days wouldn't resurface that night, Enchanted Cottage comforts or not?

The Millennium Revelation reality offered the resurgence of supernatural figures dating back centuries and even millennia; my personal nightmares always had a modern and even a science-fiction edge.

The group home half-vampire bullies who hassled me were only another twist on a common male adolescent type . . . gang members. They were minor annoyances.

My most frequently rerun nightmare was "Alien Abductee."

Now *that* was really out of this world.

Yet, I'd always be there again, flat on my back under powerful overhead lights that made my captors into featureless white-clad shadows. I'd be naked as a *CSI* corpse with the memory of a flimsy white sheet being stripped away.

I never quite knew what bound me down. Maybe it was just the paralysis of nightmare, but I was incapable of moving or of speaking.

Just as I was frozen in place now, once again in the relentless grip of dreamland.

The figures leaned closer, blocking some of the light. The needle-in-the-navel cliché felt as real as memory. I glimpsed a long thick silver instrument at the foot of the table. It was coming towards me, held in white hands with fingers as smooth and boneless as a stingray wing, more cartilage than muscle and flesh.

The giant stingray motif hovered over all these dreams, looming beyond the blinding overhead light like an albino bat with a wingspread of twelve feet.

I couldn't breathe, as if the atmosphere was water-heavy. If I couldn't breathe, I certainly couldn't scream, even when the approaching instrument vanished as it neared my torso. Not even when the hovering heads drew in until all light was gone except for a searing luminous halo behind them . . . .

I ESCAPED into another nightmare.

Something seized me and slammed me upright against a wall.

My eyes batted to close and filter out the punishing light.

They slowly adjusted to see another ring of hounding beings . . . . These had faces. Snarling, fanged, pimpled and scarred. The local half-vamp hoods were after me again for "blood and booty." Rape and a liquid supper.

I knew how to fight them off and raised my trusty diamond-dusted nail file to the nearest blood-shot eye.

My fist was empty! I was unarmed. Only a long thin chain wrapped my knuckles, a flimsy piece of jewelry, not a weapon.

I struggled, but four of them held me pinned upright against the wall. I couldn't move or scream. Something hard and metal prodded between my legs. They were going to rape me with a knife!

A scream struggled to stutter its way out of my throat, but one contorted face came too close to focus on, the bared canine fangs already dipped in fresh blood and dripping more . . . .

THE DREAMSCAPE changed, the wall behind me pounded with a salsa rhythm, echoing my rapid heartbeat, massaging my spine because I was pressed hard against it by another body.

A tongue was flicking back and forth along the edge of my lips, tickling, teasing them open for a direct inward thrust. That forward motion was followed by more lateral moves, by lips encompassing mine, lower and upper in turn, caressing.

The man's weapon was hard as knife steel and pushed vertically against my crotch.

His hands were on my bared hips, the hips his hands had exposed on the dance floor when he jerked my skirt down from my waist until it was a low-rider model slung below my navel.

He was breathing hard and so was I.

My thighs were slick. Was my body wounded from the previous dream? Menstruating? No, it was welcoming this man, my dream lover.

The man's hands and mouth were hot and persuasive, teasing my body into a matching rhythm with his subtle hip thrusts, making it thirst for conjoining.

Now I fought to hold back a . . . sensual moan.

I'm not the kind of girl to go limp against a hall wall in a dance club. Hell, I don't even dance well. But the man knows how to lead me and I want him to.

I open my eyes to see Ric's dear, dark-eyed face, to hear his Spanish murmurs of love and passion and *it's all right*. We're at Los Lobos salsa club, where the werewolves change under the full moon.

I have changed. What was once threat is now temptation, teasing, pleasing, deeply wanted. I smile at Ric, tongue-kiss him back, rock my hips hard into his . . . and wake up.

Ooh la la, what a bitchin' place to let an invisible friend down flat, Irma croons. *Um, that man was soooo habeñera hot for us! Even I could feel the fire. Go back to sleep. I want to get to the necking session in the car and the first fuck in the bathroom mirror later and our second orgasm.*

That's my business. I don't need to be reminded and I'd never put it in those crude terms.

You are almost twenty-five, girlfriend, and I am right there with you. You can't afford to give up a single rerun of a feminine thrill, not even in your dreams. And ain't Ric's Latin lover act so way better than dodging half-vamp bully boys or alien probes from Hell? Let him at me! Play it again, Samantha. And again and again.

I ignored Irma's irritation, letting myself drift back into the moment when nightmare had segued into wet dream. My nightmares had never had a happy ending before. Ric had awakened pleasure in me where I'd been conditioned to feel panic.

The deep gratitude I felt for that might have been love. I didn't know. An unwanted orphan doesn't much feel the love. I knew my body loved him. I knew the joint psychic link we'd felt when we dowsed together for an innocent cache of water in Sunset Park and found that the dead supernaturals had sealed our sensual connection.

Umm. I'd forgotten the rocking motion of his hips against mine in that dim nightclub hallway. The slick liquid glide of his lips against mine. The glint of his gold wristwatch on his olive skinned wrist. The luminous whites of his eyes against the swollen-pupil black of desire in his eyes. That narrow gold belt snaking around his hips.

I snuggled in the smooth sheets, opening my mind and heart to the possibility of Ric. Irma purred in the back of my mind. I was just more up front about it.

Chapter Five

DREAM OF THE DREAMBOAT . . .
    Ric called me the next morning for a date.

"At the county morgue?" I asked. "You have something kinky in mind?"

"Always, but this is business. Grady Bahr, the coroner, called me yesterday with info about the Sunset Park corpse couple. I mentioned I might bring a colleague. They'll make you a visitor's badge, so I gave him your name. He said you'd already met."

"Someone suggested I check with him earlier, so I did."

I didn't mention that the "someone" was Snow, who seemed to consider me his house detective at times. I doubt Ric would want me consulting, or consorting, with a guy whose hobby was addicting infatuated women to devouring onstage kisses.

"Anyway," Ric went on, "he likes you enough that he'll put you on the consultants' list like me. When can you meet me there?"

I liked it that Ric wasn't offering to pick me up. My independence seemed as important to him as it was to me. Damn, that man just wasn't making one wrong off-putting move.

"Ten?" I suggested.

"Fine. Maybe we can catch an early lunch afterward."

I laughed. "The law enforcement pro. Making a lunch date after a visit to the morgue."

"Shouldn't be gruesome. This pair has decayed down to the bones, remember?"

How could I forget? Yet those bones had communicated intimately enough with him and me, even before we'd guessed Ric's dead-dowsing abilities had hit a double jackpot in tranquil Sunset Park.

I was dying to hear what Grady "Grisly" Bahr had for us, but needed to grab an energy bar and take Quicksilver for a forty-minute run in the park across the street, then shower before leaving for the morgue.

Usually the desert air-dried sweat before it could form drops, but I did have to slather sun screen on my pale skin. And slather it on again after a shower. If I went out early enough, I could let Quick run off his leash to take great galloping loops around the far bounds of the park before coming back to me.

I knew a responsible pet owner would have him "fixed," but he'd already demonstrated one important paranormal gift. Did I want to eliminate a genetic line that could heal in this often-hurtful world? Besides, Quicksilver is smart and strong and a survivor; his offspring would be too. I'd adopted him at Sunset Park pet adoption event when I overheard he was scheduled to be put down, but one thing was clear from the first soulful gaze of his baby blues: He had "picked" me. He not only survived, but now did his considerable darnedest to ensure that I did too.

Quick's gait was loose and powerful, as beautiful as a thoroughbred's to behold. It made me wonder who had let this magnificent specimen get away from them.

I'd probably never know, like I'd never know who had dropped my infant self off on some Delilah Street somewhere twenty-four years ago. Or whatever exact day was my birthday, give or take a few. Me and Lilith? Abandoned together or apart? I needed to look into my options for tracing my "roots" as an abandoned baby, if any bureaucratic system would let me.

Not that I didn't have enough on my "To Do" list.

Right now I needed to find out more about who—what vampire, that is—had died with mob boss-hotelier Cesar

Cicereau's lovely teenage daughter in Sunset Park almost seventy years ago.

Was he her prince charming or not?

RIC WAS WAITING for me by his vintage bronze Corvette at the bland, boxy coroner's building—waiting for me and my 1956 black Cadillac, Dolly.

Dolly could have crushed the Sting Ray and maybe even outraced it. She would be worth plenty on the collectible car market, but she was my fortress, my mobile home, my soul sister, and no one was getting her and her chrome bumper bullets except over my dead body.

Which body, by the way, was feeling very lively as I took in Ric's usual business outfit: expensive vanilla-colored tropical weight suit, silky shirt and tie. The look was great for corporate consulting work. No one would ever take him for an FBI agent, already legendary in his late twenties as the "Cadaver Kid" for his knack of finding corpses.

Now he is ex-FBI and we were heading into Corpse Central to find out more about bodies we'd already found.

I say "we" because I'd contributed to this particular find. Ricardo Montoya could dowse for the dead since childhood, but walking skeptical me through the dowsing process had raised more than a pair of buried corpses. It had put us into close proximity, my back to his front, creating a sensual overload (okay, it was a mutual zipless orgasm) and my scary new psychic visions of the dead amplified Ric's inborn corpse-finding ability.

Ric opened Dolly's heavy driver side door for me, mainly to eye the pristine red leather upholstery. I knew he'd love to take Dolly out on a lonely highway outside Vegas and run her up to full speed, but he knew I wouldn't like that. He'd just have to settle for taking me out on lonely highways at full speed.

"Jeez," Ric said, slamming the door shut with the sound of a meat freezer locking, "the troops could use these in the Middle East."

When I stood up in my going-to-meeting high heels, we were nicely parallel in all the right places. We just stood there, silent, savoring the heat between us.

Ric took my elbow. "So you went out and seduced the coroner on your own. It took me a year to get an in with the old goat."

"You don't have my advantages."

"Definitely not," he agreed, grinning. Without the grin, he continued, "I want to nail the identity of the dead guy fast. You'll get the Cicereau syndicate on your tail any day now for knowing his daughter is one of the two corpses. Once the police can announce both identities, it's out in the open and you won't be worth going after." He paused. "At least you won't be worth going after in *that* way."

We stopped, gazed, smiled.

I'd never felt that odd combination of lust, love and looniness. Ric was much more sexually experienced than I, but I doubted he'd ever felt this way either. Me twenty-four, he twenty-eight, both orphans in the thrall of first love, like the bodies we'd found. Or had they found us and passed on the fatal infection?

Why did I think love was a lethal disease?

He shook my elbow a little to pull me out of my trance. "Come on, but don't lose the dewy look, Del. Bahr likes lovely young women, especially if they're alive. We want to play on our source's weaknesses."

"Is investigation work always this cynical?"

"Always," he told me, opening the door and washing us with a wall of icy air-conditioning as freezing as a casino's. Ever the gentleman. "I'll let you lead so you can cement your rapport with Bahr. I'm already on his A-list."

I nodded, glad I'd dressed in the professional on-camera clothes of my former TV reporter persona. I was even gladder that Ric was secure enough to defer to me. Circumstance had made us momentary partners; only we could make that partnership permanent and professional. The personal side of it was even trickier.

Miss Ortiz (I read her ID) gave Ric the glad eye and raised her eyebrows to see me with him. She hadn't been on duty when I'd first come here on my own.

"*Hola,* Yolanda," Ric greeted her. "The boss is expecting us and I think you have a new ID for Miss Street here?"

She passed him both IDs, ignoring me.

Ric clipped mine on my aqua linen lapel like it was a corsage. Our every gesture with each other conveyed a certain subliminal heat, whether we wanted it to or not.

He grinned companionably at Yolanda. "She's new to the coroner business, not a pro like you. Be gentle with her."

I'd never seen a guy both lead on and turn off a woman so smoothly. Yolanda couldn't help sighing. Ric might not have the Brimstone Kiss, but he sure as hell had a sterling silver tongue.

She dialed her boss and then nodded us in.

"I see why you wear suits, even in this heat," I told Ric, eyeing the plastic rectangle dangling from his own lapel. "You must get a lot of temporary ID tags in the consulting business."

He nodded, then smiled as Grisly Bahr came out in his lab coat to greet us. Even he wore an ID tag.

"Great to see you, *amigo,*" he greeted Ric. "I should have known you'd have snagged Miss Street. She's a comer."

"I thought she'd snagged you," Ric said.

"Don't I wish. Well . . . you both will like this new mystery. I want to run it past you, C.K., before I lay it on Captain Malloy."

C.K.? Oh. Cadaver Kid.

"The captain likes her crime facts cut and dried and down to earth," Ric agreed.

"This is down to earth, all right, kiddies. Way down to earth."

By then we'd walked through a door or two, down a featureless hall and into a refrigerator-cold room littered

with sheet-covered gurneys. Some sheets were alarmingly
flat, others way too lumpy in all the wrong places. I knew
the air would be icy, but that didn't completely eliminate
the stench of death, so I'd treated my nostrils with Vicks
VapoRub, a trick I'd learned as a reporter.

Bahr led us to one side of the room and pulled back
two of the really shallow sheets to reveal the bare bones
of our Sunset Park couple.

I winced to see what was left of the gently rounded
flesh of the young woman I'd seen in my Enchanted
Cottage mirror. Yet the brown bones were mostly whole
and the facing skulls seemed to be smiling rather than
grinning.

"You've placed the gurneys so they're still face-to-
face," I noted, surprised.

Grisly Bahr actually stuttered a bit. "Yes, well, *ahem,*
it duplicates the crime scene, doesn't it?"

"Don't let him fool you. He's a sentimental old dog,"
Ric told me.

Bahr gestured at the right side bones. "She was a
healthy young woman in 1946. About seventeen years
old."

I nodded, knowing and mourning all this.

Ric surreptitiously took my hand. He knew that too.

"But this guy," Bahr was saying. "This young buck of
perhaps nineteen from the length and development of the
bones, as we knew, we can now accurately date for age.
He was a robust young fellow of six hundred or so." He
eyed Ric under the shrubbery of his eyebrows and over
the glint of his half-glasses. "You got any ideas on that,
C.K.?"

Ric sighed. "It could only be . . . vampire."

"So you say. Still, you know our authorities are having
a hard time dealing with supernaturals showing up now
in all ways, shapes and forms—including from the past.
They still want to believe it's all the result of autoimmune
disease or pollution or even global warming, God help us.

"I told Miss Street earlier that the male's cause of death was one used centuries ago to kill vampires. The head was cut off and a coin put in the mouth. But that's folklore. The age of the bones is scientific fact. I fear our friends in law enforcement are going to lay it on that disease that ages kids prematurely."

"Progeria," Ric said while I was still taking in the subtext of their comments. "That's ridiculous. These bones are full-size."

Did they mean that officialdom was a tad behind on recognizing the sweeping influence of supernaturals on the history of this planet? I'd noticed that the Wichita authorities were in a state of denial, but thought that was just small-city slowness in catching up with major national trends.

Now, I wondered if all the standard authorities— police, politicians, coroners, medical and health officials and religious leaders—were behind the curve on this. In that case, any investigations I could do for Hector or even Howard Hughes would add to the human knowledge pool.

While I'd been daydreaming, the two guys were still discussing those dry bones.

"Just as well, maybe," Ric told Bahr, "if your superiors are slow to see the supernatural cropping up here. The Cicereau mob is deeply involved in these kills. If the case can be solved to our satisfaction, privately, we might all be safer. I can always get Captain Malloy to sign off on it."

"Yes, you can, *muchacho macabre*."

So Bahr thought blond Captain Kennedy Malloy was utter putty in Ric's fingers too. Didn't like to hear that.

"No use agitating the public, or the police, on some of these dicier killings," Ric agreed.

"All part of the job," Grisly told me, winking. "Don't you worry, Delilah. This fellow's saving the attractively efficient Captain Malloy for me."

So much for the "Miss Street" act.

I asked my first question. "The man's manner of death. It was enough to keep him dead for eternity?"

Bahr nodded. "Decapitated, coin in mouth. Unless someone or something with some extra strong mojo we don't know about comes along." He glanced at Ric. "I'm keeping the corpses in separate stainless steel lockers. This guy's heaped with garlic. Just in case."

Ric nodded.

Grisly Bahr shook his head. "My wife is used to the orange after-odor of the formula that banishes the workplace air of decay around here, but this new garlic overtone is driving her crazy."

Chapter Six

"SIX HUNDRED YEARS," Ric mused as we returned to the now-welcome heat outside and our sizzling cars. "Where do you want to go for lunch?"

"Someplace where they don't serve six-hundred-year-old food."

He suggested we stop at a deli en route to Sunset Road and picnic in the park; then Dolly and I would be the next thing to home.

By the time we settled under the concrete awning on the concrete picnic table, with our feet resting on the attached benches, it was well past high noon and the joggers were long gone. We'd laid our jackets aside, and probably looked like a couple of office workers on a lunch break.

If anyone had overheard us, they would have gotten over that assumption.

"A six-hundred-year-old male adolescent," I said between munching on low-fat turkey and rye. "Indubitably a vampire, Dr. Van Helsing."

Ric nodded. "We've seen a few recent converts to the clan in Vegas, but not any established vamps. What about Kansas?"

"Same thing. Half-blood vamps, usually punk kids and even some fake ones."

"Some humans like to mimic the vampire lifestyle. Artificial fangs and carotid artery cocktails."

"Icky."

Ric drank from the longneck Dos Equis at his side. He'd bought a six-pack, so I had my own and some to spare.

"If it's consensual all around, though," he said, "there's nothing traditional law enforcement can do." His pupils darkened. "And you seem to like keeping my vampire bat bite site active. Is that 'icky?'"

"Let me see." I slipped my fingers under his shirt collar on the left side of his neck. Stroked softly along the thin silk shirt fabric. Ric's eyes closed and his lips parted. I moved my hand down to feel his pounding heartbeat and strum his hard nipple with my fingernail.

"Delilah," he said. I think that was all he was capable of saying at the moment.

"I've got some buttons I can discreetly push wherever we are. You bet I like that, Señor Montoya."

He leaned close to kiss the taste of the beer from my mouth.

"I've got my weird buttons too," I pointed out. "But there's more than wannabe vamps going on. Look at the half-weres who stay in a semi-human wolf state permanently. It's like someone's been messing with the traditional mythology."

"Someone *has* been messing with all traditional mythologies."

"What Hector Nightwine calls the Immortality Mob," I suggested.

"Catchy name, but I doubt it's just one entity. A lot of big corporate money is invested in making Vegas the most hip and future-forward place on the planet. But it's hard to keep up nowadays, with new 'manifestations' turning up all over the globe."

"Keeping up with the Joneses could mean playing ring-around-the-world."

"You mean finding and claiming supernaturals nowadays is like the Space Race way back when: an international competition that's part politics and part profit? Cool idea, Del, but why would the appearance of the unhumans be anything more orchestrated than them popping up from pockets of superstition here and there?"

"I'm serious, Ric. I looked this up once as part of my job reporting the paranormal beat in Kansas. The first reports of supernaturals appearing followed the path of midnight through all the time zones. Midnight when the second millennium started."

"That's an odd thing to check on."

"Watching the dot-of-midnight celebrations progress all over the globe on TV was the key night of my pre-teen life."

"I thought *I* was the key night of your life."

"Well, *now*. But back then I was only eleven. Seeing the global celebrations and feeling a sense of world unity made me decide to be one of those reporters holding a microphone, spreading the good news."

Ric, smiling, tucked my hair behind one ear. Nobody had ever played with my hair in my life. Maybe that was *my* vampire bat bite.

"And you did indeed get to hold a mike back in Kansas. Why'd you give up your TV reporter job?"

Explaining about Lilith's *CSI* cameo role as a corpse was too complicated a subject for our flirtatious picnic. Besides, if Ric knew that my "twin" Lilith made me a universal object of abduction, or worse, he'd get over-protective and never want me running around town solo.

"Oh, one of those phony vamps, the anchorman, stole my paranormal news beat. Then his weather witch girlfriend blew away my rented bungalow. I figured I needed another scene."

"And Hector Nightwine ended up your landlord, how?"

"He can use a good reporter. *CSI* is the biggest TV franchise in the world. He needs case ideas."

"So you marched in there and talked him into a job."

"Sort of. Quicksilver marched in there with me."

"And the cottage?"

"Rental housing is sky high in Vegas and what place would take a hundred-and-fifty-pound dog?"

"He's that big?"

"He's my big bad wolf, you better believe it."

Ric frowned. "Possessive too." He leaned in to kiss behind the ear he had bared. "But you still need very close watching by me," he murmured. "And Nightwine wants you to find out who both of the corpses are?"

Nightwine and someone else even creepier.

"Right," I said. "I've suddenly got this weird ability to see the girl victim whole and alive in my cottage mirror, just like I suddenly got a weird ability to get it on in the park with a hot guy with a weird ability to dowse for the dead. So I now know she's Cicereau's daughter. Or was sixty-some years ago."

"Whoa!" Ric drew back, all business. "Cicereau's daughter. That's big news."

"I only confirmed it when I sneaked an old photo off his office computer. Then I got caught."

"That's how you ended up at his mountain lodge as were-wolf pack bait. Jesus, Del! If that CinSim butler of Nightwine's hadn't tipped me off to where you were, you'd be buried out there. I need to nail the identity of the dead Sunset Park guy fast. You'll get the Cicereau syndicate on your tail any day now for knowing his daughter is one of the two corpses. Once the police can announce *both* identities, it's out in the open and you won't be worth going after any more."

He gave me a steamy look. "You won't be worth going after in *that* way."

I leaned into his shoulder. He buried his mouth in my hair.

"Sorry to be slow on the uptake, Del. I didn't have much time right after that night to think about how and why, only what."

"I know." I took his hands in mine. They'd been barbed-wire-torn raw meat after he'd used the razor-sharp fencing material to dowse for the dead beneath Cicereau's hideaway. "How did you actually raise zombies, instead of just locating corpses?"

"As I mentioned—blood. My blood. You have to shed a bit of blood to raise rather than find the dead. At least

I do. I don't do that anymore if I can help it. I raised enough zombie slaves for those vile *coyotes* who'd owned me since I was four years old. I'd sworn never to do it again."

I cringed to hear this again, Ric's determination to never raise zombies for anyone's purpose, vile or even merely using them as curiosities. I'd thought growing up in group homes was rough. Now, to save me, Ric had revisited his years of childhood enslavement by smugglers—*coyotes*—and done the one thing he'd sworn off forever. I had to change the mood.

"Okay, *hombre*," I said, reaching under his tie to undo a button of his shirt. "Tell me how the poor orphan Mexican desert boy learned to be so slick and sexy."

I'd distracted him, as I'd hoped.

"You're pretty slick and sexy yourself."

"I was a later bloomer. You obviously managed to sow your wild oats, as they said in olden days, when I was still in knee-highs.

"Knee-highs, huh? Very sexy in the right context. Catholic schoolgirl look."

"I did that high school uniform bit. An all-girl high school. Catholic, natch."

"Good girl. I attended an all-boys prep school run by Christian brothers. We had uniforms too."

"*Ooh*, you must have looked delish in a uniform. No wonder the girls were all crazy about you." I undid another button and he caught his breath.

"As a matter of fact, they were." He was teasing back, waiting to see how far I'd go. "I was the hot new kid. I'd made the news a couple years back as 'feral boy,' but my adopted mother had given me every behavioral test in the book; taught me English, plus a few other languages; civilized manners; gave me an accelerated learning program. After that, the hotties from the nearby girls' prep school were ready to put me through every test drive they could think of."

"It must have been . . . guy heaven."

"Yeah. I couldn't believe my luck. They were all on the pill and they planned to get all the thrills they could before settling into a semi-arranged marriage with some WASP Stepford husband."

"Didn't the other guys get jealous? Wasn't being from Mexico a problem?"

"This was D.C. Lots of foreign ambassadors' kids and wealthy elite kids attend such schools. Besides, my adopted mother had taught me all the romance languages. Castilian Spanish, French and Italian. I have a gift for languages."

"Impressive. You can use your French on me any time It sure says romance. Wow. You aren't only good-looking, but smart."

He recognized the line guys usually give girls and laughed. I undid another button and slid my whole hand inside his shirt to get him back on the right track. "So what were these preppie girls like?"

"Like? For one thing, they'd never paw me in a public park, just to make me forget that I broke my vow never to raise any more zombies."

I drew back, caught.

"Not that they wouldn't paw me in a public park just for the heck of it."

I slapped him lightly on the chest for leading me on while I was leading him on. "I'm jealous."

"Don't be," he said. "I found out their game by senior year. I was the hot ethnic flavor of the year. A way to defy their parents, have some kicks and not get bored. I was just a diversion."

"That you are." I toyed with his nipple again.

"Delilah, stop that! You wanted to know. Listen, some wanted their parents to know they were seeing me, just to jerk them around. Others never wanted anyone to know but their very best friends. Guess how I found out?"

"Very best friends can be treacherous. 'Them', Ric? You were a serial gigolo?"

"Yeah. I was young, they were ready and so was I. It was too easy to be right."

"And I'm hard."

"Yes. What really turned me off was why I wasn't good enough to date for real."

"Which was?"

"It wasn't my Mexican blood. It wasn't my lurid background. One of the other guys told me why, finally, meaning to piss me off. It was that my adopted parents weren't high enough on the Washington social register."

"What did you do to get back?"

"What makes you think I did something?"

"You don't allow those you . . . owe something . . . to not pay for the privilege."

"There was this townie gossip blog. I hacked in and altered a really vicious column before it time-posted. It hit the Web and a lot of trust fund babies lost their graduation trips to Europe."

"Europe, really?"

"Especially Spain."

"Think they guessed it was you?"

"Naw, they thought they'd fooled everyone."

"So how'd you end up in the FBI?

"My adopted father wanted me to go into the military, like he had. I would have obliged him, except I knew having men ordering me what to do in that no-questions-allowed way would . . . I'd kill someone first. So he got me some internships with the suburban police, a D.C. crime lab. I had all the right qualifications for Quantico and was accepted by the FBI as soon as I was eligible. They value Spanish speakers now."

"And your special talents—?"

"I just wanted to forget about that. It'd been years. I was a privileged white-collar kid. Then they took us to the body farm—you know, real bodies in various states of decomposition. My fingers twitched for wanting a twig. It started happening again when we were examining possible death scenes. I finally picked up a dead stick and let myself "discover" a disruption in the earth. I had to go off by myself to do it, so I got a rep for being a human bloodhound on some trail only I scented. With the Millennium Revelation, lots of strange things were happening. They were uneasy about me, but also pleased by my usefulness."

"Why didn't you stay?"

"Got too hard to conceal what I was really doing. Dowsing for the dead is nothing a seriously scientific crime-solving organization wants to claim even these days. It was better I consult out of town. I'm taken for a science geek, not anything cheesy like a psychic, and I make sure to make it seem that way."

"Nobody would ever mistake you for a science geek," I said. I ran my hand over his muscled bare skin and then up under the shirt collar, stroking the side of his neck. "What were they like, those society witches?"

"Nothing like you."

"Nothing?" I challenged.

"They weren't about me or even the sex. It was all about them. They were shallow and artificial."

"But good-looking."

"Sure. They'd had plastic surgery since their pre-teens. They didn't care about me and I didn't care about them when I learned to see through the American princess façades. Not one of them could fight off a werewolf."

"But you were dazzled at first, admit it."

"No argument. I was a teenage boy. We're nine parts testosterone and one part horny. You should be glad, *paloma*, that I didn't break my heart over anyone else, so it's all in one piece for you."

"*Hmm.*"

I stroked the bat bite again, hyped to feel his carotid artery bound at my teasing touch. I could almost understand the vampire's predatory enjoyment in sensing signs of vulnerable human circulatory systems that thrust so near the surface.

"Are you going to take me home and to bed," Ric asked, "or just drive me crazy in the park?"

"Yes. Both."

My feelings for him were incredibly fierce, both possessive and protective. Was it because I'd never felt much affection at all *from* and therefore *for* other people?

Or because something of Lilith sang through my blood? In lore, the original Lilith was an Eden-exiled femme fatale, a devouring goddess, and a succubus, a "night hag" who haunted men's dreams and beds, a psychic vampire who drained men sexually.

It scared me, how deeply I wanted Ric, but I wasn't interested in draining him. Quite the contrary.

"Home," I said.

Chapter Seven

HE FOLLOWED me from the parking area across Sunset Road and pulled the Corvette into the driveway beside Dolly after I'd disarmed the gates' security system so we could enter. I unlocked the quaint wooden cottage front door with the remote.

When he joined me at Dolly's driver's door, the public kid gloves were off. He pushed me flat against Dolly's sun-warmed Detroit metal as soon as I got out.

"The last time I was here your wild wolf-dog attacked me, knocked me flat on my back on the floor and attempted to tear out my throat."

"He was just trying to get you to hold still while he licked your hands whole again."

"After that, you straddled me, pinned my hands above my head, ripped open my fly and ravished me, *chiquita.*"

"Someone had to. You'd been so wracked up from cutting your hands to shreds on the barbed wire you used for dowsing rods, you needed to feel something pleasurable fast."

"This time, I'm going to ravish you." He eyed the greenery. "Where's the dog?"

"Out probably. He has his rounds to make."

"You don't know where he goes?"

"His breed was born to run, so he takes gallops around town. I can't possibly walk him enough for the exercise he needs."

"Can you give me the exercise I need?"

"Oh, I think so." I pulled his tie knot loose, yanked the top button of his shirt free and fastened my mouth onto his bared, brown throat like a rabid bat.

His lean strong body rippled against mine, all muscle, now aroused and hard. Ric picked me up, cupping my head against his neck so my mad, bad succubus kiss couldn't stop. He bounded up the few steps to the door, pushed it open, and carried me upstairs.

He found the bedroom without help and set me down while I clung to his shoulders and neck.

He found something else without help. In no time he'd stretched my hands above my head and tied them to the large gargoyle carving of one bedpost with his silken tie. If anyone else had bound me, I'd have panicked. But I'd taken control of his hands and arms the first—and last— time we'd made love here, and understood his desire for a return ravishing.

It was play, it was deadly serious passion, it was scary and it was divine. I was pulsing with excitement, my body writhing to excite his even more. His gaping shirtfront made my mouth lunge for him, seeking any part of him to fasten on, lips, neck, nipple, but he bent down out of reach to take off my high heels. Once they were gone, I balanced on my toes like a ballerina, light and spinning. He knelt there still, then undid the side zipper on my skirt. I'd thought from the day we met he'd unzip my skirt as if it was a polite social gesture.

"Such a demure little skirt, Delilah. Opaque linen. Surely you wore it to excite me with its modesty. Is my friend the silver chain curled around your hips under here, warm and glittering? So delicate, so strong."

His forefinger touched the revealed chain and only a distracting question kept me from coming right then.

For the first time I remembered the silver familiar. Where was it? Had it morphed into the chain? No, I'd worn the real chain this morning. Was it curled into a tight little ball playing peek-a-boo in my cleavage? Would Ric find it and wonder? Would I have to explain?

I sent out an all points bulletin over my body, which was difficult to do with certain central points so awash in sensation. Ah, there it was! Formed into a toe ring on my right foot, either too discreet or embarrassed to remain in the path of major erotic stimulation. Lucky Ric wasn't a foot fetishist.

Right now his fetish was navel-gazing. And sucking. He'd pulled the gaping skirt waistband down to reveal the thin chain swagged beneath my navel, and then began kissing his way upward until he had to stand.

"And this neat white blouse that buttons down the front under the jacket you left in the car. Surely you didn't want me to rip it open, ruin it, just to see your breasts. Just to see the full tops of your breasts inside those push-up bras you wear." Buttons flew as he bared me.

"I don't wear push-up bras," I said indignantly. I didn't need them. Oh. His hands were underneath the satin cups, pushing me mostly out.

Before I could react, he reached down to pull my tight linen skirt up to my hips until it was a cummerbund.

"And you don't wear hose in the heat, of course, but, what, no panties, not even a shred?"

I murmured mindlessly in self-defense, because I did indeed wear a brand-new thong, and it still felt darned uncomfortable up my back crack. So much for Irma's lingerie advice. His finger had found that narrow bridge of silky fabric and teased it aside.

His hands ran up my bare arms to my secured wrists, linked fingers with me as his body leaned hard against my mostly naked parts.

"You like this vertical, I know, Delilah. And I'm very vertical at the moment, I think you can tell."

The more intimate Ric got with my body, the more he used my formal name. I moaned. *"Por favor, por favor,"* I murmured, knowing how much Spanish from my mouth pleased him. The hard ridge in his pants was pressing into my naked pelvis, the closed zipper welt thin and hard. I rocked my hips into it, until that welt slipped between my slick labia. I was aching to fuck his clothes again. Why did he never strip fully for me? Why did he make me always push forward to feel him? Maybe because it made me wild with desire.

"Now, my love? Are you ready? *Ahora?*"

I was murmuring his name and the word *ahora* over and over. Now, now, now.

His thigh pushed my legs apart, only a little because of the tight skirt. He'd moved a hand to work his fly open and then spread the warm fingers of his other hand on my lower back as he tilted my pelvis to receive his erection and I wrapped my thighs around his hips.

Our positions were constrained. I was constrained. My vagina was tight. The penetration was slow and tantalizing. I started to scream with release at the first hint of the first thrust, as Ric's hot mouth closed on my neck to give me my own vampire-bat suction-bruise.

He kept moving into the eye of my orgasmic storm, prolonging it as I shuddered into whimpers and purrs and then, amazingly, peaked again. Only then did he climax.

Finally, our energy evaporated. We remained locked together like the Sunset Park lovers.

"Too rough?" he asked, his voice ragged.

I shook my head violently. Couldn't speak. My emotions were as wrung out as my body.

"Not rough enough?" He sounded unusually cautious.

I shook my head again. Spoke. "Just right. *Dios*, Montoya, you sure know how to rock my world."

"And you mine." His last parting thrust made me draw in a rasping breath, then he tucked away and zipped up. As he untied my hands, he murmured in my ear, "We're going to need a good supply of shirts and blouses, I think."

He buried his face in my cleavage as my arms came down. I wrapped my arms around his shoulders, giving him the heat and nurture of my nipples. We ended in a mindless round of "*te amos,*" and this time I had a Spanish soul and meant every repeated syllable I could find breath to croon.

When he pulled back, I was flushed with satisfaction and a bit of a blush.

"Yes?" he asked, reading my reservations instantly. He *was* a cop of sorts.

"That was, that was a bit, um, lurid."

"But you liked it. You came like a catamount almost before I could penetrate you."

I blushed more. "Yes, but bondage—"

He lifted each of my undamaged wrists and kissed them, then folded the wrinkled sky-blue silk tie and put it in his jacket pocket. The gesture made my heart pound afresh. He expected to use it again. The wetness between my legs warmed with a fresh flood.

He stroked the back of his fingers against my flaming cheek, then took my pulse under the skin he'd suckled. "*Muy caliente*," he murmured, "*muy tempestado*. Don't fight it."

"You know how I feel about being bound horizontal."

"This is being bound vertical. This is different."

True, but I still felt uneasy about my wildcat self, about how easy that self could break loose at the silken touch of his tie and the mere nudge from the head of his penis.

He smiled as his face neared mine. "You like it well enough to ravage the parts of me that the past has made sensitive." He showed me his neck, the skin reddened, a new bruise already turning as dark as thunder.

I was a little shocked to see the fresh damage—and breathless. "Because it excites you and I like to excite you."

"This lovemaking excited you."

"It shouldn't have. I'm not a victim."

"Delilah. Often the things we fear the most turn us on the most."

"How do you know that?"

He chuckled. "My adopted mother, the psychologist. Oh, she didn't put it that plainly." He took my hands in his again, held them palm-to-palm as if teaching me to pray.

"Delilah, I most fear being under the control of others, but I also fear that the pleasure and release the bat-bite brought me during my youth was a sin in that desert wilderness of constant want and pain. When you use it with such wicked delight to excite me it frees me to enjoy the pleasure, because the woman I love has accepted everything I was and did and rejoices in my manhood, no matter how I arrived at it."

Tears were flowing. "Oh, God, Ric. I do! I do love you, I do want you. There's nothing wrong with you. It's me. I veer from being leery to distrustful, but it's of myself."

"I know." He lifted my hands above my head again. "But a bit of binding frees your *hembra tigre,* because you are not quite in control then, are you? Not quite responsible when I'm driving you so crazy."

I nodded. Slowly. Ric released my hands and leaned in to extract a string of sweet, deep kisses from my lips.

"Don't fight yourself, your own nature," he advised, "unless you don't want to feel like this again."

I hadn't known what "normal" or my own nature was since the Millennium Revelation. Somehow, I'd decided to fully accept exploring it with Ric. And I was liking it.

When I'd dressed again, I showed him to the door, where we dawdled over goodbye kisses.

"*Umm,*" he said during a breathing break. "You look so . . . disheveled in those clothes."

"Linen wrinkles easily," I said demurely.

His eyelids were heavy, sexy. "I could make love again, just to your clothes."

"Guess I'll throw away my steamer, then, if you prefer me mussed."

"Absolutely." He kissed me like it was the first time, long and deep.

When he broke it off, though, he was back to business matters.

"There's one thing you can't put off, Del."

He sounded sober, serious. My heart did a highland fling. I wasn't telling him everything about my investigations. I should, but . . .

"What, Ric?"

"The Cocaine groupie killing. The police still may like you as a suspect because the victim was seen pawing you in the Inferno security film. You'll need to be interviewed."

"My attorney," I told Ric, "can deal with the Las Vegas police if they want to interrogate me about the groupie death."

"You still using that Nightwine CinSim?"

"Perry Mason never lost a case or an innocent client."

"That was fiction, sweets."

"He'll be right with me all the time."

"Having a lawyer at an interrogation looks suspicious."

"They'll be star-struck, you know they will be. Perry is awesome."

"Maybe. You won't ask me to escort you there, but you'll let Mason accompany you to the police station. I'm hurt." I winced. "Meanwhile, let me work around the back door."

"With your police captain friend?"

"Colleague."

"Woman cop. Don't forget that for a moment, *amlgo mio*. She likes you."

"All the better for you. We'll talk after it's over. When can you get in?

"Soon. Perry's on permanent retainer with Nightwine, remember. I'll have him set it up. Can you promise that Haskell won't be involved?"

"I'll hold Captain Malloy's flat feet to the fire if they don't keep that lowlife out of it."

"I don't like you holding anybody's feet but mine, but I promise I'll get in for my own special grilling."

Chapter Eight

ANY SENSIBLE "SUSPECT" would have been fretting about a forthcoming date with the police to discuss the ugly matter of the Snow groupie death.

Any sexually susceptible woman would be obsessing about hot rock-star Snow instead of one of his dead worshippers.

I spent the rest of the day dreaming about sudden reruns of the *Pulp Fiction* romp with Ric. I kept checking myself in the mirror to see if I looked like a woman who'd get off on light bondage and heavy breathing for a little afternoon delight.

Even the hall mirror seemed to reflect a newly disheveled me and I wondered if my sudden conversion from celibacy would make me more sensitive to Lilith's appearances. Lilith had obviously been a hot number since the apple orchard in Eden.

So I wasn't totally surprised when my own image blurred and I saw someone else posing as my reflection.

Seeing Cicereau's daughter in my hall mirror had become less startling, but I still caught my breath. This time she seemed more real than the impish version of my double, Lilith, I'd glimpsed earlier. This decorous girl posing for her first prom photo in a sweetly modest 1940s gown was a world away from the slaughtered lovers in a forgotten Sunset Park grave.

That she'd been killed during the act of love amid a fiery furnace of sexual passion with her ancient yet teen-aged vampire lover seemed impossible. I'd psychically glimpsed them coupling sixty-eight years ago, feeling at the same time a fierce erotic desire I'd never known personally.

At that moment, the dead girl had become my bridge to womanhood. As Ric clasped me tightly from behind, an attractive stranger whose dowsing lesson had now welded our hands together on the forked twig, he and I shared the dead lovers' dying emotions and sensations.

Remembering our unintended orgasms at that moment now made me blush to see the innocent girl who'd awakened them. Ric and I had sensed and shared the lovers' last, impassioned moments, knowing nothing of their Romeo and Juliet youth. My blood heated in memory. Ric and I hadn't been actually intimate until a few weeks later, but we'd been dowsing our own depths, natures, minds, and bodies ever since.

So I stood there staring at the demure girl from a much more innocent era, the once-virgin daughter of mobster Cesar Cicereau and my inadvertent orgasm fairy godmother. I owed her a lot, including justice. Discovering her own father had ordered her killed in that harsh humiliating way shocked me more than the capital crime of murder.

Maybe that was because I'd never known a mother or a father. I'd fantasized, after each interviewing couple left without adopting me, that my real father and mother had been strong and loving and killed in a terrible accident by a hit-and-run driver and my infant self, surviving, had been dropped on a faraway corner to be found. Yeah. A fairy tale. Kids do believe them, for a while, me longer than most.

I now had the sexual experience and strength to face the dead girl fully. She wore an orchid corsage on one blue taffeta shoulder. I hadn't seen that in their double grave. I saw their clothes as bits and pieces around them. They must have been killed somewhere else, perhaps in a room at the one-story 1940s motel that evolved into today's monolithic Gehenna Hotel. They must have been picked up in the bed sheets and driven to a deep grave in empty sand desert considered remote from the minor oasis that Las Vegas was back then.

Dumped. Like dirty hotel laundry. And positioned face-to-face, as if still making love. Bastards! Perverted murderers!

My dark thoughts had obscured the young woman's image, although she was still there.

"Please."

I heard the word as if she stood next to me. My inner focus switched to the mirror again. My fingers had reached out to spread on the cool surface. Her hand had lifted to match me, fingertip for fingertip.

I could feel a buzz like electricity.

"I'm not ashamed," she said softly, "of anything you saw or felt in Sunset Park. Only that you know my father killed us."

"How do you know I learned that?"

She smiled. "I feel you too. That's rather nice after all this time in nowhere. I guess I'm like your pretty dog. I followed you home from the park."

"Pretty" was not an apt description of Quicksilver, but I suppose to a naïve teenager, he was just a big, handsome dog.

"Do you see me all the time," I asked, "or just when I'm standing in front of this mirror? How do you know what I've learned?"

"If it involves me, it just blossoms in my head. It's like I'm dreaming after a long time in utter darkness. I'm getting stronger," she said. "I think that's because you are, Delilah."

She said my name so shyly, yet with such pleasure. It made me feel good, like I'd found a friend. Life so far had thrown me competitors, not friends.

"Can you . . . live again?" I asked her.

"I don't know. Can you come in to see me?"

Probably, but did I want to? I pushed my fingers forward against the faint pressure of hers.

Yes! As my hand had passed into the magician Madrigal's front-surface conjuring mirror, my fingertips thrust through this mirror as if it were melted glass. There was no sense of barrier. It felt like a perfect day when the air is exactly your own body temperature, so you feel naked even while wearing clothes. I said so.

"I've seen you naked too," she said, smiling.

"Here? In the hall?"

"Inside the mirror."

So she'd seen Lilith too! From the other side of the mirror.

"Come in," she said again.

I had to get past my astonishment—and think.

There were many lovely creatures in the Millennium Revelation world that could speak softly and look harmless and could liquefy your soul like a blender set on purée before sucking it clean out of your skin.

Was this girl one of them? Being dead and suddenly having a lingering presence might motivate an unhuman lust for life that would take it from unwary humans.

"I won't bite," she cajoled.

That was a good point. A lot of people did bite these days, and they did a lot more weird things than appear in mirrors while dead. What was she? Certainly werewolf like Daddy. All werewolf or only part?

So I asked her.

"I'm half human. That's why Daddy punished me so severely. A true werewolf, he said before he killed us, would have never betrayed her pack with a vampire."

"He was there?"

"Of course. He had to let us know who did it."

"He . . . participated?"

Her eyes became all iris, blue like her gown. Pain twisted her features.

"He watched. He made me watch."

"Watch what? Oh. You were second to die," I whispered.

Cicereau was a freaking sadist! Yeah, you had to be a monster to run your enemies down with a werewolf pack at full cry, then mount the heads of your human victims on your hunting lodge wall. But to make your own daughter watch her first love killed . . . .

Her fingers twined with mine. They were the same exact body temperature. In a moment I no longer thought about the strange physical presence of dead flesh, no longer felt that we were not one.

This was the closest physical/mental link I'd ever had with anybody, except for Ric.

I was scared, but too eager to know her full story to break our communion.

In the mirror, a shadow was congealing behind her. I recognized Cesar Cicereau, glowering, his face white and slack, his dark eyes empty holes in his head.

Vague figures circled him, men or rearing wolves.

"They killed my darling first," she said in a hard voice.

"How?"

Her fingers slipped through mine, then stroked my palm and grasped my wrist, as I grasped hers. I was now inside the mirror up to my forearm and my face was leaning closer.

"They staked him."

That didn't jibe with the physical evidence. The coroner hadn't mentioned finding any evidence of a stake, although it could have crumbled to dust in the dry desert air in almost seventy years.

Still, I winced at the anger and pain in her light, young woman's voice.

"They held you down?"

She nodded. "And then they . . . cut off his pleasure parts."

That severed flesh would decay in the grave, leaving no evidence of the mutilation.

"You saw?" I breathed.

"Then they cut off his head."

True. The spinal vertebrae had been separated at the neck and the detached head put back in place. Grisly Bahr had found that anomaly right away, deducing the male victim had been vampire and the amputation had "killed" him for good.

"They put a chip from the proposed Inferno Hotel in his"—her voice fractured—"mouth, like the holy Host, and scattered thirty silver dollars over his disintegrating body. And then they turned their attention to me."

"Attention?" I didn't really want to know. I was feeling this, not just hearing it.

Rivers of furious blood suffused my face. If this mirror revenant hadn't been holding my wrist with a death grip, I would have made a fist, torn away, and gone Cicereau-hunting that instant.

Her sweet young voice droned on like a zombie's, no current emotion in the dreadful words.

"I was beyond despair, Delilah. I opened my mouth to curse my father—but one of his pack betas leaped down on me, raped me in a burning instant, and howled to cover my screams as he shot a silver bullet into my broken heart and body."

Bones would show no evidence of rape.

I fought to control my outrage. I was a silver medium. Maybe I could become a living "silver bullet" that would take Cesar Cicereau down, all the way down to the Hell he deserved.

At that moment, his daughter was far more real than any vision of Lilith. The mirror reflected my fingernails pressing red crescents into the girl's pale skin. We still bridged the gap with only our arms between my reality and her Mirrorland world.

I sensed she couldn't feel the pain my grip was inflicting on her. It was nothing compared to her past, anyway.

"What do you want?" I asked. My voice rasped. "To be avenged?"

"No."

No? Then why hold me captive and appalled in my own mirror?

"I want my lover back."

My breath came out so hard and fast it fogged the mirror, monetarily concealing her smooth, soft face. I could only confront her outrageous request.

I'd gladly go after Cicereau to avenge her and myself. But . . . to raise a vampire destroyed so totally no flesh remained . . . even Snow would tell me that was a fool's quest. No one reasonable would take it on.

"Who was he?" I asked briskly. I was a damned paranormal investigator, wasn't I? No task too impossible. Time to step up and live up to your own business card, Street!

She smiled like all young girls in love, damn her. "He had a very important assignment. The Old World vampires had sent him to scout a beachhead in Las Vegas."

Beachhead? What kind of word was that for this teen kitten to use? Oh. Military talk. Right. She had met and fallen for her foreign vampire just after WW II. European vamp culture had probably been as decimated as the human population by Hitler's rampage. Jews, Gypsies, gays, anyone "different" had been immolated. Why not hidden clots of vampires?

So the vamps hankered to start over in America, like a lot of DPs. Displaced Persons, as anyone who watched History Channel knew, is what refugees from the European slaughter were called then.

"The Inferno Hotel of today was a dream in your day, then?" I asked her. So Snow had claimed, but I didn't take his word on anything.

"It was a dream my father needed to stop, like all of mine."

"Your lover is not just sleeping vampire flesh." I had to make her face the facts. "He's only bones, as you are today. You, at least, have a mirror half-life. He is only history. He can't be seen in mirrors, if vampire lore is correct."

"I surfaced when you and your lover found us in Sunset Park. I floated up to the sunlight and sand, to feel you, to share our joy with you and Ric."

"You know his name?" I don't know why that bothered me more than anything, that she should know as much about me as I about her. She was dead, damn it!

"I know a lot that you know. We bonded, all four of us."

Shit! The implications were too intimidating to tote up. My first paranormally powered pairing with Ric over the murdered lovers' grave was not, as I'd thought, a psychic echo of ecstasy swiftly ended in mid-rapture. It was this very active spirit's way of drawing us into the true love that had spurred a brutal vengeance killing.

"Only the men resist." She smiled, girl to girl, woman to woman. "They are less intuitive, less trusting."

I knew I should be less trusting now.

"Isn't there someone you would do anything to save?" she asked.

A couple months ago, I would have said, *Achilles*. He was my incredibly loyal little dog who died in Kansas defending me.

Yes, I knew that was pathetic. My nearest and dearest had been my dog for almost the first quarter-century of my life. It just showed how far I'd come in a few weeks. I'd grown up in the heartland a girl who was afraid of sex more than death in a world that had suddenly blurred the lines between the two.

Was there anyone I'd do anything to save? Now I could say, *Ric*.

How could I say now that even a dead girl's hopes for the man she'd loved to death were undoable? Maybe I'd just have to find out how much of the impossible was possible in the Millennium Revelation Las Vegas.

Who and what her lover was.

Maybe in the course of doing that, I'd find out more about who and what I was.

We smiled at each other and slowly released our clasped arms.

"What was his name, your lover?" I asked quickly. That might reveal much about the vampire presence in

Vegas, past, present and future. That might explain the outcome of the werewolf-vampire war and stop another one today. One word. One name.

But someone or something was calling her. She glanced backward, fearful. With a regretful look, she faded into the Mirrorland shadows behind her and the shadowed hall behind me. My arm slipped through the dead zone of air between reality and reflection to my side.

We'd each withdrawn back into the limits of our worlds, whatever they were, but a deal had been sealed. I had yet another "client" for solving the motives for such a heinous double murder, a client who perhaps held the key clue to doing that.

Then I realized that I'd forgotten to get my new client's first name.

Chapter Nine

THE NEXT MORNING, I again scoured the daily paper.

I couldn't believe the violent showdown at Cesar Cicereau's Starlight Lodge a few days ago was still off the local media radar. Could he really keep the press in the dark about his secret mountain killing ground? What an ugly amount of power.

While skimming the Las Vegas online *Review-Journal*, I was astounded to spot an item about Caressa Teagarden, "one of the last living legends of the early film era." Seems she'd recently relocated to the Las Vegas Sunset City retirement community

I'd been assigned to interview her at Wichita's Sunset City franchise just before I left the Kansas TV station a couple months ago. Unlike senior citizens who had flocked to Sun City retirement communities until death did them part since the 1950s, senior citizens in today's Sunset Cities seemed to live on forever. Rumor had it that the North Koreans, through various experiments, had invented a method of replacing death with a "twilight awake" state. A thing like that would rake in billions. Think Donald Trump paying to be preserved in amber, comb-over and all. Forever.

I'd never met Miss Teagarden. My assignment editor said she'd "pulled the plug" on her Sunset City contract. "Died," in a way: let herself fade out of physical and even virtual existence.

Not true, apparently. I didn't fret about the cancellation at the time—I'd had bigger issues to deal with, like the sabotage of my entire career—but lies always made me want to find out what *was* true.

And now, Caressa Teagarden had popped up here. It was almost as if she'd followed me. Why?

I decided she was worth looking up. She'd been a big star in the Silver Screen days and might have known some of the CinSims I'd met here in Vegas. The local reporter gave me Miss Teagarden's number—professional courtesy—and we made an instant date.

After a short drive into the desert, Dolly and I entered an artificially maintained setting out of a movie company back lot of specialty sets. We navigated the winding, tree-shaded lanes that surrounded the picture-book community's large artificial lake and finally found a sprawling, shingle-sided cottage that read "Teagarden" on the gate.

When I knocked (no doorbell) on the arched front door, the sight of the bent, wrinkled old lady who answered almost physically knocked me over. Most people vain enough to extend their life spans by hook or crook or scientific experimentation had major plastic surgery before signing up for semi-immortality.

Caressa Teagarden was what she would have been before the Millennium Revelation at her age: a crone—a papery, somehow radiant dandelion fluff of a crone. She even used a cane, a sight seldom seen these days when everyone was forever young.

"Come in, young lady. I have tea and scones for you. Scones with currants. Not raisins! The only way to make them."

I tiptoed inside like an elephant in a Venetian glass shop.

The place was a gingerbread dollhouse, even more so than the Enchanted Cottage. Doilies were everywhere and furniture with carved curved legs broadcast the scent of lemon oil. My bottomless homesickness was sinking into the atmosphere like tired feet into a down pillow, a lavender-scented down pillow.

"Sit down, dear. You came to interview me for your . . . blog? What an ugly, modern term. I like to remember the old days, but I hope your questions aren't too prying."

"Prying? Ah. No." Star power had me by my Dorothy Gale heart. There is no place like home. Too bad I'd never had one.

My guilt at "interviewing" her for a fictional blog faded. Like many oldsters, she craved talk.

"Have a scone." She leaned close and confidentially. "It's the currants that make the scones. Very potent berries, you know. Sip your tea, dear. I've made a rather thorough study of tea over the . . . years. It's in my name, you see. Of course that's a screen name."

"Teagarden, you mean?"

"Yes, and not my first. My twin sister and I were a child act in vaudeville, Lilah and Lili Lockheart, only our real last name was Zellinsky. I went west and became a star."

"And Lili?"

"She stayed back East and we lost touch. They wanted me to play the Good Witch Glinda. In *Oz*. I declined, and it went to that vibrato-voiced ditz—oh, did I almost say *bitch*?—Billie Burke."

"Do you know why I consented to this interview?" Caressa/Lilah asked, abruptly fast-forwarding from the past to here and now, as the old will sometimes. "I need to get something on record."

About her career? Or . . . I thought madly back, trying to recall any indiscretions, any dead hunky actor I should be asking about.

"Not *that*, dear girl!"

Could the old lady read my mind?

"This generation is so enamored of digging up dirt. It's my history I wish to have recorded. My *family* history. That's more important than anything I've ever done on the screen or off it in some overdone satin boudoir. Décor was so over-the-top in the thirties."

Family history. Maybe it was the old-fashioned ambiance, but the phrase almost made me choke up. My only family history had vaporized back in Kansas at Smokerise Farm when Achilles had died.

"Pull yourself together and listen, Miss Street." Miss Teagarden's cane pounded the wooden floor, jolting me out of contemplating my still-fresh loss.

"I am the last of my family line. Oh, there are surviving cousins—first, second, third unto the loony power—but I am the last surviving descendant of Jean-Christophe l'Argent."

Wow.

Who the hell was Jean-Christophe l'Argent? And was he any relation to Christophe at the Inferno? She answered before I could ask.

"He was a famed French artisan who carved many of the most artistic gargoyles on Nôtre Dame Cathedral in Paris. The decorative gargoyles acted as necessary waterspouts but they were also thought to guard against evil spirits and monsters. Most people forget, though, that a great monster begat the gargoyles."

"A monster?"

"The fire-breathing, water-spouting, shipwrecking, human-eating dragon called *La Gargouille*, who purportedly lived in a cave near the river Seine in the sixth century. To placate this monster, murderers and maidens were annually tossed into the Seine. The gargoyles on Nôtre Dame and other medieval cathedrals were made to guard against the monster, Miss Street, and also to commemorate the dragon's dread reign."

I shivered to hear the tale of the devouring dragon and its victims and thought about rock star Cocaine's nightly entrance on a dragon's head. What evil forces could that stage effect represent?

Caressa saw her tale's effect on me. "My ancestor's work was more than what it seemed, just as you are."

"I don't know what I am. I'm an orphan."

"Ah. Give me your cup. I can read tea leaves." She snatched my empty cup. "Ah. I thought so. You have a split soul, as I do. You are surrounded by split souls, dear girl. That is your gift and your curse."

I'd recently discovered an unknown double. Of course my soul might be split. Now I had a curse?

"You're giving me chills."

"Tut. I'm just an old lady and I'm not really here, am I? I'm just a shadow of myself."

That shadow and split soul stuff spooked me, so did the names Lilah and Lili and the lost twin left behind. Sometimes I did feel I was chasing a shadow in hunting Lilith and that I'd never find a piece of family.

Caressa's knobby arthritic fingers crunched down on mine until I winced. "Self-pity is a servant who will bite you in two. This hand you feel has been wracked with constant pain for forty years."

It was crushing mine. I nodded, the tears in my eyes now from pain, not pity for myself or anyone else.

"I'll find you a book on my ancestor." She rose and tottered toward some bookshelves. Her cane prodded a low footstool into place in front of them.

"Please, let me—"

"I let you and I let you and I never do for myself again."

She swiped at me with the cane like an arthritic old cat showing its claws. I backed off, but stood guard behind her frail form as she climbed up and leaned left, then right, searching for just the right crumbling spine (not her own).

"Here. See for yourself. Jean-Christophe l'Argent, master gargoyle carver, a Frenchman famed for his work on churches."

I turned the brittle pages. The illustrations were engraved drawings, not photographs. I glimpsed twisted gargoyle faces turned to stone as if frozen in some instant of eternal judgment.

"My ancestor had other work, my dear," she said cryptically, "as do you and I."

"I don't understand."

"Perhaps you will." Her eyelids lowered. They were as wrinkled as a silk broomstick skirt.

Broomstick. Was she a real witch, unlike Glinda?

We sat again and she pressed the book into my fingers. I must take it, she insisted. I protested. It was her family history, not mine. She wouldn't let me leave without it. After all, I had followed her all this way to have an interview. Yes, she remembered that we were to do it before, but she'd had a sudden . . . displacement. Such a fuss. I was here now too, and we'd had time for a good talk. She moved between Sunset Cities, you see. An easy way to travel without leaving home.

Often her focus and voice faded as she recounted scenes from her fabulous film life. "Oh, William Powell! Yes. Born to play Nick Charles. Such a pity that the love of his life, Jean Harlow, died so young and tragically. Also a pity I can't leave Sunset City to visit him."

Her pale, watery eyes fixed on mine. I had a sense of time as precious, like a Fabergé egg. Circular in a way. Intricate and bejeweled. More than what it seemed, this humble bird shell. Rare large ostrich and emu shells from faraway lands. Pale robin's egg blue of ordinary nature. I had a sense of this time, with her, as fragile. She could be my grandmother . . . my great-great-great grandmother. My adopted grandmother.

Suddenly an object appeared between us, in her knobby fingers. It was not a scone.

The ring was almost black with age. Coiled with overdone scrollwork. Cheap. Pot metal. Old impure silver at best.

"You have listened to my life. This is in thanks. No, take it. My swollen knuckles are not for rings anymore. Besides, it's worthless, as you suspect."

Her smile was crooked, like her spine, but still a thing of steel. "You are too honorable to take anything of real value from a strange old woman." Irony curled around her words like wrought iron. "This is in thanks for recording my l'Argent family history."

The ring was too big for my finger, and gaudy, and it would probably turn my skin green. I felt proud to accept it.

HOME AT THE ENCHANTED COTTAGE that night, I put the ring next to the vase holding Achilles' ashes on the mantel. My Lhasa apso had still been with me when I'd first been assigned to interview Caressa/Lilah.

Odd that she'd preceded me to Las Vegas. I wondered why she was so vague about her twin as I headed up the stairs to bed.

Chapter Ten

IAWOKE THE NEXT DAY with dream remnants of huge stone gargoyles-turned-stalkers and a massive dragon hovering overhead while I ran for my life down the majestically lit but empty Las Vegas Strip.

Ah. A refreshing change from the usual alien abduction scenario. Scones and tea must be good for me.

I decided to go with the flow, so brunched while skimming Caressa Teagarden's quaint book from the late nineteenth century. It concentrated on the purpose and art of the carved gargoyles on medieval churches. Jean-Christophe l'Argent only got one mention, but as *the* master carver of all time.

The Internet was even less forthcoming. L'Argent meant "silver" or "silvery" in French surname traditions, but the name was rare and usually translated to Largent in English. However, I was happily browsing dragons and gargoyles and coming up with lots of lovely graphics, if no useful information, when my cell phone rang.

"I'm always calling you about police matters and appointments," Ric's welcome voice said, "when all I want to talk to you about is our investigations of the very private and personal sort."

"Why not," I asked, "when we can make progress on both fronts at once?"

"True. I'm just checking if tomorrow is okay for your jaunt to the Crimes Against Persons interview."

"Sure. Book me, Dano," I said, paraphrasing the *Hawaii Five-O* catch phrase. "Speaking of which, I had an intriguing interview myself yesterday."

"Yeah?"

"An ancient film star who's lingering on at the Sunset City west of town. Caressa Teagarden. Started in the Silents. Knew some of the Vegas CinSims personally."

"Never heard of her. What's the connection?"

"Hard to say. It was just weird. I was supposed to interview her at the Wichita Sunset City and she had supposedly canceled her contract, i.e., died, but now she's showed up here. Even before I did."

"That Sunset City setup is creepy, anyway."

I laughed. "More than CinSims? Vegas makes you pretty blasé, Montoya."

"But *you* don't. I'd suggest lunch, but I've got some *Federales* from the border coming up to consult. It's bloody hell down there between the drug lord wars, the zombie smugglers, and ordinary illegal aliens."

"At least I know you're here in town and safe."

"Same here."

We closed the call on murmured little nothings, neither wanting to hang up, promising to check in with each other when we could.

Well, I would be in town, but maybe not as "safe" as Ric would think or like.

If I wanted to know more about a long-dead teen vampire corpse in Sunset Park there was one source I dare not omit.

Snow.

JUST GETTING DRESSED to go to the Inferno that evening was a chore. My silver familiar kept flitting over my body, becoming a Thai dancing girl's slave bracelet one moment, a sleek designer torque around my neck another, then a Mexican hair comb in the shape of a jaguar.

I reached up to tear the last form from my hair, but it eeled away from my touch. I never wore the sides of my hair pushed up. The 1940s coiffure reminded me of the Black Dahlia, the era's most famous female victim and, now, of Cicereau's poor dead daughter. So the moveable silver thread looped around my neck into the form of a narrow snake chain, produced a smooth bezel and added a large faceted blue topaz.

Cool. I decided to take the hint and wear my forties white linen suit with shoulder pads big enough for a modern-day linebacker. Girly *and* gritty. It was something Ingrid Bergman might have worn in *Notorious* or *Casablanca* to meet a cynical Cary Grant or a bitter Humphrey Bogart. But the man I was going to see about a corpse was neither of those things. He was just Hell on wheels.

I ankled into the Inferno Bar on my white leather platform sandals with the, well, ankle straps. The area was awash with so many CinSymbiants—as devoted CinSim fans were called—in vintage drag it was hard to tell who were the real Cinema Simulacrums. CinSymbs dolled themselves up as their favorite CinSims, white-face and all. They gathered in droves here in the evenings, before the Seven Deadly Sins performed.

I wended my way past Clark Gable from *Mogambo* chatting with a blond Vivien Leigh from *A Streetcar Named Desire*. A CinSymb could pay personal tribute to any actor/role he or she wished. This Gable was short and stout and Vivien weighed two hundred pounds, but their costumes were perfectly in period and they looked quite dashing. The sound system was playing Big Band music that covered most of the eras represented. "In the Mood" was one of my favorites and I couldn't help swaying my hips to the choo-choo motion that made Swing king for a couple decades.

"*Wheuuut-woo*," Nick Charles wolf-whistled as I approached, turning to pull the white gardenia boutonnière in his dark tux jacket free and tuck it behind one of my ears. "'Sweet Leilani', one of Bing's best," he said, citing a Hawaiian ballad from his thirties' heyday.

"Think Snow will dig this outfit?" I asked him, taking a red-enameled steel barstool.

"White? What's not to like?" Nicky snapped his off-white fingers. The barman produced the cocktail of my invention, an Albino Vampire, in a minute flat.

"I need to talk to the boss," I said after the first, long, luscious sip. Damn, this was good! Too bad you can't copyright drinks.

"With you in that outfit, he'll be here before you can kiss that martini glass rim goodbye," Nicky warned. "Nora will be chartreuse with envy if she hears about this."

"Are you flirting with the customers, as ordered?" a deep baritone asked behind us. "Drink up, Delilah," it added, lowering a register into a soft purr. "I want to dance with you."

Why did that voice resonate in the pit of my stomach? Why did I know it wasn't addressing Nick Charles after the first question? Maybe because he was a Vegas entertainment icon or maybe because I was nervous or maybe because it came from the pit of Hell.

I took a long, long swallow of the vodka and white-chocolate-liqueur blend, then turned, ready to face the music and dance.

Snow wasn't performing until later. No white leather catsuit open from throat to navel. He was wearing a white silk Italian suit with white ostrich cowboy boots, only the roach-stomping pointed toe-tips visible, a white poet's shirt open at the neck to show off the pink ruby dog collar around his albino-white neck, and the usual black sunglasses.

I stood. Ric was tall but Snow was taller. Ric could salsa with the werewolves, but Snow could rock with the Seven Deadly Sins.

He held out his hands and I moved into his ballroom embrace.

How could so much white be so hot? White-hot maybe?

I really had no rhythm and I couldn't dance. Ric overcame that with his sexy human, Hispanic warmth. Snow overcame everything with his icy unhuman perfection and command. He led a dance partner like a cobra, fast, sleek, sinister.

I could feel his hands sucking the warmth and courage from my body as we foxtrotted around the dance floor, alone in the crowd. For such a high-profile personality, an international rock star and Vegas kingpin, Snow could become oddly invisible to the mob at will.

He pressed me close, moved his hand from my shoulder blade to my lower back, took the other to cradle it on his shoulder, then tangoed me like a puppet over the floor. I felt like a girl in a Parisian Apache dance, slung from pillar to post, winning the battle of the sexes through submission.

Snow had made a career on being ridiculously sexy. I had made a career on being totally impervious to sexy ploys. I was the objective reporter. Incorruptible. He was corruption personified. I knew he wanted me, but he wanted me ruined. That would never happen.

He stopped the sweep around the dance floor, released me. "You are really as tempting as an Albino Vampire in that ensemble. Is that why you wore it? What do you want from me?"

I quoted Patrick McGoohan as Number Six in *The Prisoner*. (I'm a vintage film junkie, occasionally even if it was on TV in color.) "Information," I intoned.

"Always your petty self-serving goals. Always nothing really interesting."

"You have got me so wrong, Snow. Self-serving is *your* modus operandi. What I want to know might help you and your Vegas empire. Interested now?"

"In what you're up to? Always."

"In what I know or don't know. Always."

He shrugged. It only enhanced the lines of his three-thousand-dollar suit. Armani, I bet. "The office, I suppose. You're so tediously dedicated to business rather than pleasure."

"Here," I retorted, "business *is* pleasure, and damnation."

His fingertip touched the blue topaz stone nestled on my breastbone. It grew suddenly warm, as did his tone. "You've been plumbing the depths of personal pleasure lately. It makes you very . . . persuasive. Come to my office, Delilah, where we can talk in private."

As if we weren't in some bizarre bubble when he moved through the public places of his empire . . . I followed in his wake, feeling a little like Captain Ahab. "Whales" were big spenders and gamblers in Vegas. I bet that Snow was a "great white whale" when it came to the top rank of hotel-casino owners.

At the door to his office he hesitated to allow me to enter first. As I did, he plucked the gardenia from my hair, inhaled its heavy, sweet aroma, and then put it in the buttonhole of my suit lapel. It had become a midnight-red rose wafting almost narcoleptic scent.

He sat in the white leather executive chair behind the desk, tented his long white fingers and let me gaze at my tiny reflection in those jet-black lenses.

I felt like a suspect up before a homicide cop. There were those "depths of personal pleasure" I'd been delving with Ric in the presence of Snow's lock of long white hair turned body jewelry, turned snitch. There was my secret plan to attempt to reform hooked Snow groupies into free women I hadn't yet done anything about. Soon.

I sighed as if bored and sat on one of the white leather and steel chairs facing his desk.

"I'm investigating the identity of the male skeleton found in the Sunset Park grave."

"For whom?"

"For myself."

There was a long silence.

Snow's pale lips smiled. "For whom else?"

This time I shrugged. I doubted it did for my vintage suit what a shrug did for his Armani. Most easily available vintage clothes that survived were ordinary ready-made. A working girl couldn't afford the rest.

"There are . . . other interested parties," I conceded, rather pleased to have some cards to put on the invisible table between us.

"Parties, plural?"

That had increased his interest. "Yes." I didn't often have a chance to sound smug in front of Snow. I kept Nightwine's and Hughes's names to myself.

"You're not saying who."

"No. I'm just saying that if you prove to be a reliable source, I might tell you the outcome."

"'Might'."

"Might."

He laughed as he swung the expensive chair from side to side. "I have my own very special and rather creepy operatives I could send to your bedroom by night to extract anything I want from your conscious or unconscious mind."

"Don't doubt it. My dog would eviscerate whatever it was, human or unhuman."

"Don't doubt it. You have interesting allies. But I have more. So, quit playing around and tell me what you know."

"Apparently your omnipotent allies haven't found this out yet," I said.

"Omnipotence is not a fail-safe substitute for one old-fashioned investigative reporter with the information-gathering instincts of Hell's pit-bull."

I kept still. Was that a compliment? I kinda thought it was and it wasn't even sexist. Must be this Katharine Hepburn power suit. She was a stainless steel hellion.

"The rumor is you're a vamp."

"The rumor is wrong."

"Then you wouldn't have any insight on who the vampire was who shared the Sunset Park grave with Cicereau's daughter."

"*Cicereau's daughter*?" He sounded impressed. "So that's who it was. Obviously Daddy Cesar didn't tell you that. Who did?"

"My sources are protected."

"Not enough."

I shrugged. Damn, I liked the effect of my buttressed shoulders. I felt like I could knock a lumberjack off a log with them.

Apparently they impressed Snow. He capitulated and answered, in depth.

"No. I don't know what vampire led young Miss Cicereau to bliss and butchery," he said reluctantly. "Vampires were keeping a low profile then. They'd let Cicereau and his werewolf pack get the jump on them. The Gallic werewolves had come to raw western America with Folies-Bergère ambitions and lots of francs. That attracted some of the more powerful Parisian vampires over too, and they had big dreams for a stunning hotel called the Inferno. The French vampires were used to a society where werewolves had been vigorously persecuted since medieval times and the vamps were civic heroes."

"Vampires were French heroes?"

"Who do you think had the ears—and probably throats of Marat, Robespierre and Danton during the French Revolution, the bloodiest political rebellion in relatively modern Western civilization history? Who encouraged the reign of Queen Guillotine and the rain of severed heads into baskets while truncated necks shot out gouts of blood? Madame Defarge was Reine of the Cité . . . and the vampires. Her famed knitting needles made fast work of any aristocrat who didn't die quickly enough. They called her needles the *Fer-de-Lance*, iron spear, after the venomous pit vipers of the south and central Americas.

"It was a world triumph for the blood-based breed. They almost got one of theirs elected president of the French Assembly. They still mourn their loss of influence in recent centuries."

I sat back, silent in the face of Snow's convincing description of events two hundred and twenty years ago.

His tales of French supernaturals centuries after Caressa Teagarden's fairy tales of devouring dragons in the river Seine jibed more than was comfortable for me.

Snow lifted a hand. I sensed something behind me and turned. His security chief, Grizelle, was waiting with a small silver tray. Two Albino Vampire cocktails sat upon it.

She did the waitress dip. This six-foot-plus tall supermodel-type with a tiger-stripe pattern in her silken black skin who could shape-shift into a six-hundred-pound white tiger did the *waitress dip* to set the glasses on Snow's desk.

"Thank you, Grizelle." He lifted his glass and held it out for a toast. "If you were a wine, Miss Street, I would characterize you as 'cheeky and amusing, but also full-bodied and effervescent, to be drunk quickly, before it spoils'."

Well! "Those who can, invent. Those who can't, steal."

I referenced the yummy white chocolate Albino Vampire cocktail I'd created at his Inferno Bar on a whim to annoy him. The bastard had simply made it the house drink, charged a mint for it, and profited from my invention.

"I'd be willing to pay you a royalty for the drink, but it wouldn't be as lucrative as what Nightwine would give you for Lilith's onscreen use."

I had been about to sip my drink but stopped before I choked. "You know about his hopes for Lilith?"

"Lilith is a valuable commodity in this town, thanks to his forensics show empire. I know about everything of value and the value of everything."

"She is a human being."

He shrugged. "That's what you want to think. She's supposedly dead. As far as we know. That makes her no less valuable. Even more so. "

"As far as 'we' know?"

"Ask Nightwine to let you attend the filming of a *CSI* autopsy. They're always done on a strictly closed set. It'd be interesting to know if he'd let you see the process."

"I've already visited the city morgue, on your recommendation. Maybe I should ask to be a background autopsy tech on the show." I thought my voice had been scorching with sarcasm.

"Not a bad idea." Snow was too obviously enjoying a long swallow of my creamy cocktail. Vampires didn't drink "vine," but neither should they suck down white liqueur cocktails. "Nightwine would love to titillate his enraptured audience with those bright baby blues you share with Lilith glimpsed, say, behind the Plexiglas of a safety shield. Rumors would run wild that Lilith still . . . haunts . . . the autopsy set. Million-dollar publicity for the show, refreshes an aging concept. Brilliant! You can give Nightwine the idea and claim it was yours, a bit of return on the Albino Vampire. He'd even pay you for it if you play it right."

I knew better than to drop my jaw. Snow thought just like the ghoul I worked for.

Still, it *was* a good idea. I'd have a chance to get to know—and probe—the film crew about Lilith's turn on the steel table, and find out if there was any possibility she was alive then. And if she might still be.

I really didn't like the fact she was putting on a show in my mirror. Maybe I was wrong in concluding that only dead acts performed there. So I played my unexpected ace, something I'd concluded about Lilith.

"You knew Lilith before she was on *CSI Las Vegas*, before she was officially 'dead' or famous."

"Why would you say that?"

"The first time I visited the Inferno, you came up and swept me onto the dance floor. I don't dance."

"You do in my arms and maybe Montoya's."

I ignored his attempt to link himself and Ric. "You also said you'd been waiting for me."

"It's a line, haven't you heard? Maybe you didn't, in Kansas."

"You left out you'd been waiting for me 'all of my life'."

"Maybe it would be impossible for me to wait for you all of my life."

"What? Poor mortal me? You're right about that and I wouldn't wait a New York minute for you. So quit the song and dance, Snow. You're good at it, but I'm good at detecting lies and evasions. *You thought I was Lilith.* You already knew her, but you hid that fact from me. Why?"

"I hide a lot of things from you. Why shouldn't I?"

That I believed. "Guess I'll just have to find them all out."

"Break a leg," he said cordially. "Anything else I can do for you today, Delilah?"

I'd barely tasted my Albino Vampire and his glass was drained. I wasn't going to be shuffled off, so I leaned back, crossed my legs, and sipped my drink that he earned the money for.

"You don't seem surprised by my mentioning Lilith's possible survival, Snow. She was presumed dead when you laid that line on me."

"I never believe any presumptions of innocence or death in this town, not even my own. What I believe about Lilith's state of being is moot, however. Her only filmed presence was, alas, as one dead. Not that this is a fatal problem. If she was in CinSim form, I'd lease her for the Inferno. I have a private club on the Lower Circles where she'd be in red-hot demand."

Every word of his speech seemed to indicate that his eyes were following every last detail of my form and face for its reproduction of Lilith. His tone was seductive, possessive, as if he owned me because he had seen and knew of, or possibly desired, her. Or had had her, in the Biblical sense.

"Lease her? Or would you buy her, at auction, like a slave?" I asked, bluntly.

He drew back a bit, as if slapped. As I had intended. I wasn't a Snow groupie to be seduced by some sexy sweet talk. I had a lot of Our Lady of the Lake Convent School backbone.

Snow lifted a pale eyebrow over the smooth black top of his sunglasses. Mr. Spock on MTV. "Now why would you think . . . one could buy . . . CinSims . . . when leasing them . . . is so much more lucrative . . . for the parent conglomerate, ISFX-MS, Industrial Special Effects and Magic Show?"

Snow was acting far too easy-going at the moment. And if he thought aiming his sunglasses at my crossed legs was going to make me jump up like Miss Muffett and shriek away, he was in the wrong nursery rhyme.

I recrossed them, higher, and sipped more slowly. Hello, Sharon Stone. Not a vintage film shtick, but effective.

A smile visited his pale lips and settled in. He lifted his martini glass, full again.

Parlor tricks that Madrigal at the Gehenna could do with his eyes closed would not disturb me, I told myself.

"I'm not here about Lilith, poor self-destructive girl," I said. "I'm here about the boy. The young man in the Sunset Park grave. I thought you might know something. Apparently not."

I drained my Albino Vampire in one long swallow and stood.

Now *he* was left holding the drink and being run out on.

"I have no clue," he admitted, his tone suddenly direct, flat. "I'm counting on you to find one. Call me your first client in Las Vegas."

"On the same case? You forget I've had two others ask me to solve the riddle. Or don't they count?"

"So be it. I'll pay you well for your results anyway."

"In Albino Vampires?"

"They're on the house now, for you."

"For how long?"

"Forever, Miss Delilah Street. Forever."

Okay, that was truly creepy. What was creepiest was that I was sure he meant that. Did he mean that I was immortal? Or that he was? I knew from experience that Snow's afterthought gifts had bite.

What it did mean for now was that I could collect three fees if I solved the identity riddle.

I doubted that was ethical, even here.

Don't sweat it, Irma advised me as we left, sailing under Grizelle's short supermodel nose as if her impressive form was not even there. *This town was always the capital of the con game they call Three-card Monte. We deserve three times what any one person would give us. We are a class act. And we are double trouble."*

Or were we a triple threat? Maybe, if I could find Lilith alive somewhere, we would be someday.

Chapter Eleven

Ric HAD "BOOKED" me into an early interview at the Crimes Against Persons, a.k.a. CAPERS, unit the next day.

Hector Nightwine had Perry Mason on tap just as fast.

I had to wonder where CinSims were "housed" when not on duty. Were they kept inert in warehouses? And what about their props, like the black fifties Cadillac convertible Perry drove up to my gate the next morning? Its color matched his black-and-white TV image, so I viewed a fragment of fifties TV film idling in my driveway.

Perry got out of the totally solid car to meet me at the cottage door and to admire Dolly parked in front of the carriage house.

"What a beauty! Where'd you get her?" He was a sharp one, recognizing Dolly's gender. Maybe it was the red interior leather and flashy white convertible top.

"Second-hand. In Wichita, Kansas."

"Kansas?" Perry seemed surprised. "Someone in Kansas must be foolish to part with a fine machine like that."

Also dead. I didn't want to mention that Dolly was estate sale spoils. It might remind Perry that he was a tad behind the times.

"Will I seem more suspicious if I come in with an attorney?" I asked as he saw me into his Caddy's passenger seat. It may have been a CinSim prop, but it was a genuine vintage automobile. I donned scarf and sunglasses for the ride, feeling *so* fifties.

Perry was a heavy-set man but he stepped briskly around the huge car frame to take the driver's seat. I reached for the seat belt I'd had to install in Dolly and saw Perry eyeing me. He had an intensely soulful gaze, but it was honed to a razor-sharp edge.

"Um—" How could I explain my out-of-era groping? "Just . . . uh, petting the leather interior."

He frowned, and when Perry Mason frowned it was enough to make Pinocchio spill his wooden guts. "Your car has a leather interior as well," he pointed out.

"Yours feels so much cushier, more L.A. than Kansas."

Perry's laughter was open and full. You might almost mistake him for Santa Claus if you were very foolish, like my mythical Kansas seller of a vintage Cadillac.

"Don't be impressed by L.A., young lady," Perry advised me. "It eats lovely young women for lunch . . . for very long, supposedly 'business' lunches. You're better off here in Las Vegas, under Nightwine's protection. Already the unsavory elements of *this* Sin City have roped you into a crime investigation."

Yeah, right. Hector was Daddy Warbucks and I was Little Orphan Annie.

Still, riding along with Perry getting stern advice on my safety felt like going for a drive with the daddy I'd never have. I'd put up with a lot of unwanted advice to savor that pleasant, relaxed, cared-for feeling. I felt a tinge of it with Ric, but the sexual chemistry was too overwhelming; it made me feel edgy and excited instead of cozy. Enough of a rewind on that!

The drive took us north. The homicide unit had its own building not too far from the fabled Las Vegas Boulevard, a.k.a. the Strip. Outside, the building was sleek and modern. The inside was absent of cliché except for a communal coffee pot.

Captain Kennedy Malloy, attired in a navy suit like an officer and a gentlewoman, or maybe a British nanny, entered the interrogation room first. This was the usual central long table and chairs, stripped to their essential forms. Apparently that's what the police had in mind for interrogation subjects: stripping me to my essential form.

"Your presence wasn't necessary," Kennedy Malloy told Perry. "We regard Miss Street as more of a witness now than a suspect."

"'Now' is a 'wiggle' word, Captain Malloy. It can quickly become obsolete in these apparently motiveless murder cases."

"Perhaps it's just as well that you see the recorded evidence."

She sat to click on a small flat-screen computer. I studied her smooth cap of strawberry-blond hair and slim figure.

Kennedy Malloy was as pale-skinned as I was under a tan veil of faint freckles. Hazel eyes. Irish, but not Black Irish like me, and not the red-haired, green-eyed boisterous lass of song and story. All business, all control, high-strung but low-key. I didn't see her and Ric hitting it off romantically.

But maybe she did.

Perry was leaning in to scowl at the small screen. "Footage from the Inferno security cameras, I take it." Malloy nodded. "Is that you, Delilah?" he asked me.

I leaned in to look, never having seen this before. I could see why Perry asked me to identify myself. I looked like a figure from a 1930s society ball in my rented vintage black velvet gown with my hair up in a chignon. Snow in his rock-concert white leather cat suit didn't look any vintage at all but Elvis spaceman. We were tripping the light fantastic—ballroom dancing— while the CinSymbs around us watched stupidly, as if they'd been bonked on the head.

Maybe seeing their idol capering among the pre-concert cocktail set had done it, or it was that invisible bubble Snow could command around himself that kept them from crowding in.

What had unhinged the now-dead groupie was seeing me actually touching the idol. Or, rather, me being touched by the idol. I'd told Snow: I don't dance, don't ask me, but he'd swept me into a fox trot anyway. Bossy bastard.

Now I saw that a strong lead could make anybody look competent on a dance floor.

It was uncanny how good I looked in CinSymb black, white and silver. With our coloring, Lilith and I were almost-CinSymbs born. Snow's albino skin and hair filmed like a silver-screen dream.

No wonder the groupie had been crazy jealous.

"Is that you?" Perry repeated.

"It must be. I didn't have a mental picture of how I looked in that CinSymb get-up."

Malloy snorted delicately. "Like you never looked in a mirror before leaving the house all dressed up for dancing."

"It's just a cottage. I use the hall mirror for full-length views and that hall is dim."

"She didn't need to look," Perry said. "Obviously Miss Street"—his chuckle rumbled as he no doubt thought of his secretary, Della, with the same last name—"doesn't need to fuss much to look well. I've always been partial to brunets."

And he winked at me!

Meanwhile, Malloy was doing a slow burn. "What is your relationship with Christophe?" She nodded at us sweeping around the floor while staring CinSymbs stepped back to make a circle. "You dance like lovers."

I'd had no idea we'd made such a display of ourselves. I'd been busy verbally fencing with him.

"He didn't ask me if I wanted to dance and, actually, I didn't. Our relationship is . . . probably best described as predator and prey."

"He does seem the type to prey on naïve women."

Naïve, I seethed in tandem with Irma. "No. I meant *I* was the predator. He's the prey."

Her hair color was too watery red for her to show much eyebrow, but one seemed to twitch with disbelief.

"I'm a former investigative reporter for a TV station. I came here on the trail of a . . . missing girl." Well, Lilith *was* missing.

"You came here from where?"

"Wichita, Kansas."

"And you think Christophe knows something about this missing Kansas girl?"

"I think he knows a lot about shady dealings in this city."

"How do you know this girl is here?"

"I saw her, on television."

Malloy nodded. "Yes, the networks and cable TV are always here filming Las Vegas crowd scenes for various shows."

I didn't correct her. Lilith had been filmed in a very uncrowded scene. Autopsy rooms generally are.

"How old is this missing girl?" Malloy asked.

"About my age."

"Twenty-four, then." Uh-oh, someone had been looking in my personal file. Maybe it was my FBI file. "There's nothing the law can do unless we find her and she's a victim of a crime."

"I know. That's why there are people like me."

"And you're like?"

I wanted to squirm. My new "profession" seemed theoretical so far. "A private investigator, I guess, but not the mean streets kind. I do paranormal investigation."

"For how long?"

"First for the Wichita TV station and, on my own here, uh, officially, a few days." That would be official in several months when a new Yellow Pages directory came out. My new Web site would be much faster . . . when I set it up.

"You get a license?" Malloy asked.

"They don't give them for my specialty."

Perry intervened. "It seems this town, and these times, could use paranormal investigators."

"If they're not jailed on suspicion of murder themselves," Malloy said sourly, licking her pale lipstick and apparently discovering it was Green Apple Sour Gloss.

I still suspected her secret heart was set on Ric and she didn't like my showing up and getting in the way. *Jeessh!* A homicide captain and a Snow groupie, both jealous of an orphaned Kansas virgin (until very recently). You'd think they'd have enough hardened Las Vegas femmes fatales to worry about.

Malloy ignored me again and squinted at the screen. "Here it comes. The hair shtick. You still want to say nothing's going on between you and Christophe, Street?"

The camera angle was at my rear. The gown was backless, but that was the style in the thirties: prim high necklines in front, tailbone-dusting plunges in back. Well, not quite that backless.

In the tape, Snow was teasing out hairpins until my chignon came undone. I remembered him making some sexy insinuation about his long white hair and my long black hair blending in the mirror over his bed. I'd figured it for a hint that he wasn't the Albino Vampire he was rumored to be, the way seducers before the Millennium Revelation used to assure girls they'd had vasectomies.

I blushed now, hoping it didn't show but knowing it probably did.

"He's very forward," I murmured.

"'Forward'? Is that a word out of a convent school?" Malloy demanded. "The man is obviously seducing you."

I blushed more. She'd hit the nail on the head. Out of Our Lady of the Lake Convent School in Wichita, to be specific. "Only if it works," I retorted, "and it didn't. He's leaving now, see."

"And here comes the frantic fan," she added.

"She's been watching them for some time from the group of people at the left," Perry pointed out.

The next scene that I did remember word for word played out with only moving lips, inaudible against the background music.

The woman, shorter and dumpier than I, swathed in a patterned velvet shawl, bent to retrieve my dislodged hairpins from the floor. She rose with three fanned in her fingers, souvenirs of the rock star called Cocaine. Addictive to her.

My hand made a motion that she could keep them.

She came as close to me as Snow had, like an unwanted dance partner pushing too near. Even on film her feverish eyes looked mad. Her hands reached for my loosened hair, fingers twitching to tangle in it.

I shook my head and my hair loose. Said something serious. Sharp. The damned woman had wanted to cut off a lock of my hair. No way was I letting a lock of my hair go off on its own.

But Snow had touched my hair when undoing my chignon, and this woman wanted anything he'd touched, including parts of me. She's the one who should have been under suspicion, not me. Except she ended up dead by the Inferno Hotel Dumpster in the back service area later that night while I went home to Quicksilver.

"This is all you have?" Perry asked.

"The women did have an altercation."

"The dead woman had an altercation. Miss Street simply stood there and defended her person from pawing."

"She didn't from Christophe, a.k.a. Cocaine."

Perry turned to me. "Did the man do more than hold you in the traditional social dance position and pull a few hairpins from your hair?"

"No."

He'd made a verbal pass and once his cool white hand had trespassed on my bare back below the waist.

The floating Inferno "eyes-in-the-sky" mirrored balls—a metaphor for the boss's ego and brass, perhaps?—had missed recording that. I saw no reason to cop to a copped feel if I didn't have to.

Perry shrugged and eyed Malloy.

"I see no reason to question Miss Street further," the captain said, "and obviously she isn't planning on leaving Las Vegas with her new career in gear."

The glance she flashed me added ". . . and Ric here."

I nodded politely and smiled.

And that's when the door burst open.

Chapter Twelve

"**Y**OU CAN'T just let her walk! What about the charge of resisting arrest?"

The man had burst through the door, legs and arms splayed to both confront and bar anyone from leaving. Haskell could have been any aggressive, middle-aged guy with a receding hairline and advancing gut when I'd I first met him over the dead skeletons in Sunset Park. Since then, he'd gotten a werewolf bite or two and it hadn't improved his looks or attitude.

"Detective Haskell," Malloy said in Ice Queen tones, "you were only to observe."

Ice Queen authority was not going to cut it with this guy.

I'd risen by instinct. Spittle was dotting his unshaven chin. He hadn't seen me since we'd tangled physically in Cesar Cicereau's office at the Gehenna before the boss's head muscle man, Sansouci, had hauled him off me.

His features had coarsened, as if halted in the middle of a werewolf change, sprouting tufts of hair here and there that were neither beard nor pelt.

His eyes seemed smaller, his nose and teeth larger, his body hunchbacked.

His anger toward me from the moment we met at the crime scene in the park had not changed, though.

"You gonna let this witch go? You afraid, Malloy, of that Meskin ex-Fed, or what?"

His sneer made pretty clear what "or what" he suspected Malloy of harboring toward Ric.

I hadn't heard anything, but Perry Mason was suddenly standing beside me, a huge black-serge wall. "Captain?" he asked.

Haskell answered, still spraying spit. I guess fangs make it hard to speak the Queen's English.

"She resisted arrest for questioning and you have her back for a tea party, Malloy, instead of a grilling? Leave me with her for two minutes and I'll get the real story."

Haskell prowled around the table's end, pushing into my territory.

Malloy was standing now too. "Haskell, you were ordered to stay out of here."

"That's what you want from detectives now? Do what they're told. I know things about this bitch, where she's been and where she shouldn't be, at the Inferno, the Gehenna. She's sucking up to all the mob bosses in town."

Wow. Haskell was a perfect case of what the shrinks call "projection." That meant accusing someone else of your own missteps.

"You selling out, Malloy? To Meskin ex-feds and CinSim shysters?"

"That will be enough." Perry Mason reached around me to seize Haskell by his jacket collar like a rabid cur. "My client came here voluntarily, not to be assaulted in homicide headquarters by a rogue detective."

"Rogue!" Haskell struggled to get his paws on Perry's hand at his nape, but it was like a puppy trying to escape the maternal teeth grip.

Perry reached into a pocket of his custom-tailored Big and Tall Men suit coat.

"Play this DVD, Captain. You'll see how Haskell arrests helpless and innocent young women."

I sent Perry a glare. He had to have Hector's security tape. I didn't want to be tagged as "helpless" and I really didn't want Malloy to see that humiliating scene.

Big Daddy was not having any backtalk. Malloy obediently accessed the DVD.

Haskell stopped struggling while his raging mind tried to figure out what was up.

I set my teeth.

It was all there. Haskell threatening to shoot my defensive dog. Me locking up Quicksilver to save him from a hail of bullets. Haskell handcuffing me by pushing me face-first against the wall, only a quick head-turn saving me from a broken nose. Haskell running his hands over me. Haskell spreading my legs by swiping the barrel of his semiautomatic between my legs . . . The words he muttered while he mauled me.

"You white-trash bitches, always bad-mouthing white guys and you turn around hot to be Meskin meat. All that good white skin wasted as black boys' and bite boys' meat." He'd pulled my hair back, hard, to examine both sides of my neck as if I were a horse for sale. If Ric ever saw this, he'd kill him. *"No freaking bite boy nibbles. Wrists clean, but . . . oh, too bad, somebody's been bruisin' 'em."*

Yeah! Him!

A sharp snap darkened the screen and ended the rerun.

Malloy looked up from the screen. "You are suspended, Detective Haskell, until further notice."

He started to swagger toward her, this petite woman in her prim suit, his big hairy hands reaching out. She did something, so fast I couldn't see it, to his thumb and his neck at the same time.

He went to his knees, growling.

"Get out," Malloy said. "And don't come back until you're told to."

We kept silent as he lumbered upright and left, literally snarling. Haskell was obviously some misbegotten half-unhuman now, but it was illegal to discriminate against unhumans in employment. That made everyone handle them gingerly. No court precedents had been set. No one wanted to be the test case.

"He doesn't belong on the force anymore," Perry told Malloy, dusting his hands on a white handkerchief.

Oh, right, men carried pocket handkerchiefs in his fifties heyday, big white linen squares. Bed sheets didn't even come in colors then. Women carried little embroidered nylon or cotton hankies. I hadn't been able to resist buying a bunch at estate sales. They were so tiny, so feminine and so beautifully useless, kinda like women in that era. What a vanished world!

Perry's arm was around my shoulders. It was like being embraced by King Kong. "I'll take that DVD and Miss Street out of here, Captain Malloy, and your apology."

"We'll need the DVD, Mr. Mason."

Perry must have felt me stiffen. "I'll take the DVD, Captain. It's private property and *we* don't intend to prosecute Detective Haskell for his abusive arrest."

Malloy hesitated, looking ready to try her thumb-lock on him.

Perry's quick smile said the matter was settled, his way. "We just wanted you to know that the detective's assertions about Miss Street are motivated by issues other than the crime."

Malloy's lips quirked, a grimace rather than a smile. I bet she'd hated what she'd seen and heard. Haskell's "Meskin" was Ric, obviously. Just as obviously, Ric and I were a visible couple. I hadn't liked her hearing and seeing that almost as much.

"Hector promised that no one would ever see that tape," I hissed to Perry as he walked me out, tight in his grasp. More for his protection than mine at the moment, believe me. "I want it back!"

"Hector only released it to me under duress."

That would have been a bit of mind-wrestling I'd have liked to see.

I staked my claim. "I shouldn't have let him keep his master copy. I want that DVD."

We still spoke in harsh whispers. By now we were outside and at the passenger side of the Caddy. Perry had parked right out front, as if he was the mayor. Haskell was nowhere visible. I checked.

"I do what's necessary for my clients. You may have the recording. It's made my point to Malloy."

"But Haskell got to see it. And Malloy. And you. Did you watch Haskell? He enjoyed it."

"I watched him. And you." He took my upper arms in his big hands to ensure my attention, that I'd look him in the eye. But I couldn't. My glance slid to his Caddy's shiny black fender as my face finally flushed. He spoke in the measured tones of an attorney addressing a jury. Or a judge.

"Delilah, we aren't responsible for how or why other people hurt us."

The words sat there and sank in. He was a master at that.

Above, the midday sun was beating down on our bare heads. I couldn't remember the Raymond Burr Perry Mason ever wearing a hat. I wondered why. The fifties were the era of men in hats, until JFK became president in 1962 and tousled hat-bare hair became male chic.

But neither of us was protected from the glaring sunlight. I realized I'd always blamed myself for those vamp-boy attacks in the group homes. My dead-white skin, my looks, the way I attracted them. My fault.

Perry rumbled on. "Rotters like Haskell always like to bother attractive young women. He's just more brutal than most, even before he . . . changed for the worse. The tape proves that. It's an indictment of him, not you. The shame is his, not yours."

"You think I'm attractive?"

"It's not a judgment call, my dear Miss Street. You don't need a defense attorney to prove that. You are a very attractive young lady and well able to take care of yourself. You were right to avoid fighting Haskell. The humiliation was worth your dog's life. A fine animal, I could see that even on the tape. I'm sure he would have given his life to save you that distress."

I nodded, tears of anger in my eyes. The group homes staff had always acted as if it was my fault I was attacked. It was because of me that nice Father Black was forbidden to take me out for driving lessons; it was my fault the other girls at Our Lady of the Lake school resented me.

But Perry Mason said it was them, not me, all along. I thought he made a pretty good case, as usual. It convinced me of my own innocence for the first time in my life. He released his stabilizing grip.

"Now I'll drive you back to your charming cottage at Castle Nightwine."

I giggled. "I thought only I called it that."

"Obviously not. I'm going to hector our mutual friend Hector over a very good dinner about his breaking his promise to you, so he'll never do it again. And you will forget about all this and have a happy rendezvous with the lucky Latino fellow Haskell is so jealous of."

"Ric. Ricardo Montoya."

"Ah." Perry's gray eyes—probably really blue in color—were twinkling as he opened the heavy car door as if it was made of cardboard. "I've met the young man. Impressive. I believe Captain Malloy has made a similar assessment."

I twinkled back. "I guess she struck out on all fronts today, then, didn't she?"

Chapter Thirteen

IT WAS TIME I started looking for Lilith to save my own skin.

I'd spotted her name on some of the discussion forums of Snow groupie Web sites like cocainefreaks.com, sevendivinesins.com and brimstonesluts.com.

It could be another Lilith or a pseudonym someone had liked. After I'd finally realized that Snow had mistaken me for Lilith the first time we met—and tangoed and tangled—at the Inferno, I was more inclined than ever to think I'd find a path to Lilith through his groupies.

I might also find out who'd killed the one who'd messed with me. Doing that would get Malloy off my case, if not Haskell.

My scheme to start a groupie "self-help" group seemed the best way to get to know the culture and its members. And the best way to do that was mingle with them during a Seven Deadly Sins show.

PERRY HAD BEEN RIGHT and wrong at my interrogation today. I was not a mirror-gazer. My typical adolescent dislike of my maturing looks was magnified by the realization that vampires really grooved on them.

Now that I'd encountered Vegas, Ric and the Enchanted Cottage looking glass, though, I couldn't avoid mirrors. I needed them to confirm my disguises. I didn't need seeing glimpses of the dead in them, but I got them. Ric and I had first made love in front of a mirror, his choice, showing me a sexy side of myself I'd never imagined. Was I becoming a mirror seeress and escape artist because I always had a mirror self, a twin?

These thoughts were circling in my head as I did a last check in the hall mirror to make sure I passed as a Snow groupie. I had a lot of range there. They ran from dewy 'tweenhood to octogenarians and beyond, in flavors from Goth to punk to country club to vintage diner.

I had butterflies in my stomach, but not because I was going to the Inferno Hotel and Casino for the Seven Deadly Sins' nightly show. That alone proved I wasn't in any danger of becoming a Snow groupie. No, I was nervous because I was going to seduce those groupies away from the object of their mania. Long shot. But I didn't have any others when it came to tracking down my possible "twin."

I wore gray contact lenses to camouflage my signature baby blues. My outfit was relentlessly denim down to the ankle boots. I didn't usually dress this urban casual—I'd been a newsroom career woman for too long—so it was a good disguise.

The silver familiar had followed my thoughts, slithering up my arm, neck, and cheek to become a literal crown of thorns. That was a little dressy for denim, but the spiky look resembled the Statue of Liberty's tiara in a funky way and I needed one touch that would get me remembered, yet not attract Snow's post-show Brimstone Kiss.

His Brimstone Kiss was supposedly the one and only admitted desire of Cocaine groupies. Their raunchy online discussions, though, proved they hankered for more. Rumor nicknamed him "Ice Prick," but nobody could speak from experience. Witchcraft lore claimed the Devil and demons had ice-cold penises. Believing Cocaine demonic might appeal to women with Darkside tastes, but I couldn't imagine any thrill from that chilly attribute, other than goose bumps.

What I found demonic was that Cocaine fans who got to a Vegas show lost both ways. Some, broke, eventually went home without the Brimstone Kiss to try again on another trip. The "lucky" ones, though, might as well have rewound and erased their previous lives once they got that mosh pit lip-lock. They moved to Las Vegas, they held menial jobs, they attended the Seven Deadly Sins performance every night they could afford, seeking a return engagement with the Brimstone Kiss. And they never got it again.

I wasn't sure what Snow was, besides addictive to his victims, but right now I was more concerned about where Lilith was, or if she even was at all. I adjusted my crown of silver thorns to look more like a custom chrome hubcap. Then I slung a hobo bag full of my new business cards over my shoulder, and bid my mirror goodbye.

NOWADAYS LAS VEGAS resembled *Lord of the Rings* country. The new forests of time-share and condo towers were narrow needles, like magicians' or hermits' towers, that offered views from every unit. Hotels dating from after the millennium favored fountains of fire and geysers of colored smoke. They all looked like pits of Hell and just the right cracks of doom to throw a pesky but supremely powerful ring into.

The Inferno was the most fiendishly lit. The sound of falling water, hissing steam, and beating flames was oddly New Age. I dropped Dolly off at valet parking.

"Don't bruise those fins," I warned. "She's a big girl."

"Sure thing, ma'am," said the loathsome, scaly demon who slipped behind the wheel. Since the last time I saw him he'd lost the temporary tan, but still wore the beaded collar, linen kilt and jackal-head mask of a Karnak employee. "I'll park this baby in a handicapped spot. A '56, right?"

"Right." Guys and cars.

"Love your bitchin' Inquisition headache band. Radically retro, like the wheels."

I should have known, I thought, touching my fingertips to the sharp spikes haloing my head.

I entered the lobby to join the flow of females pouring past the casino area for the theater at the main floor's rear. They were so tightly packed we could only shuffle forward like old folks. I avoided even looking at the bar area, where my CinSim pals Nicky and Claude Rains, the Invisible Man, hung out. This was a total undercover outing. Small mirrored surveillance balls danced above us. Tiny bubbles. Tiny bubbles courtesy of Big Brother.

None of the other audience members came here alone like me. Their Snow dependency was a full circle of enabling. I intended to break it, but first I had to break *into* it.

"You're the one," a breathless voice behind me said, "who almost got the BK a few nights back."

I nodded as everyone around me quieted. "Have any of you gotten it yet?"

Heads short and tall, light and dark, shook in disappointment. Obviously, only a few lucky souls got the post-concert smooch. I prepared myself for two hours on my booted feet, sandwiched between pushing mobs of hysterical women, my eardrums caught between the huge stage amplifiers and mewls and whimpers of my sisters-in-waiting.

Still, Snow was a compelling performer. I couldn't avoid a small tremor in the pit of my stomach. If I worked it right, I would again "just miss" the Brimstone Kiss and get a ton of sympathy from my "sister" addicts.

I only prayed one would lead me to Lilith, my Lilith, and possibly to the groupie killer.

Maybe praying before a Seven Deadly Sins concert was a bit inappropriate to both parties involved.

A screaming guitar chord announced the Sins' entrance.

Greed's lead electric guitar was the culprit. Once he had our attention, he rocked that axe like a maniac, his silver- and gold-coin-encrusted duds glittering in shades the color of money and autumn leaves: green, amber, and rust.

The female back-up singers shimmied into place. Lust's lithe black figure was licked by rhinestoned red, orange, and gold tatters of flame silk. Envy looked mermaid sleek in a strapless sequined green gown.

Anger wore his black leather jacket with a swagger that emphasized the blood-red lightning bolts decorating it. He made his bass guitar grumble and rumble, a one-man biker gang. Gluttony in patchwork velvet hung over the drums like they were a five-course dinner he needed to devour, cooking up a percussive storm. Sloth's rhinestone-slathered silver-gray jersey shirt sparkled as he drifted almost idly into supporting riffs.

All the scene needed was lead singer Cocaine.

Ear-spearing screams erupted all around me. I could see the massive gold, green and maroon scaly chest and clawed feet of a huge animated dragon descending from the flies high above the stage. Clouds of smoke and fire enveloped the stage and the mosh pit, bringing a wave of heat, light and fog, and a beastly roar from the dragon's two hideously gnarled and horned heads that were now visible.

Snow—with his white skin, hair and leather catsuit—was a glittering flake of humanity perched on one of those beetled reptilian brows. He slid down the long dragon snout, hung from a huge gold nostril ring, then dropped onto the stage just in time to take the white electric guitar Lust rushed to his hand.

His strong baritone bawled out a line about "everybody goin' down" and some hard-driving number was launched, the boys in the band shaking a tsunami of sound from their instruments, the girl singers wailing like lost souls in counterpoint to screaming guitar and frantic drums.

Having the mind-numbing music this close nearly deafened me. The long wait and longer show numbed my tingling feet to the ankles and my mind into an endless trance. By the time Snow finally pulled out the long white chiffon scarves and went trolling for clamoring female

fans, I was tired and crabby. I snapped myself to attention
again, because this was the moment I'd been suffering for.

Snow, of course, never let anyone see him sweat. He
was still pale-faced and dry as he began his concert-
ending walk along the edge of the stage while the band
played wildly behind him.

His long, angel-white locks brushed some of the fans'
faces as he bent down to loop a scarf around their necks
and draw them near. He gave them the long goodbye,
not a short kiss-off. I'd seen that from the back of the
audience. What I hadn't seen from there was that the
Brimstone Kiss was so heavy on tongue, an erotic sensual
smooch that drove deep before he released them back,
swooning, into the buoying crowd with a palm stroke to
their foreheads.

It was such a weird blend of, say, Elvis's ghost-on-
speed kisses and some Holy Roller preacher's phony
healing routine, I just did not believe it. These women
must be self-hypnotized.

Then I felt the silver familiar fast-tracking from a
punk tiara on my forehead into a heavy chain and pendant
around my neck, as if drawn to its master. I looked
down to see a giant *S* nestled in my cleavage, like I was
Supergirl.

At that moment Snow bagged my neck with a chiffon
scarf.

The women around me automatically pressed inward,
determined to help push me up toward his kneeling figure
for the final kiss.

Poison dog lips! Irma screeched in warning. I almost
giggled, except I was too appalled. The Brimstone Kiss
might be a lot of things, but that one it most definitely
was not.

I felt my elbows grasped as I was bodily hauled up, the
women pushing inward to assist my lift-off. My face was
level with the stage, then Snow was standing and I went
up and up with him.

He brought my face very close to his, holding me off the ground like a toy.

I shut my eyes and squeezed my lips shut even tighter, flinching against the forthcoming Brimstone Kiss. The only tongue that had ever gotten cozy with mine came from the butcher's counter or Ric Montoya. Or maybe Quicksilver if I wasn't fast enough to dodge doggie enthusiasm.

I felt a downward swoop and my feet hit the stage floor with a jolt.

"The *S* is for Street, I presume," Snow said. "Or should *I* be flattered?"

"More for 'sold out'," I admitted. Caught in his groupie cauldron. He could think I actually meant to be here! I was so humiliated.

"Miss Delilah Street. What are you up to?" Snow asked as he bent down, a smile on those lethal lips.

"Not up high enough for the Brimstone Kiss," I said. Okay, that was a coy answer.

And so he treated it. "See me backstage later. Use the side stairs and 'Beelzebub' for a password."

I blinked. This was an invitation a Cocaine groupie would kill for.

Snow was leaning forward to lower me back to the mosh pit. I hit the floor with a jolt. By the time I looked over the stage apron, he had retreated to the mike for the finale.

Wailing, bereaved groupies crowded forward even though the last Brimstone Kiss had been given, pushing me aside.

I let them, working my way to stage right.

The final song was a furious rock hair-raiser called "Liquid Lightning." No one noticed me creeping toward the black-painted side stairs where I confronted the creature from the Black Lagoon wearing a T-shirt labeled SECURITY. In the dark, the grayish CinSim was discreet but visibly ugly enough to repel all comers when noticed.

He smelled rubbery rather than rank, thank goodness. I breathed the Devil's B-name into his frilled side gills and Fish-face stepped aside.

Whipping around the black curtain, I entered the shadowed wings beyond.

I lurked there, my heart beating triple time, watching the Seven Deadly Sins rock out with demonic sound and fury.

I pressed myself against the offstage wall as the Sins swept offstage like a flock of demon raptors.

Snow was on me like white lightning, pressing me between his body and the wall. He spoke harsh and fast.

"You're not a groupie. You'd spit staples before you'd covet one of my Brimstone Kisses. What do you want? Why are you here?"

I decided to try honesty. "I want to understand."

"That's impossible. That is *impossible*, Delilah Street. No one understands. You pursue failure."

"Nevertheless, that's what I want."

"What you want means nothing in the scale of life and death and afterlife."

"It does to me."

"And are you that supremely important, that others should exist to be the objects of your 'understanding'?"

"Yes," I said. "It isn't just for me. It's for them."

"Them?" he thundered in a stage whisper.

"Humanity," I said back. "Oh, the humanity," I repeated, quoting the dazed radio reporter who had witnessed the hellfire destruction of the Hindenburg zeppelin almost a hundred years ago.

It wasn't film coverage, but the radio voice segment had been run over and over again, along with black-and-white film clips of the giant air-boat flame-out, for the disbelieving anguish in the reporter/witness's voice.

I was a reporter, and Las Vegas was my beat.

If Snow's eyes hadn't been obscured by the constant sunglasses I would have said he'd blinked at my reference to a seventy-five-year-old disaster that ended an antique form of air travel.

"This isn't Lakehurst, New Jersey," he answered, naming the location of the tragedy with eerie precision. "This is Las Vegas. And not that many perished at Lakehurst. If all the combustible elements in modern Las Vegas ignited, hundreds of thousands would die."

I didn't know what to say for a moment, taking in the enormity of his insinuation. Vegas was a potential tinderbox and I could be the spark? Me, the poor little match girl? I don't think so.

"Talk about self-important," I replied. "I merely want to get to the bottom of this Brimstone Kiss racket you've got going here. I hate seeing women turned into mindless zombies."

"I thought you were investigating felonies for Hector Nightwine's *CSI* franchises."

"That too."

"No laws are being broken here. Nobody's getting hurt."

"Having their free will tampered with, that's hurtful."

He pulled back to fold his arms. "They do it to themselves."

"People do lots of bad things to themselves. That doesn't mean we write them off."

"And you're going to undo the effects of the Brimstone Kiss?"

"Maybe."

"When you haven't even experienced it for yourself?" He stepped closer again.

I didn't want his faux jewel-bedecked fly grinding into my belly again, but I made myself hold my ground. Any renowned performer has learned to project charisma to the farthest, highest rows. There was a sort of magic to that, but Snow had taken whatever natural gifts he had to the mind control level. Or maybe emotion control. Not mine.

I was five-eight and not a wispy girl. Still, he'd picked me up like a leaf from six feet below the stage level. It was impossible to tell what was simple reality and what was supernatural about Snow. Whenever I defied him the slightest bit, he scared me more than Cicereau and his mob of werewolf hitmen ever could.

And, of course, my position at the moment was weak because I was really, really curious about the Brimstone Kiss.

He lifted me by the arms again, until I was level with his sculpted white face, his slick black sunglasses in which I looked no bigger than a pixie because of the convex shape.

"You want it? Yes or no?" he asked.

"No!" I shouted.

"You don't know what you're saying no to."

"With you, no is always a safe bet."

"Nothing with me is safe."

"Especially sex, I bet."

My tendency to cover nervousness with quips only tightened his grip on my upper arms. I'd probably be bruised from this, but happy just to get far enough away so I could check.

"You are audacious, tenacious and perspicacious."

"That last word is actually a compliment." I blinked at my own tiny distorted image. "You messed up."

He shook his head. "But you're best left to your own self-destructive path."

He lowered me until my dangling soles touched the wooden stage floor again and released my arms even as he turned to go.

I nearly turned an ankle trying to regain my balance. I felt like I'd been thrown back into the gene pool by God.

"Do your worst," Snow advised me. "It can't be any less disastrous than your best."

He whirled away into the darker part of the wings in that strange unseen bubble that made him invisible offstage.

I turned and made my way down the dark stairs. Most of the audience had poured out in a mass, but the groupies were still disconsolate, milling around the discarded trash of the mosh pit.

As I approached their faces turned to me like transfigured flowers to a sudden ray of sunlight.

"You jumped up on stage to get the Kiss," one breathed in the silence the Seven Deadly Sins always left in their wake after the screaming had finally died down.

"Cocaine almost lifted her on stage with the Sins and himself!" another cried.

Technically, I'd even had an offstage tête-à-tête with Snow, but they'd missed that and seen only what they'd wanted to see earlier.

Now they were gathering around me. I glimpsed the cow-eyed, adoring gazes Snow eyeballed every performance. No wonder he was pretty pleased with himself.

I pulled fistfuls of cards from my hobo bag. Denim boots and a hobo bag. Good homeless orphan wear, but not quite the battle gear I'd pick to go toe-to-toe with Snow. When I was on the ground, that is.

I fanned my homemade—well, computer made—cards and doled them out to the beseeching hands.

HOOKED ON A FEELING? The type read. WHETHER YOU'VE LANDED THE MIND-BLOWING LIP-LOCK OR NOT, IT'S TIME TO TAKE THE BRIMSTONE KISS APART SECOND BY SCINTILLATING SECOND. COME TO DELILAH'S GET-DOWN WORKSHOP AND FIND OUT ALL ABOUT IT. BOTH HAPPY HAVES AND HANGDOG HAVE-NOTS WELCOME. The next line was a place, date and time: next Tuesday at six P.M. at a former Weight Watchers spot in a strip shopping center.

Tenacious? Snow hadn't seen Kansas grit in action. We regularly endured killer blizzards that made the King of Kool look like something cool and slurpy you'd order at a Sonic Drive-in and suck down in one long swallow.

Thanks to his intervention, I now had the reputation of not only "almost" getting the Brimstone Kiss, but of clambering up on stage to chase it. Delilah Street, Pursuit Instigator.

The upcoming groupie gig might help me find Lilith as well as defend myself from suspicion of murder. It was still a personal pursuit, a side issue, maybe an obsession.

The Sunset Park lovers was the crime I was being paid to investigate and I was about to catch a break on it.

When I got back to the Enchanted Cottage, flushed from my success with the groupies and dangerous encounter with Snow, an intriguing message awaited on my answering machine.

Right now, all I wanted was some quality sleep time. I'd have to wait until tomorrow to deal with it and needed some advice from a local anyway.

Chapter Fourteen

WORD WAS no unescorted mortal woman came out of the Sinkhole alive.

Naturally, I was planning to meet my very first unknown client in the Sinkhole. And no, I'm not immortal. Yet. If I didn't intend to be, I'd have to be on my guard.

Then I thought about whom . . . or what . . . I might be meeting tonight. The message machine tape featured a low, hissing voice, like all whispers. I listened to it several times that morning.

It said if I wanted to know more about the male skeleton—"the bone boy"—in the Sunset Park grave, I should meet my informant tonight at a place called Wrathbone's in the Sinkhole. The name had been spelled out so I got the initial *W*.

That gave me a clue to my mystery source and actually reassured me. I had my suspicions. Not too many people, or other entities, in Vegas knew—or guessed—about my quest besides Ric and my clients: Hector Nightwine, Snow, and Howard Hughes.

I'd need two things to enter—and leave—the Sinkhole: a disguise—so I wasn't hounded as Lilith—and serious weapons, both defensive and offensive. Oh, and a third thing: A way to find where the blamed place would be tonight.

The Sinkhole moves, you see, a mist of Hell's breath floating in the brimstone heat of the dark desert air like a nightmare oasis.

Post-Millennium Las Vegas is still paranoid about bad press. It may host a helluva lot of supernatural forces in 2013, but they all must fit the sales model. Even a pestilential pit like the Sinkhole attracted a certain kind of tourist. Being hard to find was an extra kick. And getting out was a lot harder than getting in. Or so they said.

"I HOPE you're planning on taking your hellhound to the Sinkhole with you," Hector Nightwine, my boss, said, sounding a teensy bit guilty, when I told him of my expedition in his manorial office that afternoon.

"Quicksilver is not a 'hellhound,' he's just a poor rescue dog."

Hector snorted. He does an awesome snort, being a bearded man of size and a connoisseur of blood-red wine, bizarre food forms and vintage films.

"And I'm Orson Welles," he sniffed.

Actually, he *could* be in Vegas nowadays, where the line between life and death is thinner than a honed straight razor's edge.

Quicksilver, who combined the huge size of a wolfhound with the disconcerting conformation and features of a blue-eyed 150-pound wolf, lifted his grandma-eating-size muzzle from his paws to whine like an abandoned puppy.

Hector snorted again. Majestically. "That dog could have outdone the heroic Rin Tin Tin in the early movies. He knows just when to second your extravagant lies."

"I can use loyal backup," I said, "especially since your damned show has made me the world's most wanted woman."

"Isn't that what all women want?"

"Not this one. Not this way." I ticked off my many pursuers on my fingers. "Cesar Cicereau of the Gehenna Hotel thought he could use me and then tried to kill me. Any creep who mistakes me for your highest rated *CSI* corpse, Lilith, wants to sell my hide to the black and blue division of the blue movie trade. The Las Vegas Metro Police Department's Detective Haskell has been bitten unhuman, into an even more loathsome variety of bully, and wants me either convicted of the murder of a Snow groupie or just plain dead out of revenge. For all I know, this mysterious 'client' wants to lure me into a meeting for some fate worse than death."

A sliver of smile peeked like a maggot from the corner of Nightwine's small, pursed candy-apple-red mouth.

"There are a lot of fates like that nowadays, my dear. Surely you're taking the Cadaver Kid along?"

I shrugged. If I was going to be a serious investigator, I needed to prove to him and myself that I didn't need a white knight behind my every move around Vegas.

Nightwine took my reticence for the affirmative, as I'd hoped.

"Very wise. A good dog and a good man are what a girl needs most in these perilous times."

"I thought you didn't like Ric."

Now he shrugged, a lot more impressively than I had. The shoulders in his burgundy brocade smoking jacket were mountainous. "Montoya's FBI, but at least he didn't stay in long. The Feds keep trying to close down my City of Dreams."

"City of Nightmares."

"As I said, my City of Dreams."

"I don't know why you're going all soft on me now that you're my landlord. You've always wanted me to find out who the guy in that Sunset Park double grave was. I've got a stake in your new vintage murder concept TV series. You were gonna make me a living-dead star, keep Lilith's mystique as a *CSI*'s hottest corpse yet going. Remember? I couldn't do anything more dangerous in this town than get mistaken for Lilith."

"That's all true," he admitted. "I only fret because you're still new to Vegas. Good luck, Delilah. Do check in when you get back. Godfrey will be anxious."

"Right."

I left Nightwine's sumptuous office, Quicksilver at my heels, to find his man Godfrey lurking and listening in the hall. Godfrey's amiable, middle-aged starch went splendidly with his formal butler's garb. He escorted us down the back stairs to the kitchen exit with a monologue of warnings underscored by the castanet click of Quick's nails on the wooden stairs.

"The master means well, but underestimates the sturdiness of his employees, Miss. He is used to dealing with staff less, er, physically fragile than a mortal such as yourself. The Sinkhole is not fit for woman or beast. Mr. Montoya is not so accustomed to Las Vegas and its quirks yet that he would make a reliable guide. I knew a poor chap from Bangalore—"

"Godfrey," I said, "that sounds like the start of a naughty limerick." When we hit bottom at the large kitchen floored in big black and white marble squares like a chessboard, I turned to face him. "Besides, I know what I'm doing."

Godfrey's CinSim face and garb were all black and white and shades of gray. He was a blend of actor William Powell and the disguised rich-man-posing-as-butler from *My Man Godfrey*, a classic nineteen-thirties screwball comedy.

I knew that beneath the slick film image the heart of a zombie *didn't* beat, but Godfrey felt solid when touched and his fully human concern touched me.

"Godfrey, I have to learn to live in this pretty nasty world I've found myself in, just as you have. I'm not tied to any particular place, as most of you CinSims are. A girl's gotta do what a girl's gotta do."

I nodded at Quick to follow me. We skedaddled out the back door, but not before Godfrey called after me, "Remember you're from Kansas. There might be some ruby red slippers somewhere to whisk you home in a pinch."

Poor Godfrey. He believed in movies almost as much as Nightwine did.

IT WAS ONLY thirty yards across the cobblestone driveway to my digs. The sharp, reassuring sound of Quicksilver's nails still shadowed me. That dog was my fanged guardian metronome.

The place I rented from Hector was as cute as dimpled and spit-curled Betty Boop, the cartoon flapper. I fell in love again with my literal Enchanted Cottage every time I saw it. I considered it a real-life version of a vintage Disney cartoon cottage made for bluebells and bluebirds circling the front door, and sometimes they actually did.

Hector had added a lot of modern comforts, including a Jacuzzi and convection oven, but the cottage remained an unfolding origami magic show of kitchen witches, yard trolls and other usually invisible manifestations that came and went on their own quirky schedule.

Once home again, I caught up on the newspaper and current events and domestic chores that didn't get magically done by the shy household help before preparing an early evening snack.

"Better eat, drink up and be merry," I told Quicksilver. "We're going where you definitely don't want to consume anything you don't have to in self-defense."

I could soon hear him lapping up a tsunami at the kitchen water bowl while I changed into my impromptu Sinkhole outfit. As a TV reporter in Wichita, I wore business casual for the job. Here in Vegas I was going places where I needed clothes that would protect me from fang bites and claw burns.

I'd learned at an early age that bluff was the best disguise.

The use-softened black biker leathers I'd found at vintage clothes emporiums along Charleston would have looked Hell's Angels Goth with my black hair. Especially if I slapped on some vampire-red lip-gloss.

But after I struggled into the leather low-rise jeans, the knee-high boots, the spandex knit top and funky suede-fringed seventies vest, I pinned up my Black Beauty mane and pulled on my new short blond wig in the classic twenties/seventies Sassoon/so Neurotic Now bob that curves under your chin like twin scimitars.

The perfect disguise. Blonds were so plentiful in this town three hundred miles from Hollywood people literally couldn't see their faces for the façade. And the town sprouts wig shops like a transvestite creates female celebrity impersonations. Then I popped in gray contact lenses with no correction that obscured my morning-glory-blue eyes. Delilah, meet anti-Lilith.

The mirror accomplished the introduction. When the tall mirror ending the hall to the attic bedroom suite wasn't playing tricks and I wasn't in disguise, it reflected me in all my Snow White coloring and Lilith glory.

It was odd that the world thought Lilith, and therefore me, her double, beautiful. I'd always hated my dead-white skin and dead-black hair that reminded every vamp and half-vamp in the New Millennium universe that I came corpse-pale, just what they were looking for in a woman and a fast-food combo. I'd been fighting off vamp-boy bullies since puberty. It got so I'd rather fight than fornicate, even when I'd finally had a chance to do the latter.

I was making friends with my own image since I'd met Ric, though. His savvy, warm and winning personality and hot Latin blood were melting my Black Irish heart and hormones. I'd never had a boyfriend, only bad dates. I'd never had a lover or an orgasm. All that was past tense now and I'd wanted in the worst way to ask him to escort me to the Sinkhole.

Which is why I wouldn't. I don't like being dependent on other people. It only gets you hurt in the short run and makes you weak in the long run. Orphan's axiom. Dogs, on the other hand, offered unconditional love and unflagging doggy breath.

I slapped on some Lip Venom. I always carried the tingling, lip-plumping gloss because it made me feel lethal and viperish. Then I finished pinning on the wig with twenty copper-blond hairpins and was ready to go, except for donning the used cop utility belt I'd found in a pawn shop behind the Harley-Davidson souvenir shop and café.

It made me look hippy, but in a big baaad don't-mess-with-*moi* way. I kept the baton and heavy flashlight and added a couple kitchen knife hilts for show.

No cell phone. You could be identified by them. Las Vegas was full of dead zones, anyway. Nor did I have lots of relatives and friends to send pics of the infamous Sinkhole.

So where would I find the elusive Sinkhole, a notorious place where human and unhuman lowlifes did sex, drugs, armed robbery and grievous bodily harm to each other and any suicidal straights who wandered in?

I drove Dolly downtown near the crime district for starters. I wasn't worried about my flashy vintage ride even though it was hot enough to melt. It had its own special security system.

Soon after hitting town, Quicksilver had broken out a side window to escape the locked car and defend me from a half-werewolf biker gang called the Lunatics. The window was a one-off, long since vanished from even junkyards and online auto-part dealers. I mourned loudly about the impossibility of replacing the window when I got home and parked Dolly in the driveway of the Enchanted Cottage.

The next morning, I found the window-glass in place and intact. Ever since, when I parked Dolly in iffy areas, a nasty poison-green aura haloed the car. I figured it was pixie halitosis.

If I could bottle that arsenic glow, I'd have a really innovative method of car security. Nobody in Vegas messes with pixies, I'd learned fast. They're the equivalent of supernatural fleas: tiny, hungry, able to leap from one host to another in a single bound and bite. They cursed as much as your average American teenager, but real curses, not just bad words. Curses corrosive enough to move all the hair on your head to your toes.

So I left Dolly in the parking lot of a new high-rise time-share. Quick and I trotted through the Downtown "Experience"—a blocks-long barrel vault canopy, ninety feet high at its peak, that combined a pedestrian mall with a not-at-all-pedestrian sound and light show.

The venerable Four Queens Hotel and Casino had been reinvented as an exotic Temple to Ishtar, Medusa, Isis and the original sexpot Lilith. No Delilah. I guess overeager hair stylists aren't sexy-scary goddesses, even though it's *sooo* hard to stop them from snipping too much off.

Overhead holographic images evoked great world tragedies of fire and flood, featuring thousands of screaming, falling bodies hurtling right at you. There were no sappy Celine Dion renditions of "My Heart Must Go On." A rock band howled to back up their death agonies.

Tourists in Capri pants and Bermuda shorts were gaping open-mouthed at the kaleidoscope of destruction playing out above, tiny camcorders attached to their cell phone earjacks, so they could look and shoot instead of point and shoot. They resembled Borg wannabes. Creepy! Quick and I passed them like dust on the wind.

I headed for the area's outskirts. I figured that the Sinkhole would find you if you wanted it to. Or if you looked like you belonged there.

Amazing how even the biggest tourist attraction in the world makes room for sleaze. I was soon walking along unkempt strings of one-story shopping centers. Half of the shops were deserted. The other half sold fortunes, cut-price show tickets, lottery tickets, exotic lingerie and massages.

Beside me, Quick growled. I put my hand on his shoulder. It reached my hip. He was three times the size of most wolves. *Good dog!* The thin silver chain with a cross around my neck coiled like a snake and slithered down my black-knit sleeve to my wrist. It became the mace-like spikes on a leather wristband.

If my unwanted bodyguard was showing its fangs, we must be nearing the Sinkhole.

Quicksilver's hackles rose under my fingers along with his prolonged, low growl.

Good. We were there. Now all we needed was not to "get into" anything. I was hoping to tap the same eerie psychic energy that had helped me find the Sunset Park bodies when co-dowsing for the dead with Ric.

FIRST I FELT the heavy metal beat from the Downtown Experience quicken under my feet, through the thick leather soles of my motorcycle boots. It rumbled on and on, like Quicksilver's growl.

The sidewalk broke into smaller blocks, then heaved, then shattered.

The ground was giving way underneath us! I curled my fingers into Quick's thick black leather collar studded with silver-dollar-size moons in phase from crescent to full If he hadn't been born half wolfhound, he would have been all wolf. As it was, he hated werewolves, even half-werewolves.

My punk leather wristband tightened hard enough to take my pulse.

Pounding. My pulse pounding.

Spinning. My head was spinning, the low-rise buildings around me were falling down, together. Ashes, ashes, all fall down.

We fell. Together. My fingernails digging into my own palms, Quicksilver's sharp wolfish muzzle tilted up at the moon.

And then the carnival music rose up to snap at our senses. We rode a merry-go-round of sound and fury screwing deep into the earth. I held on to the dog collar for dear life, Quick's and mine. No wonder it was called the Sinkhole.

We plunged, bucked, gained our feet and braced them. Stood.

In another world.

I looked at the slick, wet pavement, smooth as glass. Exotic heavenly bodies reflected in its surface, but when I looked up, all was matte black. No firmament, neither stars nor neon signs. I realized I was looking *down* through black glass. And the starry heavens were below us.

I inhaled deeply.

Quick looked up at me with blue eyes paled to mirror silver. I saw myself reflected in them: blond biker chick with icy gray CinSim eyes. Not really me. How would my skittish informer recognize me? I figured it had to be someone from Cicereau's mob. Cesar had tried to have me killed and failed. No one knew that but Ric and Cicereau's people.

Looking around, I heard the hiss of roller blades. Teens in black neoprene jumpsuits whizzed by on their narrow runners, one crouching to cruise between Quicksilver and me.

"Watch it," I yelled after the cheeky speed demon.

"*You* watch it, biker bitch!" the kid hollered back. "Watch me score rings around you."

Not what I was here for. I ducked into the nearest dark doorway. Two "doormen" stood guard at either side of the entrance: tall, lean figures so cadaverous they looked like candidates for Vegas coroner "Grisly" Bahr.

Even though their stinking breaths were as effectively repellent as laser security beams, we evidently passed muster and went through the doors. A flash indicated I had been photographed. Quick squeezed his eyes half shut. Don't modern security measures make your blue eyes blink?

My own eyes, with the gray contact lenses acting as indoor sunglasses, scoped out a mixed bag of supernatural sleazes at the crowded bar. They were all checking me out, visible drool decorating the corners of their mouths. No other women here. I retreated, Quick doing the back step with me until we were in the eerie, windless echo chamber of the Sinkhole's main drag again. It exhaled the same artificial pumped-in air of the Downtown Experience topside.

I checked the name of the first establishment we had seen, "Mudflaps' Limbo Bar," and joined the oddly silent figures shambling along the street. In the smoky fog, it was hard to make out their faces.

After ten minutes of what felt like walking on a treadmill, we didn't seem to have gotten anywhere. Could this be an outpost of Hell, a true "Limbo" of some kind? If so, the creatures of the underworld and overworld would mingle. One thing made the place really weird: the background chime and chuckle of slot machines was missing. There wasn't a casino to be heard down here. Unreal.

As if responding to my mental critique of the silence, distant wailing instruments began to play. Quick sat on his haunches to bay up at the moon. Well, where a moon would be. I saw someone had turned on a huge blood-red planet of shifting light that bled through our smoke Plexiglas sky like the Devil's nightlight.

Then I spotted a sign in soft white neon: *Wrathbone*. This must be the place.

INSIDE, WRATHBONE'S was as dark as the Devil's left nostril.

The clientele crowding the bar and tables were a mob of human and unhuman cutthroats ranging from such past masters of villainy and oddity as Jack Sparrow's pirates to werewolf and vampire gangs to the *Star Wars* cantina denizens. Large white neon hieroglyphs lit the bordering dark brick walls. I didn't want to stare at any one individual or object because I didn't want to encourage attention. I was the most recognizably female person there and one of the few humans.

Maybe the creepiest unhuman in the place was the mummy wearing a black trench coat, felt fedora, dark glasses and black leather driving gloves in the corner.

Was he a Cinema Simulacrum or a Cinema Symbiant? His wrapped linen was wedding-day white and looked as crisp as priest's collar against the black accessories.

Had any of the classic thirties and forties mummy movies featured fashion-conscious mummies in contemporary clothing? No. They were all naked under the wrappings, and this one might be too. The creature lifted a spread-fingered hand to wave me over, hoisting a convivial low-ball glass with the other gloved hand.

A single chick out for the evening in the Sinkhole had a lot to consider.

Was this just a barside come-on or my blind date? Blind he certainly seemed, with those impenetrable glasses and a slit of black for a mouth. How he could sip a drink, I didn't know.

I'd find out soon enough. Besides, of all the unhumans eyeing me hungrily, he looked the least able to bite me. Sitting with him for a while would give me a chance to size up the other customers.

As my eyes adjusted to the low light, the décor became easier to grasp at a glance: what I'd taken for neon tubes were an endless chorus line of luminous skeletons hung with their hipbones at eye height. Some wore tatters of clothing. Some could be still hosting tatters of dried flesh. Tasty.

Yet, with their gaping eyeholes and Jolly Roger grins they seemed a carefree bunch. Their clothing ranged from bandoliers to bandanas and a Hawaiian shirt. The one that wore nothing but a bone necklace looked naked.

Them dry bones also packed a lot of weaponry thrust between ribs and hung from scapulae. I was hoping this was some sort of corny Western bar six-gun guest storage system, but a quick glance at the other patrons assured me that they were all more seriously armed than I was. Chains and shivs and daggers and semiautomatics, oh my.

I decided a mummy in a trench coat couldn't have been packing more than a semiautomatic or a sawed-off shotgun, so I headed for the only friendly face I saw, because it had no expression.

Quicksilver kept at heel all the way to the table while every eye in the place still in sockets shifted to watch us. I wasn't sure whether my dog or I was the bigger attention-getter.

"Grab a seat, doll," the mummy said.

"I'm surprised you can sit. Talk about tightly wrapped," I murmured as I pulled my captain's chair close to the table. Quicksilver stood guard beside me, his head at my shoulder-level.

"I'm not a mummy," the creature said in a flat baritone. "They were even dumber than zombies. Could only travel in that same slow, ineffective lurch. Get them mainlining Red Bull, they'd have had something. As for having mummy sex . . . You into peeling off Band-Aids forever as foreplay? I didn't think so."

He pulled out a lighter and a cigarette case and soon had a cancer stick twitching between his white-gauze lips. I couldn't help feeling nervous, as if I was watching Dorothy's flammable Scarecrow puffing away.

"Relax, Miss Street," he muttered under his breath and the cover of bluish smoke. "We're the normals here."

I almost recognized the whisper this time, and frowned. "Do I know you?"

He leaned in, extended his free gloved hand and pinched my thigh under the table.

"Ouch!"

Quick growled and snapped, but Cigarette-smoking Man's gloved hand was quicker than a magician's wrist action.

"Oooh," he drawled. "That's my quick-step girl. Glad I saved your, uh, carcass. Can't pinch an inch there. You are one smooth lady."

"What are you doing here?" I asked the Invisible Man, disgusted. Yes, he'd saved me from being torn into shreds by werewolf gangsters, but I'd hoped to meet some real Vegas unreals tonight.

"What am I doing here, doll? Seeing you in private," he smirked through the head wrappings.

We'd first crossed paths at the Inferno, and later the Gehenna, when he was truly invisible. He lived to pinch butt. I guess you can't blame a mad genius scientist who was probably a nerd when he became invisible in a 1933 film of his same name: *The Invisible Man*. Even the most depraved CinSim groupie, or CinSymb, wouldn't want to get it on with a celebrity you couldn't see.

"How do you manage to get around so much?" I asked. "The other CinSims are chained to their venues."

He paused to catch the eye of a passing half-werewolf waitress, the first obvious female I'd spotted, pointed to his empty glass, then in front of me. "I hope you like Old Fashioneds," he said. "I don't want that cute furry trick hanging around overhearing us while taking our orders."

"I've heard of the drink," I said. The cocktail had been out of fashion for more than half a century, almost as long as the Invisible Man. "You hang at the Inferno. Why was it necessary to meet here?"

He leaned close, whispering. "Christophe is a liberal master and I manage to get out on various missions for him, but this is a private meeting. Just you and me."

Mention of Christophe made me wonder what the silver ball and chain transformed from a lock of his albino hair was now. Aha! The token had subsided into a discreet locket around my neck. When I opened it, I found a tiny mirror version of my current disguise. I bet Snow would get a private kick out of seeing raven-haired me in platinum-blond guise!

Thinking about Snow always scratched my skin like invisible briars. I pushed those thoughts away along with the locket I snapped shut.

"Was following me when I was whisked from the Gehenna to Cicereau's lethal Starlight Lodge one of your assignments for Snow?"

"Not just every dame gets to call him that, you know," the Invisible Man answered, evading the question. "If you weren't alive and were a CinSim he'd have you doing hostess duty at the Inferno in a New York, New York minute for taking such a liberty."

So I thought about Christophe again. I had to. The silver locket on my breastbone stirred at the mention of his name and nickname. It crawled up my forearm to circle cozily around my biceps. *What big ears you have, Snow.*

All the better to hear you with, Delilah.

What big teeth, I thought, and then couldn't help adding. *Bite me!*

Wait! Was I issuing a smart quip or a death wish? It was hard to know the difference in this town.

"I don't know whether he's bad or good." The Invisible Man twisted a paper cocktail napkin in a gloved hand. "He—like your boss, Mr. Nightwine—does deal straight with us CinSims, though." I looked up from my alien accessory, surprised.

The fedora was nodding. "Yeah. CinSims know who our friends are. You, lady, are on the 'A List'."

"I—" Was surprised. Touched. Not sure I wanted to be in a category with Snow and Hector Nightwine, but, hey, I'd never had many friends. To be taken for one sounded . . . kinda cool.

The black leather glove had captured my hand just as the waitress dipped to put two murky orange drinks down before us.

"Have a fun evening, you two," she wished us, showing fangs.

Was her other half vampire? I wondered what kind of tip we could leave her. Blood or money?

And I really couldn't lead the Invisible Man on. He wasn't my type. Not that I have one. But now that Ric and I have been . . . *wow!* I do think about things like monogamy. Besides, he was middle-aged, squat and reminded me of

Cesar Cicereau, the werewolf mob boss, at least physically. From my recall of his movies, as played by character actor Claude Rains, he was as sexually appealing as a demented toad. And that mad, disembodied laugh . . . . Call me shallow, but a vintage character actor could never rev my melancholy Irish pulses.

Ric. *Now* we're talking different. There aren't a lot of Latino movie leads for reference, but think early Ricardo Montalbán, pre-*Wrath of Khan* days, but with a lot of that fierce, sexy edge. *Wrath of Khan,* the *Star Trek* movie! *Wrathman. Wrathbone.*

I glanced at the Invisible Man. "Do I call you Dr. Jack Griffin or Claude Rains?"

"Either one. Frankly, my dear, I don't give a damn. Speaking as Dr. Griffin, I am brilliant, but quite mad from being invisible, and speaking as Mr. Rains, after all these decades stuck in the role, I am mad to take on other personas. Claude was claustrophobic and the black velvet suit I had to wear against black velvet to appear invisible for the film didn't help even my sanity. I find myself role-playing all over the map, and you will notice that I crave human contact, even of the rather crude sort. Being a Las Vegas attraction makes us CinSims part of a very exclusive twenty-first century Rat Pack, sometimes all in one package. Some of us can go country or pop. I brought backup." He nodded at a spot along the crowded bar.

And there was raven-haired Ricardo Montalbán himself, lean and muscled in swashbuckler shirt and tight pants, in his Latin lover persona, not as the older (but still suave) Mr. Roarke of Fantasy Island. And decidedly not as the still-older and brutally wrathful Khan, a notable movie villain in his sixties with long gray hair. Still, you did not want to rile this man.

And . . . oh, my God, there was Basil Rathbone as Sherlock Holmes, also lean, both of mind and body, smoking a pipe and eyeing the cast of unhumans with eagle-sharp eyes from under his deerstalker.

I smiled at the Invisible Man's inviting two CinSims associated with the word "wrath/rath" on this outing. I'd have to find out where this unlikely pair was usually stationed before I left.

The Sherlock Holmes CinSim would never notice my Lilith lures, but Khan-to-be looked interested already. I'd rather flirt with the youthful leading man Montalbán . . . maybe a water baby idyll, like he'd had with swim star Esther Williams in *Neptune's Daughter*. I was beginning to see the commercial appeal of the CinSims to the public. Fantasies fulfilled, from a casual meeting to a long, hot mating, only *not* in living color.

But . . . no thanks. I had the real deal. My deal. Ric. Whom I should have asked to escort me here, except I was trying to prove to him I didn't need him as protection. Or to prove it to myself. Who was I kidding?

Claude gestured for the two CinSims to join us. As they sauntered over, I eyed the rest of the clientele over the rim of the cloying drink. To us middle-class Kansans, they'd come across as the scum of the earth: gang bangers, bikers, low-rent muscle and hitmen, robbers and muggers, carjackers, sex and drug addicts. And those were just the humans.

I played the game of guessing which were the unhumans. There were enough CinSims here that some had to be CinSymbs. It struck me that today's Las Vegas was a city of strong dualities. Good/bad, lucky/unlucky, rich high roller/poor sucker, powerful men/weak but sexy women, faux/real and now, of course, alive/dead.

Chapter Fifteen

So far the Sinkhole had been the usual guy venue: alcohol, cigarettes and 3-D TV sports, plus a few rough-looking women lined up at the bar.

Now I was mesmerized by the famous personas heading toward the Invisible Man's table, two CinSims familiar from my pre-teen reading and cable TV-watching days.

Basil/Sherlock was looking as bored and unhappy as Mr. Spock at a picnic, but Ricardo/stock Latin lover character was eyeing the crowd. His eyeing got more personal the nearer he approached.

"Why did you want to meet me here anyway?" I asked the Invisible Man as our new companions joined the table.

He leaned nearer to whisper even more softly . . . and put a leather glove on my knee. "It's the only place in Vegas that isn't monitored by the powers that be or the police. That's why it moves around. It's the only place CinSims dare assemble, and are tolerated as free agents."

"*Are* you free agents?" I asked, glancing at all of my Three CinSim Stooges: Sexy, Asexual, and Horny. Snow White never had it so good.

"*Shhh!*" The Invisible Man eyed the unsavory ranks of supernaturals and debased humans surrounding us. "It's to everybody's advantage to keep a safe zone private. That doesn't mean that very bad things don't happen in the Sinkhole. They simply are not official business in the rest of Vegas."

"What entertainment venues host our new friends here?"

"Entertainment," Holmes spat. "Certainly not."

"These two are . . . privately owned. Like Hector Nightwine's man, Godfrey."

"Owned, not leased?"

The fedora nodded.

"How does this happen?"

"The . . . purveyors announce auctions. All interested parties are free to bid."

"This smacks of outright slavery." Which was exactly what I'd suggested to Snow, and which he'd denied vehemently.

"Viva Miss Delilah," Montalbán hailed my indignation in his silken tequila voice. "It is even worse than the studio contracts I signed when I first came to Hollywood from Mexico. Those old time moguls were bastards, but at least they loved making movies. Our current masters only love making money."

"CinSims have been legally declared intellectual property," the Invisible Man explained. "Our base material is anonymous and the actors who played us are, in most cases, dead—"

"And if some are not?" I asked. "After all, people are extending their life spans in some form or other, or being revivified all the time, if they're rich enough."

"The studios, or whatever legal entity has succeeded them, get a royalty, as do the actors or their estates. But since a CinSim is a true amalgam, the courts have ruled, so far, that we are a new creative entity and belong to those who cobbled us together from the dead and the flickers of vintage film strips."

"You sound almost proud of your unique status," I told the Invisible Man.

"Why not? I was and am still typecast as a mad scientist. I salute what science today has done to blur the lines between art and technology, and even life and death, to preserve what were mere half lives as whole lives."

Montalbán was meanwhile eyeing my butch leather outfit. "This is most unfeminine," he said, caressing the next words. "No scarlet silks, no ruffles, no jewels." His autocratic tone softened. "But I like it. I like it very much."

"Who is your . . . master?" I asked.

"Mistress," he corrected smoothly. "I was won by a woman, of course."

Whoa. My inner girlfriend, Irma, spoke up for the first time on this expedition. *"Does she rent him out, do you think? I'd share with you, even though you won't with me."*

I rolled my eyes at no one in particular. Dealing with two "Rics" was beyond my modest experience of a social life. Still, I could see that my Ric, less suave and more direct, shared that certain sexy something with the young Ricardo Montalbán.

"What about Sherlock?" I asked Claude, since the great detective was keeping aloof from the conversation.

"He won't say who commands his services," Claude admitted, leaning close to whisper. At least this time he had something interesting to say as well as another squeeze of my knee to execute. "But don't let his attitude fool you. He's here to learn the ways of the Sinkhole and to use them in the future."

"When the CinSims rebel," I guessed.

"*Shhh!* We trust no one here. I wanted to tell you in this safe zone that your escape from Cesar Cicereau's hit squad has infuriated him and his lieutenants and soldiers. Rumors abound that his organization 'bungled' an operation. That's the first kiss of death in mob circles. We CinSims have our ways of learning things. That's why I called you here."

"You don't have information for me on who the Sunset Park male victim is?"

"No. I know you're after that secret even though identifying the female victim nearly got you torn apart by werewolves. Trouble is, word of that showdown in the mountains is arming the opposition too. Cicereau's people, and werewolves, have IDed your boyfriend, Ric. They're not happy with him gunning down their muscle with silver bullets. He should be wary too. Those of us CinSims who've preserved a sense of self and free will can help you, but we are sadly few."

He glanced at our table partners. "And you can see we are limited by the roles in which we were preserved."

Which meant that we had young skirt-chasing Montalbán to deal with, not the seasoned actor who projected *The Wrath of Khan* on movie screens more than thirty years later. It also meant that Sherlock Holmes was present in the brisk, ultra-effective form of Basil Rathbone's 1940s portrayal, not the mercurial eccentric that Jeremy Brett portrayed to great acclaim forty years later.

I assumed that Rathbone's dazzling real life and onscreen fencing skills were still available in this Holmes enactment. The literary Holmes had practiced *baritsu*, a fictional Asian martial art Conan Doyle invented decades before such skills showed up routinely in twentieth century action novels and films. Too bad Sean Connery's James Bond wasn't available, but the youthful Montalbán had wielded a mean sword in pirate movies.

A thought occurred to me. "Are any of the CinSims in color?"

Claude drew back in melodramatic shock.

"No! It's the silver nitrate in the old films that both destroyed the strips and now preserves our performances. Look at mine. I had to convey my character and emotions with voice only. Not since the Silents had an actor met a more demanding challenge, if I say so myself. More rumors say that a color process is under development, but, frankly, all that gaudy hokum diminishes and distracts from the power and polish of the classic black-and-white format."

He sounded as snobbish as Hector Nightwine. In fact, I wondered if Hector might have leased him, not Snow. Being invisible, he could go anywhere. Snow had

once appeared to recognize him, but that may not mean
he leased him. My rotund boss had an appetite for the
bizarre. Whatever, I had time to inquire into that later in
places less unpleasant than the Sinkhole.

"So why do you want to hire me to find out who died
with Cicereau's daughter?"

"Cicereau's a big guy in this town. His CinSims
work under the worst conditions in Vegas. We like his
fur ruffled and you're pretty good at it so far. Plus, you
escaped his forced labor operation.

"Even a magician with supernatural connections
hasn't been able to do that. That makes you our hero.
We can watch your back if you'll go for Cicereau's front.
Another thing—"

Claude hunched closer. I could see my white-blond
self reflected in his dark sunglasses like I saw myself in
Snow's shades. The similarity was unpleasant.

His gauze lips barely moved as he whispered. "The
vampire CinSims are all disappearing. All over town.
Even at the supernatural chicken ranches out in the
boonies."

"There are vampire brothels?"

"Of course. Any flavor or twist of supernatural you
want, male or female or question mark. They say the
chupacabra three-way is out of this world."

Chupacabra! Irma made herself known. *Ric's seen
one in the Mexican desert; you've seen the tracks of one
in a Kansas cornfield. What's a monster animal doing in
Nevada houses of ill repute?"*

Good question. The *chupacabra* was known as a
goat-sucker, a blood-sucking creature that left its prey a
desiccated sack of bones. How this could be put to erotic
use without resulting in death was beyond me and I was
thankful for that.

I thought of Count Dracula, the motion picture CinSim.
Was Howard Hughes snapping up all the Vegas vampire
CinSims for some reason? Could be. He shared Hector

Nightwine's love of vintage films and had a billionaire's need for one thing more. Control. He'd been a "force" in Vegas once, he wanted back in, and vampires had been out of power in Vegas since they'd lost out when the city was being founded.

Hughes had hired me to discover the identity of young Miss Cicereau's boyfriend, another piece in the power game. Of course, Nightwine was also my client. If we knew the whole story, we'd have Cicereau on the ropes. Nightwine could film a slightly fictionalized version of the murders and Cesar would be toppled by the publicity and outed as a known . . . what was the word for killing a daughter? There were words for killing mothers and fathers and sisters and brothers, but I knew none for offing offspring. The ever-unpopular "child killer" would have to do it.

Snow, another power player, also wanted to know who had died with Cicereau's daughter and, like Hughes and Hector, had "hired" me to find the answer. Now here I had a fourth set of clients—rogue CinSim conspirators.

"Chickie-baby," a loathsome, lusting, derisive male voice growled into the haze of my macabre reverie.

The worst part was that I recognized it, even if the speaker didn't recognize me.

"Why's a hot babe like you sitting with these lame CinSymbiants, huh?"

The man had taken my tablemates for wandering tourists dressing up as their favorite hotel CinSims. That was a mistake.

He'd also grabbed the nape of my black leather vest.

That was an even bigger mistake.

Before I could even begin to tell Detective Half-balled Haskell to take his hands off me, Quicksilver, who'd been as still as a statue following our conversation, sped like a speeding bullet for his throat.

Haskell went down on the floor, with Quick growling and worrying at his most vulnerable areas—throat, gut and crotch.

"Back! Off!" I ordered, careful not to use the dog's name.

Haskell had glimpsed Quicksilver once, but had never heard his name. At the time, Haskell's attention was fixed on me, so I doubt he had even registered the wolfish breeds Quicksilver combined.

As far as I knew, since our round at the Enchanted Cottage Haskell now had only one ball left and was three times meaner than before. I didn't want Quicksilver snacking at his crotch because I was sure that *no* balls would make Haskell almost supernaturally dangerous. The last Sinkhole attack on him might have started something like that already. In the post-Millennium Revelation world, it was vital to watch out who, or what, you were bit by and how often.

Ric had gone incognito into the Sinkhole; someone, or something, had inflicted nasty extra damage on Haskell's body parts after Ric left him unconscious.

I had a few friends capable of the same vengeful instincts as Ric on my behalf. Quicksilver's gusto for the crotch area made me wonder what he did on his solo midnight runs. Nightwine could have sent one ugly CinSim of a customer after Haskell once he'd viewed the security tape of the cop mauling me in his very own treasured Enchanted Cottage.

At that moment, the silver familiar moved from my neck to make a chain-wrapped fist of my right hand, reminding me that maybe Snow could spy on me through the artifact. Even he might not like the corrupt fuzz hitting on his newly-wired toy.

All speculation was moot now. Haskell didn't know that blond Sinkhole Biker Girl was Delilah Street.

Quick had obeyed my command, a growl warning his prey that this was just a temporary truce. I took a deep breath . . .

. . . and expelled it as hot-tempered Ricardo Montalbán hauled Haskell up from the floor.

"*Puerco! Hijo de puta!* You dare accost a woman sitting at my table?"

And Montalbán essayed a fist to the chops that laid Haskell back down again.

"I'm a representative of the law," Haskell screamed at the lowlifes gathering around.

Sherlock Holmes bent down to blow pipe smoke into Haskell's face. "If this is a representative of the law, I'm the Dalai Lama."

Then Holmes hauled him upright without losing a breath to puff out smoke.

"How shall we expel this noxious snake? Is there a vampire in the house? Bites and blood-sucking are extremely effective ways of dealing with snake venom. I confess that I do not believe in vampires, but one would certainly be useful in this instance."

The Invisible Man had doffed trench coat, hat, sunglasses and gauze and was now invisibly pummeling Haskell about the head and chest like a frantic windstorm.

"Take these thugs into citizens' arrest!" Haskell shouted, dodging unseen blows.

The problem was one of the few human bodies in the place was looking picked upon. Visiting tourists, CinSymbiants and human riffraff rose in a wave from the wide-screen sports TVs at the bar and the small cocktail tables anchored by some CinSims of their choice.

"That's okay, officer! I'll help," a beefy man in Bermuda shorts and a Hawaiian shirt called, wading into the battle. "Hang in there," he added, an unfortunate choice of expression for Half-balled Haskell.

When he accidentally wopped the Invisible Man in the back with a fanny pack, I was forced to push him aside.

"Bitch!" a woman with pink hair and a nose ring screamed, heading for me.

I was more than ready, but she was plucked away before she could hit me with her faux-Prada bag.

A half-dozen half-were bikers waded in, their chains chiming. I pulled the nightstick and found it as effective when poking as when striking sideways. My chain-wrapped fist was scuffing lots of biker leather as I dodged return blows, getting into the rhythm of something I'd never participated in before, a brawl. With these allies—and no deadly weapons out as yet—it was kind of invigorating.

Then I felt my arms pinned to my side by someone unseen and unwelcome and really strong behind me. We hadn't figured on vampires joining the fray.

I turned to snarl in that direction . . . and faced off a tattoo freak with a smear of black beard. He picked me up by the waist, spun me around behind him, and proceeded to stomp Haskell in the nuts. Or where what was left of them would be. Nice.

Quicksilver was nipping neatly at the thick ankles of the tourist couple while Holmes and Montalbán were engaging the gathering crowd aching for a fight with quaint but effective fisticuffs. I dodged around my unsavory would-be rescuer to back up Holmes and Montalbán, but was again grabbed and pinned, my back to his front. The whole scene was really beginning to look like *The Three Stooges Meet the Monster Jamboree*.

I couldn't enjoy the comic aspects in the custody of another mauling male. I twisted hard to take another look at my rescuer/meddler. He was a smoke-and-brimstone-streaked guy wearing Eau de NASCAR pit-stop cologne. Not attractive unless vintage auto exhaust turned you on.

I started to order him to back off, when he rubbed the back of one tatted forearm over his sooty brow, eyed me hard, and said "Whew. All this action gives me an adrenaline junkie itch. Let's go somewhere and fuck, babe."

Babe! Really offensive language always brought out my Our Lady of the Lake Convent School warrior maid.

I managed to slew around in the creep's grasp, fighting to pull far enough away to kick him in the nuthouse.

Quicksilver was pushing between us, growling and snapping at the same target I coveted.

My attacker had snaked around, clutching me as close as a shield, and was once again behind me, holding me tight. Too close for Quicksilver to hurt him without taking a chunk out of me. I struggled, panting, at hearing my warrior dog whimper in sheer frustration.

"And you thought I couldn't disguise myself in the Sinkhole," the man whispered against my ear as my head thrashed to butt him under the jaw and get myself loose.

I stopped fighting. And was silent, hearing only my ragged breathing. And his. Fury became something quite the opposite, or maybe just in a different mode.

"Hell, Montoya," I whispered just as softly. "Why wouldn't I panic? That thing felt a foot long."

"I *thought* you were interested."

"So is Quick."

"You don't have a way to tell him to back off before I let you go and expose my crotch to his two-inch fangs?"

"Quick. *Down.*"

The dog went to his stomach, still growling.

The eager-to-assist citizens and gang bangers were backing off, tamed by a first-class pummeling from some formidable CinSim superheroes. My friends held Haskell, but looked ready to rush my captor. I shook my head no. Violently. They looked carefully away, confused but aware that our new ally was more than friendly with me.

Ric rocked his pelvis into my backside until my pulses hummed like a vibrator, still whispering into my tingling ear. "Your place or mine? I think we have explanations, at least, to exchange."

"Yours," I whispered back. "We'll drop Quick off at the cottage."

"First," Ric said, "I have to secure the loose vermin. Wrathbone's might lose its hospitality license if we left this piece of shit crawling around."

While Haskell writhed, pinned facedown like a cockroach by Montalbán and Holmes, I forced myself to bend down and lift up his black satin bowling club jacket. Tawdry taste. I found some shiny new cuffs on his belt, probably the ones he'd used on me. I bent down to wrench one hand behind his back as Holmes bent the other wrist at a painful angle and brought it around.

Haskell screamed curses when I snapped the cuffs shut. Sweet.

I rose, nodding at my gang of three CinSims, who looked disheveled but unbowed. The Invisible Man had hefted his wrappings and clothing over one arm, so I could tell where he was.

"We better split before we look like co-conspirators," Ric warned me.

He took my right arm in custody and this time Ricardo Montalbán growled softly, not Quicksilver, who'd overcome the diesel smell to ID the man in Cheap Thug guise.

"Ricardo Montalbán, meet Ric Montoya, my partner in crime-solving," I said quietly. "Ric, Mr. Holmes and, er, part of Dr. Griffin. We need to leave first."

Ric, eyeing the restless crowd, barely registered my famous associates.

"Gotta make this exit fast and in character for this dump," he told us all in a low voice. In a loud, blustery tone, Ric ordered everyone within hearing, "Better drop this cuffed crap topside for the street cops to find."

His booted toe prodded the struggling and cursing Haskell's side. "Meanwhile, I'll take up *this* trouble-maker myself."

I was startled to feel a shiver of cold run down my left arm and to hear a metallic clink. My obliging body jewelry had morphed into a pair of handcuffs. One clasped my wrist like a bracelet, the other dangled open. Ric grabbed the open cuff and locked my wrists behind my back.

No one regarded us openly as we left, Ric shepherding me like a captive, Quicksilver shadowing us both like a bodyguard on a leash. Just another dicey situation in the Sinkhole with someone likely heading toward a nasty fate. Didn't matter who or what. Ric acted like an undercover cop but he might be crooked or an impersonator. Maybe one more unescorted human woman would not be leaving the Sinkhole alive.

OUTSIDE WRATHBONE'S, we paused in the soft white neon light of the sign while Quicksilver eyed Ric's hands on my wrists and growled the soft friendly warning he reserved for people I know.

"It's okay, Killer," Ric told him. "It has to look like I'm an undercover cop taking your roommate out of here to jail." Quick liked being addressed man to man, and relaxed.

"Did Nightwine tip you off about where I was going?" I asked.

"Got it first try. The Fat Man has a surprising paternal streak when it comes to you."

Nightwine was mostly protective of my commercial possibilities as a Lilith/Maggie stand-in, but Ric didn't know about Lilith yet and would want me off of Hector's premises if he knew about the man's scummy commercial interest in both Lilith and me.

"You know," I told Ric, "now that I've seen the Sinkhole, I've got a couple of new theories about who really maimed Haskell after you beat him up and left him for what passes as street-sweeper meat down here last time you visited incognito."

"Yeah?"

Passing people didn't even glance at us. I must have looked like a hooker chatting up a client with bondage tendencies. I nodded toward Quick, who was following every word we said like he could lip-read. He probably could.

"I had to lock Quick up at the cottage when Haskell charged in or the creep would have shot him. The dog goes out alone at night a lot. He could have trailed Haskell's scent to hell and back. He was not happy about being shut out of the action or what Haskell was doing to me."

Ric eyed Quick. "Possible."

"Or . . . Hector could have loosed a really nasty CinSim on Haskell."

"A paternal meddler, maybe, but I don't see Hector Nightwine as the Black Knight riding to the damsel's revenge after the fact."

"He was really upset Haskell had crashed his security devices and violated his property."

"And you're his property too?"

"In a way, in *his* mind. He's hired me to research crime stories for his shows and I live on site. Sometimes I think he confuses me with one of the staff CinSims."

"Anyone else in your circle of suspects?"

Yeah, Christophe, a.k.a. Snow. Pointing that out would tip Ric off to the fact that another man, one he regarded as beyond a bad guy, had roped Ric's girl with a permanent silver lariat, now masquerading as handcuffs.

Snow was like Nightwine. He owned so much of this city and so many CinSims that he tended to confuse that with owning people. A lot of mobsters and lobbyists make that mistake. Not that Hector was a mobster. He was too egocentric to even have henchmen.

"You must have felt a lot of satisfaction," Ric said, "cuffing Haskell in return for the brutal way he searched and cuffed you at Nightwine's cottage."

"You must have enjoyed kicking him in the family vault."

"Not as much as whoever"—he glanced at Quicksilver, panting amiably as he lay on the slick Sinkhole street, tongue limp in a forest of sharp white fangs—"really maimed the bastard."

"And you must enjoy cuffing my hands behind my back." I grinned as Ric suddenly realized he had me in a very compromising position.

"I'm used to seeing a sexy thin silver chain around your hips." He released my second wrist as I pretended to fool with the one shut cuff. "When'd you add concealed handcuffs and a pseudo-cop belt to your walking-around wardrobe?"

"Found 'em at a second-hand store," I said, now pretending to slip the cuffs into a belt pocket. In reality, the instantly liquid silver ran up my arm and back down my side to my waist, where it became the spitting image of the thin sterling silver hip chain I wore. "They were so shiny and new I couldn't resist them. You know me and silver."

"You sure there isn't some Latina in you, *Querida*? You wear silver so well. Your jewelry always rocks."

Well, it came from a headlining rock'n'roller's head. I was speechless. Ric took that as a pleased response to his compliment when I was scared stiff he'd guess the nature of the silver familiar.

"You should resist your faux law enforcement tendencies," he went on. "They could get you into serious trouble sometime."

So could Snow's morphing lock of hair.

Ric still had custody of my right arm and used it to steer me through the ambling tourist traffic. Quick was up and heeling alongside me like a service dog. Which he was to me. He kept so close to my outside leg that he reminded me of Achilles.

"I sort of had to go into a trance to get here," I said. "How do we get out?"

"Trance, huh?" Ric's grin was white-hot against the black, two-day beard smudge. "Like you went into in Sunset Park when we first met. You're full of surprises. The rest of us just take the completely natural mobile spiral staircase."

I stared at the ornate wrought-iron corkscrew that appeared out of the smoky air like something very Jules Verne glimpsed in a London pea-soup fog. "You're telling me this thing moves?"

"Think of it as the Devil's auger to the Lower Depths."
He hitched up my arm to help me onto the first step. They
were higher than ordinary ones. Quick brushed past to
bound up three risers sniffing the iron, the smoke, the
upper air.

Meanwhile, Ric had mounted close behind me. Nicely
close. As for climbing the spinning spiral staircase, we
didn't need to move. It was as if we'd all jumped on a
passing tram to Nowhere.

I wanted to grab the smooth metal handrail, because
the stairs were indeed swirling around. The effect was so
dizzying I closed my eyes, fighting nausea.

"We're here," Ric whispered in my ear.

My eyes opened to see downtown take shape around
me, a panorama of darkness stabbed with slashes of light.
Quicksilver was nosing around ten feet away, chasing the
phantom scents of hundreds of pedestrians. We stood by
a hole in the street bounded by a metal-pipe fence and
orange safety cones.

"How does anyone know this hole in the ground from
any other street-repair site?" I asked.

"It's always near downtown and the manhole cover is
a Celtic design."

I peered at the pierced metal circle. "Celtic?"

"The assumption is that the fey folk created this
underground retreat. With the green spaces declining,
they've had to turn to the cities, and this desert environment
isn't welcoming of the fey. Some of the stuff going around
now is fairy stories, plain and simple. Some isn't. The
anthropologists are still trying to sort legend from reality
and delusion from actual experience." Ric made a face.
"It's no delusion that the Sinkhole is a reeking, rank evil
place. Let's get away from here."

It took a couple blocks' walk to reach the tourist-
crowded areas and recognize landmarks.

"You parked by the Four Goddesses? Great," Ric said.
"I'm there too."

Dolly was not hard to find.

At my car, Ric stood back to take in the faint fluorescent green glow haloing it.

"Some funky Hector Nightwine safety alarm," I explained.

He didn't know about the Enchanted Cottage oddities, either. I didn't want to freak him out any more than I had to. He had one stunning paranormal power. I had, and was surrounded by, a whole growing flock of weird little quirks I was still figuring out.

"The Caddy sure looks too toxic to steal." He glanced over to study me as thoroughly as he had my car. "I wouldn't have recognized you except for the dog." He paused long enough for our stressed-out pulses to beam us into a more intimate mode. "You make a hot blond, *chica*."

"Guys are always suckers for a bleach job." Compliments still made me want to make excuses. "I wouldn't have thought you'd have one rough edge in your high-end city slicker wardrobe, and here you show up with razor-cut seams on your jeans and a jaw primed to give beard burns."

"So you like?"

"You do dark well," I agreed demurely.

Ric picked up my return cue. "Undercover needs to be extreme, Blondie," he said in a mock street growl. "Speaking of which, the nice folks at Wrathbone's expected me to do something bad to you. I'm the law and it'd be suspicious if I didn't give you a strip search."

His eyes were doing a good job of that already; the effect was a world away from Haskell's impression of a tough cop. "That super-sexy utility belt is LVMPD property. Take it off."

I unbuckled without a word or a moment's hesitation, and then let the belt slip slowly off my hips. Our surprising, disguised personas gave us a new way to express our insanely intense attraction, playing hard and fast into our fantasy roles. It was as I'd discovered while salsa dancing with Ric at Los Lobos. Letting him lead at moments like this made me hot.

I watched Ric's fingers expertly probe the contents of the belt's various pockets and holsters, swallowing hard.

He looked up. "If you're going to be a scofflaw, you need some better defensive weapons. Silver-hafted stilettos. I don't recommend silver bullets; guns are two-edged swords in close quarters, excuse the mixed metaphor. You need more street cop stuff. Mace, for one. A taser for another."

"You sure you want me equipped to drop a man helpless to the ground at the push of a button?"

He smiled at my comment. "Depends on who the man is." He set the belt on Dolly's fender so gently I nearly swooned as he turned his attention to me again.

"Nice vest." He fingered the long fringe on my used leathers. "Take it off. I have to make sure you're not carrying concealed."

"And you aren't?" I looked where it was relevant.

"Strip."

I shrugged slowly out of the vest. Didn't want to give the nice undercover policeman any reason to panic. In fact, I had him breathing hard already.

"That tight knit top really juices up your breasts," he said. "Take it off."

Here? Outdoors in the empty night? It might not be empty any minute. The notion was exciting. Besides, the big bad strange lawman made me do it. *Si, señor,* Irma growled in my mind. *Give and you shall receive, chica.*

I torqued my torso to eel out of the spandex knit, down to my black sports bra. My thin silver chain shimmied on my hips, where I usually wore a chain with him in mind.

He parked a thumb in my navel to stroke the chain. Even that tiny bit of mock penetration had me ready to writhe with excitement, except that Ric caressing Snow's lock of hair once-removed made me feel oddly incestuous.

"Nice low-rise jeans." Ric was still exploring. His finger stroked along the top edge just above my pubic bone, hidden until now by the top. A sudden vertical jab down inside almost made me jump out of my skin . . . and my skin-tight leather.

"This short little front zipper is going to drive me wild until we get home." Ric tugged on the metal pull. I felt an answering tug from deep within, my muscles straining to pull something inside, that teasing finger, that eager erection I'd felt in Wrathbone's.

Ric curved me back against the convertible top. The night was warm, but I shivered. His other hand brushed over my breasts, along my ribs, down my hips, and past my navel to the ebbing edge of the jeans' band.

His mouth started at my throat and slipped down my center, his teeth finally biting the zipper pull and tugging until I spasmed, arching toward his face and mouth.

"*Mi amor*," he whispered into my pelvis, as shaken as I was by our mutual sensual connection. He pulled away, brought his face up to mine.

I was quivering. "You get off on bare torsos, *señor*. Any reason?"

"You always want to know 'why' about everything, *mi periodista*."

I recognized the Spanish word for "journalist."

"Yes, I am one. I have a *muy grande* need to know."

"Now you need to know why I like to caress you, where and how."

"It's because all this is new to me."

"In my case, it's because of those filthy *coyotes* who held me captive in the desert. I kept the herd animals between myself and those evil men. I knew, even as a *muchacho*, that nothing was safe from them. But they had magazines. Porn. The only thing I had to read. The crude photos repelled me, but one magazine had a photo of a belly dancer glittering with gold coins in a fringe beneath her breasts and in a circle of gold at her hips—all swathed in sheer silk. That bare midriff with mysteries above and below, that an ignorant boy could safely covet."

I smiled at him, letting my glance fall to his dingy neck, expert applied camo makeup rather than dirt. A wrinkled bandana circled it, covered something. "There are things an ignorant girl can covet too."

We froze, my heart pounding at the thought of soon teasing the love mark I'd made on his throat and kept bruised and tender, the site of a boyhood vampire bat bite. That had been his first innocent, unconscious turn-on and I'd learned to use it.

Quicksilver had endured enough of our sensual games that aimed straight at the heart of love. He thrust his furry head and neck up at the sky and celebrated, or protested, human lust with an ancient, long and mournful canine yowl.

Chapter Sixteen

SINCE DOLLY was protected from vandals by pixie halitosis, we took Ric's vintage bronze Stingray Corvette, which was always thief bait despite its expensive security devices.

Quicksilver stood dancing from forefoot to forefoot twenty feet away, wired to race the Corvette home. Even my skimpy top and leather vest barely fit in the so-called storage area, but I liked the ambiguous privacy of the small, low, throbbing car that had the road feel of a very large and intimate vibrator.

Sometimes the intensity of our physical reactions scared me.

Both of us were orphans. I was never adopted. Growing up in group homes made me defensive and emotionally cautious. Ric was from a poor Mexican family of water dowsers and ended up used by a gang of *coyotes*, the heartless desert rats who take money to guide illegal immigrants through the Sonora and Chihuahua Desert wilds into the U.S. There the *coyotes* often abandon them to death by dehydration. They gave real coyotes a bad name.

After the Millennium Revelation, illegally imported zombies from Mexico began fueling the entertainment industry as technology and magic combined to create whole new industries. Young Ricardo Montoya was forced to find and raise zombies so they could be sold into servitude. Somehow he got away and grew up to be the man I'd recently met: an educated, attractive, sexually sophisticated drop-out from a good government job who dressed like a *Gentleman's Quarterly* white-collar stud.

I wasn't a former TV reporter for nothing. There had to be a whale of a backstory between the man in the present and the illiterate boy on the brink of puberty living among men worse than animals could ever dream of being. That boy had relied on visions of Our Lady of Guadalupe as an ersatz mother figure until a dancing girl in a porn magazine collaborated with a vampire bat to bring him over into manhood one moonless desert night.

Me, I'd come out of puberty with holes in my memory and a phobia against lying on my back.

Somehow, though, Ric and I had a healing effect on each other.

Our cars said a lot about us. Dolly was a 1956 Caddy Biarritz, a classic car. During my self-supporting student days I'd survived by living on other people's castoffs and learned to love the plunder to be found from families who didn't honor their own history—history I would have given my blood for, if vampire bites could deliver such a thing.

Dolly was a battleship: flashy, big, slow, ponderous, but with enough hidden power under the hood to tow Superman. She was my fortress. Ric's small sixties-era Corvette was fast, sleek, powerful, the perfect escape car.

And now here I was a passive passenger in Ric's car, and liking it. Group home Delilah was easing up. How could I not like it? Ric drove the sports car like he did me, an easy hand on all the gears, shifting them silkily . . . when he wasn't shifting he was caressing my bared midriff.

His fingers were teasing my thin silver hip chain, which put me in a ticklish position again in a couple ways. Caresses were one butterfly wing away from tickling, and this chain wasn't the department store one I'd bought, but yet another shape-shifting incarnation of a lock of albino hair from Christophe/Cocaine/Snow.

So Ric toying with Snow's sending gave me the edgy feeling of being in a threesome nobody knew about but me. Me and my silver shadow.

Ric quit toying and pushed three fingers tight inside my leather pants, under that ridiculously short zipper.

Man, that hombre does know how to rattle our cages, Irma kibitzed.

Yeah. As much as I reacted physically, I knew a significant part of my new sexual thralldom was emotional empathy. I longed with every bone and drop of blood in my body to find the last, hidden key to Ric's past and heal any wounds still borne by that brutalized boy in the desert. And maybe I would. Someday.

THE COURTYARD to Ric's house, hidden behind six-foot-high pale stucco walls, resembled a square in Old Mexico with its huge central fountain plinking away like a watery harpsichord.

A girl could feel like Zorro bait pressed against a stucco wall in the warm, velvet dark, surrounded by the heady scent of a flowering vine while six feet of hungry male sucked the sugar from her lips. Much better than being vampire bait. Much better than being horizontal, although Ricardo Montoya was luring me more and more to that inclination.

His hands were on my bare hips, stroking, caressing, until my pelvis was seducing his as much as his mouth subverted mine.

Move your booty a little to the left and do a yoga pelvic tilt. That oughta hit him where it hurts so good—

Irma was a slut. So I complied. Ric groaned and pulled back. "We better find a room, *mi tigre hembra*."

His tigress. *Yes!* We lurched inside together, mixing lip locks with forward progress. *God!* Now I knew what all the Top Forty hits were about.

The kitchen was dark and vaguely reflective, the living room dark and mysterious. The house sound system greeted us with an instrumental Latin beat, softer than salsa. I knew he was taking me to the master suite, where we'd first made love. It had been in front of a mirror.

Sometimes I fantasized that it had been my double, Lilith, doing the wild thing, not me. Now that I knew I had mirror connections, I wondered if that was why my first joining with a man had resulted in climax. I'd had outside help.

I tried to avoid looking at the low platform bed as we came in. Beds cried for the missionary position and I wasn't ready for that. The warm, throbbing, sloping hood of Ric's Vette was scary enough, yet I wanted to be there again.

As we entered the bedroom, the bathroom lights had come on: frosted globes above the over-the-sinks mirror, a softly glowing chandelier over the sunken tub. He nodded to a curve of glass blocks.

"I'm going to shower off the temp tattoos and Sinkhole Scumboy. Feel free to look around."

"Shouldn't I wash off Biker Chick too?"

"You're perfect the way you are. Don't change one sexy thang." He vanished behind the wall, still dressed in his disreputable Sinkhole disguise duds.

Well, that was clear. No lingering, naked shower together. I'd seen so many shower scenes in TV movies I was disappointed. On the other hand, at least it wasn't *Psycho*. Shivering a little at the memory of Janet Leigh getting knifed to death in living black-and-white at the Bates Motel, I accepted his invitation to snoop. A reporter is an incurable spy. I opened one of the bathroom's two walk-in closet doors. And walked in.

The clothes were neatly hung on two levels. Men wore only separates. No need for a long gown rack. My vintage stuff was more long than short. I moved among the garments, caressing them, inhaling Ric's cologne and the natural scent of soap and skin under it. My sense of smell had become sharper since our joint dowsing experience in Sunset Park.

Every piece was natural fiber: tropical weight wool suits and silk or silk-cotton blend shirts. A built-in set of

drawers increasing in depth from top to bottom started
with a shallow jewelry drawer of gold cuff links, a
bracelet I'd never seen him wear, a slender neck chain
with a medal of some kind. Below was a sea of silky
boxer shorts, all black, below that, socks just as silky in
shades of beige to match the desert climate of Las Vegas
and its surrounding Mohave Desert.

I heard water running, hitting tile, and considered
walking in, totally dressed.

No. Ric needed his distance. Just as his clothes were
all selected to cosset his body and cosseted me by proxy,
I'd been selected because I suited his body and mind and,
hopefully, heart and soul. So he said, but could he really
know me well enough so quickly to be sure?

Ties were on a pullout rack. All silk, all subtle, all
long and smooth and fully packed . . . *oops!* Irma was
influencing my objective reporter's instincts.

I suddenly realized the pitter-patter of shower water
had stopped and moved back into the bathroom proper,
like any good girl caught snooping with very bad, even
confessable, thoughts.

Or . . . into the bathroom, vastly improper.

Ric's hair was damp, yet still thick and smooth. He
was semi-naked and the semi part of that was what was
so interesting. He wore black satin boxer shorts and
a matching black satin robe, open and hanging off his
broad shoulders.

*Introducing, in the center ring, ladies and ladies, the
Cadaver Kid.*

I hated the brutal so-called sport of boxing. I loved the
boxer in the room with me. Kinda like the "hate the sin,
love the sinner" religious motto.

His skin was sleek and brown as amber, his pecs taut,
his abdomen a subtle six-pack. If I was a Jockey or men's
cologne advertising director I could get the Cadaver Kid
such an endorsement deal . . . but I'm selfish. He was all
mine.

"Wow," I said. "You look even better wet. And you're all mine."

Original dialogue is not a reporting requirement.

His laugh was the advertised music to my ears. Most of all, I wanted to make him happy. We walked into each other and then stayed there.

"Ric," I said finally, choosing my words to get the information I craved, "I really didn't recognize Sinkhole Slimeboy. All your clothes here are so smooth and soft and sensuous. I understand why you'd love that after having been burned to a cinder as a kid in the Mexican desert, but damn it, sometimes I fantasize about being fucked by just your clothes. Is that normal?"

His laughter reverberated against my hypersensitive skin and bones. I felt like a very happy drum.

"No, it's not normal, but I feel the same and, anyway, are *you* normal, Delilah?"

I swallowed hard. That question had dogged me all my life. "Probably not. I just want to understand. How can *GQ* guy co-exist with Sinkhole Slimeboy?"

"How can edgy, virginal Del co-exist with tigress Delilah?"

I just laid my cheek on his chest and rubbed my Lip-Venomed mouth over his nipple until he bent to take my mouth with his.

"You want to talk?" he asked finally.

"A little."

He lifted me atop the granite sink surround, my back to the mirror. "You want to know about Ricardo Montoya, FBI agent."

"You. I want to know about you."

"Can't we just fuck?"

The bad, blunt word revved my momentarily idling engine. "Sure. But I don't smoke. I won't want a cigarette after. I'll want information."

He closed his eyes. Opened them. "What do you want to know?"

"*Need* to know. That's what we call it in the reporting trade. The need to know."

Ric searched my eyes, then nodded and waited for my first question.

"Just . . . how you escaped that awful background, that rotten start in life."

"Like you did?"

"In your own way." My fingertip brushed the corner of his mouth. "Talk, Montoya, or I'll torment you for hours in bed."

"It couldn't be worse than this," he said soberly, then sighed. "Okay. The facts: You know the *coyotes* made me find the dead and raise them as zombies. Even as a four-year-old I knew what I did was wrong. The dead want to rest. But I was a small child, bewildered that my family had traded me to these monsters."

I inhaled with a hiss. "Traded! And here I always longed for a real family, my birth parents—"

"My people were untaught peasants, Del. They didn't understand a boy who could only dowse for dead things, not life-giving water."

"Do you have any memories of them?"

"Only of standing alone, over the dried-up body of some small desert creature. When the *coyotes* came, saying they'd heard I was useless but could employ me, they passed me on without a thought."

"How awful."

"When you're poor, you must be worth the beans to feed you."

I leaned my forehead on his satin shoulder. "How could the zombie trade be starting up then, before the Millennium Revelation?"

"The MR was a public announcement. They don't call it the "Revelation" for nothing; nothing happens overnight. Evil is always ahead of the curve."

I nodded. "I want to know about after. Right after you got away from the *coyotes*. How."

"One day U.S. border agents raided and collected my uncouth masters. They rounded up me with the goats and burros."

"And?"

"And." Ric took such a deep breath that my head on his shoulder heaved up and down as if riding an Atlantic swell. "The leader was ex-military, a decorated major-turned-D.C.-bureaucrat doing a final, pre-retirement field assignment. I was considered a feral child. His wife was a Georgetown University psychologist. They had no children. I was a 'fascinating case'. I went home to them, which included a couple years in behavioral labs."

"This was better?" I asked, horrified.

He nodded. "Better. My . . . adopted mother is a brilliant analyst. She pioneered a method of breaking through to abused or isolated or autistic children with me."

"And adopted you."

"Not officially. That's why I'm Ric Montoya, not Phillip Burnside, Jr."

"How did you get your name?"

Ric smiled nostalgically for the first time since I'd known him. "She and I sat down with a baby name book and a surname history book. We went through Latino names that didn't remind me of my keepers. That's how my father got leads on the identities of the captured *coyotes*, who weren't talking."

I could picture that. The sophisticated American career woman and the wary, half-wild Mexican waif poring over name books as if they were fairy tales. Although randomly named, at least Ric had a memorable moment about the occasion. He wasn't named after a street like me.

"Why didn't they formally adopt you?"

"They were a couple complete unto themselves, never wanted kids. I became a canvas on which they could paint something permanent, a tribute to their union."

"You make them sound so . . . cold."

"They were people of the mind, not the emotions. They gave me my mind back and let it expand a thousand times. I'll always be grateful. I'll always be ambivalent. Do I love them or do I owe them? Do they love me or do they love what they made me become?"

"Adoption is so . . . major."

"Maybe *not* being adopted is not so bad, *hmm?*" He kissed me softly on the neck. "I have no quarrel with them. I respect them and do anything they want as long as I don't lose any part of the self they worked so hard to find and develop."

"They don't always understand that."

"No. An understatement. They were not happy when I left the FBI to consult. But they don't know about my dowsing facility." Ric grinned. "So now I have the same family issues as any ordinary American kid."

"And I still envy that."

"Don't. You're not alone any more. You *are* my family, Del." He pulled me close to him, my legs straddling his hips, our pelvic heat melding. He whispered a Spanish phrase, "*Tu vestir mi consuelo,*" or something.

I knew most of the words. *Tu.* You. *Mi.* Me. *Vestir.* Dress. Clothe. *Consuelo?* Wasn't that a woman's name? I still didn't know much Spanish, but I did remember an Italian nun at Our Lady of the Lake—Sister Maria Consolata. Her name meant "consolation, comfort."

"You clothe me." *Consuelo* made it, "in comfort."

I broke our kiss to brush my lips against the faint bruise on the left side of his throat, the heart side.

"Then put me on," I whispered.

Chapter Seventeen

FIRST HE HAD to extract me from the skin-tight leather jeans he lusted to remove without laying me horizontal.

This became a long, inciting process involving sliding and turning along the walls, kissing and laughing and breathing hard all the way through the bedroom into a room I'd never seen. By then he could lift my bare butt atop a cold marble table top and shimmy the leather off my legs, one by one.

He was kneeling before me and his mouth was at my center. "Do you have your Lip Venom with you, *amor*?"

"*Sí, señor,* but I'm tingling enough already."

"Never too much," he murmured through kisses.

I wanted to lean my head back and howl like a . . . wolf, not a coyote. Instead I giggled.

"You laugh?"

"Your five o'clock shadow tickles." He pressed harder. "*Oooh*. Now it feels so nice and rough." I growled the last word a little.

That made him pause, pick me up, and deposit me half sitting on a circular red leather lounge. I reached up to pull down his boxers and slid onto my tailbone, still half-sitting. He braced his arms on the back of the low sofa and pressed his pelvis into mine.

The tension of *not having* was overpowering the tension of almost having. I recognized the taut pain of anticipation in my inner muscles. "Now," I breathed. "Now."

"*Ahora*?"

"*Ahora*!" I repeated desperately, clenching my hands on the satin lapels of his robe.

"*Ahora*," he repeated, finally pushing inside, moving as I did to repeat that sublime act, over and over until we tumbled together into shudders and screams, pleasure wringing us out along every *simpático* nerve in our bodies.

I sat half-upright but still laid out, throbbing, clinging, even crying.

Ric was murmuring comfort, even as his lips sipped up my tears. Was I all right? Nothing hurt?

Hurt? Hell, I was quivering with gratitude, lifting my hips hard into his to protest any separation, overflowing with emotion and . . . love.

It wasn't just the peak of orgasm. It was the high of total human connection. I almost understood the Snow groupies at that moment.

Ric was nuzzling my face and murmuring sweet Spanish nothings. His open, verbal passion was a rare gift, I understood. And after all that he'd been through. *Te amo, te amo,* we murmured, each lost in vying to express our emotions. Separate but blended. Incoherent yet mentally in touch as perfectly as our bodies.

I listened for other voices, other objections. There was nothing. Even Irma had left the building. It was just Ric and me and we were utterly and completely enough.

EVEN GREAT SEX isn't the answer to everything, I was discovering. *Mi amor* was a lawman. He'd needed answers as much as a journalist did, maybe even more. Catching me in the sated backwash of climax was a great time to interrogate.

"How did an innocent émigré from Kansas become the target of Cesar Cicereau and his hit pack of werewolves?" he asked, applying the torture of constant caresses.

After teasing more details of Ric's sad and shocking childhood history from him, it was time to confess that I didn't have any.

"I wasn't his target," I admitted. "A few weeks ago my exact double was autopsied on Hector Nightwine's *Crime Scene Instincts V: Las Vegas* show."

That made Ric sit up and take notice and more liberties. "Double, *paloma*? Hard to believe there could be two as uniquely smart and sexy as you."

"Lilith," I said. The name made him frown. "Yeah, another shady lady from the Bible. She gave her last name as 'Quince'. Hector says she'd arranged to kill herself for the autopsy. I spotted her post-mortem, so he says."

"Your exact double, the hair style, everything?"

"Just like a man to not notice that I don't have much of a 'hair style'. It's just a shoulder length blunt cut. And so was hers. She even wore my tiny blue topaz nose stud, which was a creepy coincidence."

"Yeah, where is that bashful little punk touch you had in Sunset Park when we first met?" His forefinger stroked my nostril.

"I quit wearing it shortly after I got to town and found out everyone's looking to find and grab Lilith. She apparently had so much sex appeal as a corpse that her image is the heart of a growing media empire."

"For Nightwine, great. Why have you been hiding this from me?"

"Maybe I'm afraid you might catch Lilith fever and forget me and go for her?"

"Jealousy is always a good motive, but I don't buy it in your case."

"I'm that secure?"

"No. You're that solitary. Jealousy grows in a crowd. So why didn't you tell me?"

"Lilith is so popular everyone wants her image or the person they think is behind it—me."

"They'd kidnap you?"

"That's what Cicereau did. He wanted to make me a celebrity magician's assistant in his house act."

"'Make you' being the operative issue. So he wasn't just out to stop you from investigating his daughter's murder? And you didn't tell me? *Chica*, we're not just lovers; we're partners."

"I know, but it's hard for me to think like I'm not alone anymore. Anyway, I got away the first time, but while I was at the Gehenna I was able to snoop in his personal computer—"

"Delilah! He surely had safeguards that would reveal what you did and where you went in his system."

"No. Cicereau is a technophobe. He never noticed a thing."

I didn't mention that Cicereau's right-hand muscle, Sansouci, had. Ric would want to put me in purdah if he knew how many big, bad werewolves I had aggravated in this town. His concern for me was welcome after my years of being institutionally ignored, but his protectiveness had an Old World fierceness that I couldn't let hamper my freedom.

"He noticed enough to catch you and ship you to his hobby hunting range in the mountains," he pointed out.

"Yeah, well, I had to go back to the Gehenna for proof and Haskell was looking to work for Cicereau and trapped me."

"Is that why Haskell is still stalking you? You escaped the bastard at the Gehenna?" Ric was indignant.

"Not completely, but sufficiently. Anyway, even the werewolves despise Haskell. Me, they wanted to use and then they wanted to kill when they decided I wasn't docile. That's when you rode to the rescue up in the mountains."

"Indirectly, you can thank or blame Hector for that too," Ric said. "I was astounded to find Hector's CinSim butler waiting at your cottage door when I got worried that full-moon night and came to find you. He told me about Starlight Lodge. I never dreamed CinSims had that kind of smarts or freedom."

"Hector knew nothing about it," I told Ric. "I don't know how the Invisible Man manages to slip his Inferno leash and get around town, but he saw me kidnapped and tipped off Hector's man Godfrey."

"So Godfrey was acting on his own too," Ric mused. "Fascinating. Was that the Invisible Man in the washed-out Ace bandages at Wrathbone's tonight? Or were your male companions all CinSymbiants?"

"Hey, good question. I took them for the real unreal thing. IM taking off his bandages for the fight proved it in his case."

As usual, though, Ric's skeptical ex-FBI agent instincts made me reconsider what had happened at Wrathbone's. It could be hard to tell CinSims from their CinSymbs.

"The police go undercover at Wrathbone's, for your information," Ric added.

"Great, so some of the CinSims and CinSymbs present could have been narcs. And then there was Haskell, not exactly undercover. Or even on active duty, come to think.

"That bastard! I didn't know he'd messed with you earlier at the Gehenna too. I wish I'd *really* hurt him."

His partisanship made me smile. I saw and heard the racist cop dismiss Ric as a "Meskin" in public and Ric kept his FBI-agent cool. The same cop laid a few fingers on me and Ric was ready to skin Haskell alive.

"I'm serious, Del. Kennedy Malloy told me she'd love to bust him off the force, but the police association would have to defend the sonovabitch."

"*Captain* Malloy," I said, invoking her title. "No wonder she's such a good police source for you, *amigo*. You have a thing for blond authority figures, as you just proved when you disarmed and strip-searched me in my Madonna wig. I bet she has a thing for you."

"You'd be wrong," Ric said, "and she'd be wrong. I have a thing for raven-haired reporters-turned-private-eyes."

He teased the bobby pins out of my platinum blond wig and threw it aside, releasing my hair to my shoulders. "I need to feel those midnight Rapunzel tresses of yours brushing my thighs and your lips brushing something else."

He slid down level on the sofa, pulling me down with him. I'd recently learned that I have no problem lying horizontal if I'm on top, and I set to work demonstrating exactly that.

"HOW DO YOU SLEEP?" Ric asked much later when it was obvious we'd be spending what was left of the night on his red leather sofa.

"You don't want to get too close. I get ex-orphanage nightmares, so I might kick you."

"Kick away, you won't hurt me. No, I mean given your hatred of being on your back?"

"On my stomach," I answered, stretching face down to demonstrate.

Ric whistled something sexy in Spanish under his breath that I needed my Street Spanish dictionary at home to translate. He thoughtfully explained in English, "Nude, white-skinned, black-haired woman face down on red leather—would be quite the *Maxim* cover layout. I can work with that."

And so he went to work. His fingers teased the bottom of my butt and then strummed between my thighs. I burrowed deeper into the smooth leather, lifting my pelvis in lazy, content trust, all three of those conditions utterly alien to me before I'd encountered Ric. I loved being his sex object and making him mine, and was finally discovering what all the hooting and hollering about sex was for.

Ric *hmm*ed his pleasure at finding me receptive for more, which only made my core heat flare along my nerves like liquid mercury. Not being able to see what he was doing ramped up my excitement.

He stopped doing anything for a moment and I lay there throbbing with sweet anticipation. I couldn't imagine not welcoming anything he wanted.

His voice came closer as he pushed higher along my side until his face was buried in my hair, his lips at my ear.

"Were you raped, Delilah?" he asked in a whisper. "Is that what's kept you unplumbed for so long? It's all right. You can tell me."

"But it's not all right! I don't think so. I don't think that's what happened."

"Something happened."

"Yes! No! I don't remember."

"And you feared it and it caused you pain?"

"Yes!"

"Does our having sex cause you pain?"

I tried to sort my tumultuous feelings, not wanting to hurt his. "Yes. But only a . . . little."

"You're virgin-tight, Delilah," he said tenderly. "Intercourse may be painful at times."

"Yes, I know. *Muy delicado*." I tried to diagnose my feelings, the sensation I welcomed yet feared. "This, right now, it's just the pain of wanting so badly. I know it precedes pleasure. That old . . . other was only . . . pain. A lot of pain. And fear."

Ric sighed. I could feel his lips drizzling kisses on my neck and ear through the veil of my hair.

"Was anyone there?"

"From my nightmares, little gray men."

"Like ETs?"

He sounded so startled I had to stifle a laugh. Here I was, half-fucked, and we were discussing my very personal alien invasion nightmares. It occurred to me that Ric knew exactly how and when to draw out my most-buried fears and secrets: FBI man in bed.

"Were any of them women?" he asked.

"Women? No!" My reaction was visceral. Even I recognized that. I reconsidered. He was right to ask. "I suppose some of them could have been. I never thought of that. Why do you ask?"

"You went to an all-girls' high school and say you don't remember a lot of those four years. Girls can be vicious bullies."

"No! Some of them were snobby bitches, but the nuns would never have allowed it and they had eyes in the back of their habits."

"And what about the child abuse scandals in the Church?"

I was growing impatient with the interrogation. "That was mostly priests. Besides, what does it matter now, when you're holding me on the aching edge of an orgasm? Fuck me or forget it. You know you want to."

The relentless interrogator turned silk-voiced seducer. "You like me needing so bad to get inside you."

His words excited me. "Yes."

He swept the hair off of my sweat-damp neck, then strung a necklace of kisses around it as far as his lips could reach. I was melting with the need to have him inside me.

"I've always felt you flinch a little at first penetration. If you were abusively invaded, Delilah," Ric whispered, "you need to get past it. Sick people hurt others sexually because it mis-wires the lines between pain and pleasure. Whoever, whatever hurt you inside, it can be all pleasure now. Feel it. Feel how good what I want makes you feel."

Ric's voice was as soothing as a lullaby. "Don't worry, Delilah. We'll solve the mystery of your nightmares. We'll go back to Kansas. Investigate. This night, you're not dreaming. We're not dreaming. We're having sex. Does it still hurt a little? Or does it just hurt so good?"

I thought about it: his weight half on me, compressing my agitated nerves, this sudden, frank interrogation delving my lost past traumas, the throbbing tingle between my legs feeling oh-so-exciting.

"It hurts only because I want what you can give me more this instant than I ever have."

His hot fleshy tongue plunged into my bared ear as he finally pushed inside me. I was awash in salty, wet hot desire.

We murmured our litany incoherently. Our names. The word of love.

Amor.

And when I could feel him nudging the mouth of my womb, I felt completely sated, a sublime satisfaction at again accomplishing this for him, for me, every cell in the surrounding tissues touched and responding to such perfect possession, mine and his, that my panic popped like a bubble and vanished into the past.

Some dark veil in my mind dropped away.

"All right?" he asked.

I nodded and twisted my face over my shoulder as his mouth met mine and we siphoned warmth and wetness from each other until he broke the contact.

"And now—" Ric's deep voice was saying as his brushing fingers merely touched my clitoris.

I erupted in a Vesuvius of moans, almost fearing surviving such a seismic orgasm. Rip-roaring was the only way to describe the roller coaster of a climax that had me screaming and hyperventilating.

Ric's hot hands bracketed my pelvis as it shuddered, then slowly withdrew. I just wanted to lie there savoring the waning aftershocks.

He settled beside me, throwing a leg over mine, the sides of his black satin robe covering me like wings. That recalled my night flight with Bela Lugosi's Dracula, another escapade I didn't dare tell Ric about. I was beginning to feel like a compulsive liar. Intimacy was a tough exercise in trust.

Also, I'd never literally slept with anyone before and was nervous. I fought to exile my regrets and bask in the afterglow. His body was warm and comforting. I was beginning to feel drowsy. I felt safer totally exposed and plumbed on this makeshift sofa-bed with Ric than in the Enchanted Cottage. I hoped I could stay nightmare-free until morning for once.

I WOKE UP the next morning—first and nightmare-free— and rose on one elbow. Light was filtering down from a skylight I hadn't noticed the night before. The black satin robe was wrinkled beneath us, and Ric still slept beside me, face down too.

I smiled as I admired the way his dark hair curled on his nape, the sight of his brown, black-haired forearm still around my hip, the same swarthy, very masculine leg lying between my snow-white limbs. He would make an impressive werewolf.

I didn't move, not wanting to wake him, feeling what I never had in my life, sexually sated but also vaguely maternal and tender, something I'd never show him when he was conscious.

For the first time, I felt a surge of loss for a best friend forever girl buddy, someone I could whisper with about what we'd done and compare giggling intimacies. Was it good? Was it naughty? Normal? God forbid that I shouldn't be apple-pie normal.

Hey, what am I, chopped liver? Irma demanded.

You've been AWOL, I told her.

Just knocked out and knocking back in sensual paradise. That was an awesome fuck and a mind-blowing, bitchin' orgasm, girlfriend. And you want to worry about it?

He thinks I was assaulted, I told her, and myself. He thinks it's good therapy for me to confront it.

Right. Mr. Self-sacrifice. And you don't consider a killer orgasm good therapy? I give up. I'm going back to my wet dreams.

I was glad she retreated. I wanted these rare moments alone with Ric, when he was blissfully unconscious, as I'd been last night after he'd delved the depths of my psyche and my body.

Some shadow pattern overlaid his bronze, hairless back. Maybe the skylight had built-in miniblinds for sun control.

I put my hand out, palm down, but the shadow didn't show there.

Surprised, I looked down again. The pattern was made of spokes and bars, but too random for blinds. My heart started pounding like werewolves were hot after me as my stunned brain recognized what I had seen. My body wanted to rear away, run, but I didn't dare wake him now.

He stirred under my scrutiny and rolled over on his back.

His change of position allowed me to slide out from under him as slowly and smoothly as I could, and over the back of the sofa to avoid waking him. I didn't even collect my clothes that were strewn on the floor, but crept out into the hall, then paused, leaning against the wall and shutting my eyes.

Apparently secrets, trust and intimacy issues worked both ways. Ric had lulled me into confronting the vague ugliness of my past, but I'd soothed him into revealing an even more obvious proof of his even uglier past. And he was worried that *I'd* been assaulted?

Even shut, my eyes saw the raw grotesque pattern radiating out to cover all of Ric's back to the shoulders and waist and sides. Welts as thick as my forefingers, seeming to tunnel under his skin like invading parasitic giant worms.

Whip welts.

What monster would do this?

Where could I go with my forbidden knowledge? What could I do with it except conceal it? How?

I snuck back into the den to retrieve my clothes, then raced to the master bathroom and dropped my clothes there, turning on the shower. The house's computer system responded to my activity by turning on a morning radio show in the kitchen.

Leaning against the shower's glass blocks, I adjusted the water until it was warm and stepped under it. The hard-rain patter of the massaging showerhead matched the flamenco-beating of my heart. I stood under the head as needles of steaming hot water pummeled the top of my head.

And then my tears came, running in rivulets to mingle with the pouring water, washing down my face and chest and all the way to my toes and down the drain that was swirling away all this noisy, rushing water, including my accompanying sobs.

I'd never been a crier, but now I understood and wished I didn't. This was the one thing he hadn't told me and, therefore, the one thing I didn't dare ask him about now. He'd been so careful, but he'd gotten carried away last night, like I'd been carried away.

No wonder he loved that we had met and connected spoon-style, my back to his front. No wonder he dressed in expensive clothes. I remembered buying a fifties Dior suit at an estate sale once and having it altered by my usual tailor. "It *feels* so good on," I cooed about my find.

She'd nodded and said, "Money buys comfort." As well as love buying comfort.

No wonder I could never put my arms around Ric, comfort him. My full, encompassing embrace would be scouring. Now I had one more thing, one major thing, to conceal from Ric. I wasn't good at that, lying by omission.

Stop bawling, Irma said. *We've never done that, no matter what.*

"We've" never been in love before.

"I'm so screwed," I wailed aloud, in the thunder of the shower.

So is everybody. You just have different ways of doing it. We were always "different."

I'd never talked back aloud to Irma before, fearing that would put me clearly in the delusional category. Now I couldn't stop, hiccoughing through my sobs and the smashing patter of water on tile.

"But it'll be so hard to hide."

Pity is always a tattletale. You can't afford to feel it for a proud man.

"He was only a boy, then—"

My hands made fists. I pounded my palms against the wet tiles until they burned.

I hated feeling helpless again, unable to protect where I was protected. Yet I dared not wallow in my discovery here and now, in Ric's refuge of soft clothes, gently falling fountains and metallic, chuckling chimes. All soothing, all comfort he could put on, like me.

I brushed the heels of my hands over my cheeks, washing away saltwater and chlorinated city water.

"You're up already," Ric called through the aural storm of shower water and chirpy morning radio music.

Did he sound a trifle wary? I must pull myself together and fix that. I must fix a lot more than I realized.

"I woke up when it was still dark and listened to the house play, um, 'Raindrops Keep Falling on My Head'. Dumb song. Man, that is some sensitive sound system. I'll be out in a couple minutes."

"Fine, I'm dressed already. You can wear this for now."

I glimpsed the black satin robe being tossed to a bench outside the shower.

Shit.

I COULDN'T BEAR donning his robe and finally ventured out fully dressed. My "motorcycle mama" leathers seemed pretty silly by daylight in a kitchen. Ric handed me a mug full of coffee and caramel-flavored cream.

"Sit down like you're planning to stay a while," he urged. "We have lots to discuss."

Did we ever—and nothing that was relevant to what I'd just learned. I wanted to lie on the floor, kick my hands and feet and scream. Instead, I took the mug, sat at the breakfast bar, took a long sip and a deep breath, and said, "What's next?"

Orphan's motto.

Ric took another of the stools. "Don't worry, *chica*. I know you didn't mean to do a sleepover, but the pooch is fine on his own and Hector won't kick you out for crossing Nightwine cottage lines for immoral purposes."

I produced a smile on cue. "I've got actual paying customers for the backstory on the young-old vampire in the Sunset Park burial site, so I'll follow upon that. What about the zombies in the mountains?"

Ric made a face over his steaming cup of tricked up java. He was back in the pale smooth suit and the tie, the silky, stylish stuff that was his trademark. The daily disguise.

"I've already been up there, hunting, and I'm going again later, after some appointments. I can't find them, which is worrisome. I expected them to scatter, though. Unchained zombies are like migrating Monarch butterflies. They mill around, heading for Mexico on their own hither and yon schedule."

"Can't you just let them go there?"

"To get nabbed and 'napped by secret Immortality Mob 'agents' at the border? I wouldn't let that happen to Haskell's crabs."

"But what will you do with them? They're raised now."

"I know." Ric sighed and rubbed the back of his neck. "And I don't know."

I shuddered at the simple gesture.

"But they're my responsibility. I can't just leave them there while Cicereau calls in a wagon train of construction machines and combs the mountains until he mows them all down into reburied shards of flesh and bone."

"You've seen the heavy equipment moving in?" I guessed.

Ric nodded. "Those earthmovers drive slower than a funeral cortege."

"Most of those guys Cicereau's werewolves ran down and killed were crooks, weren't they?"

"Some were unlucky gamblers who welched on bets. Some were probably just schmucks who got caught in the mob crossfire by mistake. I can't let any of them be used and abused further, by anyone."

That Ric. He was one sexy saint. I almost lost it again, but sipped scalding coffee while I corralled my emotions.

He tapped his buffed fingernails on the granite countertop. Even his hands were cared for, smooth, sexy.

"Okay," I said carefully, smiling even more carefully.

"Why so shy this morning? Was it what I said, or did, last night?"

He'd sensed my mood, of course. Lying had never been my long suit.

"No, *amor mio*." I put my hand over his. "Nothing you did. Ever."

I wished to hell that I could say that about me.

Chapter Eighteen

Seeing the Enchanted Cottage again when I drove home that morning reminded me of the scarred film couple who had fallen in love under the place's spell in the film named for it.

Scars were just that: evidence of past pain. They had no power to hurt again, unless we let them. Although it pained me that Ric had been brutalized as a child and still felt enough shame to hide the traces, he was healthy, well-adjusted, successful and more concerned about my past traumas than his own.

I wondered if we could really root out the truth about my phobias if we went back to Kansas. There was a lot more truth to root out here first.

Now I settled into every-day tasks. Quicksilver greeted me at the door with fevered licks at my face.

"Yes, a walk. A run, rather. Just let me change."

I freshened his water and food bowls and ran upstairs to change into terrycloth shorts and jogging top. I knew I'd need another shower when we came back and grabbed a protein bar on our way out the door.

Sunset Park's red-dirt paths attracted joggers because of the trees. The ducks were quacking around the lake, the sun was still bearable and I felt almost as strong and sleek as Quicksilver. Even Kon Tiki, my name for the lone, Easter Island stone head on the little artificial lake's sad excuse for an island, seemed to wink at me as we raced past.

Once back at the cottage, I resolved to stop dwelling on personal discoveries for a while and concentrate on what I didn't know, and needed to, here in post-

Millennium Revelation Las Vegas, where so little was what it seemed.

I felt a rising dissatisfaction with my opposite number, Lilith. Glimpsing her a couple days ago in my mirror, pert and sassy, had sharpened my fears that she was indeed dead. If so, my quest to find her, my main reason for being here in Las Vegas, was pointless.

Was my theory that I only glimpsed the dead in mirrors right?

Achilles was still a no-show there, but he was just a dog. He meant much more that that to me, of course, but maybe in the world of immortals dead dogs are only glimpsed crossing the Rainbow Bridge to disappear thereafter into a vague hereafter.

I was having trouble with the Vague Hereafter and maybe I should start dealing with it right here and now.

I showered and changed into jeans and T-shirt for the day and then went into the hall.

The mirror was tall and narrow with an elaborately carved wooden frame.

This narrow hallway kept the light to a minimum. Shadow was the mirror's natural environment.

I traced the carvings with my hands, realizing close up that it was a frame of demonic and gargoyle faces, some human, some beastly, some horned and barbed. It seemed the glaring eyes and open maws I traced yearned to trap my fingertips in their shallow three-dimensional surface of carved and polished wood.

I was glad I hadn't fetched a flashlight. Light would only emphasize the shadow creatures I sensed framing the mirror.

The mirror itself was cool and glassy. My fingertips skated over its even surface, finding only their own reflection. I did rather fear finding the Wicked Queen in it. After all, I was a latter-day Snow White, pale of skin, dark of hair.

I laid my cheek against it and saw a shadowed swath of nose and chin. Mine.

And my reflection was oddly immediate. I pulled away and flared my fingertips on the surface again, making pale spider legs. Yes, this mirror used front-surface glass too, which would be very odd for a literal fairy tale artifact.

Madrigal was right. Reflections without the sixteenth-inch of intervention of glass necessary with most mirrors felt different. For me, a silver medium, the effect joined reality with something usually unseen but deeply real.

"Lilith," I called softly. "Are you still there? I'm coming through."

I heard an echoing giggle. But that could have been vagrant pixies watching me from the mirror-frame shadows. Pixies had a rep as secretive, malicious little beings. The equivalent of magical dust mites, they were present everywhere, sucking up the detritus of our unknowing human lives.

Or did Lilith stand just out of sight and giggle at my struggles to find her? What was "just out of sight" in a mirror?

I pushed my face and body close to the blue-tinged glass. Blue like a pale topaz. I thought of Ric and made love to the mirror, opened myself to it, something I couldn't have done, or imagined doing before. I was not group home Delilah or Kansas Delilah any more. I felt more deeply, wished harder, needed more, wanted more.

I wanted inside this mirror.

So did my silver familiar. It stirred around my wrist, its usual sleeping location, and split into five cold, flowing beads as liquid as mercury. In an instant, my thumb and four fingers were ringed in silver at every joint.

I could feel my heart beating frantically as I pressed my icy, be-ringed right hand hard against unforgiving glass. My breath seemed to fog the surface with frost white. Snow-white . . .

Oh, my God, did Snow himself have some key meaning for me, my life? Why hadn't I linked the nickname's significance to me and my fairy tale coloring before—?

The mirror's surface was milking over, growing opaque. Nothing was clear as I forced myself—my body, mind, spirit, will—into nothing.

For an instant I was sheathed in ice, in cold so stunning it froze my blood, thought, senses. And then . . . I was in a dark hall again, only it stretched as far as the frozen eye could see.

I shook myself free of the closed coldness of fear, remembered the warmth of openness, of trust, or maybe faith. I literally shook myself. And felt my mortal form reassemble, take shape and heart.

I'd been there. Now I was Here. Just what I wanted.

I walked forward, into the long dark.

NOT A WIZARD or a psychic or a magician, I soon realized this world inside the mirror would show me what it wanted to, when it wanted to.

I moved on, feeling my arms, my thighs moving as if I was strolling in Sunset Park.

I was solid, I was mortal.

That might be a big disadvantage here, because I was also unarmed except for my uncontrollable silver familiar.

Whoosh!

Young Miss Cicereau swept into place straight ahead, right where I was walking. Into my path. I glimpsed a shadow of the Easter Island head on the island in Sunset Park. It had witnessed Rick and me finding her body there. . . .

Here she was a tender 1940s teenager in a velvet and taffeta blue gown.

"You look so familiar now," she said, surprised. Apparently she had forgotten our earlier linkage in the mirror. Was time all helter skelter in Mirrorland? I couldn't assume it mirrored my world in any way. "You look like my daddy's girlfriend, Vida."

Her casual reference shocked me speechless.

Vida!

I didn't want to be compared to the woman Howard Hughes had made into a vampire so she could turn him in turn. Double bastard! She'd been Cicereau's mistress thirty-some years before becoming Hughes's hot ticket to immortality.

While I mused on sexual and spiritual betrayals, the girl was drifting away from me into Mirrorland's vague shadows.

"Wait! I'm not Vida."

She paused. "Of course not. I know that. You seem so nice. Not from here. Las Vegas, that is. No one from here is very nice."

"It's a gambling capital built on sin, crime and sex."

"Yeah, sure. Does my dress look all right?" She turned, as if I were a mirror she consulted.

"Lovely. I'd adore having it myself."

Absolute truth. Until now, I'd never thought of my freaky mirror as a vintage shopping mall.

"Daddy complains it's too 'old' for me." She sighed. "They are awfully puzzling and, gosh, scary, aren't they?"

"Men?" I ventured.

"Parents. My father is so antique."

Little did she know. She was seventeen going on eighty.

"What about your . . . boyfriend?" Lover, I figured, was not a word virginal 1940s girls tossed around like toast. Or dice.

"Krzysztof? He's so dreamy."

Bingo! She gave me the first name. Just that simple. Ask the dead girlfriend straight out. Row, row, row your boat, life is but a dream. "Christophe." Very suspicious name.

I took a deep breath. Interrogating a corpse can be tricky.

"Where did you meet Christophe?"

"Oh, in the casino. Where else would I meet anyone? Daddy doesn't allow me anywhere dangerous. He keeps me inside his own little kingdom."

"What does he look like?"

"Daddy?"

"No. Your boyfriend."

"Golly, a real dreamboat! Tall, chiseled features—"

So far, so bad, so Snow.

"—blond hair, wind-gilded skin, perfect manners."

Nope. Just the usual bronze god still desired today.

"He's European?" I guessed.

"*Umhmm*. Polish. A prince. But he's traveling incognito. No one must know."

And they hadn't known. No one had a prayer of knowing for almost seventy years. A corpse buried in Sunset Park was gone for good . . . unless a man who can dowse for the dead came along ready to impress a woman, who didn't know she was a silver medium, with a dowsing demonstration . . . and bingo. The dead rise. And identify themselves at long last.

"That locket," I said. "It's so sweet. Something valuable Christophe gave you?"

She lifted it away from her breastbone to examine it fondly. "Only sterling silver, but it had been his mother's. She told him the right kind of silver was more valuable than gold."

I lifted my open palm and she crossed it with a warm silver heart that seemed to throb and burn against my skin. Something pure enough, perhaps, and strong enough to make memories as well as memorabilia.

I saw ghostly portraits in the empty double-heart-shaped interior. One was of a woman in a 1500s headpiece. His mother. The other was of young man with short hair, a blond mustache and goatee, wearing a single, small hoop earring. He could pass as a rock star or actor today, but in the 1940s he would have looked like an Errol Flynn swashbuckler wannabe. No wonder Cicereau's daughter had lost her girlish heart.

The name *Krzysztof* was engraved on one side, and *Sophie* on the other.

Aha! An eastern European spelling, not French. Still, vampires must have cousins somewhere.

Both mother and son had been vampires, I realized, as I watched the engraved heart-shaped trinket weep a discreet drop of blood, perhaps an illusion performed only for my eyes.

Two women had treasured the locket, Krzysztof's mother for centuries and Cicereau's daughter for only days or weeks, perhaps, as they had in their separate generations treasured the same young man. I closed the locket and gave it back to the girl.

Cicereau's daughter had faced a pre-ordained fate.

As for Lilith . . . .

"Did you give him a token with your name on it?" I asked.

I needed to think of her as more than "Cicereau's daughter," his mere possession.

My question startled her. She froze like a woodland fawn.

"There was no time. There is never time enough. You'll learn that too."

The young woman hid the locket in her tight fingers and turned away, vanished.

I turned to retrace my steps in the void. Walking out of the mirror meant walking into a shiny black curtain. I was back in the hallway, cold and shivering, dizzy, unable to focus. The more time I did in Mirrorland, the more my body paid.

I was sad to leave my first mirror friend with no more intimate a name than my soubriquet from the old song, "Jeanie with the light brown hair."

Still, I had what I needed most, the bone boy's name. Krzysztof. Now I only needed to find out who he'd been and for how long.

Chapter Nineteen

NOW THAT I had two dead chicks and a guy to investigate, I was alternating between my paying and personal case loads.

With a big fat new clue in my quiver, it was time to concentrate on the Sunset Park case. Bad timing, though. My usual three days of menstrual agony hit me hard, as if the mirror was punishing me for teasing a secret out of it.

I wasn't about to run with Quicksilver in the park, but I'd always worked through menstrual cramps with a stiff upper lip, so late that afternoon I donned my pseudo-cop clothes and duty belt. Quick and I shared a roast beef sandwich snack in the kitchen before going out to get Dolly on the road.

I was going trolling in blond disguise again, this time on the Las Vegas Strip opposite the glittering sprawl of the Gehenna hotel and casino.

I needed updated info and insight on the werewolf owner, Cesar Cicereau, and wanted more specifics on magic, mirrors and me. Before I'd escaped Cicereau's pack of hit-werewolves at Starlight Lodge and before *mi amor*, Ric, had obliterated a bunch of them with his silver-bullet-spitting Uzi, Cesar had hoped to mount my head and hide on his hunting lodge walls. Was I still a wanted woman? I should be able to find out from an inside man. Madrigal, the indentured magician I'd been forced to work with briefly, who had first abetted my Adventures in Mirrorland, might just be him.

After valet-parking Dolly at the hotel-casino opposite, the towering Babel, and hiking to the Strip, I paused to admire the Gehenna's façade, an angular forest of glittering verdigris and copper glass towers. Only someone who knew the owner for a werewolf would realize the colors suggested a forest at sunset, both the tranquility of nature and the hot blaze of blood at the end of the hunt.

Since a couple of Cicereau's goons had abducted me from Sunset Park to first bring me here and I'd escaped the hotel through the vast bowels of its service systems, I wasn't sure where to enter.

Quicksilver growled softly beside me, recognizing our former prison.

"You can't go inside," I told him. "You were with me on my previous visit and the boss man's men would recognize you."

His wolfish ears perked and angled at my every word. Almost-humanly expressive pale blue eyes seemed to pick up my meaning instantly and reject it. He whined his frustration, but when I said, "Stay," he sat on the hot sidewalk.

I hated to disappoint Quicksilver. He'd saved my life more than once. And I'd saved him from Haskell's bullets. We were partners.

So I told him to nap under a high-riding pickup truck and waited until he drag-tailed to the spot and circled to lie down. I also adjusted my street-cop utility belt sagging with various nasty tools of the trade.

With my black leather pants and motorcycle boots, a short-sleeved black shirt, and kiddie souvenir gold "shield," I looked enough like one of the city's numerous security personnel to pass for a hotel security guard. The outfit was hot for Vegas, but you can't have naked cops, and I wasn't about to don the seriously non-serious khaki shorts real Vegas cops wore. I needed all the gravitas I could muster.

I fluffed my chin-length platinum wig and adjusted my aviator-style sunglasses, then joined the tourists taking the escalator up to the bridge over the Strip.

Las Vegas heat in early summer can singe your eyelashes off, but it's dry heat and you don't have to worry about anyone seeing you sweat. The black leather belt was old enough to squeak in the dry air, announcing my presence with a nice air of gunslinger.

By the time I pulled open the huge copper door handle of the Gehenna, I was still dry. I plunged into the hotel's dark, icy interior, leaving my sunglasses on and waiting for my eyes to adjust to the extremes in light.

I hadn't bothered to wear my gray contact lenses today, not expecting to deal with anybody who'd recognize my natural baby blues.

At least, I hoped I wouldn't have to.

A major problem was weaving my way through the mammoth hotel's public areas to the theater, far at the rear, and its even more distant backstage area. The casino area was right off the main lobby. Once I worked my way through the crowds there, the chime of slot machines masked the jingle-jingle-jingle of the belt's attached handcuffs.

These cuffs were the real deal, not another handy-dandy manifestation of the form the silver familiar had taken in the Sinkhole. I'd stopped and bought a pair at a sex toy shop on the way to the Gehenna. Hey, this is Vegas! There are way more of those than cop shops. I'd also picked up a couple of canisters of pepper spray at a sporting goods store.

Checking above for surveillance cameras, I noticed automated birds twittering away in the canopy of stained glass leaves above the gaming tables. Clever. The small barn owls with the 360-degree swiveling heads must be mechanical cameras. Their unblinking yellow-glass stares were capturing the images of every passing person.

It was hard not to bump into tourists who stopped unexpectedly to coo about the "cute" animated birds in the faux foliage. Right, cute. Those eye-in-the-sky birds had probably X-rayed their clothes down to the skivvies and recorded their credit card and driver's license numbers and their retinas.

The weight of my police duty belt and its array of defensive weapons had taught me the law enforcement swagger. That walk kept the tourists respectfully out of my path and the real security guards subtly nodding to me as I moved deeper into the behemoth of a building.

Illuminated signs guided me through a couple blocks of casino. Near an arcade of pricey shops, the theater entrance beckoned with a marquee framed in the usual round light bulbs. The house would be "dark" yet, until the 7:00 and 10:00 P.M. shows. I pushed through the blank door.

"Hey," said a voice behind me. "It's closed."

I turned to face a security guard dressed like a Robin Hood merry man.

"I know. I'm on an errand for the boss. He left his Blackberry here."

The guard was a young guy, jumpy. Not good. So I blathered on.

"I'm just saving Sansouci the bother, but if you want to bother him to check, it's okay by me." I hit the word "bother" twice, ominously.

"Ah . . . no. That's fine. We don't need to bother Mr. Sansouci. You go get it."

"Thanks, bro." I waved him toodleloo and ducked into the absolute dark inside, grinning. As I'd guessed, the staff knew Sansouci was no one to trifle with. Not that I hadn't tried, the last time I was here, with middling success.

Now, the magician Madrigal I could handle, if I could only find the guy.

I walked down a raked aisle between rows of seats, finally doffing the sunglasses and letting my eyes acclimate until they could focus on the "ghost light" to the left of the stage far below. It's an old theater tradition to leave one light on so anyone coming in doesn't trip over all the technical equipment in the wings.

Given that Madrigal was something of a real magician, I didn't trust that one small burning bulb a bit.

The stage seemed deserted, but I walked slowly up the access stairs at the side of the house. Madrigal had an exclusive contract with the Gehenna, perhaps for eternity. None but he used this stage, none but he set it up.

Out of the corner of my eye I saw the ghost light soften, then flare. At the same instant, a gossamer steel net fell over my shoulders. Before I could pull any weapons from my hip-slung belt, I was jerked off my feet, swinging upside down and being drawn up into the high flies above like a wriggling fish on a line.

I kicked hard to grab the super-strong filament and twist semi-upright before all my belt trinkets fell to the floor and my wig hairpins pulled out.

Meanwhile, I felt a narrow ribbon of cold metal climb my torso under my clothes. It emerged out my short sleeve, twining my arm down to the wrist. *Presto-change-o!* I had a charm-bracelet chain dangling the cutest miniature wire cutter you ever saw. A Break-in Barbie accessory. There should be such a doll!

Pulling the implement into my hand, I began snipping links of the net that was forming around me. The fibers—stringy, gelatinous, yet strong—snapped. More formed to replace the broken lines as soon as I severed them.

My so-called wondrous opposable thumb was aching from my desperate, machine-gun fast motions. I knew I was up against Mother Nature. Well, a perversion of Mother Nature. Madrigal wouldn't hurt me, much less kill me, but I knew nothing of the sort about his fanatically attached pair of magician's assistants, Sylphia and Phasia.

A doll-small, gorgeously girly face penetrated the broken links to rub cheeks with mine. Her iridescent skin was colder than the side of an ice bucket.

"We don't want you back," she whispered, her voice like wind, or rushing water, or the pass of a dagger near your neck.

"I'm not back," I said. "Just visiting."

Phasia's supple serpent muscles tightened around me inside the entrapping mesh her spider-sister Sylphia had woven around me. Phasia was the serpent-sister of the two.

By now I was hiked so high above the dark stage floor below that snipping net fibers would be suicidal.

"Phasia!" My cry came out a whisper. The serpent-familiar was tightening her coils on my chest and lungs and heart.

I could feel the wire cutters lengthening and growing like a sterling silver vine toward Phasia's iridescent-scaled neck . . .

"Let her go," a voice thundered from below, its deep tolling power vibrating through all of us, felt by all three.

I was released so quickly that my lungs burned from a massive inhalation. I plummeted down fifty feet to the black floor below and the figure of a man making a small vertical island on it.

I wanted to shut my eyes, but resisted, seeing that it was a race to the finish. The lengthening silver rope tied around my wrist flung upward to loop around a pipe high above and shortened fast to stop my fall . . . just as my body landed, cradled in the muscular arms of the man bracing his legs below.

The metal rope released above and fell coiling into a delicate chain around my neck.

Madrigal lowered me to the floor, still glaring up into the darkened flies.

"Behave yourselves, spawn of Darkness. Dead humans on our doorstep will inconvenience Cicereau."

He eyed my blond wig and black leather, then let my boots touch the floor.

"You're trespassing," he said. "You have no business here. Leave and count yourself lucky."

"But I do."

Perhaps my voice sounded familiar. He paused in turning away.

"I *do* have business here," I explained.

Madrigal turned back to me. He was built and dressed more like a World Wrestling Federation champion than a magician. The Gehenna Hotel billboards advertising the magic act depicted him as a strongman and the homicidal assistants twin Tinker Bells.

Competition-level muscles made his tawny skin look sculpted in age-darkened bronze. His thick dreadlocks gleamed like beaten metal. Magicians came in three major stereotypes. The long-haired lean and elderly Gandalf type with flowing gown and beard was one. The short and muscular athlete type like escapologist Harry Houdini was another. The modern model was lean, limber, and dressed to kill, either in formal tails or spandex Las Vegas glitz. Madrigal was in a class all by himself with his unique shtick: power lifter with demonically delicate assistants.

While I reacquainted myself with his hunky persona, he stared at me, clearly annoyed. Any visiting female threatened his spooky and possessive familiars; I wasn't doing as I was told and leaving.

"I need to know more about your front-surface mirror," I said.

And then he got it. A fingertip flipped my blond wig off-center.

"Delilah? You were lucky to get out of here the last time. Cicereau is so angry that he's destroyed all surviving film of your image, despite its commercial value, even on security tapes. He calls you 'Lodge-leveler'. He lost twenty-three prime werewolf soldiers at Starlight Lodge last full moon night."

"My image would be worth a pile if he claimed I was Maggie."

"He knows that and no longer cares. Attempting to coerce you into becoming the world's first Maggie in live performance has cost him more than you would have earned him. He's extended my contract fifty years, without any increase in pay."

"I'm sorry, Madrigal!" And I was. "It wasn't my idea to get tangled up in your act or with your assistants."

He sighed and massaged his trunk-thick neck. "How can I get you out of here fast, so neither you nor I suffer further?"

"Tell me about your mirror magic. You know I have some link with the looking glass world beyond. I manifested it here for the first time. I need to know why and how."

"Why should I tell you anything?"

"Why are you so hostile?"

"Why are you playing ignorant? You know far more than I about mirror magic. You were able to abduct the mirror image you left behind here by using remote viewing after you left. Even I can do no such thing."

"I don't know how I did it, Madrigal. I didn't do . . . anything. I felt desperate to leave no part of myself, of my soul, here for Cesar Cicereau to exploit on his theater stage."

"And so to save some infinitesimal part of yourself from nightly nude exposure on a stage, I and my assistants are indentured for another fifty years."

"I didn't know taking . . . it . . . away would cost you anything. How? No one knew about it but you and I."

"Even after the lodge slaughter, Cicereau would have gloated if I'd had some remnant, some illusion of 'Maggie', to add to the act."

"Hector Nightwine would have stopped it anyway. Legally, the image and the nickname are his."

"Possessing that tame remnant would have placated Cicereau even if he couldn't use it on stage."

"How?"

Madrigal looked uneasy.

"How?"

"For his private . . . use."

"You bastard!"

I stepped out of his reach and flicked my wrist with anger. The silver rope still attached to it snaked around his neck four times, tight.

"You're trying to make me feel guilty for taking back a stolen sliver of myself you were willing to pimp out to Cicereau. I suppose you already do that with Sylphia and Phasia."

The living metal rope tightened.

"No." Madrigal stood very still, all his mighty muscles clenched.

My attack was bluff. I knew his possessive familiars would soon swoop to his rescue.

"They'd kill him," Madrigal said, "and he knows that. Only I can control them. Besides, they are too petite and childlike for him. He likes statuesque women."

Statuesque. I'd never been called that before. Another ego boost. Still, I was a piker in the statuesque department compared to Vida, the dramatic brunet in the 1940s photo I found of Cicereau and friends, including Sansouci and Cicereau's soon-to-be slain daughter.

I relaxed my tense muscles and particularly my right wrist. The rope slid away from Madrigal, twining my right arm up to the biceps and adding a striking snake's head to both ends. It was at rest, but not disarmed.

I was amazed and a bit repulsed by how fast it responded now to my muscle tension and thoughts. It was becoming an unconscious part of me, like a devoted pet.

Madrigal looked pretty amazed too. He eyed it with loathing and wariness.

"All right," he said. "You've convinced me that we've sinned against each other equally." He shook his braided mane with some self-disgust. "These are dark times in a dark place. Come with me. I'll show you everything I know about mirror magic."

Chapter Twenty

THE EBONY BEADS terminating Madrigal's braids clicked like Quicksilver nails as he led me backstage.

Madrigal's mirror was tall enough to put on a closet door to examine your best duds in. Standing before it, I found it tall enough to show even him from foot to topmost dreadlock.

I looked like a character from a space comic: blond, blatantly armed and busty.

I didn't need to use my new intimidating persona anymore. Madrigal was resigned to taking me on as a temporary apprentice just to get me out of the Gehenna . . . and his dreadlocks and his dainty familiars' lethal webs and toils.

"Front-surface glass is a relatively unknown but ordinary product," he said, tenting his big strong fingers against the mirror to make a spider image and giving me the full scientific spiel.

"It's made by vacuum-depositing a highly reflective aluminum coating onto the front of the glass. You get only a single, perfectly clear refection. With ordinary mirrors, you get a faint refection from the front surface, plus a strong reflection—filtered through glass—from the silvered backing. And your fingers couldn't *touch* their reflection—there would be the thickness of glass in between. The multiple reflections of ordinary mirror glass blur the image compared to the brilliant clarity of the front-surface variety."

"Why do you use it onstage then? I'd think a magician would want to blur perfection."

"Cameras and camcorders nowadays have awesome magnification and quality. I can't even afford a thirty-second of an inch of difference in manipulating certain illusions."

"But you're a real magician."

"Yes and no." He nodded up to the flies, where his agile familiars hung waiting in the dark. "They're the magical creatures. I was just an offbeat magician with a little act in a traveling carnival. I found them feral in the California redwood forest. I took them for wild children. I didn't know them then for the Dread Queen's subjects."

"You mentioned her before when you first explained who . . . or what Sylphia and Phasia are. Who is she?"

"Maybe the mundane world knew her as Shakespeare's Titania, maybe as Queen Mab. I figure her as a Mother Nature goddess, benign at times, destructive at other times. I believe she rules all the fairy spawn that have shown their faces since the Millennium Revelation: pixies, nixies and the like. I've never seen her, mind you, perhaps that's why I'm standing here now. Her wrath will move mountains, I hear, and I inadvertently kidnapped two of her creatures. They've possessed me. Together, we've created an 'act' that will save our lives. Even the Dread Queen will not enter the hellish head hotel of the werewolf mob. Werewolves prey on the small fey folk, you see."

"Cicereau's werewolves? I thought they were after human game."

He shrugged. "True, but fey queens aren't always in touch with the modern world. She's a suspicious creature, from what I hear. Arbitrary."

"Like the Red Queen in *Alice in Wonderland*?"

"Yes, prone to offing heads, whether they be floral or human."

"That's why you stay here."

"I'm caught between two equally unpleasant forces. But my association with Sylphia and Phasia has lengthened my life. I can wait."

"Then what you do with the mirrors is merely magician's tricks?"

"I myself mostly, yes. Real magic is too unreliable for a nightly act. Sylphia and Phasia can play between here and there with mirrors."

"And my 'tricks'?"

"Were quite astounding. Sylphia and Phasia have never transported themselves through the mirror beyond the immediate area, just to the flies and the stage. It's handy for my act. Where you went, I'm not sure, but you left no shell of yourself near the stage area until I worked with you. And Delilah, Cicereau didn't know how right he was. You and I could have invented superb illusions, but we'd probably have been sent to Starlight Lodge to be eaten before that."

Madrigal was watching me carefully, but I didn't react. He didn't need to know I'd used his offstage mirror to slip into Cicereau's private office and snoop.

"Why can they and I move through mirrors?"

"I don't know. They're sisters, of course, but yours was a solo act."

Or was it? Was I accessing Lilith in the mirror? Did she sometimes assume my exact form by mimicking my dress? Was my mirror simulacrum only a shadow form or Lilith in bondage to my actions? Did we just miss meeting in that timeless, spaceless plane?

I pushed my hand at the slightly aqua surface, so like a pale natural blue topaz. My fingers melted into tepid air and stirred the mirror surface into ripples, as if it was water.

Madrigal's hand struck snake-fast for the surface and tapped on ungiving glass.

"For you it melts, for me it freezes over like ice." He frowned, then took my wrist in his hand and guided it to the mirror, through the mirror.

This time the mirror was an opaque pool of mercury, shimmering but solid, reflecting a distorted version of our hands, his totally solid and mine half-submerged.

"The mirror bends to your touch, not mine, although I can use your limbs like a puppet master to penetrate it. I must try this with Sylphia and Phasia. It would make a spectacular illusion."

"It's not an illusion, that's the problem!"

"Your problem, not mine." He smiled grimly. "You'll just have to do as Cicereau's humble house magician does: experiment with your equipment to find intriguing new uses and effects for it."

"Aren't you afraid of losing Phasia and Sylphia in the mirror world if you send them in too far or for too long?"

"You I wanted to lose," he said, smiling. "Them, not. Without them Cicereau would axe my act, and perhaps me. He was furious to lose 'Maggie' in her docile remnant form."

"He saw her? Me?"

"Yes, in the mirror. But don't worry. He thought my magic produced her image. When you jerked her out, however you did that, I had to confess to him that my 'spell' had weakened. Cicereau doesn't tolerate weakness in any living thing around him."

"So you got in dutch with the boss over me and my shadow. Sorry."

"Cicereau runs hot and cold. He was a lot angrier about your physical form escaping from Starlight Lodge. How'd you manage that?"

"No smoke and mirrors, just running and dodging and a little help from my friends."

"One of them that big lupine hound?"

"Actually not. Quicksilver was safe at home that night, like a good dog." Not quite true. He'd been out on errands of his own. But he wasn't talking and I wasn't asking.

I returned to the central question.

"What am I to think about my new gifts for manipulating mirror? The only thing I did with mirrors in Kansas was put on TV makeup goop in them."

"So much came out after the Millennium Revelation. My girls"—he nodded up to the flies where they kept invisible watch—"your gifts. Don't let anyone fool you, Delilah. Magical talent, paranormal gifts are like DNA characteristics. The pattern for them lies hidden somewhere in the physical body. Magic, which so often depends on natural things for its spells and enchantments—"

"Eye of newt?"

"That's from a play. Made up. It's more useful to think of magic as herbs with their many healthful effects and uses and to consider science as the drugs and medicines that are synthesized from the raw material of nature."

"You're saying science and magic have things in common?"

"Of course. That's what makes a big corporation like the Industrial Special Effects and Magic Show so profitable. Take the governmental experiments in such a woo-woo effort as remote viewing. That's been going on for decades."

"You mean people seeing things happening from a long distance away, via their minds? That's never been proven possible."

"You do remote viewing, from what you tell me, in your funhouse mirror at home. Perhaps the Millennium Revelation brought out a lot of dormant gifts in the humans, as well as legions of unhumans.

"What is mirror walking, Delilah, except remote viewing in 3-D?"

Chapter Twenty-one

MIRROR WALKING.

Was that the name for what I did? I mulled Madrigal's words and ideas after I left him and the theater area.

Maybe what I'd told Captain Malloy wasn't bullshit. I *was* a predator. I'd come stalking three men in the past twenty-four hours: Snow, Madrigal and now perhaps the most dangerous of all.

Meanwhile, mirror walking was of no use. I could only walk around the immense exterior of the Gehenna hotel and casino as day turned to night, hoping to catch sight of my next prey leaving. The constant movement helped me forget my killer cramps, and I looked like Security making rounds.

Quicksilver was with me, but on "shadow" alert. That meant he remained invisible until needed. He was such a brilliant dog. I only told him "shadow," once, and he had my back with nobody the wiser.

So I could pretend to be a tough mean street-walking investigator and know I had an awesome ace in the hole. In fact, Quicksilver was so discreet even I forgot about his presence at times.

Finally, I spotted a black-clad man leaving the massive hotel's back service area. It was after ten P.M. but I thought I recognized the man's not-quite-muscle-bound movements, as graceful as a Grizelle's in white tiger form.

He was big and tough, but had a brain. And, more important, I thought, a sense of humor. And he was definitely heterosexual. My newly awakened senses told me that. My newly awakened senses also told me he had recognized my newly awakened senses.

True, he had seen me escorted off the Gehenna premises to become dog meat or werewolf meat, if there was a difference, but I'd sensed a tad of regret. In this town even tads of regrets are hard to come by.

I was willing to bet that an urban werewolf's daily sex lust was stronger than the monthly, moon-driven killing lust. One must live to kill another day. I had no idea where he'd go, but was prepared to dive into the Sinkhole's migrating underbelly again, if necessary. Instead, he led me to a private club off the Strip.

The windowless entrance was disturbingly unlabeled. I could be entering a sex or a fight club. The clientele could be gay or straight or blended. Human or unhuman. Or blended.

Hey, these motorcycle boots were made for riding, so they're going to walk wherever they want to. Attitude is all. I'd learned that in the group homes.

After taking off my fake badge (but leaving on my police belt, around here it would probably just be taken as fetish fashion), I approached the blank door and kicked it a few times, then stood to the side.

It opened, a long black gun barrel sticking out.

"You going to use that thing or just think about it?" I asked in a husky tone.

A man's head came peering around the door's edge.

I pushed the door with all my weight and caught gun-barrel and gunman's neck in the crack and pressed for dear life. Mine.

"I'm here to see a man about some business," I said. "You think I might do that?"

Sputtering curses, he eyed my motorcycle boots and tight leather pants through the crack, then my mirror-shaded eyes and angel-white hair. I'd learned from the Snow mystique.

"Ah, yeah. Our clients like your breed of cat."

Hmm. Would that be biker chic, tough chick, or ambiguous human/unhuman stock? Guess I'd have an opportunity to find out inside. I showed the doorman a lot of teeth—either a smile or a feral grin, you choose—and eased in when he opened the door.

Inside was totally smoky. It smelled like a pot factory cheek-by-jowl with a cigar bar. Very guy. I sighed internally to see some eyes that shone green, gold and silver in the half-light. Lots of unhumans here. Lots of bad boys. Where was my particular bad boy?

I started swaggering around the room, hunting. I felt so undercover. It would have been fun if it hadn't been so dangerous. Finally, in one of several booths along the perimeter, I spotted my prey. He was sitting alone nursing . . . an Albino Vampire.

My eyes opened wide behind the mirror shades. I'd invented that drink at Snow's Inferno Bar. Why was the muscle for a rival hotel-casino owner downing such a girly cocktail in this haven of testosterone?

I approached as quietly as I could.

"Sit down," Sansouci said, not looking my way. "Order you one?"

When I said nothing, he hefted the white cocktail in its martini glass and added. "I figured this would tell you where I was sitting. The drink is getting legendary at your hangout, the Inferno Bar. Order one. The cretins here will stop thinking I've lost my edge and realize I was just using it to troll for a hot babe."

Damn! He'd caught me tailing him, and worse, guessed who I was, wig and all. I sat.

"How did you spot me?"

"I didn't."

Before I could follow up on that mystifying comment, a barmaid in a black leather frilled apron and cap appeared. "Um, sir or whatever?"

"Scotch. Straight up," I said for simplicity's sake.

She wriggled away, exposing a short bustle of white eyelet.

"Amusing," he said, eyeing my outfit. "Your boyfriend know you're out on your own?"

"Boyfriend?"

Sansouci put his fingers to his temples, as if massaging a headache. "Don't be cute. You're too clued in for that after the showdown last full moon at the Starlight Lodge. You should know the cast and dénouement of every bad scene in Vegas goes out on the CinSim telegraph. So what's your deal here? I'm listening."

"You're not going to call out the canines?"

"Lupines. No."

"Why not? You let me be taken off to Starlight Lodge to be eaten."

There was a pause. "That's not the way I'd like to see you eaten."

"So. You're a sexist pig among wolves." As a career woman, I always deflected sexy talk on the job. Although there didn't seem to be much point any more.

"I like you, Delilah. I like your looks and your style. You don't want to hear it, one of us can leave."

"'Like'. You allowed to do that a lot working for Cicereau?"

"You think?"

"No. Listen, you know I'm taken. I might like you, though, under other circumstances."

He smiled around the edge of the Albino Vampire. "That not lying stuff is a weakness. You're not above seducing me a little to your side."

"Not now. But that's all show and no go."

"I know." The waitress dropped the scotch in front of me. Sansouci gave her a twenty-dollar bill, told her to keep the change, and switched our drinks. "I have a weakness for 'show'. What do you want?"

"I need to know about Cicereau's history."

"Why?"

"A dead girl."

He went quiet. "You're just a girl yourself, you know."

His voice was morose. So maybe he was physically thirty-five, a decade older than I. Plus a few more decades supernatural time. Just how long were werewolves living now, as opposed to then?

I bit my lip. I was such a faker.

"But with guts," he added.

This time *I* went quiet.

"You really want to dig up all that old stuff?" he prodded.

"No. But I have to."

"Why?"

"She's asking me to."

He reared away from me, his head against the high booth backboard. "Who?"

"That's one thing I need from you. Her name. I call her 'Jeanie'."

"Like in a lamp?"

I shook my head. "Like in the old song about the girl with light brown hair."

"Yours isn't light," he said, leaning forward, speaking fast and low, "but black as night. If you were a werewolf, you'd be almost impossible to see on a midnight run."

"If I were a werewolf I would have changed with all the mobsters at Starlight Lodge last full moon. You'd make a handsome werewolf, though." I nodded at his own black hair stroked by dramatic strands of silver.

His smile had an odd edge. "Thanks. So you've imagined me in lupine form."

"Why didn't I see you when I was running for my life from the pack?"

"Cicereau doesn't reward his lieutenants that way, only the soldiers."

"Was killing his daughter and her lover back in the forties a job for the lieutenants? For you?"

He took a long swallow of his drink before answering. "She was sleeping with the wrong supernatural."

"A killing offense?"

"Not . . . usually. Maybe just marking, or maiming if Cicereau was in a bad mood."

My questions were making Sansouci uneasy. He twisted on his bench seat.

"Her lover was vampire." I made it a statement.

His fingers turned the low thick glass in front of him around and around. "Yes."

"Why were they killed with two different weapons and buried together?"

Sansouci licked his lips. His big knuckles tightened enough to shatter the glass. I was glad he wasn't in werewolf form.

"This is why Cicereau is beside himself about them being unearthed. He's furious you escaped the hunt and that his crew was shredded by zombies. He figures you had something to do with that, but he doesn't know you were involved with revealing the bodies too. There could be an all-unhuman pow-wow called about this."

"Sorry to get all the supers in a snit. Finding the dead couple was an accident."

But I wasn't so sure now. Ric had been dowsing in Sunset Park for reasons more serious than entertaining kids and hick girls from Kansas. He was a consultant expert in finding the dead. Who had he been working for when we found those buried bodies? The police? Or someone way less official? I couldn't let Sansouci see my doubts.

"I know the female victim was Cicereau's daughter. All I'm asking for right now is her first name."

"Why do you want to know?"

"I don't want to know. I have to."

"Why? Cicereau already hankers for your head for escaping his trap. Why keep maddening the beast?"

"I'm the one who found them, rotted to only bones. It was like unearthing Romeo and Juliet. I'd never seen anything that awful. I have to put them to proper rest. They have to be reburied by others than their murderers."

"This is a mission?"

I nodded. "I see dead people."

"And Montoya digs them up. Yeah, I know his rep. Cadaver Kid. Oh, beautiful! You and Mr. Mojo Man are about to become prime targets in this town, you know that?"

I nodded and sipped the Albino Vampire. "This is really good, isn't it?"

"Yeah." Sansouci sounded odd. "Really good," he added in a different tone.

"Why do you come to this place, for the Albino Vampires?"

"I figured I had to let you catch me someplace. This is quiet, private and in a bad enough area of town anything could happen to you and no one would much notice."

"So *you* could happen to me?"

"Maybe. It's dangerous for you to be here whether I am or not. What made you think I'd help you? Why me?"

I made a face. "You like me? I like you? You like-a-me and I like-a-you . . . "

I'd gone into that vintage film ditty from a quaint musical called *Meet Me in St. Louis*. I was always living through something once removed. No wonder mirrors were my thing.

"Don't." Sansouci wasn't looking at me, but his voice was strangely thick. "Nothing is ever that simple. Nothing is what it seems. No one is. Not even you, angel-face."

"That expression is so Bogart as Sam Spade."

"The man had integrity."

"I think you do too."

The silence held for a long time.

"You haven't the slightest idea," he said.

"That's why I need you."

He eyed me hard. "Don't sling words like 'need' around like that. They're weapons."

"I didn't mean to . . . hurt you."

"What the fuck makes you think you can?"

"Because . . . I'm instinctively fond of dogs. Because . . . I see something in you, big bad werewolf. Maybe a bit of humanity—"

"Don't." He half rose and glared at me across the booth. "Don't go looking for humanity in Las Vegas after the Millennium Revelation. In me or anyone like me."

"What are you like?"

He sat back down. "You don't even know enough to be dangerous. You *are* danger."

"What are you like?"

His teeth grated the glass edge as he drank again, swallowed, drilled a glance at me. His green eyes glittered like a rain forest after a downpour. He really did look like he'd like to eat me, the hard way. "I'm not werewolf."

So why should realizing that someone is *not* a werewolf scare the shinola out of me?

I kept my fingers casually loose around the foot of my martini glass. I didn't move.

But my mind and heart were racing together. I'd convinced myself that Sansouci favored me over Detective Haskell. I thought it might be because of my girlish ways. But girlish ways hadn't saved Cicereau's daughter. I'd told myself that an unchanged werewolf was domesticated, like Rover. That they were normal except for the three-or-so-day moon madness thing. Not too different from the average woman with PMS.

But Sansouci wasn't a werewolf. I'd never see those strands of silver gleaming on a noble canine brow in the moonlight. Well, at least I wouldn't have to drill him with a silver bullet or Quicksilver wouldn't have to run him down and tear him to pieces to protect me.

"You tell *me* what you are," I said quietly.

"'Humanity'," he quoted me with derision. And a shade of bitterness? "You're looking in all the wrong places for all the wrong things, little girl."

"I have to start somewhere."

"You're not going to stop, are you? You're going to pick away at the immortal wounds in this town until you bring apocalypse down upon yourself . . . and everybody else."

"I just want to put a ghost to rest. It's me she stares at from my hall mirror, so tragically unhappy. She was no more than, what? Seventeen?"

"Loretta."

"What?"

"Her name." Sansouci washed his face with one big hand. I'd never see him with a sharp furry snout and mini-mountain ranges of fangs, with dark curved claws on those big hands. What *would* I see him as? More than this, certainly.

"Loretta," I repeated. "It's pretty," I decided, picturing the blue-gowned girl in my mirror.

"Seventeen." Sansouci answered me like a robot, still distracted about facing what had happened to the boss's daughter.

He was staring into his drink as if it was a magic mirror with Loretta's young face floating in it.

"Loretta was a cute girl," I said softly. Sansouci was in a semi-feral state at the moment. He might snap my neck as easily as look at me. "I suppose she was just the boss's underage daughter to you."

"Not quite." He clipped off the words like spit.

I knew I looked puzzled.

"I was her bodyguard."

"Oh." And then I saw. "For a long time?"

"For a long time, as human reckoning goes. Since she was a young child."

"And then your orders changed overnight?"

"Then everything changed."

"Why?"

"You have your mirror-maiden's first name. You should get out of here before I decide to eat you, Little Red Riding Hood."

"You're not a werewolf and anyway, the moon isn't right."

"Any night is a full moon for my kind." His eyes glittered with anger. "You pretty young things look so sweet, so tender, but you play with the fire of your own body heat without reckoning on pushing everything male over the edge."

"Blame the victim?"

I jumped when his fist pounded the table and grabbed the stem of my Albino Vampire to keep it from tipping over. I was partial to the drink even if it was a rip-off. His heavier glass just washed expensive Scotch over the side.

"'Love' is the poison that killed Loretta Cicereau," Sansouci said. "'Humanity' was never in the game. I don't have any of it anymore."

"You wouldn't be so angry if you didn't."

That huge hand caught me by the back of the neck and dragged me out of my seat and across the table until he could whisper in my ear.

"What am I? I am vampire. I am a daylight vampire. Every day and night is prey time for me." I felt his teeth and then tongue brush my pounding carotid artery. His breath was lukewarm on my face, not hot like a canine's. Like Quicksilver's. What was a vampire doing working for a werewolf mob? He was still spitting words like nails.

"You came to me. You followed me. You put me to the question. How did I know you tailed me? You're menstruating. I can smell your blood. It's like catnip to a tiger. You're so ready for me. I can take you to places darker than the Sinkhole and make you enjoy it."

All right, I was really scared now. Human or unhuman, this was a man who'd been asked to jettison his protective instincts to kill the young girl he'd guarded. That he'd hated doing that was to his credit. That he'd do the same to a girl he admittedly liked was pre-proven.

I faced down his angry stare, though, literally shaking in my boots, but nowhere else, until he broke the impasse by brushing his lips hard against mine, a sharp fang raking my bottom lip. I was shoved back into my seat, tasting my own blood.

At least I was proven right. My pasty-skinned looks attracted vampires. Even the big boys. They wouldn't want to use me up too soon. Waste me outright. I really shouldn't be alone with this guy. As he had tried to tell me.

I wondered how Loretta had felt when her own bodyguard as well as her father turned on her.

"So you killed her," I speculated, not believing I was pushing a super and a murderer to confess. Inquiring reporters need to know the way vamps need to suck O-negative.

"I didn't stop it." He leaned back against the high wood booth. A vampire with a conscience. He'd been waiting decades for someone to confess to and I guess I'd do.

"She knew?" I asked softly.

"She knew." He closed his eyes. "I didn't want to see her that way."

"Dead but not undead?"

The green eyes opened a slit. "Having sex like that."

"You don't seem to have any problem with me and sex."

"I've never been your bodyguard."

"I see. It was a territorial thing. Her father must have felt the same way."

"We knew it was going on. He wanted to send a message to the vampires."

"That's why the chip from the never-built Inferno was thrown in the grave along with the thirty silver dollars—as a symbol of her betrayal of the werewolf clan."

He nodded.

"And the live mutilation of the boy, her rape and shooting?"

Sansouci's lips were full and well-arched, but now they became a stark line before he finally spoke again. "She told you that? Cicereau wanted to send a message to me. The media spins werewolves as the cuddliest of the supers, all that fur, but they can be the most savage. Vampires would never waste bodies and blood that way."

"And what did this brutal message say?"

"There'd been a twenty-year lull in the werewolf-vampire war. Now he was stating things had changed—he'd mercilessly put down any vampire insurrection, starting with me."

"This was decades before the Millennium Revelation," I confirmed.

Sansouci laughed. Not a happy sound. "The Millennium Revelation marks the moment when you humans got the picture. We supernaturals had been out there all along, dismissed as myths in modern times and persecuted as monsters in the Dark Time."

"Why are you telling me this?"

He finished the scotch. I realized I'd at least lived to see a vampire drinking something other than blood. I needed to find out what daylight vampires really were, what drove them, and what limited them. Soon. Maybe Ric would know. Or Snow.

Meanwhile, I sipped my Albino Vampire. It contained all of my mouth-pleasing favorites in liquor form: white chocolate liqueur, vanilla vodka, and a delicious drizzle of yummy raspberry. If this was a "last meal" at least it was a corker of my own invention. And it lulled the constant drill of my cramps. What more could a girl ask for?

"The Albino Vampire is the house drink of the Inferno Hotel," I said suddenly. "What's it doing here?"

"Christophe owns this place. It's called the Dead Zone."

"Then why did you choose it for our chat?"

"It's the only unhuman watering hole the werewolf mob avoids because Christophe owns it."

"And you're a vampire seeking a hideaway, if only for a few hours."

"So much for running you down to eat you."

"No, I doubt vampires are much for chasing their victims. We come to them."

He shrugged as if to say "Well?" Here I was.

"But I didn't know what you really were. So why are you running with the werewolf mob?"

"Wolves were extinct on the British Isles by the end of the seventeenth century, were extinct in Europe by the twentieth century and in France by the 1920s. But here in the U.S. southwest, wolves hadn't quite been hunted to extinction in the 1930s and forties. It suits werewolves to live where there can be confusion between a natural wolf population and their own packs. Think of them as like . . . the Mormons."

"The Mormons!"

"They weren't welcome elsewhere, they were persecuted and driven out, so they migrated to a desert wilderness no one else wanted and built an empire."

"Are wolves polygamous?"

Sansouci laughed again. "No, but they are polyamorous." He'd leaned closer, like a big bad wolf. "Why? You want to try werewolf love? I have connections."

"One human at a time is plenty for me," I said quickly.

He nodded. "Montoya is a useful ally for an amateur like you. For now. For a human, he knows the score."

That prickled. "But not about the werewolf-vampire war."

"No. Because I'm telling *you*."

"Why me?"

"Because you asked. Because you're the only human to ever escape Cicereau's Starlight Lodge run-down, and because I want to see that bastard eat sand." He grinned.

"You're thinking I could be your tool," I told him. "For revenge. If you've worked for Cicereau all these decades, why do you want revenge?"

"The vampire empire, which has deep European roots, and—more importantly for this country—English as well as Eastern European, was ageing. All civilizations rise and fall. We were used to rising again, but the New World was riper for a carnivorous tribe, like the werewolf packs—especially the French ones, who were the most active—than our vampire way of loose associations and, forgive me, lone wolf operations."

"You didn't play well with others, including your own."

"Delilah, you do have a way of nailing the situation."

The waitress was back. Sansouci ordered another round. When she lingered with flirting on her mind—she was wearing a blood-red velvet ribbon around her neck and precipitous cleavage—he swatted her rear bustle and told her to get lost until she had drinks to set down.

We kept silent until she returned with our orders and left again.

"I invented the Albino Vampire, you know," I said.

"No kidding. So you get a cut of your own drink profits?"

"Snow stole it."

"Snow?" The word was sprung like a wolf-trap.

Not everybody used Christophe/Cocaine's nickname, I guessed, but probably everybody knew it.

"We've had words."

Sansouci was quiet, recalculating. "*You*—on nickname terms with Christophe? I don't like it."

"Is he a vampire?"

He shrugged. "I don't know. No one does. He could be. He certainly has made Cicereau nervous."

"You should like that."

"I do." He smiled. "I just don't like you being on cozy terms with him."

"If you consider hatred cozy—"

"Any strong feeling is dangerous in Las Vegas these days. Beware, Delilah."

"He's a thief."

"So is Cicereau."

"And you?" I asked.

"No. I'm not a thief."

"I believe you."

"You shouldn't."

Sansouci lifted my fresh Albino Vampire drink from the table to taste it. "Congratulations on your bartending instincts. A sweet, seductive girly drink, but with unsuspected kick."

"Thank you. Snow added the cherry at the bottom."

Sansouci lifted the glass to eye the cherry bobbing like a succulent blood clot in the crimson tint at the bottom, then me. "He might have a sense of humor too, but I wouldn't bet on the humanity."

"I don't bet on anything."

That seemed to settle things between us. Sansouci returned my Albino Vampire.

I shrugged this time. "About the werewolf-vampire war."

"I'm a hostage in it," he said.

While I sat stunned, he hunkered over his unwatered scotch like a character from Hemingway or maybe even Melville, and gave me the straight story in a long, unwinding riff of smothered fury.

"The sex and gambling trades seemed natural to the new wave of French vampires arriving in the New World in the early twentieth century. Night work, a constant supply of pliable pretty women, profits. So we hit Hollywood. Rudolph Valentino was one of ours. And a whole bunch of accountants. When the rumors of a lousy desert crossroads becoming a mob destination came up, we wanted in. But the werewolves had been there decades before. You've heard of the Native American Ghost Dance?"

I nodded. "We had an Indian population in Kansas. Something like the last stand against the whites. Didn't the Indians believe that the ghosts of their ancestors would join them in a final battle to banish the white man?

Late 1800s. They thought their Great Spirit had given them bulletproof shirts. The Indians lost."

"They lost their shirts," Sansouci corrected me, "magic shirts to repel the white man's bullets. The local Paiutes around Las Vegas here were the tribe that revived the Ghost Dance and that forced all the last stand battles here and elsewhere. The odd thing is that they did have magic shirts."

"They did?"

Sansouci rolled his eyes. "In a way. We vampires had infiltrated them. We could have taken bullets all day. There'd been enough instances for them to believe that. But the werewolves had been playing on the Paiutes' cultural reverence for the natural world. For 'Brother Wolf'."

I winced as I visualized the confrontation between Indian and cavalryman, between vampire and werewolf. The gullible Indians had been massacred. The werewolves had driven off the vampires, able to rend their undead flesh before the blood-sucking fangs could get near enough to drain them. A game of rock, paper, scissors that drew blood.

Sansouci ran his tongue around the rim of his scotch glass, panting as if he'd been there. Perhaps he had.

"We needed a truce," he said. "I suppose the vampires were the losers. We withdrew to distant 'reservations'. The werewolves stayed. But there was an exchange of hostages to ensure peace."

"You and—?"

"I don't know who the werewolf hostage was. I was already assigned to Cicereau."

"You must have been somebody to be valuable enough to be a hostage."

The eyes glittered again, but his tone was bitter. "Have-beens are worthless. I'd had leadership ambitions, being the first daylight vampire with the advantages that meant. I wanted to overtake and boot out the werewolf mob, reestablish vampire supremacy. Instead I've been serving the enemy as a damn go-fer for decades."

"And you don't know who the vampire who died with Loretta Cicereau was, really?"

"Really. It was a huge secret, as was the identity of the werewolf who went over to the vampires. Truthfully, any leaders we had left were pretty lame."

"How did Cicereau take over, not only the vampire presence, but even the werewolves? He doesn't strike me as prime alpha material, like you."

His grin was feral. "Flattery will get you more than you want." He went on. "Cicereau was the land agent in those days, a former voyageur. He excelled at collecting pelts. Now he wanted geld. Gold. Money. The werewolves were happy to trot around on two legs then. And their lives were extending. Word was the dry desert sun and air was prolonging their lives. I doubt that, but something was.

"Day was our enemy. We vampires lived forever, so some of our elders from the old country worked to create a daylight vampire, one resistant to this savage desert sun. I was the first successful result, so I was indentured to Cicereau to secretly scout the wolf pack and its territory and pave the way for a vampire resurrection."

"What is the secret?"

"Some of it was so simple it's not a secret: wearing sunglasses in daylight. Dark glasses weren't in usage until the early nineteenth century and then not common until the twentieth."

Of course I immediately speculated about Snow. "And you're telling me all this because—?"

"Because it's moot. Decades later, when Loretta crossed family lines to mate with a vampire, Cicereau figured out we vamps had only gone underground, not retreated. He demanded the Blood Price for the vampires breaking the bargain.

"Blood Price?"

"The werewolves would kill the errant vampire lover. The vampires would kill his daughter." He sipped his scotch. "But we wouldn't have killed Loretta Cicereau, literally 'wasted' her, or the boy. We would have turned her, increasing our numbers and political clout that way. We can't easily reproduce like werewolves."

"Whoa. I've never heard a whisper of that! Vampires *can* reproduce?"

"In rare circumstances."

"How rare?"

"A human woman with the just-right blood type, and more than that, the right genes."

"How do you find such a rarity?"

"Assuming you want to, endless taste tests, my dear Miss Street."

I wanted to swallow, hard. Is that why his fang had scraped my lip? Gathering a bit of blood type?

He leaned closer, smelling my fear. "Yes, you taste especially sweet, Miss Delilah, like your cocktail. But I'd have to have more to give you a true assessment."

I felt my pulse jump just then, knowing that was the worst way to let a vampire sense me. This sure wasn't some wannabe anchorman bloodsucker. Sansouci was the real deal and he enjoyed seeing my skittish nerves as a sign of his power.

His green eyes snapped with wicked amusement as he leaned back again, watching my chest with two-edged interest as I fought to even out my breathing. "But we don't hunger to reproduce that way. It's time-consuming and awkward and entails sacrifices on the part of both human and vampire. We prefer to choose our recruits full-grown. That's another major difference between vampires and werewolves."

Did that mean that vampires avoided sex? He didn't act like he did.

He went on. "In the Old World model, both breeds agree that humans are prey. That is natural. It's also natural that vampires and werewolves compete over human prey. Vampires like to draw out our feeding, letting our victims linger, savoring the meal, like spiders. Werewolves must gorge on prey over their few feral days of moon-full, killing and devouring like berserkers. If we blend bloodlines, we could have vampires who kill their prey before sufficient blood is drained."

"Can you drain the dead?"

"It's not as physically and psychologically satisfying. And once it stills, blood rapidly loses its flavor and sparkle. As for werewolves, if they were to hoard their kills, they could neglect to finish killing and devouring before they turn human again."

"Messy."

"Messy. It would forever destroy the natural balance of supernatural life and death and stir humans to unite and hunt us all down."

"Poppycock! Talk about a worst-case scenario. You sound like a global warming campaigner or a social scientist. Vampires have bitten werewolves. I know that. I've seen the half-weres here; have even been attacked by them."

"War is one thing. Love is another."

"I didn't know that vampires and werewolves *could* love."

"Anything can love. And anyone can be destroyed by it. Witness your petitioner in the mirror. What can you do for her, except feel pity?"

"You might be surprised." I was getting angry. The supernaturals were as hidebound in this town as the humans. Still, I'd found a fount of knowledge and was determined to drink him dry. Excuse the expression.

He didn't seem surprised that I could see the dead in mirrors. I suppose that was a minor human talent these post-Millennium Revelation days.

"You do have some tricks, for a human," he admitted. "I don't know how you broke into Cicereau's office twice or how you managed to sandbag me once. It won't happen again."

"I know," I answered. "I was just lucky."

"And lucky that Haskell is such a loser that even a crime boss like Cicereau hates his half-were guts."

"Maybe you couldn't help Loretta way back then, but you helped me plenty."

"What did I do?"

"Nothing." I lifted my cocktail glass and waited for him to chime rims, projecting my most appealing girly vibes. "That was a big help."

He nodded and toasted my admission. He could have tipped Cicereau off about my ability to break and enter, but he didn't. That also left him on shaky ground if he wanted to squeal on me to Cicereau now.

"Tell me about being a daylight vampire. Does a guy like you get to rock around the clock? When do you eat, drink?"

"You looking for a dinner date?"

"Maybe."

Sansouci had spilled as many guts as he was going to this session, I figured. I might as well find out how personally dangerous he was.

He leaned back. "You still have a little blood on your lip."

"How careless of me." I pulled out the tiny, mirrored lipstick case that fit so well into one of the police belt's pockets, then dabbed at my lower lip with the tip of my little finger. It burned.

I checked Sansouci. He was sitting back looking stoic, but intent. I imagined he'd looked like this when he had witnessed the "preview" of my enforced Gehenna "act" with Madrigal.

I'd been magically suspended in air, nude, with a huge boa constrictor twining my legs and torso to hide the naughty bits. Madrigal had bent down as if to kiss me and instead extracted a ruby-jeweled apple from my mouth.

Decadent remnants of Eve and Eden and the serpent and apple would certainly appeal more to a long-lived vampire like Sansouci than the werewolf nation.

I opened my tiny Lip Venom bottle, tilted it upside down on my fingertip, and dabbed it over my lower lip, painting on a stinging, sparkly swath of juicy cherry red over my nicked skin.

"Nice," he said. "I can smell the spices from here. They mix well with your blood type and natural female-in-heat scent."

My pulse raced again. The trouble with trying to seduce someone just a little is you can seduce yourself a lot. I'd assumed werewolves and vampires would have extra-sensitive senses of smell. I didn't know it was this keen until he'd told me.

"So how do you get your blood suppers? You're not into butchered animal byproducts—?"

"Shut your mouth! I have a harem." He sounded satisfied and smug, like a man trying to impress a new girl.

Okay. I could feel myself looking shocked. But that didn't ruin the moment. If anything, it got him explaining more.

"A daylight vampire has twenty-four hours to feed. No need to drain any single . . . source . . . to death. Just a shallow bite, a few minutes or hours of slow, sweet sucking and fucking and I'm good to go until the next assignation. No one loses anything but time."

"They must come to you, since you're on call with Cicereau."

"Sure. You want I should pencil you in?"

"I'm not a serial supper."

"For you, I've got time for a six-course meal with a selection of appetizers and desserts."

Girl! Irma was frantic. *You have* got *to let me loose in this town. You don't want to be the six-course buffet, let me at it!*

"Still can't hide the fact that it's a one-way street, Sansouci. They give and you take."

"I give too," he said.

I chose not to examine that claim. "Thanks for explaining a few things." It's always good policy to appreciate a source.

"Thanks for the drink." He snagged my almost full Albino Vampire glass as I rose to leave.

Something . . . my Lip Venom or my blood, had left a crimson swipe on the wide martini-glass rim. I had a feeling that Sansouci was going to be nursing my signature cocktail for quite a while after I left, girly-looking or not.

Oooh! Irma cooed. *Shivers of fear and a strange anticipation.*

I realized then that danger was indeed an aphrodisiac.

Sansouci wasn't a half-vamp, a juvenile delinquent, or a ham actor who'd hit it big and come back as a CinSim. He was the real deal, a Las Vegas 24/7 vampire, hungry for primal things like blood and sex. Including mine.

Irma had a point.

Chapter Twenty-two

B Y THE TIME I left the Dead Zone I was a little zonked. Whether that was on pain, Albino Vampires or the stress of interviewing a vampire with no warning, I didn't know.

I also had a lot of hot new info to process.

Sansouci was a vampire, not a werewolf, and a *hostage* as well?

A hostage free to move about the city.

They'd done something like that in the Middle Ages, when knighthood was in flower and honor was a word that came with a capital *H*. Rulers would guarantee their word and their willingness to compromise by sending their sons to an enemy's court.

That's why Sansouci hadn't run with Cicereau's rabid werewolves to track me down and tear me apart at the Starlight Lodge in the mountains that night.

He couldn't.

I'd like to think he wouldn't, but he was still a supernatural, and they tended to prey on humans. The xenophobic militants who wanted the supers exterminated en masse might be, ah, right about that.

"Sansouci" meant "without care" in French. Insouciant was the English word for it. Happy go lucky. I imagine Cicereau had christened his hostage that in a taunting moment. Sansouci must have had a lot of cares over the decades, especially when his special charge, Cicereau's young daughter, had been marked for death.

I'd have to ask Loretta about that the next time I was able to play Alice in Mirrorland. I was thinking hard about a lot of things. If I could find out the identity of Sansouci's opposite number—the werewolf prince who was sent over to the vampires—I'd know more about the vampire/werewolf war and also satisfy the demands of Howard Hughes, the CinSims, and Snow, get myself out from under having to deal with that mostly unsavory crew, and maybe have some fresh clout as well as dollars to spend in the New Las Vegas.

Self-congratulation is always a dangerous game. For one thing, it lulls your instincts.

I knew that even as the snarling, fanged beasts darted from the shadows and went for my throat.

Shadows. *Shadow.*

"Quicksilver, attack!" I shouted, drawing the two new pepper spray containers from my patrol officer's belt like twin six guns.

The attacking canines were large and hunch-backed, maybe eighty pounds each, with huge boar-like, small-eyed heads armed with carnivore teeth.

They danced in and away, nimble circus dogs, attacking and retreating cannily, their jaws ajar and snapping . . . animated bear traps.

Tall, pointed ears.

All the better to hear your location, my dear.

Broad, fanged snouts came snapping inward again despite the fog of tearing peppers.

All the better to smell your location, my dear.

Long, clawed forelegs scratched gouges in my leather pants.

All the better to claw your legs out from under you, my despised two-foot.

I'd drawn the cop baton and started flailing it.

I batted one creature away, cringing at the crunch of jawbone shattering.

I liked canines. It'd be easier to club werewolves, because I knew from personal experience that the attacking kind were mad, bad people underneath. But this might just be a pack of homeless dogs . . . *ouch!* One had grazed my wrist with a two-inch-long fang.

A leaping gray shadow smashed that critter to the pavement, rolled it over, and disemboweled it with the savage slash of a forepaw.

Maybe Quicksilver was more defense than I could stomach.

When green-black blood leached out of the claw trails, I admitted to myself that some very icky supers were trying to make meatloaf out of me. This was not Lassie and friends.

I had to stop being squeamish fast. The creatures seemed to come springing out of the asphalt at me. Maybe they'd smelled my menstrual blood, as Sansouci had. Ick. That was a lot less interesting. It had grossed me out that Sansouci knew, not even so much from a prey/predator perspective, as from a woman/man one.

But the attacking creatures weren't going to let me wallow in squeamish sexual oddities. They leaped to push me down.

I booted a couple away for Quicksilver to deal with, spun to guard my back and found my silver familiar had climbed the cop club and was now a high-gauge chain lashing left and right like a metal whip.

Canine voices howled louder than frustrated demons as I beat the ugly creatures away. One clawed over the ebbing bodies of its pack to lunge for my throat.

I heard a battle growl too long and deep for even Quicksilver as big human hands seized the beast's neck and nearing fangs from behind, wrenched once, and tore the head half off.

My stomach got queasy again, whether from the cramps, the close call, or the savage attack that saved me, I couldn't tell. I knew I'd just seen an embattled vampire in action, seeking not the blood needed for its own life, but the blood of another's death and destruction for the pure sake of it.

"Back to back," Sansouci ordered.

I was more than happy to turn away from his unrecognizable, fury-snarled face and fangs. So many of the black-backed, sand-colored dogs were launching themselves mindlessly into the air that I didn't have time to process Sansouci's terrifying new visage.

I slashed my chain right and left like a sword. Although it was a limp one, the lethal strangling curl of linked metal jerked three of the beasts off their feet. Quick joined us, dancing around in a circle, lashing out and slashing the fallen milling legs and leaping torsos with his fangs while we attacked heads and backs.

My arms were aching from the recoil of my awkward weapon and my boots were slipping on bloody pools on the pavement.

Then, all at once, the lunging animals were gone.

Even the fallen bodies vanished in a puff of powder.

I was too exhausted to do more than let my silver chain swing to a stop and lean against Sansouci's back, steeling myself to turn around and confront his vampire face.

Quicksilver sniffed in a wide circle around us, whimpering with frustration at his vanished foes. Not even a fallen body to howl over. Were these ghostly shapeshifters? Humans who could assume animal shapes and then shed them?

I pushed away from Sansouci, took a deep breath, and waited for him to face me. Quick came to my side, giving that low gargled growl that meant business.

"They're gone." Sansouci sounded as surprised as I must have looked.

And he looked human again, his face everyday stoic, handsome enough to set Irma's heart a-pitter-patter.

Mine was still doing the tarantella in my chest. "You looked like a vision from a nightmare."

He shrugged his big shoulders modestly—complimented!

"Not your nightmares, Delilah, but I'd bet you have some doozies. We just encountered something new under the Las Vegas sun. Or moon."

He glanced at the sky. The moon had waned to half.

"Then these creatures weren't—"

"Not werewolves. Demon pariah dogs, maybe," he said. "At best."

"And at worst?"

"Some new deadly shapeshifters in town. Stronger than wolves even. I'd guess some freakish hybrid. Jackal or hyena in them, maybe."

"Those are native to these parts?"

"No more than you are."

"And you have no idea who, what or why?"

"I'm not the intrepid investigator. You need me any more?"

I wanted to flash on that last assumption, the implication that I'd needed him at all. "Nope. We're fine without you."

"For now." He bent to take my hand. Quick leaped up, growling. But Sansouci only raised it to the pale moonlight. "One scratched your wrist. Better have that tended by a more-than-mortal doctor. Never know what hidden dangers supernaturals may be harboring. I doubt they disintegrated. They were just called off. For a while."

He bent to kiss the top of my hand. I smelled his breath as his smile seemed to graze my face, my lips. It reeked of white chocolate and raspberry and scotch, not blood. As if none of this furious slaughter had happened.

I turned to regard Quick, who was licking his silver ruff into place and looking super satisfied. When I looked back, Sansouci was gone.

I held up my wrist. The skin was already red and puffy, infected. God knows what venom those bloodthirsty scavengers carried.

Quick's front legs stretched up my body so he could wrap his long, warm tongue around my wrist, as if following Sansouci's directions. Who's the best holistic healer in Las Vegas? Dr. Doggie Howser.

My skin felt a rush of heat, followed by icy cold. My wound had been cauterized, then flash-frozen in an instant, like a CinSim zombie. A subtle green tinge to my vision vanished. I'd taken it for a ring around the moon, not a noxious fog rising from my wound.

"Are you all right?" I asked my wonder dog.

Quicksilver's snout wrinkled with distaste, and then his long pink tongue rolled out for an evening stroll as he grinned.

He was fine. Sansouci was fine.

Too bad I wasn't fine. I was puzzled and worried. And the top of my hand still tingled from a bloodless kiss of Albino Vampire.

Chapter Twenty-three

I DROVE DOLLY home to the Enchanted Cottage, downed a couple of Darvons and gave Quicksilver a midnight bath in the Jacuzzi tub. He loved the jets.

He seemed to take my checking for wounds as an extra thorough petting, grinning and panting and wagging his tail. He was, miracle of miracles, free of fang marks, so I towel-dried him and let him go rinse his mouth of jackal or hyena or whatever hair and blood at the kitchen water bowl.

I cleaned the dog hair out of the drained tub, refilled it, and took a long soak in fresh, steaming hot water, letting my aching belly, back and thighs sink against the pummeling jets. Not my time of the month to play Superhero Street, even if I was used to toughing it out through the paralyzing pain. A career woman didn't want to look wimpy on the job. I particularly didn't dare look wimpy on this job.

While wrinkling in the tub—the silver familiar retreated into a thin metal ribbon holding my hair up out of the water—I thought about Sansouci's startling confession.

Why would he tell me that? He was betraying his boss/master, Cesar Cicereau. Was he planning to break the agreement of sixty-some years ago and desert Cicereau and the Gehenna? Was it part of a vampire comeback? Or was it what he said it was? He thought he could use me to topple the werewolf mob.

I shuddered to consider what he really was: a daylight vampire. Able to withstand sunlight, fuck as well as suck, and do both delicately enough to leave a woman healthy and hearty and ready for the next round.

It was no secret why he enjoyed being so cooperative. I'd finally faced myself in a mirror enough to understand what I hadn't back in Kansas. I was a natural-born Goth girl, with death and resurrection built-into my dramatic black-and-white coloring. Most ordinary girls figure out pretty young what their type of look is, and who their type of guy is. What attracts what. I'd been repulsed by the half-breed, pushy, hungry vamp boys I attracted, but had finally encountered a mature vampire with a smooth barside manner.

I was a slow learner, but I was making giant strides.

Okay. So Sansouci might be attracted to me. That might mean I could use him.

It didn't mean for a moment that he wouldn't try to use me, whether I survived it or not.

SITTING BY MY LAPTOP on the bedroom dressing table—even my increased makeup use was still light enough that I used the surface as a computer desk—I sipped a glass of the Bailey's Irish Cream I'd saved for cramp and cram nights since college and cruised the Web for scavenger dogs.

I came up with jackals and hyenas. Both were native to the African and Indian continents. Jackals were sand-colored, sharp-eared and foxy, smaller than wolves. What had attacked me and Quicksilver were clearly hyenas, which I'd thought as the third-world version of wolves. No such luck.

Hyenas were bigger, stronger and weirder. They had a bear-like look because their rounded ears and small heads seemed out of sync with their thick, solid bodies, and their back legs were shorter than their front ones.

The weird part was that these heavy-set creatures—who could go carnivore or scavenger—were considered to be related to dainty, agile critters like meerkats and mongooses.

In fact, they were such formidable beasts I was awed. Quicksilver and I had beaten them back, even with an assist from Sansouci in full fang, not that I'd gazed long on his handsome face in carnivore mode.

The spotted hyena seemed to be the variety most partial to digesting all my most inedible parts outside the Dead Zone. Although the hyena bite is bone-crushing and bear-trap strong, the beasts' best survival weapon is industrial-strength stomach acid that can turn bone, gristle, tooth, claw and hoof to liquid nutrition.

And then there's that eerie, taunting, ghostly laugh. Some African tribes thought the hyena laughs were calling the name of their next victim.

Oooh. De-lie-lah-ha-ha-ha.

My name lent itself to hyena mockery, but I'd yet to hear the creatures laugh.

I had to wonder why some naturalists consider this gibbering kitchen trash compactor as having intelligence near that of apes, but there was no doubt why the hyena's reproductive system made them the eternal object of fear, superstition and hatred.

I read on with interest, so much so that Irma started reading over my shoulder. Or whatever.

Oh me-oh-my-o. This is better than Animal Planet *porn. Did you see that? Hyena females dominate the smaller males. Wow. Complete control over who, or what, gets the goodies. This is where Women's Lib has gone! And what a physiology. Gross.*

I read on about the female hyena's outsize clitoris, a pseudo-penis that also functions as vagina and birth canal. I wondered about her cramping problems. Could account for being really nasty-tempered.

All modern hyenas live in arid environments like African savannahs and deserts. Check for Las Vegas. Close. Their ability to digest all the hard, horny nasty bits got them associated with gluttony, uncleanliness and cowardice. African witches and sorcerers are thought to fly on them or shift into their forms. And many tribes regarded them as inedible and greedy hermaphrodites.

Ooh, said Irma. *Hyenas couldn't be eaten, so they'd naturally multiply in peace. And people believed in "werehyenas," like we didn't have enough wolves and tigers and bears "wereing" around after the Millennium Revelation?*

Even Ovid, the Roman poet, thought the hyena changed its sex from male to female and back again. No doubt due to that large, multi-useful clitoris.

I sat away from the computer screen, needing to think.

WHY WOULD ANYONE sic supernatural hyenas on a girl and her dog in Las Vegas?

What had I done to rile the mongoose-meerkat mob? Just the idea of these small fur-bearing creatures, born to be stuffed toys, sending hyenas after me made me smile. Yeah, a mongoose could fight and kill a cobra, but it was still just a small furry animal designed to root out poisonous vermin.

Hyenas were big, formidable predators. Guess that was why they'd turned up in Las Vegas: desert environment, big hotel moguls, predatory mob bosses and supernaturals.

So who did this four-footed gang work for? I couldn't see Cesar Cicereau needing a hyena pack to compete with his werewolves. And Snow . . . he'd never underwrite any beast as greedy and clumsy and mismade as a hyena.

I pulled out an older drawn map of Strip attractions. The unending building boom outdated maps faster than shoe styles. Which were the African desert-themed hotels? Problem was, most were history. I discovered a Web site about Vegas hotel implosions adorned by fireworks, with photos and videos, just another form of larger-than-life entertainment.

The aging desert-themed hotel-casinos had been key targets of destruction. Was that an accident, or someone's master plan?

The Dunes had been the first to go, in 1993, making way for the Bellagio. The Sands had fallen in 1996 for the

Venetian. The Aladdin had gone bankrupt in the eighties and risen from the ashes of a 1998 implosion with a whole new Arabian theme, opening in August of 2000, just before the Millennium Revelation.

The terrorist attack of September 2001 had made Arabian themes unmarketable and the hotel had morphed into Planet Hollywood by 2007.

In 2001, the venerable Desert Inn took a dynamite dive to become mogul Steve Wynn's namesake high-roller palace, the Wynn.

I moved on to other sites. In 1993, twenty years ago, one last oasis of desert mythology went up at the south end of Strip. My fingertip pinned the shape of a pyramid to the tabletop. The Luxor had been the first Egyptian-themed hotel in Las Vegas, and Egypt was in North Africa.

Luxor was the modern name for ancient Thebes. Vegas bigwigs back then had liked the implication of "luxe" in the word. The Luxor's pyramid shape boasted a light beaming from the peak that was visible in outer space. It once had an inside waterway with "Cleopatra's barges" giving tourists a lift.

That idea had been lifted from the first boutique Vegas hotel, the Crystal Phoenix, which had pioneered the idea of a "Love Moat" back in the day. Now the Venetian had its gondola canals, the Inferno its "river" to gambling "Hell" and the massive new Karnak, built a year ago in 2012, had its own "Nile."

And an eighteen-foot-high statue of a hyena-headed gambling god in the main casino. I suppose for the Egyptians, Lady Luck had two faces and possibly two genders.

I remembered the demon parking valet at the Inferno who'd noticed Dolly when he parked her. He'd worn the beaded collar, linen kilt and jackal-head mask of a Karnak employee.

Maybe I had an "in."

BY THE TIME I'd finished researching on the Web, it was
4:00 A.M. After another hot Jacuzzi soak for my cramps,
I doped myself up on more Darvon and curled up with
two old-fashioned rubber hot water bottles in soft fleece
coverings I'd found in the bed.

I'd spent ages on my feet on hard surfaces yesterday
and felt just like a beat cop: I ached from the soles of my
feet, up my legs all the way to my waist. Girls just want to
have fun, as Cyndi Lauper sang.

This wasn't the kitchen witch's territory, so I didn't
know who or what my bed warmer was, but my cold feet
and cramped tummy appreciated the thought and I slept
like a lamb, Quicksilver on the area rug by the bed, until
mid-afternoon.

Holy hyenas! I needed to burn rubber, and not the ones
filled with cold water in my bed. Ric had left a message
on my cell phone, but I'd call him later, when I had
something to tell him.

"This is a solo outing," I told Quick after I threw on
some casual clothes and got myself down to the kitchen,
where a fresh hot bag of McDonald's awaited me. The
kitchen witch was an extremely practical supernatural,
and always knew when I needed a fast hand in the food
department.

He growled, so I threw him some of my precious limp
French fries.

"Really, Quick. My aching, crampy back needs a
break from that heavy fake cop gear I'd need to wear so
you could get into the hotel-casinos with me as a K-9 dog.
Next time, buddy."

Those heavenly blue eyes watched me with eerie
understanding, even about the cramps part. Meanwhile,
that big maw snapped up every fry I tossed its way.

Within an hour, I breezed Dolly past the Inferno hotel
again, pausing at the entrance until my guy in Egyptian
drag came back from hot-rodding other cars into parking

slots. If parking valets aren't going to abuse your ride by gunning them into the garage at warp speed, they're going to fall in love forever. He immediately spotted me, or, rather, Dolly.

It was a relief to not be the center of male attention for a change.

"That's my ideal prom girl. Those are fins to kill for," he said, admiring Dolly's sleek black flanks.

"Sorry. I'm just pausing. I'm not parking her here."

"Let me just run her through and out again. I promise I won't make her squeal. Too loud."

"I'd need to know some things first."

"Yeah?"

"Like why you wear your Karnak outfit parking for the Inferno."

"The big boss don't mind," the demon said with a shrug that dislodged some large orange scales from his bare upper arms, "and my Inferno uniform hasn't arrived yet. I don't think the big boss likes the Karnak much and is glad I was hired away."

"You mean Christophe?"

"I don't know who. I only heard that the big boss liked my outfit and since I paid a fortune for it myself— the Karnak is cheap for such a big joint—why not wear it here? I mean, almost everyone is eligible for going to Hell, right? Even ancient Egyptians."

"When exactly did the Karnak open?"

"Jeez, lady, I don't know. I was only summoned a few lost souls ago. Fairly recently. It's run by a foreign outfit. Vegas moguls are building all over Asia now, so Vegas is getting new blood too. I like working for the Inferno a lot better."

I cocked an eyebrow. "Why?"

He grinned, showing gray-green pointed teeth. "A better class of vintage car comes through?"

"Okay, you can take her for one run through the parking garage, but no racing!" I slid out of the driver's seat.

"Sure, sure," he said insincerely, hopping into Dolly's bench seat—yuck, what a color clash: orange scaly skin against fire-engine red leather!—and screeched away into the garage's dark maw, a dragon's head designed as a mini gate of Hell.

"Do you need some assistance?" a deep, icy voice inquired behind me.

I turned to see Grizelle, Snow's security chief, in human form. She was a towering black woman whose skin bore the tabby pattern of a house cat. Not a tattoo, natural. She wore four-inch Manolo Blahnik spikes. I liked her better naked in a fur coat, in plush black-and-white tiger stripes with six-inch claws.

"No, thanks," I told her. "I'm just passing through. The parking valet should return with my ride any minute."

Grizelle folded arms clad in emerald green silk to match her eyes and glowered. Apparently people weren't supposed to loiter in the driveway, and I suppose my jeans, sleeveless gauze top, sneakers, and glittery tourist fanny pack weren't up to the Inferno's dress code. Fanny packs were pathetic, but they left my hands free and held what I needed. Plus, it was great camouflage. Usually I dressed a lot more formally when I visited, but then I was seeing Snow, not parking attendants. I'd always found as a reporter that it was wise to dress to the druthers of whomever you were interviewing.

So I didn't bother chatting up Grizelle.

"I'd be happy to answer any questions you might have," she prodded.

"No, you'd be happy to *know* any questions I might have," I told her.

"The boss puts up with a lot from you. I won't," she warned me.

"You don't think I don't put up with a lot in turn?" I lifted my wrist to display the silver familiar, now changed into an Egyptian dancing girl's slave bracelet with rings on every finger and chains linking them to the broad sterling cuff. "It's kinda clumsy to shift Dolly with all this hardware hanging off my right hand."

"I don't know anything about that," she said. "Only that you shouldn't be interrogating the help."

"Hey, we were just talking cool cars. Don't you have a hobby?"

"I do, but you wouldn't want to know what it is." Her dazzling bleached smile featured pointed teeth.

A squeal of brakes hailed Dolly's return.

"Smooth as a Black Russian," the demon valet announced, hopping out. "Ask for Hermie at the Karnak. Tell him Manny sent you."

Grizelle still stood guard, frowning, as I slipped behind Dolly's huge steering wheel, shifted into drive with a clatter worthy of old St. Nick, and accelerated our way into Strip traffic.

Ten minutes later Dolly and I idled in the shadow of the Karnak's looming black marble façade, a thick stone forest of soaring massively broad pillars looking too crowded to allow anything but an anorexic between them. The overall effect was to dwarf and awe puny humanity.

I'd quickly checked out the real Karnak on the Web. It was the world's largest temple complex. Las Vegas's usual overblown theme architects had done such good job of capturing the reality that one could hardly take in the actual shape of the building from this close. I glimpsed a monumental gateway bracketed by two tapering towers and flagpoles topped with crimson banners. Of course, in Vegas they always went for the gold: blinding, sun-shot gold glinted from the pillars' capitals and the tops of two glassy black obelisks on either side of the entrance. The effect was massive, imperial, and cold, despite the blistering afternoon heat.

Meanwhile, I needed a parking valet-cum-guide.

"Hermie?" I asked the row of kilt-clad demons, all wearing instant tanner so their scales were a matching shoe-polish brown, giving them the look of upright alligator boots. No wonder Manny hadn't fit in. He liked to flaunt his colors.

A parking valet wearing a headdress with fetchingly spiral Hathor horns leaped forward. Hathor was a female cow goddess, so wearing her headdress could be considered cross-dressing for a male. I wondered if demons could be gay, not that it would bother me. I held up a fifty-dollar bill. "Manny said you'd treat my car right. Why don't we breeze into the garage and discuss it?"

"Scoot over, miss, and we're gone."

I did, watching his clawed fingernails—enameled purple and chartreuse—curl around the wheel. I was sure pimping out poor Dolly today. I owed her a high-speed desert drive this afternoon to air out her vents and upholstery.

"Thanks, Hermie," I said in the dark, deserted spot he'd parked Dolly. "I just wanted to get the lay of the land inside from someone who knew."

"Hermesaphritus," he corrected me.

"And 'Manny'?"

"Manniphilpestiles."

Humph. Where is Rumplestiltskin when you need him? Irma grumbled.

I'd turned on my cell phone voice recorder to get these guys' full formal names. I'd heard demons were proper name nuts, wouldn't answer to anything else, and had no idea if I might need one of these scaly little rascals again someday soon.

"Delphine Delgado," I told him, keeping my own name secret. "I'm new in town and I need to know a bit about the Karnak. When it was built, why this particular décor."

"You a cop or something?"

"Heavens no, Mr. Hermesaphritus. I'm a scout for *Women's Werewear Daily*. Animal-headed supermodels are the rage in all the hip rag mags nowadays. We might shoot a big fashion spread here."

"Don't we have a PR person who could tell you all that?"

"Of course, and I'll check in there soon, but first, I need the inside dope. I want to know all the fascinating nooks and crannies that only the staff sees, places that would make absolutely fab fashion-shoot backgrounds."

Hermie was looking dubious, even downright scared. Scared demons get big purple goose bumps and it is not a pretty sight on all those scales, even if they are tanned a toasty brown. Obviously, very low-level demons staffed the Karnak service areas.

Hermie confirmed that by reeling off a list of visitor no-nos. "You stay in the designated public areas. You don't wander. The security guards here would just as soon bite your head off as look at you if you're caught somewhere you shouldn't be."

I had a feeling he was speaking literally. Okay, I'd been warned. Quicksilver was not with me. I was on my own. I'd just have to do my darnedest to keep my head while trying to nose out why yet another big Vegas hotel was setting the hounds on me.

I left Dolly in the dark, with Manny spit-polishing her steering wheel with demon-knows-what, and walked back to the entry area for a date with an ancient empire.

Chapter Twenty-four

THE ENTRYWAY consisted of a double row of massive black pillars that squeezed out all the Las Vegas sunlight and made you feel your way inward. You felt like an archeologist exploring a lost temple in the noonday sun that drove Englishmen and dogs mad. Vegas could vie with Egypt for that.

As I moved between the close-set columns, my hands started out dancing off the hot stone, and then jerking away from the flash-frozen inner row of pillars that had turned icy cold from the interior air-conditioning.

I never encountered an actual set of doors, but soon stepped into a vast echoing chamber too wide and high to be called a mere lobby. It was more a gigantic reception hall, anchored at the far end by a thirty-foot high statue of Anubis, the jackal headed god of the dead. Nope, my attacking canines had not been jackals, which had a leaner and less hungry look.

Egyptian figures painted on tomb and temple walls were usually pretty lean and mean and lithe. Their art style of showing bodies facing front and heads in profile made shoulders wide and hips slim, a posture savvy female fashion models adopt today.

The towering statue portrayed Anubis striding forward, a broad-shouldered, slim-hipped hunk of black stone surmounted by a sharp-eared and sharp-muzzled canine head wearing a golden headdress. He carried a gold staff, wore a golden kilt, and matching, uh, accessories and had pointed ears the Big Bad Wolf would envy.

Given the importance of burial rituals to the Egyptians, I shouldn't have been surprised that the Karnak was a massive tomb of a place. Tourists scurried like ants from the gilded reception desk through various painted and hieroglyph-incised interior pillars to the elevators, the Pyramid Tomb Trail, the Sphinx Theater, the Nile Barge Ride, the Valley of the Kings Shopping Mall and the Necropolis Casino.

I edged along the hall's hedging pillars until a steady *ching-bah-ching* of slot machines overpowered the constant echo of shuffling shoes and raised voices. Hermie had told me not to miss the hall leading to an adjacent high-roller high-rise that was off-limits to the public and the regular staff.

It was lined, he said, by mummy cases—supposedly real mummy cases with real mummies inside—and ended at a chariot of solid gold that was rumored to descend and whisk special guests to a secret lower level crammed with authentic tomb treasure.

What intrigued an ex-reporter the most was the off-limits part, not the glitz and the gold. Not so my silver familiar. Just the thought of treasure had the silver slithering restlessly over my skin, gathering and spreading thin to cover my chest with a wide, cold Egyptian collar, front and back. Like me and the CinSymbs, the thing had an uncanny urge to dress for the proper period surroundings.

There were no mirrors in the corridor except the polished black granite behind the parade of mummy cases on either side. No mirrors meant no mirror magic to use for a quick exit, if I had the ability to use it here and now which, after my talk with Madrigal, I thought iffy anyway.

I eyed the giant coffins on either side. These mummy cases were an awesome seven feet high, many gilded and brightly painted with fantastic creatures and mysterious, to me anyway, hieroglyphs.

At the far end, the golden chariot gleamed, a delicate yet useful object attached to a rearing pair of black marble horses. I couldn't see an exit from the charmed circle where down lights from above made the chariot look like it was constructed from liquid fire.

A nasty series of creaks and rustles kicked up behind me, flowing after me in a distant wave. I was getting close to the chariot and didn't want to turn back to look.

And then something stepped out from around the steed statues, backing its confrontational stance with a basso growl and a hideous laugh that echoed into a roar down the corridor and back again. The laugh would have been Boris Karloff-corny in an old horror movie, but here it was utterly spine-chilling.

This was no indignant high roller upset by some nobody approaching his elite retreat. This was one of the beasts that had attacked me outside the Dead Zone. In the glaring light I could study its powerful, hunched shoulders and fang-filled jaws.

Behind me the rustle and creak had escalated to a constant murmur of oncoming motion. I should be panicking at that eerie flood of sound, like an oncoming infestation of locusts, but I'd been studying more than the chariot in the nearing niche where Toothy might soon floss his fangs with my bones. I'd been analyzing the entire vignette.

Toothy lowered his brutish head, reminding me of a mythical hellhound who guards the gates to horror and despair and eternal torment. I started loping, making my strides long, and then even longer.

With that momentum, I vaulted up and over Toothy's gnashing fangs and into the golden chariot. It shivered on its wheels, but I leaped again, touching the front guardrail with one foot, and pounced onto the back of the nearest stone horse. I was content to balance there for a moment, then slide down to cling, arms and legs braced on the broad back, hands wrapped around the gold leather harness.

Meanwhile, the hellish hyena-hound beneath me was hurtling its powerful but awkward body at the smooth stone stomach of my eight-foot-high mount. Only then did I look over my shoulder, and shudder.

All along the corridor I'd passed, every painted coffin lid had swung open. Talk about unhinged! A mummy had stepped out of each to inspect me. They now stood at attention in two lines that narrowed at the other end, like a vee of flying geese, making a return escape impossible.

I was sealed in by a double line of animated mummies, their age-browned cerements coming undone enough to offer a peek-a-boo look at the dry bones and desiccated skin beneath.

It was a stalemate unless the mummies decided to rush me. Their wrappings were old and frail. I could unravel them quite a bit before they could return the favor with my own plump, moist and firmly attached skin, although I didn't fancy the clawlike look of the hands that had escaped their bindings.

I figured Toothy below me was all muscle and no brain and wouldn't find a way up my mountain of marble horseflesh.

So all I needed was for a human high roller to amble along and pick me up as a good luck piece. No one came, and the mummies remained in formation, not attacking but forbidding retreat. And rescue.

This was beginning to feel disturbingly like house arrest. I couldn't go anywhere and they wouldn't. I propped my feet on the other horse's back and waited, feeling the stone warm to my body heat beneath, even under my aching back. What were the odds that I was the only truly living thing in here?

There is a weird Zen-like feeling you can tap into when it's too late to panic and too early to whine. A treed possum must feel like that. We'd all settled into our assigned places. Even the hyena had stopped filing its nails on marble horsehide and sat quietly below, rather like Quicksilver, waiting.

I supposed I'd ultimately fall asleep and fall off in a couple days, but doubted I'd get that relaxed about my situation. I'd tried my cell phone to contact Ric the minute I was ensconced on the horses, but this stone mausoleum was an "out of service area." No surprise there.

I distracted myself from a panic attack by studying the hyena, which was an odd combination of the canine and the feline. The Egyptians worshipped cats, I knew, and probably liked dogs since their jackal-headed god of the dead, Anubis, was canine. It was hands-down the most fascinating ancient empire on earth and the first great civilization to fall in love with life, death and the afterworld, and the trappings of all. The Egyptians devoted great resources to continue their existence just as it had been before death.

Then I recalled Hector Nightwine's amazing statement about the Egyptians, or about zombies, rather. He said the mystery of how the Egyptians built the pyramids was solved not by huge numbers of slaves or stunning engineering, but by zombie labor.

I eyed my tightly-wrapped honor guard. Really, weren't these mummies just zombies by another name? They were both the walking dead, no matter the culture or time that spawned them. Was one of those embalmed forms down the hall that much different from one of Cicereau's desert-dried hit victims from the forties, give or take a few thousand years?

They were all human remnants who, revived and linked by magic, could pull a barge-sized block of stone as well as anyone alive. I doubted the Egyptians used their embalmed and dressed-for-the-afterlife mummies as grunt labor, though. It would be the bodies of slain enemy armies and never embalmed at all. Zombies weren't good for much else than cannon fodder and stoop labor and mindless rampaging, were they?

All those old forties movies, though, featured an embalmed and disappointed-in-love mummy who awakened to find his lost princess mummy-love and avenge himself on those who'd done him wrong millennia before. He hadn't struck me as the smartest roll of gauze in the sarcophagus. Okay, it was linen.

My mummy guard of honor, though, got the bitumen and bandage treatment; they were a step up from mindless stone-pushers, but not by much.

These specimens were the sad-sack sort, the Scarecrow in multiple just waiting for some Dorothy to come along and liberate them. So who turned them off and on, and released the hyenas? I was being allowed to ride bareback on the chariot horses with limbs intact for a reason.

Something made the hyena perk up its ears, stand up, and then back away. I wasn't sure I wanted to see anything that backed off this mad dog a couple of millennia removed.

From around my steeds' noble chests shuffled a nondescript, pale little man in a baggy white suit, perhaps five feet tall. His hair receded as much as his chin, and with his protruding eyes, it all added up to the look of a deadly snake.

The hyena began a low cackling that made the hairs on my neck, head, and not-recently-enough shaved legs stand up. *That'll teach a girl to neglect personal beauty routines,* Irma whispered, just as the snaky little guy spoke.

Why was I not surprised that he used a soft lisp that slithered over the marble walls in a sibilant echo?

"You're trespassing on private hotel areas, miss. You are also mocking and defacing a sacred tomb fixture."

"I'm saving my ankles for leaving as soon as I can," I said, nodded at the cackling hyena.

"Tut," the little man said.

"I'm serious. That thing was ready to chop me off at the kneecaps."

"Tut," he repeated, regarding the spotted hyena. "Stand down."

The creature burst out in eerie, ugly laughter and then stepped back against the wall, on guard with the mummies.

The man regarded me with large, sorrowful eyes drowning in upper and lower bags. His gaze was as intense as Perry Mason's, but chillingly regretful. "I'm afraid I'll have to take you to the reception hall, even though you are not an invited guest."

Now I knew him! The reflected amber glow of the golden chariot had bathed his pale complexion and clothes in its glory. He was a CinSim, but one of such a monochromatic ashen gray that his borrowed 24 karat tan had made him look warm-complexioned and human. My vintage fan mania makes me nothing but a quick study when it comes to CinSims.

"Mr. Ugarte, I presume," I said, naming his character from the film, *Casablanca,* in which he'd worn the same white, sweat-stained tropical suit he wore now. I didn't forget that Peter Lorre's other iconic film role—another Bogart classic—had been as the greedy thief, Joel Cairo, in *The Maltese Falcon*. And that title bird was a black figurine that, despite its fictional sixteenth century origins, looked very much like a depiction of the Egyptian god Horus, the falcon.

Of course Peter Lorre would be here at the Karnak in CinSim form! He was a natural. And he veered from playing truly creepy villains to effete, slimy losers. Luckily, Ugarte had been the latter.

"Let me help you down, miss." He extended a small, soft hand.

I hesitated. The Lorre/Ugarte hand was eons better than a blackened claw, but I was still freaked from taking Dracula's cold, cold hand not long ago.

"I won't bite," he lisped like a back alley seducer.

"No, but Tut will."

"Not now. Come down."

The trouble with wanting to go where you're not supposed to go is not being able to leave when you're found out. I braced my hands on my horse's broad hindquarters and slid down its swelling side to the floor, grabbing onto the real leather harness to ease the impact.

"This chariot is the biggest funerary item I've ever seen, even on PBS."

"You should see the hundred-and-fifty-foot-long funeral barges. The Karnak contains much that is fabulous and rare and beyond price," Ugarte spoke with the limpid lust of a small-time thief, "but most of that is not open to the public."

"I saw a big sign for an artifact exhibition off the, er, lobby."

"That is open to the public at twenty dollars a head"—he surveyed mine as if referring to literally detached heads—"but you will have a private audience. A pity. The management is quite severe with tomb robbers."

"I wasn't going to take anything!"

"Even memories can be stolen, alas."

"I forget a lot. I've already forgotten most of my childhood and school years."

"Is that true?" Those glassy eyes stared at me without blinking. "I'll mention that to the twined godheads, but you are hardly able to swear that your adult experiences are as forgettable as your youthful ones."

"No," I agreed, thinking of all the dangerous, dead—and therefore memorable—individuals and circumstances I'd encountered here in post-Millennium Revelation Las Vegas in just a few weeks. "I can't."

I watched Lorre pull down on one of the horse's reins. A soft whirr of gears had the chariot and its horses sinking like a stage effect—in fact, Las Vegas was full of stage effects that lowered much more extensive scenery to the regions below. I doubted we were headed for a simple backstage area.

I was glad to see Tut's drool-slavered snout snapping fruitlessly above as the animal peered down into the pit our departure created. Lucky I'd left Quicksilver home. He was a mighty dog, but the Karnak hyena was creepily supernatural, and that was even without knowing whether it was a shapeshifter or not.

Lorre stopped to light a torch on the wall with a pack of matches impressed with the name KARNAK in bold type. Matches?

Grab 'em, Irma advised. *Might come in handy in this low-tech dungeon.*

Irma usually didn't come out to advise me unless the situation was erotically dangerous or physically perilous, I'd come to realize. Call her a foul weather friend.

A stroll by torchlight with a Peter Lorre CinSim through the innards of a reconstructed ancient Egyptian temple was definitely not hot, so I slipped a hand into his baggy jacket pocket and snagged the matchbook for a souvenir.

The yellow stone road was a smooth ramp that led upward. The passage was narrow and harrowing to anyone with a smidge of claustrophobia. I'd never had an opportunity to test my score on that, but was beginning to pay attention to my breathing rate.

"You see, miss," Ugarte was droning like a bored tour guide, "this is a true pathway of the dead. No civilization since the Egyptians has quite given the afterlife its due. That is why the modern world is so fascinated by all things Egyptian.

"And now you will see what few humans have, the last and most glorious embodiments of the gods honored in the temple of Karnak."

Chapter Twenty-five

WHEN LORRE/UGARTE stepped through an opening, sweeping the torch aside with a dramatic flare and *whoosh* of its flame, I was stunned by the huge space revealed.

A right royal mess I've gotten myself into, I thought as I was led into the inner sanctum of a royal tomb.

This was no stone burial chamber, richly appointed but relatively small. This was the Mall of America—Cecil B. DeMille and Donald Trump style—redone in Egyptian Baroque.

I gasped to take in the vast glittering, gilded chamber, the rows of animal-headed figures, more than life-sized statues, alabaster urns, inlaid chests—all guarded by coils of gigantic venomous snakes. The lavish low furniture on carved wooden animal hooves and paws poised as if about to come alive and hunt me down. Almost every inch of space on the towering walls was incised with painted figures and colorful hieroglyphs.

A many-stepped dais at the space's far end was surmounted by leopard-upholstered ebony thrones virtually tattooed with solid gold and lapis lazuli inlay. A pair of huge albino cobras occupied the positions of honor, and anyone could guess who they reminded me of, swaying with their hoods flared. White. Deadly. Christophe. Cocaine. Snow.

Vegas verged on being magical at duplicating world landmarks, but mere reproductions of these treasures would be too priceless even for Vegas. A modern billionaire with close to Pharaonic wealth must have either bought or recreated the priceless past. The real thing, though, wouldn't have survived in such glorious and perfect condition, so I was back to Daddy Gargantuabucks. Of course, being escorted into a nameless billionaire's secret treasure vault didn't augur well for making a return trip out.

Whoever was behind the Karnak had heard enough about me to set the court hyenas on me. When that failed, I'd obliged them by coming to this mountain of basalt and, if I didn't devise an escape plan, probably would soon slip into a sarcophagus as an unsuspected tribute to the royal mummy, like a pre-dynastic servant killed to accompany the ruler-god to the afterlife. But why? What had I done to tick off the Karnak mob? I'd surely find out soon enough.

The floor was wall-to-wall Mediterranean-blue tiles, lapis lazuli with gold flecks.

I felt like I was walking on water. I couldn't help but move farther into this incredible vision. I knew I'd never see its like again, if I lived to see anything again.

Oddly, the lavish setting cheered me up. People who needed such pomp needed witnesses . . . impressed, awed, cowering witnesses. Disciples.

I sensed the Ugarte CinSim shuffling silently by my side. Our footsteps were muted by the sound of flute and drum, not an American Revolutionary marching band, but a quintet of musicians against one wall, looking as if they'd just stepped off its painted surface.

Their dress was tomb-painting typical: wigs and diaphanous, pleated linen kilts for the bronze-skinned men; high-waisted, long pleated linen gowns with mere bands covering only the nipples of the breasts for the women.

The music was oddly atonal, both jumbled and flat. I recognized harps decorated with semiprecious stones. There were also lyres, drums, rattles, and tambourines.

I could believe that this was an area reserved for elite guests, and then I reconsidered. This area was not for any hotel guests at all, no matter how many millions they gambled.

This fiercely luxuriant death-themed palace was for unwanted guests, like me.

Still I couldn't keep myself from gaping at the riches beyond belief as I moved forward to the processional music, not fretting about retreating or an escape route. Perhaps the swaying white cobras had mesmerized me.

Maybe I thought such civilized surroundings wouldn't be the scene of bloody murder, mine.

Maybe I figured the CinSim was obviously allowed to come and go.

Maybe I just was going to worry about it after I found out what was going on.

Maybe I would take two Darvon and wake up in the morning in my cozy Enchanted Cottage bedroom.

Wait! Maybe I wasn't worrying because my subconscious had noticed that I was surrounded by burnished reflective surfaces, if not outright mirrors, and that my silver familiar had split and morphed into pair of cobra-shaped twining bracelets on my upper arms.

I'd bet my developing silver medium ways against this flood of high-karat gold any day. I'd come within twenty feet of the thrones and paused when the music silenced. So I stopped.

The cobras slunk over the chair backs to guard an inlaid screen that made a wall behind them. Figures stepped out from each side of the screen, bizarre doubles of the ancient Egyptians painted on the walls.

Their beauty amazed me. Both had the profiles of the famed bust of Nefertiti, the queen as sleek as an Egyptian hound in her proud carriage and long, lyrical neck. Both wore the high and wide, flat-topped headdress her statue did. Both had skins the color of terra cotta and eyes edged in thick sweeps of kohl.

They were startlingly small and delicate, almost fairylike. Neither, minus crown, could be over five feet tall. Elegant, slim, rich miniatures of their civilization's oldest genes boiled down to perfection. As I took them in from headdress to sandaled toe, I confirmed that they were man and woman. And blushed.

Yup. I guess it still shows that I'm from Kansas. Here I am in a monstrous, magnificent necropolis, probably a candidate for embalming myself, and my face feels as hot as a country yokel's at a State Fair hoochie-koochie show.

The man's diaphanous kilt, the linen sides crossing on a curve at the front, still showed his genitals through the double-layer gauze. And the woman . . . well, not only did the central bands that went over her shoulders barely cover her tattooed nipples, but the empire-waist skirt parted at the bottom of her breast bone, breaking totally away to reveal the rest of her nude torso and legs in front.

Both of their pubic areas were shaved and liberally decorated with tattooed hieroglyphs. Similar funky tats appeared elsewhere on their bodies as well.

Hmm, Irma said. *Wouldn't mind having one of these, way more artistic than modern ones.*

I ignored her and turned, shocked, to see how Ugarte was taking all this.

He stood like a bashful penguin behind me, toes out, hands in jacket pockets, head down. Had we some ancient sand beneath our feet, I would have expected him to stub a toe in it.

And he was probably used to this duo!

At least the full frontal view vanished when they took their seats in tandem. They moved in eerie harmony, like paired Dobermans I'd seen, littermates trained together.

Their sandaled feet rested on small stools and their hands on the elaborate chair arms. Their profiles turned to each other in imitation of a tomb wall painting.

"This is the one?" the man asked.

"Yes. Her lion hound is a remarkable warrior. Our hyena-kas were forced to return to their bodies here."

"She could be comely, although she is large and cumbersome."

The woman's delicate features made a moue of distaste. "I prefer the sources we find in the lands of the morning sun, Kephron. They are quite trim and portable."

"And she has disinterred and is seeking to withhold He Who Is Born Again and Dies Again, the dead one we wish to dwell in our house and memory?" he asked.

"She is an asker of questions and that is always annoying, especially now," she answered.

"She is quiet at the moment, Kepherati."

The man turned his face forward to fully inspect me. He was as beautiful as the woman in the same exotic, almost precious way.

Either they were fabulously wealthy delusionists, or I was regarding actual Egyptians who spoke English. Who would the ancient Egyptians' true descendants be? Two thousand years of invasion would dilute any race. The modern-day Copts were Christians who had converted in the early days of the disciples. They claim that when the Arabs invaded Egypt in the seventh century, they kept themselves apart and never intermarried. This could be some sect that revived the ancient ways and resembled their long-ago forebears the way you saw ancient Mayan temple faces on living descendants in Mexico and Central America even today.

Kepherati had turned with him to eye me also. I got a cold chill icy enough to make my vertebrae chatter. Their speaking so freely in front of me implied the assumption of utter power or the assurance that if they didn't like how much I heard, I could be easily offed.

"Those arm cuffs are lovely in design," the woman said. "Give them to me." She stretched out a slender brown arm, tattooed at the wrist and inner elbow. I saw tattoos ringing her neck and had glimpsed designs on her inner thighs and even peeking out from around the backs of her knees.

He was tattooed in all the same places, including the elaborate ones circling his nipples.

As Kepherati lifted her arm a heavy wave of exquisite scent, spicy and musky and sweet, swirled around my face. It was so overpowering I almost raised my forearm in turn, preparing to take off the armlets. Of course I couldn't.

"I can't," I said.

"You can and will do anything we ask," she said in a soft husky voice.

"I cannot. This . . . silver design is as permanently attached to me as your tattoos."

Their profiles consulted each other in silence.

Kephron turned back first. "Skin is removable."

Another icy chill up my spine. "This design is mobile. It moves to avoid its own destruction."

"Ah." Kepherati clapped her tiny hands together. I noticed that her fingertips were stained red, as well as her nails. "Such a clever accessory. I want it more than ever now."

The twin arm cuffs became living serpents and circled down my forearms to fill my palms with thick silver hafts. My fists held a pair of intricately scalloped and edged battle axes. That startled even me, who was used to playing canvas for the silver familiar's shape-shifting ways, but I liked being so seriously armed.

The pair lifted their outer hands.

A wave of shuffling and rattling echoed like thunder and lightning in the massive hall. Behind me, Ugarte swallowed a cocker spaniel whimper of despair.

I watched the walls, as if suddenly papered by a mob, sprout brown and black bodies glittering with metal weapons. The painted figures had come to life, and then some. Perhaps they'd always been three-dimensional figures, only standing so still that I mistook them for bas-relief sculptures.

"Pharaoh's armies will use your decoration's blades for toothpicks," Kephron warned.

The paired battle axes melted onto my hands and again became cuff bracelets. Even my defensive talisman knew when to back down.

"Which pharaoh do you speak of?" I slipped a finger into my jeans pocket to turn on my cell phone voice recorder, thinking I could look up a historical reference to identify these creatures when I got away. If I got away.

"*We* are Pharaoh," they said in unison, their heads tilting together. "Kephron and Kepherati, Lord and Lady of the Two Lands, son and daughter of the God Sethmose and God's Wife Sethset, may they live forever."

And then I got it. The dainty couple before me was not only a product of royal Egyptian breeding, but of inbreeding. I'd heard of dynastic marriages between siblings, between progeny and parents even. As I stood there wondering if the silver familiar was only fastened to me until death did us part, I realized that Keph and Keph were more than siblings, they were twins. And married lovers.

The mind boggled. If I got out of here with my skin and silver familiar intact, I'd be doing a ton of Groggling the Web on ancient Egyptian customs and artifacts ... artifacts like the twin pair of golden sculptures bracketing the incestuous royal couple.

I eased my cell phone from my pocket enough to shoot a few photos, hoping I captured the throne scene. The sculptures were odder than any ancient Egyptian items I'd ever seen. They stood about five feet tall, like the pharaonic pair, and resembled flower pots impaled with a long, leafless stick from which what looked like a headless animal was tied by its tail.

Dead dog dangling. More likely a cat. Here I'd thought the culture revered felines.

But maybe this was an ersatz Egyptian cult. Much more likely. And who was this person of theirs I was trying to disinter? I wasn't trying to disinter anyone. That was Ric's job, Cadaver Kid territory.

I had nothing to do with the disinterment of anything, not even a zombie.

And then I got it. Sunset Park. Ric had joined with me to dowse for water, and he'd unearthed the two dead bodies. One was He Who Is Born Again and Dies Again.

"The dead bone boy," I said aloud. My normal tones seemed almost shouting in that echoing chamber.

Kepherati forgot my bracelets.

"He is not dead, just sleeping," she said.

"He is only bones," I said.

Kephron nodded. "Yes, but we can raise the dead from ancient bones, even if they are no longer in their wrappings."

"But, his bones aren't ancient. He's only been dead six hundred years"

"Yes, Krzysztof is a mere boy compared to us." Kepherati stroked Kephron's smooth brown cheek. "Yet he is a prince, and descended from the founder of a royal line that lasted for almost three centuries. Of course, that is nothing compared to our descent of many millennia. Prince Krzysztof is a mere newcomer, really, but better than modern stock. He is an ideal beginning for our purposes." Kepherati ran her ruddy fingertip over her consort's lips.

"Good," Ugarte hissed in a low whisper. "If they make the beast with two backs their conjoined Eye of Horus will be upon themselves, not me."

I recognized his reference to a sacred protective symbol that was also a hieroglyph of the eye. Some said today's "private eye" expression came from that ancient icon of godly oversight and protection.

I agreed with Ugarte, miserable weasel that he was. This creepy couple needed to get it on with each other and forget about us.

Their profiles were sipping from each other's lips, a passionless yet sick sort of symbiosis. Kepherati turned her face toward me again.

"Why did you disturb the boy's sleep before we had time to reclaim him?"

"I . . . I didn't know you existed, or how important he was. Besides, I thought he was slain for eternity."

"This is a modern age," Kephron lectured me in the same cold tone. "We also have refined our methods of interring and . . . disinterring. Even long-dead bones may rise—in the proper hands."

It was hard to believe the Egyptians were still after zombies, even skeletal zombies.

"Speaking of proper hands," Kephron added, leaning toward me with almost more lust than he'd shown his consort, "I've heard of bodies recently rising to the surface at Caesar Cicereau's Starlight Lodge."

"You're surprised that bodies were buried out there?"

"Nothing surprises us," they replied as one, like twins.

If Lilith was indeed my twin, and I found her, and we showed any tendency to speak in unison, I'd skip out forever and ever, amen.

If she showed any incestuous tendencies, I'd . . . I didn't know what I'd do, besides not doing it.

"How did these bodies rise?" Kepherati inquired rather politely.

Sure, like you'd say, "How'd you do that hairstyle? How do you dial 911?"

I'd tried to dial out on my cell phone again, surreptitiously, and it wasn't cooperating. Of course, if I were a cell phone I wouldn't wake up and work in this temple of blocked signals and dedicated necrophilia.

I answered with a question. "How would I know how these bodies rose?"

"You were there," Kephron said.

"There were others present, Beloved," she reminded her consort. "Cicereau's wild werewolves and dozens of the walking, unembalmed dead they call 'zombies' now."

"Kin," he agreed, "but not the quality we seek." His liquid, black-lined gaze returned to me. "You are correct. You were *not* alone." He eyed his mate again, significantly, as if they had just won the lottery, before he questioned me again.

"And you say you do not know how these zombies rose?

"I was busy trying to stay alive," I answered, trying to be as vague as possible. Who knew what these beings were or wanted?

"An overrated activity when being dead is so much more interesting these days." Kepherati smiled. At least her painted lips lifted slightly at the corners.

I understood I was among an unfashionable minority, totting up in my mind who among my circle I knew for sure was alive: Quicksilver. Ric. Hector Nightwine was iffy, and the CinSims were questionable. Caressa Teagarden was semi-alive. Among my enemies, Cicereau and the werewolves were all too alive. Howard Hughes decidedly was not. Sansouci was lively, but not alive. Snow was an enigma. I didn't know if he was good or evil or just self-serving, much less alive or dead.

"She'd mummify well," Kephron told Kepherati. Their lips met again as they spoke. I almost thought they read each other's lips or breath, if they had any, as much as spoke.

"She would be difficult to reanimate and even more difficult to kill. She has too much of a lust for life," his sister-wife replied. "She would destroy outer and inner wrappings in a silly struggle to remain breathing. She would go to the other side flawed, and thus come back flawed."

Yay for flaws! Irma chirped. *For such old sickos in the mud these two are really borrring! Let's ditch this dive.*

Easy for you to say, I mentally chirped back. But Irma was right. I was seriously disinterested in hearing more about my forthcoming flaws as a mummy.

"There must be a servant of Anubis involved," Kepherati decreed, eyeing me again.

"Is it the dog that runs with her?" They knew about my daily morning runs in Sunset Park with Quicksilver?

"He is not a desert dog," Kephron said, his straight nose barely wrinkling. "He is thick-furred for the northern wastes and large, like her."

I breathed a sigh of relief for Quicksilver. Wolves used to inhabit desert climes but I was glad to hear the Royal Pains disparage his breed. No dog mummification wanted.

"There were wolves at Starlight Lodge," Kephron went on, musing only to his identical twin, like a man addressing himself in a mirror. "Our sybil serpents—" he waved at the hooded cobras swaying like palms behind the royal pair. For a moment I thought he'd said "civil servants." Maybe that's exactly what they were. And vice versa.

"Our royal spies," he went on, "reported that the desert snakes saw wolves. Some were partly disembodied, like our own ka-sendings on four feet. Perhaps *they* raised these briefly dead people."

I nodded along with Kephron. If he considered corpses as old as seventy years "briefly dead," I wouldn't argue. If "ka" meant soul in the Egyptian old order, the hyenas were undead too. Nor did I want Kephron working his way around to Ric's presence and identifying him as the force able to uproot the dead.

I figured the more of these icy-hearted Egyptians who stayed lost and forgotten and dead, the better. Their society was obviously formal to a fault. Even lust was ritualized, obvious from the flaunted but oddly sexless genitalia and tattoos.

I'd known nothing about lust, except being the unwilling object of it, whether blood lust or sex lust, until I met Ric, but I knew it was impulsive, untidy, and best taken with generous dollops of love.

I didn't feel the love here in the heart of the ex-Egyptian empire at the Karnak Hotel and casino. In fact, I really thought I ought to be going.

"Your ka-sendings," I mimicked their expression. "Those were the killer hyenas I ran into outside the Dead Zone club?"

"You did not 'run into' them," Kepherati said coldly. "They ran into you. They were sent for you. We wished to interrogate you in ka form. Had you been compliant then, you wouldn't be here walking and talking as a living person. Your northern warrior-dog and your vampire servant and you yourself damaged the temporary bodies of our ka-spirits."

So they'd wanted me dead, a spirit to drain of information and toss aside. They'd underestimated human will. And I'd like to see Sansouci called a "vampire servant" to his face, but it chilled me that they'd known what he was when I'd just discovered it last night.

Speaking of faces, theirs were still glued to each other. No wonder their eyes seemed a trifle crossed, like those of some Siamese cats. Such soul-searching postures left them deaf and blind to actions on the fringe.

I eyed the many polished surfaces of the great chamber. Mirrors in their day had not been glass, but buffed metal. I wondered if my silver mediumship was supple enough to slip through metal as well as silver-backed mirror.

If it wasn't, I risked smashing my atoms on hard bronze, not soft silver.

But I was alone, with no one else to worry about, besides Irma.

Go for it, chickie-baby. These far-too-friendly he-shes creep me out. They won't even notice we've left the room.

I doubted that, but this was probably the best opportunity to try something.

I checked Peter Lorre as Ugarte. He had tuned out like an abandoned hand puppet and stood inert a few feet away. He had led me here and his usefulness was over.

Mine was too, as far as I was concerned.

I glimpsed my own image, small and wee, in the sun disk headdress between the horns of a magnificent statue of Hathor. The goddess was sometimes portrayed with a cow's head; this headdress wasn't on a bovine head, though, but on the usual attractive head an Egyptian woman.

The statue was maybe eleven feet all, even seated in a throne chair. A Royal Uraeus, the hooded cobra, was centered on her forehead. Her white gown was tight and she wore beaded anklets and armbands. The figure's skin was painted a yellowish hue, her jewelry in red, blue and green with gold accents, but the sun disk was the purest, most polished metal surface in the vast chamber and it wasn't gold, but silver for some reason. Then I got it. No, it wasn't a sun disk, but a *moon* disk. This was a moon goddess.

Madrigal wasn't here to amplify my mirror-walking abilities. I was about to risk a fatal concussion on a weird do-si-do with a quasi-reflective surface. Risk not, reap not.

I sent my mind leaping up into my own pixie-sized reflected image, tensed my muscles and pantomimed the mental leap with fast, fearless action. First up to her cold sculpted lap, feeling oddly like one of those mini-adult doll-size painted Egyptian children.

Then I dove upward to her elaborate headdress, imagining the two-foot diameter moon disc as a cool silver pool I could dive into. I felt a cold crash of cymbals in my brain, a jolt to every bone and muscle in my body.

As I crouched there, chilled and shaking for what seemed a truly split second of time, I saw the tomb painting of the slim Egyptian pair in profile, their shoulders and chests faced out, frozen in some eternal throne room.

I was not timeless. I had a heart and head that needed to start ticking again. I leaped behind and beyond the tray-sized disc on the figure of an ancient goddess. I passed through another split second, utterly blank and black.

Then it was as if I was speed-dating Mirrorland.

I was shot through a tunnel of shadowed time and space, fast-forwarded past all the eerie places I'd had access to, including the Sinkhole or maybe even deep space.

My body emerged in cold water, upright, and my eyes blinked open through a curtain of liquid to see a crowd of squealing tourists backing away from the spray my appearance here caused. They started clapping.

I stood there dripping silvery strings of water in a Karnak fountain that spit golden discs of gambling chips from a small cow's mouth into a huge pool. Apparently I was taken for a performing acrobat. Tourists stood nine-deep around the fountain, still clapping as I waded out of the water, pulling my dripping hair back from my face.

I paused to bow my head and curtsy, then hopped over the shallow rim of the fountain onto dry marble.

"How do they do it?" a she-tourist asked a he-tourist. "They must have a trap door in the statue someplace. Then she tumbles out, pre-sopping, to look like she came from the fountain."

I looked up at the twelve-foot high statue of the goddess Hathor, seeing my dripping reflection in her mirrored moon-disk headdress. My head ached as if it was holding up that huge symbol. Thank you, ma'am.

All I had to do next was slip through the crowds, past the guards and out of the Karnak's dark shadows into the blazing desert daylight of Las Vegas.

I shuddered from the combination of my wet hair and clothes in the meat-locker air-conditioning and a sense of having communicated with too many of the dead way too closely.

Among the weirdly attired bellmen, security guards and roaming performers, one wet woman in tourist duds was eminently overlookable.

I finally burst back out on the Strip, basking in the blare of sunlight and heat.

Hermie was waiting with Dolly, top cranked down. He'd obviously taken several unauthorized joy rides, but he was back here when I needed him.

"Home, James," I said, hopping into the passenger seat.

I'd never let anyone, even Ric, drive Dolly before, but I was still shaking, fuzzy-brained, and seeing double from my mental-physical leap through solid silver. And my menstrual cramps were killing me, although they proved I was still alive and kicking.

"Where is home, doll?" Hermie asked, obviously hoping for a long journey and a huge tip.

I wasn't about to lead anyone from the Karnak to Hector Nightwine's estate and my small piece of home, sweet heaven on it. I puzzled for a moment.

"The Inferno and make it snappy," I said, pulling out some dough to get him back to the Karnak and grinning at the idea of a demon needing cab fare.

Funny thing. After my brief inspection of the Karnak, darned if the damned Inferno didn't feel like home.

Chapter Twenty-six

"**Y**OU WENT to the Karnak? Alone? *Jesus,* Delilah!"
Ric had caught me on the cell phone coming back from the Inferno in Dolly. We'd met on the far fringes of a Sonic Drive-in lot. Now we were leaning against our parked cars and exchanging sour little nothings.

"Why are you getting so bent out of shape? It's a tourist attraction, for God's sake."

"It has an evil reputation."

"Worse than the Inferno?"

"Maybe. People have been disappearing there."

"People?"

"Yeah. Humans like you and me. The Karnak is an even newer player on the scene than the Inferno and nobody knows much about it."

"Nobody until now."

I'd been ready to bubble over about all I'd encountered there when I intercepted Ric, but I was reaching the threshold of my endurance of running around like normal with the constant pain throbbing in my stomach, back, and thighs.

"You scouted the place?" he asked, finally getting curious instead of overprotective.

"The place scouted me. I had an accidental audience with the owners, I think, and they are into attack spirit-hyenas, drawing out precious bodily fluids—a.k.a. embalming—ancient Egyptian sexual perversity, Old World depravity and death and tattooed genitalia."

"You found all this out in how long?"

"Uh." I checked my wristwatch. "Four hours."

"And you couldn't leave me a message before you went because—?"

"I was just Strip-hopping. I didn't expect to find out anything interesting. Once I was inside, the Vegas Strip's famous inhospitality to cell phones kicked in."

"But you did find something and probably it was dangerously interesting and nobody knew where you were."

"*I* did."

"No one who could sound the alarm if you didn't come back. I'm only worried because I care, Del. If you'd had parents, you'd have known about making sure the ones who love you know where you are."

A girl is supposed to go all gooey when she hears those words from male lips. *I love you*. Especially from deeply familiar male lips. Maybe I would have on another day, but today I hurt and just felt antsy, like I did when my dreams pinned me flat on my back and vague bad things happened to me. I felt a panicked need to dodge.

"Does this mean I can't go anywhere without you?"

"This means that you shouldn't go anywhere risky without telling me, or at least leaving me a message so I know where to send the coroner. Grisly Bahr would love to get you naked under his high-intensity lights."

I made a face. "He likes me, but he's not sadistic about it."

"Okay, I'd love to get you naked under his high-intensity lights, but not dead."

Only Ric could make me laugh and blush at the same time.

"See how oversensitive you're being, *chica*? If you worked on my FBI team, I'd ask no less. Okay. You're an independent operative. So don't *ask* me to go somewhere you think warrants investigation, but don't forget to *tell* me where you are."

"The law enforcement version of the armed forces' issue-ducking credo: don't ask, but *do* tell."

"Right." He was laughing now too.

"Please don't rag on me, Ric. I had to leave the Karnak via a very rough exit, and I'm still feeling a little shaky.

Plus, I've got menstrual cramps that could wake the dead."

I'd never confided my female troubles to a male before. Letting him in was my way of making up, and also getting him off my back.

"*Querida.*" He drew me close, fanning his hands on my lower back where it felt like a guillotine blade was pushing in. My equally aching belly was tight against his pelvis. That male metabolism warmth was sandwiching my pain between his hands and torso. His body heat made me feel instantly better and I couldn't muffle a purr of contentment.

"Sorry," he whispered. "You're coming to my place for some sangria and heat and massage. And then you can tell me all about what you found out today." His kiss before he let me loose promised that I wouldn't get to do much talking at all.

But it all sounded wonderful to my worn body and mind.

"I'm in your custody, ex-agent Montoya. P.I. Street reporting in, but I need to do some errands first."

FIRST, WE STOPPED by Hector's estate to check my cottage and see how Quicksilver was doing. His food bowls were empty, his water bowl was half down, and he was out on doggy business of his own. Good. He wouldn't complain about my going off with Ric. I refilled both bowls, which were the size of large casserole dishes. Stainless steel, though. I grabbed my messenger bag with the fresh reload of tampons. Really romantic and just what a P.I. who should be packing a semiautomatic and spare clips needs.

I was happy to leave Dolly parked there. I didn't feel like driving for once.

Sliding low into Ric's Corvette took a lot of pressure off my aching back and environs.

Ric started the therapy as soon as we were off the Strip and well on the way to his house. When he didn't need to shift the car, his right hand was pushing inside my clothes and caressing my skin in lazy patterns that—heavens to Betsy!—interrupted my fiendishly resistant cramp pain pathways to the brain.

My toes curled in my sandals.

"So tell me about the Karnak," he asked.

"It's kinda hard to concentrate on that right now."

He glanced over, his dark eyes even darker. "You shouldn't be out on the edge when you're feeling lousy."

"Actually, it *gives* me an edge. You don't want to irritate me just now."

"No irritation, just soothing."

My belly was almost numb from the hypnotic caresses. Ric brought his fingers to my mouth. "No trespassing there tonight. I'll just have to find another way in." He thumbed open my lower lip, then penetrated my mouth, his thumb pushing between my teeth and against the roof of my mouth.

The shaft of pleasure that arrowed through my belly made my feet flatten on the floorboard and my mouth turn into a suction machine, keeping his thumb captive.

He laughed at the fierce physical pull of my response. "I need to drive this baby," he said after a moment, reclaiming his thumb and the stick shift.

Whew. I contemplated the possibility that *not* having sex might be as exciting as having it.

The Vette turned a corner and then another, rocking me in the semi-recumbent cradle, and we were home. His home, anyway. Ric could never relax at the Enchanted Cottage as I did here, mainly because he didn't have an overzealous guard dog on duty.

He escorted me inside, arm around my waist, stopping only to pull the day's mail out of the box as we passed. The sky was darkening, long past twilight. Gravity was helping my cramps make a comeback, big time, on Broadway. Standing Room Only.

I almost welcomed having the leisure to do nothing but experience the agony, knowing what Ric would and could do to make me forget it.

Chapter Twenty-seven

THE NEXT DAY I woke up early at home, fully recovered, not to mention rethinking dreading my next siege of cramps if I could have them under the healing hands of Dr. Montoya.

Irma was still reduced to inarticulate purrs.

My new hot doc drove me home post-"treatment" so I could get the prescribed "bed rest" on my own turf. I awoke after a dreamless sleep sated and satisfied I'd accomplished a lot despite my crampy days.

I'd discovered Loretta's name, IDed her lover, learned why Loretta and her literal prince were offed, and unmasked the Karnak crew, which should be plenty of info for my four weird clients, Howard Hughes, Hector Nightwine, Snow and the CinSim Boys, but I'd neglected my personal quest for Lilith.

I'd need some time to report to everyone but Hector, and he could wait too. My clients didn't exactly keep regular office hours.

Now I needed to switch from mummy zombies to voluntary zombies. I was hoping the Snow groupies might provide a connection to Lilith or the groupie killer, but I also wanted to know why Snow's Brimstone Kiss was so addictive and encourage them to move on to a real life.

Kisses and kick-ass action, either martial or pre-marital, had not been on my personal road map until Ric happened along.

Being vampire bait from a young age and troubled by alien abduction nightmares, I'd found hovering mouths about as attractive as Great White Shark smooches. Thanks to Ric, I had glimpsed what these bedazzled rock-star groupies were feeling. I wonder if they realized they were better off not getting the Brimstone Kiss, rather than eating their hearts and psyches out for a return engagement that would never come.

Me, I'd rather be free than ecstatic. Maybe that was why I'd never been tempted to use drugs.

I READIED MYSELF for my first Snow groupie self-help meeting like a girl throwing a shower for several best friends at once. I'd never thrown a party for anyone or had anyone throw a party for me. Not even a birthday party. Especially not a birthday party.

This was going to be just girls and fun. Lucky I had the whole day to prepare, because I had to go shopping and buy paper goods and a flower arrangement. I didn't expect the kitchen witch to help me set up an event as unique as this, although I hummed "Whistle While You Work" and snacked on healthful plates of fresh veggies and cheese all afternoon. Thanks to some kind of kitchen witchery, I could never eat down to the bare china.

Rick called about ten that morning asking, "Awake yet, are we, Sleeping Beauty? Need any drive-by kisses?"

I laughed and couldn't stop, I was surrounded by bags and bags of foil-wrapped Hershey's Kisses at the moment.

"I love to make a grown woman giggle," he said. "Just checking in, *babe*." He was starting to call me that as a tease, now that he knew I loathed the word. From him, though, not so much. "Good news. I've finally rounded up all the Cicereau zombies and got them employment at Wayne Newton's Arabian horse ranch. They're going to learn to rope and ride and they'll have plenty of first-rate security." He chuckled at the idea of city-bred mob zombies amid the tumbling tumbleweeds. "I've been contacted for a meet with some Mexican consular folks. It's at the Luxor and I expect it to last into the afternoon."

"Don't worry. I've got some projects of my own."

"Where'll you be?"

"Just a little shopping center off Charleston. Safe as houses, like they say."

"Okay. Play mum. You know you'll tell me all about it after."

"You too."

"I'll call as soon as I'm done," he promised.

We closed on the usual murmurs, not quite mushy but darn near.

Back to the party plans. I figured a room where mostly women came to fight the Battle of the Bulge had a pretty good aura for fighting an addiction to a Kick-ass Kiss.

The place I'd rented for this evening came with a huge stainless steel coffee urn and kitchenette. I brought a gourmet blend and made a batch. A couple of trays filled with ice chips hosted soda cans and bottles of energy drink.

Some things, all the women at WTCH-TV swore during break periods, were better than sex. Certain gourmet flavors had a kick as good as, or possibly even better than, sex. I'd taken the lessons of those girly sessions at the TV station's break room to heart.

So I'd brought an array of snacks to tempt all tastes: Huge glazed doughnuts big enough to serve as a lifesaver rings. Carrot cake slathered with sweet cream cheese icing. Double-fudge German Sweet Chocolate Cake.

If music is the food of love, maybe food is the antidote to obsession.

Dolly's huge trunk toted all my supplies and I was on site and set up by 5:30 P.M.

Like any nervous hostess I was wondering if the music, Enya, was too mellow, and the coffee, Starbucks, too strong. I was particularly proud of two giant brandy snifters at each end of the serving table, both filled with Hershey's Kisses.

While I waited for the audience to arrive, or not arrive, I nervously adjusted the sterling silver necklace of dangling silver "kisses" around my neck. Matching chains ringed my wrist and ankle. And an adorable pair of icy silver "kisses" swung from my earlobes. Which were not pierced. And which never wore earrings. When I moved, I chimed like sleigh bells, are you listening? It was too, too corny but I knew I had to expect this kind of harassment from the silver familiar for messing with Snow's concert kissing shtick.

AN HOUR LATER my cheeks were warm with success. The large room was packed with everything from Goth girls to giggling Red Hat matrons.

The chatter noise level was high and the four major food groups—fat, salt, sugar, and caffeine—had dwindled to crumbs and empty paper cups.

Most of the women had shucked off their mules, tennies, high heels and biker boots to sit on the circled folding chairs. Content, they finally regarded their hostess with interest.

"You may be wondering why I've gathered you all together," I began.

They laughed as expected at my murder mystery opening line.

"How many here have had the Kiss?"

A smattering of hands shot up.

"And not?" Many more hands.

"I'd like the Haves to sit on the right side of the circled chairs."

"And the Have-nots?" asked a red-haired women.

"May sit on the left side of the room."

"'Left' is right," the redhead shouted as she moved. "You're sort of in the middle, ain't you?"

I nodded and kept that very place. "Yup. An almost-ran. So. Let's hear the Haves describe the Brimstone Kiss. Isn't that what the rest of us are all dying to know?"

The nods and murmurs were so unanimous that the Haves visibly preened.

"Just start anywhere. The first touch of his lips."

"Not there," said an ethereal girl wearing a wispy pixie haircut. "The first sensation is being buoyed up by the crowd, this human wave seeking to wash aground on the stage floor."

Hmms of agreement punctuated her testimony. This was beginning to feel like a revival meeting.

"Then," the girl went on, running a hand over the back of her neck, "he snares you with one of his white silk scarves. It's as smooth and strong as spider-silk. Your head lolls back—"

Ummms of empathy. Women on both sides of the room are rocking left and right, right and left. A woman on the right leaps to her feet, her head thrown back to testify in her turn.

"The scarf pulls you up, up, up. It's as strong as steel. You feel you'll never fall back."

"And then," the first girl went on, her voice vibrating with triumph, "his lips reach mine."

Yesss! the crowd croons.

"How do they feel?" the inquiring reporter puts in. "I need hard evidence."

"Soft as silk. Cool. Like a fountain in the desert. I feel the tingle of electricity meeting running water. Heat and meltdown. And then—"

Yesss, the women hiss, eyes closed, feeling the moment.

"His tongue."

"His tongue speaking in tongues," the women shout.

God! They loved that their rock idol was soul-kissing strangers? Wasn't that . . . unsanitary? Not that I didn't get the rocky mountain high part.

"The tingle starts in my lips and wraps me in an electrical storm of satisfaction."

Tingle. Kinda like my Lip Venom gloss. Snow has some kind of built-in Lip Venom? These women could *buy* the special effect. I need to hand out Lip Venom samples along with the high-sugar desserts. Wonder if the manufacturer would donate?

"The tongue is killer!" the wispy young woman declares. She is now shouting. "The back of my throat starts vibrating and then I'm thrumming all over, but deep in my throat the spasms start and they don't end. They just don't end. Wave after wave of absolute pleasure. Then I just fall away. I feel his icy palm on my forehead and the connection is broken. I'm still twitching with the sublime spasms. I guess he's gone, but my body is still possessed by the Ghost of his Brimstone Kiss."

Silence. Some of them recognize the sensations. I can tell by their dreamy eyes and slack lips. Some ache for the sensations. I can tell by their closed eyes and deep sighs.

A few, like me, remember and recognize similar symptoms.

As the chant of "Ah, men" goes up in the room, I inhale the bracing aroma of strong coffee and come to the only possible conclusion.

Snow's Brimstone Kiss bestows multiple orgasms.

Try to compete with that using a coffee klatch and a fistful of chocolate candy.

THE SECOND ACT of my private self-help group was even more interesting. All the Have-nots began to testify, rising one by one and baring their souls and their libidos.

The longer this went on, the more I wanted to shrink into the floor like the Wicked Witch of the West and disappear. Not because I can't take forthright talk, although that's a bit rough for one of my genteel and ignorant convent school background, but because I'm starting to feel guiltier and guiltier.

As the talk turned to vibrators and jackrabbits, which I learn are not wild hares, but a super-powerful variety of vibrator, I began to see that the Have-nots *have not ever had* a sexual orgasm. Some of them must be seventy or older.

Surely there is an Orgasm Fairy somewhere who sees to women like this. No?

Here I thought I was one of them. After all, forty percent of girls, good or bad, don't, according to statistics. Yet, despite my anxieties, my handful of assignations with Ric have all been orgasmic. I must be a freak! He must be a stud! Of course, there haven't been that many encounters. I could crash and burn any minute. Or not crash and burn.

And I should stand up here telling these poor women to just get over it? Cocaine. Him. His Brimstone Kiss. I feel like the Grinch who stole Christmas. The Witch who would steal the ruby red slippers. The reporter who announced the deaths at Lakehurst.

Guilt won't help me find Lilith. Plus, it was time for me to try to wean these women off the instant orgasm dream.

"But," I pointed out to the Haves, "not one woman who's got a Brimstone Kiss has ever gotten another, right?"

Disconsolate heads shook. "No, not even anyone on the online chat groups."

"So you're all pining away for something that will never happen again. But, cheer up! It did happen. You're way ahead of the Have-nots over there."

I did not see happy smiles.

"Tell me about your jobs, what you do for a living." I started pointing and they started talking.

"Waitress" comes up frequently. "Cocktail waitress" a bit less frequently. These women say the pay isn't union, but the tips are good. Others are fast-food restaurant employees. Wal-Mart greeters. Grocery store clerks. Every job is in Las Vegas to be close to the source.

"Do you really want to spend your lives underemployed waiting for something that may never happen?"

There is silence, at least, if not lively "No's!"

"Wouldn't you like to be free of your obsessions, able to date men who stand on the same level as you do? I'm sure some of them out there kiss pretty good."

This merited the "No's" I was looking for earlier.

"Don't you know in your heart of hearts that there's more to life than chasing something that hard to get? The perfect man or a hormone high? And how long does the Brimstone Kiss last, anyway?" I asked the Haves.

"Until he moves on," one woman admitted.

"To the next fan girl. Whom he leaves coming down without a parachute. You have to catch the lucky girl to keep her from banging her head on the concrete floor. And does Cocaine care? No."

Frowning brows told me I was making progress.

"Once again, it's all the guy's way and the women can wait. And wait. And wait. Don't you want to be free?"

They eyed each other uneasily. One hand wavered up, then down, and then fluttered up again. It's on the Have-not side.

"I'm sick of explaining to my family why I'm wasting my doctoral degree in education out here in Vegas slinging cottage fries."

Another Have-not stood. "I'm sick of living with four other girls in an overpriced apartment."

And another. "I'm sick of standing on hard concrete for hours almost every night until my ankles ache and paying high dollar for it and getting nothing."

High dollar. That's right. Vegas show tickets are over the moon. These women are paying plenty for a mere chance at a smooch.

"How much a night do you pay?" I asked, my calculator out. They rose and shouted numbers one by one. "$142!" "$135." "$122." I toted it up when the roll call was done.

"Two thousand and eighty-five dollars, ladies. You give that up every night to gamble on getting a kiss. I bet the odds are better at any slot machine and twenty-one table in Vegas. I bet the odds are even better for the right vibrator."

They are all standing, milling around, restless.

"Ladies, the Hershey's Kisses in the brandy snifter on your left are all white chocolate. As smooth and creamy as you-know-who. If you can't give up the dream, take a handful of them of them when you leave.

"The ones on your right are dark chocolate. Smooth and creamy and also chock full of flavonoids that are good for your health. Those who are willing to try five Cocaine-free nights, take a bunch of those. Eat a candy 'kiss' every time you think of Cocaine. For you those of you in 'withdrawal'—every time you think of Cocaine and manage to replace that thought with something else, reward yourself with a piece. Put your email address on the sheet on your way out. I'll set up a Yahoo! group list to keep in touch."

With nods and smiles, everybody signed up, but almost everybody filed up to the white chocolate jar. Eight, looking furtive and ashamed, drew from the dark chocolate jar. I'd hoped for the other way around.

A few "good children" always want to linger and talk to teacher after the class. Six gathered around me.

"Why are you doing this?" one asked. "You actually stormed the stage to get to him. Are *you* taking home dark chocolates?

"You bet," I told them, digging out several while they watched. "I'm tired of being called a Cocaine freak. You are too, aren't you? I just wanted to make that man answer to putting all us women in states he's unwilling to satisfy again, or leaving us out of the so-called ecstasy night after night. What a cheap trick to get loyal fans to show up for every performance."

"I hadn't thought of that," mused a portly woman in her sixties. "That it's just a come-on to get him publicity."

"He doesn't even have to tour to get screaming hordes. You're the hometown team. You'd think he could at least make sure you all got something to remember him by. And what's the use of a mind-blowing orgasm, or series of them, if you can never get one again? Either way, he wins and you lose. Every time."

They nodded listlessly, not entirely convinced, rolling the teardrop-shaped candies in their hands. Their color choices weren't visible to me.

One said, "Hey. I think I'll start a Web site and discussion group on this."

"Say," I followed up, "I hope we can attract more Cocaine fans. You ever talk to some online? Lilith, for example?"

"Oh, sure. Lili's a deep-down fan," said one, nearly stopping my heart.

"She's hinted she's a Have," a second woman chimed in.

Oh. No. That was me chiming in mentally as I jumped to hear Lilith spoken of so matter-of-factly. *Lili?* I could see how the nickname would evolve. And I would be "Lilah."

There was something eerily twinlike about those diminutives, even if I hadn't now known that Caressa Teagarden and her twin sister were named that from birth. I shivered as if someone was walking over Lilith's grave, and mine, and the damned cutesy silver "kisses" jewelry chimed some more.

Could there have been *two* abandoned infants left in different places? While I followed that thought, my reluctant prey drifted away after some quick good-byes.

I put the sign-up sheet in my Baggalini, cleared away the trash and loaded the brandy snifters in Dolly's trunk.

Lili. A twin sister named Lili. I choked up as I locked the door. I'd been alone so long it was scary to think I hadn't been born to be a solo act.

Hey, kid, Irma said, *you got me all these years. You don't need some upstart with a cutesy, kissy name. Who d'ye think you are? Delilah and Lilith Street, the Mary Kate and Ashley Olson of the supernatural set? Chill.*

Right. I didn't need two of me to get in trouble. Their "Lili" was not my Lilith and even my Lilith was a phantom, a filmed delusion. Or maybe not.

Quick was guarding Dolly in the drive-through area out back. The shopping center night lights only covered the parking area up front. It was odd that Snow's side was the light and my side was the dark. What an ironic role reversal.

I took a handful of the dark kisses out of the snifter. It was even more ironic that I was probably thinking of Snow as often as the most infatuated groupie. For quite the opposite reasons, of course.

Dolly started on the first turn of the ignition key. Quick leaped in the open window to ride shotgun, his tongue already lolling out in joyous anticipation of the wind rippling his fur all the way home to the Enchanted Cottage.

At least somebody was having a good night.

Chapter Twenty-eight

Working with the Snow groupies was wearing. They were so bloody single-minded.

About 8:00 P.M., I kicked off my mules and settled down with a glass of Beaujolais in the cottage parlor, brooding about Lilith. The more I chased her in the real world, the more remote she seemed. Maybe my handy-dandy magic mirror was the way to go after her. Chase her in Mirrorworld and run her down.

I checked my cell phone: no messages and Ric was not answering. His meeting at the Luxor must have run late, big time.

So I sipped and simmered, feeling both tired and wired, an unpleasant blend of emotions caused by inactivity.

When a knock came on my sturdy Hobbit door, I set down my wine glass and jumped up, ready to rake Ric over the coals for being AWOL. Then I planned to fan some intimate embers fast. I was not only getting used to physical affection, but craving it.

"Where have you been?" I demanded, sweeping open my arched door and resolving to make him wait for a more welcoming greeting . . . at least a minute.

"At the main house, of course," Godfrey said. "May I come in?"

I shut my mouth and nodded, standing back.

"Master Quicksilver?"

"Out on his nightly run."

"Sorry for descending on you with no notice," Godfrey said, sleeking the sides of his hair back with his palms.

Short notice or not, his formal butler's attire was impeccably as black and white and as unruffled as his demeanor. Did CinSims sleep? And, if so, did they dream of animated stuffed sheep?

The sight of Godfrey's dapper, pencil-thin mustache and wavy black hair, formal air, and usually twinkling gray eyes always filled me with fondness. Those eyes were darkly sober now. A CinSim, being a white, black and silver entity, couldn't turn pale. If one could, I would say Godfrey was as white as a ghost right now.

"What's wrong, Godfrey?" I checked the mantel clock keeping company with Achilles' dragon vase and Caressa Teagarden's ring. It was almost midnight.

"So sorry to intrude, miss, but my, er, cousin at the Inferno has managed to convey a rather alarming message."

CinSims had doubly convoluted relationships, since they were both actor and role. William Powell's delightful embodiment of Dashiell Hammett's tippling playboy detective, Nick Charles, was leased to the Inferno Bar. His definitive leading role from the 1930s screwball-comedy film, *My Man Godfrey*, held forth as "our man Godfrey" at Hector Nightwine's estate.

"*How* did you get Nicky's message, Godfrey?"

"Ah, you know. The blower. The horn."

"The telephone?"

"Righty ho."

"I thought Nick couldn't leave the bar area."

"Bars always have phones. Don't they?" Asked with innocent duplicity.

I gave up on nailing down CinSim communication modes. "What's so urgent?"

"He had a message from another CinSim, a displaced person, in fact. That poor fellow is somewhat mentally garbled from deserting his post. This . . . ah, errant CinSim had been contacted by yet another seriously-rogue CinSim. Now the second chap is at the Inferno Bar and desperately needs to see 'a raven-haired beauty with blazing blue eyes'."

"Nice snow job, Godfrey." CinSims from earlier eras were gallant flatterers of women, I'd discovered. I was beginning to like it, but not believe it. "And, of course, Nick Charles immediately thought of me."

"He is a rather fine judge of both female pulchritude and gin."

"*Pulchritude*, Godfrey?"

"An old-fashioned term, I admit. I hesitate to call a lady of my acquaintance a 'hot number' to her face, although my cousin Nick Charles never would. But then, that's the Gilbey's talking."

"So Nicky suggests I toddle out in the middle of the night to go see this fuzz-brained CinSim at the Inferno Bar."

"There is no 'middle of the night' in Las Vegas, miss. It's the town that never sleeps."

"Okay. I'm at loose ends, anyway. What's this wandering CinSims's name?"

"Oddly enough, Rick. With a 'k'."

That perked me up. "You sure it isn't the real Ric without a 'k'?"

"We CinSims are as real as rain, Miss Street." I'd never heard Godfrey sound so stiff. "At any rate, should you choose to see this fellow, cousin Nicky advises—and I quote—that you 'crack out your swankiest evening gown and dancing slippers'. Apparently the muddled CinSim is quite a ladies' man and, as Nick, not Rick, said, 'A gorgeous dame might unzip his lips and his amnesia'."

"Despite the comic relief with the flattery, you think this is serious, don't you, Godfrey?"

"I have never known my detective cousin to be so urgent. He actually sounded sober."

"Good grief! I'd better zip over to the Inferno to rendezvous with this mysterious amnesiac. That happen often to CinSims?"

"Certainly not. Our minds are even sharper than our components' faculties, thanks to, er, multiple influences."

His brow wrinkled. "Being jerked untimely from our environments may, however, cause some damage. What will you do?"

"Dress to the nines and drive to the Inferno to dazzle this Rick into sanity and spilling whatever beans his black-and-white-head contains."

MANNY THE DEMON actually admired *my* sleek flanks in midnight-blue velvet instead of Dolly's slick black Detroit metal ones when I arrived at the Inferno and left her for valet parking.

These thirties' silk velvet gowns were second skins. Talk about being panty-line prone! You didn't dare put underwear beneath them, whether you were Jean Harlow or Delilah Street. This one wrapped across the bodice and featured billowing and tucked sleeves and the usual bias-cut skirt that clung like static to the wearer's butt and thighs. In other words, it was a classic man-trap I'd usually never take out of my collection closet.

The "demned elusive" silver familiar had converted itself into a two-inch wide rhinestone belt that shone like a galaxy against the deep, dark universe of blue velvet.

I carried a silver mesh Whiting and Davc clutch from the period and did indeed wear "slippers," a blue-sequined version of the ruby red pumps Dorothy had to hang onto in Oz.

If this outfit didn't shock the CinSim known as Rick into babbling more than his full name, rank and serial number, I would lose my faith in vintage elegance.

The Seven Deadly Sins had already performed and retired from the stage, leaving the regular tourists holding the dance floor that surrounded the Inferno Bar.

I flashed on myself in the mirror behind the Tower of Babel of liquor bottles at the back of the bar. I'd accessorized my outfit with a rhinestone tiara, a popular look in the period, so I looked like the Queen of Romania.

And so Nick Charles said when I approached him.

I cut to the chase. "Where's this Ric imposter?"

Nicky sipped from his ever-present martini glass. "Better have an Albino Vampire before you approach the fellow. He's been drinking the house bourbon."

Hard bourbon just wasn't a Vegas drink. We like our vices more elaborate here.

I looked at the martini glass with its opaque white brew turning crimson at the very bottom. I decided I needed to improvise something extra, something more stimulating for a drunk and dislocated CinSim.

I told the bartender as I eyed the usual wall of liquor bottles against the back mirror, "Something new, Lou. Pour two jiggers of the Inferno Pepper Pot vodka, a jigger of DeKuyper 'Hot Damn!' Hot Cinnamon Schnapps, and two jiggers of Alizé Red Passion passionfruit, cognac and cranberry blend. It needs a jalapeño pepper on the rim if you use a martini glass, but leave both them out for now. Use a tall, footed glass and bring it to me down the bar in three minutes."

I took my Albino Vampire in hand and sauntered to the bar's darkest end.

Holy star power! I instantly recognized the long-faced guy in the rumpled white tropical Bogart suit. It *was* Bogart in his second-most-iconic film role, Rick Blaine of *Casablanca* fame.

Bogey had always been more rough-cut than handsome, but he looked confused and morose now. As I hitched myself up on the barstool beside him, he flashed a sullen glance from under untidy brows, eyeing the Albino Vampire.

"You drinking milk, sweetheart?"

"With a kick. Try some?"

"Nah. I don't drink booze I can't see through. Those are dames' drinks."

"You noticed." The point was, he hadn't, but now he gave me the once-over and obviously liked my vintage look.

The bartender brought over a tall, iced glass the color of a blood orange.

"Try this instead of that straight rotgut," I urged.

"I can't quite see through it."

"You can't quite see through my gown but you still like it."

He eyed the bloody cocktail. "What's this called?"

What name would appeal to a tough guy like Bogey? "A . . . Brimstone Kiss."

"Sounds like something you'd sip on all night long and I'd knock back in couple slugs."

There were two ways to take that line so I sat pat and kept quiet.

He took the glass and a long swallow, then smacked his lips and nodded. "Volcanic. What's a classy dame like you doing in a gin joint like this?"

Good. He thought he was in his own Casablanca bar. "The same thing you are. Trying to forget."

"No, I'm trying to remember." He took another bolt of Brimstone Kiss and made a face at the heat, which warmed his unfocused gaze as he took another look at me. "Black hair, blue eyes. Somebody told me about a dame like you, before I fixed it with the Nazis and the corrupt Frenchy and got out of town."

"Out of Casablanca?" I'd always wondered what had happened to Rick after he saw Ilsa off in that plane the midgets were readying for take-off. A famous fact about the movie was that the plane was a model so small the producers hired midgets to be shown working on it in the background. They may have been the ex-Lollipop Leaguers from *The Wizard of Oz*.

Maybe Ilsa and Victor Lazlo were going to Oz to escape the Nazis.

"Yeah," Rick said now, frowning as his CinSim programming took over again. "I wasn't supposed to leave Casablanca, ever, but that weasel Ugarte showed up again and said I had to find a dame. Black hair, blue eyes, easy on the peepers. You fit the bill on all counts, sweetheart."

"Thanks." I sipped the Albino Vampire, buying time to calm down. "Ugarte" had been played by Peter Lorre, whom I'd just seen during my dangerous expedition to the Karnak.

Nicky, the high society private dick, was right. This CinSim Bogart had an urgent message for me and it was coming through a fellow CinSim with a double "real/reel" life link to him. And a connection to the truly creepy crew at the Karnak!

I felt a pinch on my blue velvet butt that indicated the Invisible Man was here, and goading me on. That cinched it. Claude Rains, a.k.a. the Invisible Man, had played the corrupt French inspector in *Casablanca*. Apparently, Claude was joining Nicky and Godfrey in urging me to give Bogey my prime attention.

I didn't know their motivations, but my own interior warning system was on red alert now too. Something huge must have happened to have the CinSims uniting to overcome their bondage and get to me.

"How is Ugarte?" I asked carefully, not wanting to spook the displaced CinSim.

"Not good, but then the greasy little con man doesn't deserve 'good'. God, this booze is worse than the stuff I serve in my own place in Casablanca. I've been burned to the core by a classy dame before or I'd take you and your big blue eyes home with me."

"Where is that now?"

"Uh . . . dive called the Noir Café Parisienne. Downstairs, I think. Say, what is this place?" He hunkered over his lowball glass of bourbon, brooding again and tuning me out.

I nodded Nicky over for consultation. "He's an Inferno house CinSim?" I whispered.

"Quite right," Nicky confirmed. "From one of the signature theme clubs. There's a place for every taste in the lower depths. I heard him mention that miserable lowlife, Ugarte. He's from *Casablanca*, but that CinSim isn't on Christophe's payroll."

"Then how would Rick get a message from him?"

Nicky cleared his throat and downed some gin and vermouth mouthwash. "Sometimes we CinSims have vague memories of the other characters in our 'set'. Sometimes we don't. I remember Nora and Asta, of course," he mused nostalgically. "They would look swell hanging out on a barstool here."

"Does the hotel allow pets in?"

"Asta is not a pet," Nicky said indignantly, quashing a hiccup.

I agreed. The lively wire-haired terrier had been a child substitute for the sophisticated sleuthing couple . . . until the movies had put a real baby into the fourth sequel. The series was killed with the fifth. Hollywood, and now cable and broadcast TV, was always killing series that way.

I frowned like Bogart as I thought aloud. "So a CinSim can't even move from one venue in the same hotel to another?"

"Not without breaking its lease conditions and that does something to the old bean." He tapped his forehead. "Maybe they have us microchipped. That Ugarte must have broken his house rules too. And violently. Most unusual, and disturbing. Then Rick here started muttering about blue-eyed, black-haired dames into his bourbon—vile stuff!"

"I get that you think I'm the only black-and-blue woman in the world, but how did you get to Godfrey about it if you CinSims aren't supposed to cross venues to contact each other? You two 'cousins' collaborated before when I was kidnapped by the Cicereau werewolf mob. Not that I'm not grateful, but what's that about?"

"Nightwine and Christophe keep lighter leashes on their CinSims."

"Why?"

"They got a heart?"

I rolled my eyes. "Please."

"They have an interest in the bigger picture in Vegas and they find us useful beyond being mere cosmetic curiosities."

"Hector and Snow are secret allies?"

"Nah, just brothers in individual enterprise. They don't like mobs moving in and taking over."

"Isn't that a little late for Vegas?"

"The Strip reinvents itself every day, Miss Street. Look at you. *Hmm*, don't mind if I do again. Nora would look splendid in that gown. What's wrong with our friend Rick there? I thought some female company would unlock his lips."

"I haven't really tried yet," I whispered, spinning back to my dour drinking partner. "Hey there, Mr. Blue."

He glanced up, weary and worn and unreachable. *Casablanca* had revealed that the cynical Rick had a sentimental, even a self-sacrificing streak. Better play the queen of hearts.

"Mr. Blaine," I said, all breathless, taking on pleading (*ick*) Mary Astor tones from *The Maltese Falcon*. Some of those thirties supposed femme fatales were manipulative wimps. "I've got to get out of Casablanca. The Nazis think I'm a spy. You *know* what they'll do to me. Mr. Ugarte said you had some letters of transit. I can pay whatever you want." I put a fake little catch in my voice that Sam Spade called Bridget O'Shaughnessy on in *Maltese Falcon*, widely available on DVD. "What*ever* you want."

Rick Blaine's unfocused eyes raked me. "Yeah, I got the documents and you seem to have all the right accessories too."

Holy shit! Irma intruded. *You've done your vamp act a bit too well. Let me handle this poor bastard for you. All of us girls have a bit of groupie in us. Except for you, Iron Virgin.*

I tuned her out and concentrated on redirecting my source.

"I've got to get away to save my husband." Mention of a spouse usually put off the rogue womanizer and Rick had been forced to come to terms with Ilsa's marriage in the movie.

I saw some of that cinematic pain speed through Rick's glance. Then he reached into his suit pocket. For a precious visa I didn't really need?

He pulled out . . . a tiny case.

Rick frowned at the object. "This thing isn't what Ugarte left with me for safe-keeping. It's in the same pocket, though. I must be drunk."

I stared at what lay in his hand. It was wildly out of period with *Casablanca*, but not contemporary Las Vegas. It was my Lip Venom case, which I must have lost during the leap through the Egyptian goddess's moon-mirror headdress.

I'd been too woozy from crossing physical barriers to even notice it was gone.

"Ugarte said this was just what you needed," Rick droned on. "He said it was a matter of life and death that I get it to you. I feel like death, but I have. Mission accomplished, sweetheart. Now get out of my joint. I want to drown my sorrows in all that gin myself."

I edged off the bar stool and backed away, surprised and amazed and scared.

Peter Lorre—and somehow I thought the actor and not the CinSim had successfully struggled to escape his role to accomplish all this—had violated every physical law governing CinSims to get this to me, and had shaken Humphrey Bogart loose from his distant Inferno station to do it.

I wondered what the Invisible Man and his cohorts Sherlock Holmes and Ricardo Montalbán would think of such a feat and what it could mean for a future CinSim insurrection.

Mostly I wondered whose life and death depended on my getting the message that Rick Blaine had brought me tonight.

Chapter Twenty-nine

"LOITERING AGAIN?" a harsh voice asked.

I looked up, expecting Snow. He usually hassled me in the Inferno Bar.

Instead, it was his security chief, Grizelle, wearing heavy metal and black leather like a motorcycle nightmare goddess. The boss must be recovering from the Seven Deadly Sins performance. How do walking, strutting unhuman rock-star vibrators relax after the show?

The only things on my cell phone from my Karnak visit were photos. I needed more inside info on the Egyptians fast. The Internet would have that.

"I need a computer," I told Grizelle.

"They sell them online and at mall kiosks."

"*Now*. I need a computer right now!"

"Tough."

"It's a matter of life and death, at least so your CinSim over there says."

Her green eyes, brightened as they glanced Rick's way. They radiated fury.

"One of our CinSims? At large without permission? He must return immediately to his slot in the lower depths."

"Glad you can take the lost sheep in hand. First, Miss Bo Peep, point me to a computer."

Her head lashed back to me, white dreadlocks whipping against her black velvet cheeks. "You presume."

I said nothing, but my silver familiar loosened a string of rhinestones from my belt and whipped it around her tabby-shadow-patterned bare black forearm.

Her glossed lips snarled, but she backed down. "Use the one in the boss's office. I believe you know the way. It's empty."

"Fine. And, Nicky—" I turned to find my dapper ally looking a more than a little dead-white around the gills. "Please send me an Albino Vampire there. Snow said they were on the house. Eternally."

Grizelle glowered at Nicky. Nicky shrugged. Behind them, Rick Blaine glowered at his half-empty Brimstone Kiss glass, then eyed Grizelle with manly appreciation. Grizelle glowered at Rick.

I figured it was a draw all around and headed through the dancers and then the wandering crowds and the casino to Snow's office far behind the main floor.

The cell phone was in my metal mesh vintage purse, an unlikely partnership of technology and style, of current events and past fashion.

Despite its cool, metal sheath, it felt like a hot potato in my hand.

It felt heavy beyond the few ounces it weighed.

It felt like a matter of life and death that might mean the world to me.

How DID the human race accomplish anything before the Internet became the fountain of all knowledge—good, bad and unreliable?

I tended to think these heavy thoughts because I was sitting in the tufted white leather chair behind Snow's desk, accessing the Internet from his desktop. What extremes of evil might be found on it with some adept snooping on my part?

But I was here to deal with grave matters of my own, not the state of Snow's soul.

Getting on Groggle always made me feel like I was cheating on a test in school. It was sinfully easy to bone up on any subject in a half hour or so. Obviously, I needed to research ancient Egyptian culture to get a handle on just what the Karnak was and what might be going on there.

First I confirmed that no Egyptian pharaohs had been named Kephron or Kepherati, and no royal twins ever had jointly ruled the Upper and Lower Kingdoms.

The sixty-four million-dollar question about the lavish managerial setup at the Karnak was who, or what, the over-devoted head pair were. Were they actual surviving ancient Egyptians hiding out? Were they deluded wealthy modern wannabes? And what were they doing in Las Vegas?

People today, fascinated by the richness and beauty of tomb treasure and the royal lifestyle, might think progressing to the afterlife was a high-end adventure tour. Not so. It was terrifying, Groggle revealed. The Egyptians didn't have things like *The Book of the Dead* and *The Book of the Netherworld* for nothing

According to one reputable-looking Web source, the spirit went to a Hall of Judgment, which sounded a lot like the two Kephs' reception chamber. After passing seven gates, the wandering corpse had to face the judgment of Osiris, god of the netherworld, in a weighing of the heart ceremony in the presence of Anubis, the jackal-headed god of the dead, and the whole darn Egyptian set of forty-two gods. The heart was the only organ left in the body just to star in this final ceremony. A Weight Watcher's fear of the weekly scale was puny by comparison.

Could Las Vegas be the eternity that lurked beyond the ancient Egyptian river journey of the dead? Were there so many Egyptians here at the Karnak because they'd been crossing over for centuries? The royal twins' reception hall was beneath the surface of the desert. An entire Egyptian necropolis and city could lurk under all this Nevada sand, a secret Area 51 for aliens from Earth's past inner space, rather than outer space.

I kept skimming some of the hundreds of Web sites on Egyptian customs and beliefs, looking for a reason for

the Kephs being in the here and now. I played hooky too,
taking a detour to museum sites, comparing the loot there
to what I'd seen in the netherworld at the Karnak hotel.
Even if it was reproduction, the Karnak stuff was worth
millions.

A Web page about the tomb of Tutankhamun
reminded me of the attack hyena that shared the young
pharaoh's cute modern nickname, King Tut. I gazed on
color photos of the boy ruler's impressive mummy case,
tomb furnishings, the gold and lapis lazuli, the exquisite
collars and bangles.

Talk about a vintage treasure trove! Art Deco style
was influenced by the art and artifacts Howard Carter
discovered in Tut's tomb. I loved that period, but Art
Deco furniture would never fit in the cozy late-forties
atmosphere of the Enchanted Cottage.

But the gold, piles of it, was beautifully wrought. And
the tall gold lily in the pot, maybe five feet high . . .There,
found in King Tut's tomb, was the duplicate of the pair of
artifacts flanking Keph and Keph's paired thrones!

I opened my cell phone and took my first gander at the
photos I'd managed to take surreptitiously while a guest
of the royals. Yup, the same paired artifacts.

I went back to the Web site, eagerly reading the text
beside the online photo.

The weird dangling forms I'd seen both online and at
the Karnak were Imiut fetishes!

So what were Imiut fetishes? A stuffed or decapitated
animal skin tied by its tail to a pole which was, in turn,
inserted into a flower-pot-like stand. The skin, usually from
a leopard or a bull, was sometimes wrapped in bandages.
Its tail often ended in a papyrus flower. In some depictions,
the skin dripped blood into the pot. Gruesome!

The ones in Tut's tomb and the Karnak throne room
were stylized, gilded versions.

The fetish was originally connected with a god named
Imiut—"He Who is in His Wrappings," wrappings as in

"mummy." He eventually became an aspect of Anubis, the jackal-headed god who evolved into the gatekeeper of the underworld and who protected the dead as they journeyed there. Anubis wasn't so much a death god as a god of dying and therefore associated with embalming and funerals. He was also the patron of lost souls and therefore . . . gulp! . . . orphans.

We have a patron, Irma crowed.

I sat back in Snow's cushy chair, sipped the Albino Vampire Grizelle had sent, and then huffed out a sigh. My shoulders ached, not just from being hunched over a computer screen but from holding up the slippery silk velvet of my vintage gown, which wanted to become an off-the-shoulder style. Who knew sedentary scholarship could be so wearing?

I drank deeper of the Albino Vampire to unchain my brain and relax my shoulders. The alcohol had an immediate effect of loosening my inhibitions and opening my mind. I leaned toward the weird onscreen image again. Something about these ghoulish and oddly undecorative decorative objects had bothered me from the moment I spotted them. It had been suspicion at first sight.

They simply weren't grand and gorgeous enough to flank pharaonic thrones.

Like I'm an expert in Egyptian funerary objects. Still . . . I studied the dangling beheaded object. It gave me the creeps and seeing a pair of them placed so close to those entwined twins creeped me out even more.

Headless skins were hardly an elegant accessory for a throne room. Keph and Keph had intentionally placed symbols of . . . embalming . . . next to their thrones?

Reading further, I found the blue lotus—the lily topping the golden pole—closed nightly only to reopen with the morning sun and was a symbol of rebirth. So a symbol of dead flesh combined with one of renewal . . . could this odd object embody a ritual by which the dead were returned to life?

I wanted to pound my head to jolt out the fugitive thoughts rattling around the far reaches of my brain.

Were Keph and Keph flanked by evidence that they had been buried but still lived? Did they flaunt the Imiut fetishes that were meant to entomb them for eternity as banners to show what fate they had escaped to enjoy a double undead life hereafter? To show they now lived forever? Immortal undead . . . vampires?

What if Howard Hughes wasn't the flower of Vegas vampiredom? What if these warped, hidden creatures were the king and queen of the ancient vampire breed and they were gathering armies under the city?

What if they weren't the only ones? That would explain why the Imiut fetishes were found in Tut's tomb and in others going back to the First Dynasty. The fetish is still considered "strange" by Egyptologists despite its link to the bandages used in mummification.

King Tut had died young, about age nineteen. So had Loretta's European vampire prince—except Prince Krzysztof died the vampire's true death six centuries after his fifteenth-century birth: beheaded, then buried in Sunset Park. He remained in his grave for sixty years until Ric and I found his skeleton with a coin in the skull's fleshless mouth. Could Tut also have been beheaded, proving him a vampire?

Alas, an article I found online written by modern radiologists said the original 1925 autopsy X-rays showed the skull attached rigidly to the cervical spine, but further research revealed intriguing contradictions. Those same radiologists, examining better X-rays taken in 1968, noted a "bright beaded line" of solidified resin that might have masked a possible severing.

The mummy was stuck fast to its coffin by hardened embalming liquids used to anoint it, so Howard Carter's team cut it into large pieces. (Poor Tut!) They sliced off the arms and legs and halved the trunk. But—and here my instincts quickened—King Tut's head, cemented to its lavish golden mask by the solidified resins, was severed by the archeologists and removed from the mask with hot knives. So he *had* been beheaded in 1925, millennia past his burial date.

Egyptian antiquities authorities now guard his mummy as closely as Quicksilver guards me, but they did allow a CT scan back in 2005. This examination showed a fracture at "the first cervical (topmost) vertebra and the foramen magnum (large opening at the base of the skull)." There was, according to the scientists, no way to know if this happened during the ancient embalming process or if the rough handling by Carter's crew caused it. The king may have been decapitated back in 1327 BC after all.

One way or another, more than three thousand years ago or less than one hundred, Tutankhamun had lost his royal head.

I also had a huge "Aha!" moment reading this extremely suggestive notation about the Tut skull scans: "He has large front incisors and the overbite characteristic of other kings of from his family (the Tuthmosid line)."

Of course, even in the post-Millennium Revelation world authorities like to hush up finding vampires under every cultural icon. No one would thank an amateur like me for this theory.

Long teeth and beheading might not be proof of vampirism, but they were clues my theory could be right. I found others.

Vegas Coroner Grisly Bahr had said that the Sunset Park bone boy's head had been cut off and a coin placed in his mouth because that was a tried-and-true old European method of killing a vampire forever.

Might not the ancient Egyptians also have had vampires and used the same decapitation method to destroy them forever, sans the coin? My research revealed Egyptians didn't use coins until the Greco-Roman era, a thousand years after Tutankhamun's reign.

Yet were there, layered among Tut's wrappings, items that functioned like the coin in the mouth to keep a slain vampire dead?

Studying detailed drawings (reproduced on a Web site) made when the mummy was first unwrapped, I noticed many of the one hundred and fifty or so amulets and articles of jewelry on the body were clustered around the neck. But many items were also centered on the chest and forearms and in the pelvic, thigh, lower leg and scrotum area. Pretty much everywhere I'd spotted tattoos on the tandem Pharaohs.

The Book of the Dead prescribed the various placements of these pieces, so they were probably potent magic, even more effective than coins.

Maybe the scientists wouldn't buy it, but I found further proof for ancient Egyptian vampires in the fact that juniper was probably used in the embalming materials. In later European tradition, juniper, hawthorn and ash wood are recommended for staking vampires. Likewise, keeping a branch of juniper or holly in the home supposedly helps protect it from vampires.

Maybe that's why so much resin was used on Tut's body. It was literal overkill.

If Egyptians had entombed vampires, the Imiut fetishes featuring headless animals dripping blood could have been a warning to future generations that the tomb's mummy was a beheaded vampire and not to be interfered with. That meant even beheading might be circumvented. Certainly Keph and Keph thought they could resurrect the beheaded Prince Krzysztof and it was possible someone had revived the royal pair themselves centuries earlier.

And those tattoos I'd noticed . . .

I called up Groggle again and searched for major artery locations in the human body. A "play" vampire, like Undead Ted, the anchorman at WTCH-TV, would want to bite a neck, but avoid the carotid artery there, just under the skin. A seriously hungry real vampire would want a royal road to the blood source. I found artery sites in the neck, wrist, inner arm and knee, groin and inner thigh, the very sites where Kephron and Kepherati bore tattoos. Their mostly bared bodies had acted as billboards advertising their breed and habits.

That answered the "vintage" treasure versus reproduction question. Vampire Egyptian artists and sculptors could replace aging monuments and furnishings endlessly.

Oh, my God. Who did I warn first? Ric, of course, but who would believe us? Who would have the will and power to confront this undiscovered cabal of vampires, or even believe the urgency of some major force dealing with them?

First things first.

I needed to let Ric know so we could figure this out together. If only he hadn't been out of touch since mid-morning. Damn Las Vegas' notoriously spotty cell phone reception on the Strip and off! I took out my cell and hit redial. Again, voice mail. Where *was* he?

And then the true, awful meaning of two CinSims's unheard-of struggle to escape their venues to reach out and communicate hit me like a bolt of lightning.

My cell phone hadn't made or accepted calls underground at the Karnak *either.*

I had to place my dawning, stomach-churning suspicion into a logical scenario.

The royal freaks had taken an interest in me and were annoyed with me because they thought I'd disturbed the bone boy's sleep before they had time to "reclaim him." Then, their interest deepened because of the showdown in the Spring Mountains with the Cicereau Mob werewolves. They'd been fascinated that zombies had been raised to help defeat the werewolf packs. When I'd been in their royal clutches, they'd asked more about who had raised the dead than about me. A "servant of Anubis," they concluded, must have been present.

I'd assumed they were interested in zombies, since they commanded companies of them in the form of mummies and Egyptian warriors.

Were they really interested in Ric's abilities to raise the dead? Were they after not merely the bone boy, not merely zombies, but long-laid-to-rest vampires reborn, the age-old powerful vampires so absent in the Vegas of today? Except for themselves.

Ugarte had sent me Casablanca's "Rick" as a messenger for two reasons.

One, this Bogart persona was already working at the Inferno, a hotbed of CinSim defiance. Peter Lorre/Ugarte had a second major film connection with Bogart, so maybe he could use some form of telepathy to break the "Rick" Bogart lose from his venue. But how the heck could he pass on the Lip Venom case I'd dropped during my athletic escape leap? Maybe he had somehow gotten to the Inferno in person. I blinked. My eyes felt as dry as my little gray cells.

I'd nail down the Lip Venom transmission mystery and nuances of CinSim inter-species communications later. Right now I needed to concentrate on the other key part of the message.

Casablanca Rick was the perfect messenger, not only to spur me to examine the cell phone photos I'd taken of the fetishes, but because Ric himself, my Ric, couldn't come. Only the CinSim Rick was available. He was used to remind me of my own Ric, and to make me realize that he was in danger. Terrible danger.

That had to be why I couldn't raise Ric's cell phone. The twin pharaohs already held Ric prisoner. They needed him to raise the old vampires hidden here and maybe elsewhere.

And Ric had walked right into their trap: his appointment at the Luxor today with the "Mexican consulate" people. The Luxor had been one of the first Vegas hotels after the Crystal Phoenix to create an internal lobby waterway. They'd discontinued it years ago, but the channels might well still exist beneath the hotel-casino, a quick way to smuggle anyone anywhere. I'd practically led them straight to him. I hoped like hell I was wrong about Ric being held captive, because the thought made me desperately fearful.

After being forced as a boy to raise zombies for misuse by the Mexican smugglers, Ric had sworn never to raise the dead for another's use and abuse. I knew he'd never consent to share his secret of dowsing for the dead or his skill. I guessed the spoiled Egyptian rulers would never accept anyone's defiance.

It would be a struggle of wills to the death, Ric's death.

How long had he been out of touch? I hadn't heard from him since ten o'clock, hours before my groupie gathering. My brain was as fried as the Bogart Rick's had been.

I stood up from the desk, the huge white leather chair spinning away from me, almost knocking me off my feet as my mind juggled huge questions.

How to penetrate that fortress beneath the Karnak? Who was mighty enough to fight Pharaoh's army and marching zombie mummies? How could I save Ric from a fate worse than death? From the curse of eternal living death he would loathe with every cell in him? Servitude of any kind after his enslaved childhood was unthinkable.

How could I rescue Ric?

I had to.

Now!

Chapter Thirty

"I SEE YOU'RE ABUSING my hospitality and my office furniture," a cool, deep voice said from the doorway. "So where's the party?"

Snow, still dressed from his stage show, stood in his office doorway looking like an alabaster statue in his white leather catsuit. His ever-present sunglasses seemed to be taking in my midnight-blue velvet gown, not my desperate all-business face. At least they inspected me from top to bottom.

"I'll abuse more than that before I leave," I warned him. "Listen. I've uncovered an unthinkable scenario for Vegas and the world. I need back-up. I need . . . Grizelle as a six-hundred-pound tiger. I need Genghis Khan and his hordes. The Egyptian vampires at the Karnak have a zombie army and they're holding Ric captive!"

"Egyptian vampires? You must be drunk on Albino Vampires." Snow's sunglasses nodded at the half-full glass on the desk. "Grizelle said you stormed my office in a mad fury, but you're dressed for a waltz, not a rescue mission."

I was sweating bullets in my frail vintage velvet gown, melting from the agony of every single second of delay, but I didn't care. I realized there was another reason the CinSims had called me to the Inferno. Who but CinSims would know what the hotel must harbor on its many secret underground levels? If it was indeed modeled on Dante's Inferno, it could house an army of horrors below.

"Look, Snow. You've finally got what you want: me begging you for something. I need your help to save Ric. I don't care what you are, I don't care what you do, I just know you're the only . . . whatever . . . in Vegas that can bring any force up against those demented demigods at the Karnak."

"And how do you know demented demigods run the Karnak?"

"They sent their hell-raising sacred hyenas after me, so I got curious and paid them a visit two days ago. I found a hall of mummies, warriors who step out from walls and a sick pair of siblings who think they're a pharaoh in duplicate."

"Sounds like the usual spectacular Vegas theme hotel."

"This was *under* the hotel."

"Why would these escapees from a Cecil B. DeMille spectacular want Ricardo Montoya?"

"Are you brainless? He's the Cadaver Kid! They want him to find dead bodies. Hidden, undead vampire bodies, lost for centuries. You said yourself the vamps were driven out of Vegas during the founding days seventy years ago and wanted back in."

"I had more modern vampires in mind."

"Well, *they* didn't! There's no time to debate this. They've got an army down there. You happy with that in the neighborhood?"

He said nothing.

"Those monsters have had Ric for almost eighteen hours, for God's sake!"

"God is not in Vegas."

"For pity's sake."

"Pity is not a commodity in Vegas."

"For humanity's sake."

"Humanity is not worth much to many these days."

Didn't I know that from my orphanage rearing?

"Why are you so sure you need me?" he asked.

"You fight dirty, Snow. That's why I need you."

His smile was slow. "That's not why you need me, Delilah. You need me because you need Ricardo Montoya."

"Bastard! Loveless, soulless monster! You have Grizelle. You have your whole Inferno hotel security force. You have whatever evil creatures inhabit the Lower Circles of your Hotel Hell. I can tell you now who the vampire was who died with Loretta Cicereau."

"That's a very small matter in the fate of Las Vegas and its hidden founders and masters and mistresses and ignorant human occupants, including you. Why should I get involved?"

"I don't have time to haggle with you. You want me to beg? All right. You said I would someday and I will. I'll take your damned Brimstone Kiss now."

"An army of support for one kiss? You expect me to attack a neighboring hotel-casino on the basis of that?"

"Yes! The groupies are too easy for your ego. If you're a vampire, you'll want to destroy the upstart vampires who are trying to take over your territory anyway. If you're a fallen angel, you'll want to look better in my eyes and redeem your own shoddy soul. If you're a demon, you'll want to soil my soul. If you're just a very bad man, you'll want to humiliate and conquer me."

"And why would I want that?"

"Because you need to bring someone else down to your damned, lost level and I'm finally willing to go. For a price."

He licked his dead-white lips. Honest to God. Or Gehenna.

He was nervous, or hungry.

Whichever, it was all about me and the desperate spot I was in.

Not because I'm Lilith's double. Not because I'm a woman and supposed to be conquered. It's because I have nothing but true love in my heart and desperation in my soul. I'm awash with frantic, selfless fear and devotion. If I could trade my life for Ric's, I would. But I can only try to rescue him, at any cost. I'm a tasty treat for anything evil under the sun.

He was infuriatingly slow to respond. "I told you that one day you'd beg for it."

"It?" Even now, I wanted to be certain of the price.

"The Brimstone Kiss. You are the temptress, Delilah, who never wanted to be tempted."

"I'm not tempted. I'm desperate, like any other soul in Hell."

"They're desperate to get out. You're desperate to get in."

"There's no time. Do it."

"There is a price," he warned.

"With the Devil, isn't there always?" I knew this was the most desperate negotiation of my life or my death.

"Perhaps. Perhaps you just think so. Bad press, you know."

"Get to it, Snow."

He tilted his head to consider me, the dead-dark sunglasses winking with the overhead light reflections, adding false life to his hidden eyes.

His long white locks, that's how I always thought of them—as locks, bondage—swooped into a silver shimmer as his head tilted. His hair was seductive, gleaming like his slightly opalescent skin and lips. And fingertips. If this wasn't the base material of my marauding metal ball and chain, I might actually like to feel it feathering against my bare skin. Just where, I wasn't prepared to imagine.

"A kiss," he said. Or hissed.

That disconcertingly white eyebrow lifted above the top rim of one black sunglass lens. What *were* his eyes like? Pink like the Easter Bunny? Or crimson like a sated vamp's? I'd celebrated his rumored reputation as an Albino Vampire myself with the cocktail I'd created in his dishonor.

Right. Irma was being mum. I could still imagine her comment. *Drugged slavery while you wait, with one perverted loving gesture.* I'd seen the results on the groupies. Of what use would I be then to save anyone else, much less myself?

"I've seen your groupies sleep-walking around goo-goo eyed, wraiths, automatons, like Stepford wives. You seem to need a pretty big harem. No thanks. I'm into one-on-ones."

"Old-fashioned."

"Alive and well."

"And independent."

I didn't answer that. I wasn't very independent now, and knew it.

"Except you have obligations. One kiss. Then you can have anything you ask."

"Does it come with an apple?"

"It's just one kiss, after all," he said.

"Addicted zombiedom is my only option?"

He put a pale, elegant hand to his pale, elegant, sculpted chest. Warm, living Carrara marble? *Maybe* living. "Are you sure that's the only outcome?"

"I know what happens to your kissees."

"But not what happens to you."

"I'd be different?"

"You are different already."

"Just another trophy for your ego, anyway."

"Just your only opportunity to save Montoya. He wouldn't want you to sacrifice yourself in the process, you know."

I took a deep breath. "I know."

"All this drama over one kiss. Surely even you have done that before."

"Yeah, you're Mr. Eternal Experience. Have you ever considered you might really just be . . . shopworn?"

"You're taunting me because you're afraid."

"You bet." What the hell! Well, *his* hell. He was the only option I had. "All right. Sentimental fleas do it. Let's do it."

He seemed truly taken aback. "You have to actually say 'yes'."

Was this like having to invite in a vampire for your own destruction?

"Yes!" I sounded exasperated even to myself. It wasn't the dazzled wimpy 'yes' he'd expected maybe.

"A kiss can't be rushed," he warned.

"Not a Judas kiss, no. It has to sink in slowly, like slime."

"It will take what time it takes. Do you agree?"

"Anything. Just . . . get started."

"How is that to happen?"

I shrugged in helpless fury, picturing Ric in the hands of the ancient undead, the unhuman, those determined to extract the secret of his cursed gift of giving animation to the lifeless. To force him to raise the dead he'd sworn never to violate again with his power.

Then Grizelle was suddenly at Snow's back, wearing a heavy metal leather wetsuit from hooded head to booted feet.

He handed her a device like an iPod on which he'd hit several buttons in succession. "Contact the first tier to bring their best fighters. Roust the second tier of our own forces and contact the enemies I highlighted."

"How will you move such a force openly through Las Vegas?" she asked.

"I won't. Miss Street and I will need vampire-fighting gear. I think you can guess her size."

Grizelle's gaze nearly fried me on my bones. "She's coming with us?"

"She's our Joan of Arc," Snow said with a tight smile. "Now leave us. We have some business to finish while you're mustering the forces."

Grizelle hesitated. For only a second, but she did hesitate.

Snow's frown lines above the glass frames set her in rapid retreat, already beating out a tom-tom rhythm on the device.

Snow turned back to me.

The sunglasses studied me from head to foot.

"You must forget everything else but this, for the duration," he said. "You must accept it totally. Any worry or withholding will have dire consequences. Furthermore, I won't accept the deal as done if you falter. It will all be for nothing."

"Fine. I have one condition," I said.

"You're in no position to bargain, but what is it?"

"You ditch the sunglasses. I won't sell my soul to anyone who can't look me in the eyes."

His silence seemed endless, but he finally peeled off and tossed the sunglasses aside.

I didn't even glance to see where the hateful "shades" fell.

His eyes—!

The pupils weren't just albino pink, like I'd imagined, but deep magenta, faceted like jewels, blinding to look into. The sunglasses weren't worn to protect an albino's weak unpigmented eyes and eyesight, as I'd assumed, but to protect others from his searing glance.

I stood there blinking, my eyes watering.

"It begins then," Snow said. "You can't go back."

Shit! Who ever could?

I stopped trying to talk him into anything, just let out a long deep breath, buttressed by the taste of the Albino Vampire still on my tongue, and awaited my fate.

Not that I wasn't worried. I hoped that even a trio of orgasms in triplicate couldn't enslave me body, mind and soul forever, or even half an hour. Yet, what if there was some other addictive element to the Brimstone Kiss?

And, worst of all, by submitting to another man's intimacy, I was compromising my love for Ric. To save him, I'd have to betray him.

I just wanted us to be together again, the same as we were. Ric the same. Me the same. Surely a mere day couldn't destroy that? Who was I kidding? An hour, the wrong hour, had destroyed love time and time again in lives immemorial.

So my knees and soul were shaking just as hard as I stood there, waiting to be sold down river.

Snow tilted his head the other way. Damn, he had good hair! A girl would kill for that hair. Then his hands reached up . . . crimped into my blue velvet gown at the gathered vintage shoulders and pulled it open to my waist.

I was naked beneath. The brutal stripping action made the ebbing velvet feel as raw as duct tape searing my skin as it was torn away. Already it was more than a kiss. It was complete surrender.

His hands cupped to capture my naked breasts.

Something icy flowed over my heart.

Not fear, nothing inner. I looked down where Snow's half-lidded magenta eyes were focused.

Whoa. Major exposure, sans bra. I felt a chill silver flood rising. Instant silver bustier, courtesy of his own initial manufacture.

The pale lips smiled. "You have a way of winning allies," he murmured.

His flesh-seeking hands had captured the cool silver expanse of a metal mesh bustier that had sped to cover my bared breasts.

"You've formally surrendered, Delilah. Release your familiar."

"But it's *yours*! It's your unwanted, leeching familiar made of hair-turned-metal. I've never been able to take it off or make it release me. It simply wanders my body, as your hands do now, taking on whatever whimsical form suits it, tormenting me with bad memories and ugly questions."

His head with its long white strands shook slowly. "Mine the lock of hair, yes. Yours what it became, what it made of you and you of it. I've never commanded this snake of white hair turned goad and guardian. And you must know that."

"No!" I didn't. "Not for an instant."

"I can't give you the Brimstone Kiss while you wear it in any form."

"I can't get it off!"

"But you can let it leave."

Let it leave? That simple? Not fight it? Just let water flow downhill, silver melt into hot metal, worry wilt into wishes. Just . . . let it go. Just click my heels and go home? Then what was all this *for*? I stopped questioning, rebelling, and sighed.

My metal bustier turned warm and pliant, flowing up Snow's wrists and arms, where it formed matching metal gauntlets that warded his forearms.

My talisman was cozying up to my bitter enemy. He was armed while I stood half-naked before him. I felt an absence so intense that it took my breath away. I'd loathed the daily reminder of his meddling, yet felt as if another defensive curtain had been ripped away.

Then . . . I felt free.

Again.

It was like getting a rotten tooth pulled. I'd gotten used to the daily ache and now glimpsed utter liberty. *Yes!* I had only to pull away from his fingertips and I'd be free of Snow and his possessive toys. I was moving. . . . shaking him off like a bad dream, of which I'd had plenty.

"Montoya," he reminded me.

We both stood frozen as statues. Some classical subject, a Greek god in human form pursuing unwilling nymph. Me starting to twist away. He starting to tighten his grip on my naked forearms so the pale marble would seem as pliable as bread dough, flesh sinking into flesh, only everything was stone inside.

I shivered from cold or fear or fury, or all three. I felt all three states, holding still to submit when every muscle was poised to twitch with revulsion at being here, doing this.

Ric would say no to my deal with the Devil, with his last breath. I knew he would never submit to the vampires who held him, not the boy who had resisted the human *coyotes* who had abused him unimaginably time and again. He might be already dead, lost, and this sacrifice was futile.

To save Ric and our love at the price of being mauled and put in thrall to another man's kiss, no matter how supernatural . . . I knew I was forsaking what I cared for most for the mere chance to save the person I cared for most.

But this was my deal.

I shut my eyes, feeling Snow's cool hands finally closing on my undefended breasts, and shuddered. His thumbs touched my nipples to harden them.

"C-c-cold," I stuttered, an explanation for my apparent arousal.

"You'll be warm soon. Very warm." He pulled me closer. "Open your eyes. You wanted to see."

I batted them open. Looking into his eyes no longer made me blink. The pupils had expanded into black bottomless pools, the gemstone facets a mere ring of glitter around them.

Snow desired this. Snow desired me, my surrender.

Remaining still defied every screaming nerve in my body.

I kept my emotions battened down, dead. I made myself into what I thought a zombie was: a mindless, will-less shell that felt nothing, cared nothing, only shuffled dutifully to do others' bidding . . . .

Snow's hands continued to caress my breasts; harshly would have been deliverance, but his gestures were as delicate as a surgeon's. I felt like Lilith on the autopsy table, mock-dead, or dead, what did it matter in the face of a fatal violation of the flesh?

His face bent towards mine. I kept my eyes open, staring straight ahead, dead ahead. I should have known I wouldn't get by with the sudden, deep, passing Brimstone Kiss of the mosh pit.

"Just one kiss," the pale lips moved.

My freedom! My heart's willing slavery.

I shrugged, but his hands never lost their custodial grip. I lifted my chin and, by default my face, my lips.

He pulled me toward him, bent his head to touch his ivory-cold lips to mine. Kiss Death, while you're at it, Delilah. Embrace a statue, snuggle up to stainless steel, become a body on an autopsy table, motionless, unfeeling, a sex object for the lifeless at heart.

His lips met mine, then his tongue.

It was unexpectedly, shockingly warm. Hot. Feverish. His fingertips on my naked shoulders almost sizzled.

As I'd feared, his kiss was not the hit-and-run lip lock he doled out from the stage, which he'd end like a revivalist minister with a palm to the forehead that pushed the recipient down and away to be borne away on a litter of mosh pit bodies.

It was more like a 132-car pileup on a misty mountain road, a series of domino-falling shocks that just kept on coming. It was a dozen, then a hundred, yet his lips never left mine, just nibbled, teased, probed, stroked, sucked. When his tongue took control it moved like a silver snake, fast, sleek and deep into me, into my very heart and soul, which I felt as a molten drop of forgotten memory, silver mercury, at my center, behind my navel, spiraling out to my every extremity.

I hardly felt it when he pressed my bare chest against his and moved his hands to my throat and the nape of my neck, on shoulders and cheeks, all to position me for endless variations on a kiss.

His breath smelled of frost and he tasted of Albino Vampire. Or maybe that was me.

I could feel the overpowering and inevitable response like a slowly building volcanic eruption from deep within the landscape of my soul.

The tremors made my hands shake so much that I curled them into the edges of the white leather that lay open against his pale chest, hairless, scarred by silver lightning bolts.

My knees were shaking, but his hands were holding me up by the face alone. And still he continued the slow, sensual exploration of my mouth, and now my throat felt the irresistible pull . . . my throat aching as if it was between my legs, tightening, tautening, so much so that a hoarse moan sought escape.

In a moment all my muscles inward and outward would erupt in spasms of orgasmic abandon.

I would be lost and the deal sealed.

Except . . . I remained clenched on the brink and did not plunge over.

Did not climax, not in triplicate. Not once.

I screamed anyway and swooned like a damn Snowaholic, then fell into black velvet darkness illuminated by heat lighting strikes and the thunder beat of my overstressed heart. It felt like red-hot death.

Chapter Thirty-one

IBECAME CONSCIOUS again still pressed to him hip to hip, mouth to mouth, my bare back draped over the upholding bar of his forearm.

Snow suddenly broke the kiss, a curse under his exhausted breath.

I couldn't stand on my own power and my lips remained parted from the Brimstone Kiss.

He cursed again, so softly I couldn't hear the word or what god or devil he invoked.

That arm moved, lifting me tighter against his chest, part bare lukewarm skin, part cool bleached leather. His hands molded me to him, circling on my back, in the tendrils of my hair at my neck. I knew the lassitude that possessed me. I'd met it with Ric. Postcoital stupor. But this had been only a kiss. Hadn't it?

He took advantage. He shifted again until my lax lips became a bezel for his erect nipple. I gritted my teeth. Not reciprocal. Never reciprocal.

But I was so sleepy. So very sated . . .

And by now, my body was mindlessly stimulated.

I finally stirred, my arms struggling to push him away. His chest rumbled against me, under me. His heartbeat was steady, strong, and rhythmic. Heartbeat. Proof he was not a vampire, although some post-Millennium Revelation vamps could be a different breed abiding by different characteristics and rules.

I shut my eyes. He pressed my head against him, his hand tangled in my hair.

The distant part of my mind I'd deadened for this dreaded moment noted that I was still sleepwalking like a zombie succubus, or some recently killed creature whose nerves and muscles still twitched with counterfeit life.

He seemed somehow uncontrolled as well. He loosened his grip.

I shook my head until I seemed to hear something rattle inside and reared away, pulling my gown shut, pulling my mind and will together.

I'd suffered the Brimstone Kiss. For ages longer than the most frantic mosh-pit groupie.

And I had not climaxed, not even once, and especially not many times.

Good! For once it wasn't Irma talking in my head, only me. Loud and clear. *Go suck yourself, Snow! I'm done! It's over. I fulfilled my part of the bargain and I bet you didn't even get off yourself. Too bad.*

Ordinarily, my invisible inner friend Irma would be this spitting mad on my behalf, but I'd exiled her far inside. Not even she could witness my voluntary degradation. No one would know of this but Snow and myself, and that was two too many.

I had only hollow threats to offer, but the words came from my soft center, spit out hard. A mirrored threat. From me to him. I was good with mirrors.

"Someday *you'll* beg to kiss *me*. Someday everything you value will be at risk."

"And what will you do, then, Delilah?" he asked.

"Something you won't like. And I'll use you as coldly as you used me."

I was drawing myself up in indignation, trying to banish a sickening wave of inner disgust at what my outer self had done, when I noticed that Snow was standing dazed himself.

The sunglasses were in his hand and he was putting them over eyes that were all glittering magenta facets again.

"I'm sorry, Delilah," he said.

Could I believe this? What nerve!

"I'd hoped you'd be the one woman in the world who's impervious to the Brimstone Kiss. I'd really hoped it was you."

My righteous anger revived me, and my temper.

"It was me, right here and now. And I'm here to testify that this rotten deal did not result in giving me one orgasm, stud. Not one. Zero, Mr. Multiple Answer to a Woman's Prayer. I did not come from your infamous Brimstone Kiss. You are a dud."

He actually smiled. "Your spirit is remarkably resilient. A good thing. We have a man to free from a nexus of vampires. Would you rather do it naked? Without the services of your familiar?"

The word "naked" scorched me; the word "familiar" also, but I now knew the artifact for shield and weapon.

While I stood there, gathering strength, trying to escape the strange, timeless bubble in which he could wrap himself at will, he held out his arms for me to see.

The forearm-long silver cuffs called to me.

We are yours, they said.

And I realized that I was . . . free . . . of the silver familiar. Free of Snow's unsuspected attachment. Of his lock-of-hair turned trap.

I'm not sure I believed Snow in saying that it answered only to me, but it had even shielded me against its source tonight. It had saved my flesh if not my soul a few times earlier. I was used to its incursions, its presence, and its useful applications as a weapon of defense and aggression.

Yet it was of Snow. I wanted nothing of his to ever touch me again.

But I could use it. Especially now. To save Ric.

So my recent state of mindless sexual thralldom was not the most humiliating moment of my life.

That moment was still forthcoming.

I lifted both arms straight out. Let Snow's pallid fingers that had so recently twined in my hair touch my shoulders.

And the silver familiar came weaving and quivering, warm and liquid and enthralling, over my skin, melding with me, arming me, perhaps disarming me.

SNOW SNAPPED his fingers.

"Grizelle, Miss Street needs clothes more suitable to stalking vampires. I need to change myself. Of course, as usual, we have no time whatsoever."

I turned to eye his security chief who'd appeared from nowhere again. She must have seen me plastered half-naked to her master's body like a temple virgin, to which I was still way too close. I wanted to descend to the ninth circle of his ersatz Dante's Inferno and stay there for eternity.

Grizelle had no time for my sensitivities, but snapped shut her cell phone.

"You will require actual outfitting," she said, finally glancing my way, mightily imposed upon. "Follow me."

I did, finally, understand the phrase "mortified to death."

But this wasn't about me and my pride or even my sanity.

Grizelle led me to a cool, blue-lit room where she pulled black leather catsuits from a row of Ikea-looking white wood and glass cabinets.

"I suppose you want to retreat to human-style privacy," she said, waving me to a room around the corner.

She'd made modesty sound like the refuge of the feeble-minded.

I dashed to the security of some privacy, letting my tarnished, once-loved vintage gown fall into an abused crumple at my feet. My slick thighs reminded me my body had responded if my mind and will hadn't. Then I thought of what Ric might have faced and be facing. That knocked me out of my self-pity party. *He* was my beloved, not some demonic manipulator, and he was worth any price I could pay.

The tight pants zipped up the side and the leather was steel-studded everywhere to foil vampire teeth, but the creatures had supernatural strength that might allow them to tear your head off without a tooth touching you.

To counter that, a ninja-style hood and neck-and-shoulder piece reminded me of what the older nuns at Our Lady of the Lake Convent wore despite modernization, a very medieval wimple, only here the same form was studded black leather instead of starched linen.

Somehow, I suspected that nun-like starched linen might be the better defense.

I cringed there naked while changing, imagining what those good, long-gone nuns would think of me right now . . .

An image of a bare female arm thrusting a sword out of a body of water was so vivid in my mind it almost knocked me over. *Excelsior,* a female voice—not Irma's—said. Not Excalibur. *Excelsior.* Onward. Upward. I guess that meant I couldn't sink any lower than I had earlier tonight. Even Irma was still AWOL. Her usual nervy, naughty advice wouldn't be welcome after an encounter like that.

Okay. Joan of Arc had heard voices too and she didn't let that stop her. In fact, she let that start her.

I pulled on the thigh-high, flat-heeled boots that shielded my femoral arteries. My returned silver familiar assumed the likeness of steel mail for the second time in an hour, forming not a bustier but a protective vest up to my ears and down over my knuckles like the long, fingerless gloves prom-going girls in Loretta Cicereau's day would wear in pastel shades of lace. Nothing could easily breach my elbows and wrists, or the vulnerable neck where both carotid and heart-bound jugular came within almost kissing contact of each other.

There was nothing lacy about my protective armor except its amazingly light weight. I bounded around the corner, regrets shoved far away for pawing over later, thinking only of confronting the literal fiends who assuredly had Ric and who would assuredly do far more vicious things than kiss.

Chapter Thirty-two

I HADN'T COUNTED on Grizelle leading me to an elevator occupied by Snow.

In fact, I came to a dead stop when I saw him.

He was clad in the same studded and hooded black patent-leather wetsuit as Grizelle and me, but without my familiar's protective silver-mesh vest. The familiar wouldn't go undercover tonight. I caught Snow glancing at me and my fury surged.

No. I had to keep cool and think. That's what I had to contribute to this mission: my knowledge of the Egyptian bloodsuckers and their minions, of the chambers I'd seen and those I could only guess at.

I could also speculate about what the Inferno brought to the table. I'd assumed Snow had unsuspected resources and powers. I'd suspected he could or would fight the Karnak bunch, but I'd had no idea how battle-ready he was or why.

Why was the Inferno so well equipped for fighting vampires when so few purportedly survived in Las Vegas? Or was this gear designed for fighting more than vampires?

Snow's angular face looked scarier framed in severe black instead of his flowing white mane. He still wore sunglasses, but the lenses were gray, not black. However he looked or whatever he wore, he was the last monster I wanted to face tonight but the first I'd like to hurt.

"I'll walk," I said, looking for a nearby EXIT sign that would indicate a staircase.

"Not possible." Grizelle grabbed my arm and propelled me into the small, bullet-shaped glass capsule. She placed me firmly on her right and stood between Snow and myself. We all faced forward.

The stainless steel door closed and the elevator shot downward, scenes like a film on fast forward rocketing past the curved glass walls.

Okay, I'm a vintage film nut. This descent reminded me of that hokey thirties' Gene Autry Western-space movie serial, *The Phantom Empire,* where the cave's elevator led to a hidden futuristic world beneath the singing cowboy's Radio Ranch.

"This is a joke, right? Why are we going down?"

Snow answered without looking at me.

"If the Karnak vampires have as many guards as you say, we'll need to mount an expedition. We can't move a force that large along the Las Vegas Strip without attracting notice."

A force? That sounded serious. For an instant my heart lifted. I didn't dare be hopeful. Ric could be dead by now.

We whisked past areas as vast and dully dark scarlet as the planet Mars and as crowded as some World's Fair of the fey and unhuman. I glimpsed mutant beasts and humans, monsters and vistas of fire and ice. The levels pulsed in turn with such colors as lusty red, poison green, gold, the rust of shed blood.

"The Seven Deadly Sins," I whispered.

"Consider this a theme park under construction," Snow said. "The plans are secret, so I expect you to honor that."

A theme park of Dante's Inferno, of Hell itself!

No one can say this Snow dude isn't cookin' on all four burners, Irma put in.

I didn't answer her, but she made not one more risqué remark about my recent indiscretion.

The elevator whooshed to a sudden but smooth stop and its doors slid open.

All around us ancient stone pilings formed wide arches. This was the foundation of the many stories of vast modern theme hotel above us. It looked like an old sewer system; I heard water lapping at stone even through the hood. I touched my ear and felt a metal mesh that amplified hearing. High-tech accessories in a low-tech environment.

So this was the cistern of Hell.

It stank.

Not of sulfur and brimstone . . . hated word! . . . but of damp mossy stone and still, oily, fetid water. *Under* Las Vegas?

"Call it my subterranean river Styx," Snow said, answering my unspoken question. Had the damned Brimstone Kiss made him able to read my mind?

He and Grizelle began striding alongside the dark, broad water.

I followed, scenting an odd tinge of brimstone in the damp air underground. Maybe it was just the reek of my conscience.

We walked for what I guessed were three Las Vegas Strip blocks. I figured we were at the back of the Inferno layout.

The area opened up into an underground plain of stones and arches. Through one of the arches rows of huge freight elevators were disgorging men and women wearing the same metal-imbedded wetsuits we did, except they were less shiny, and had Inferno security force badges on the shoulders. They were pulling trolleys loaded with racks of weapons, everything from machine guns to shotguns to swords and axes to flame-throwers.

Behind them came another cadre of wet-suited people.

I froze when one of the new men walked up to me, a sword belt hung over one shoulder and a nasty-looking machine pistol on a bandolier over the other, squinting to fix my face in his focus.

"Sansouci." Only the green eyes gave him away. In the fury of a fight, we'd know our own by the uniform only. And it would be a furious fight, given the weaponry.

I eyed Snow's back. He'd believed me, at least, about the numbers and killing instincts of the Karnak crew.

"You're here because—?" I asked Sansouci.

"Christophe convinced Cicereau the Karnak vampires posed a clear and present danger to us all. I'm guessing that you're behind this."

"Why?"

"Ever since you hit town, things have been going to Hell." He looked around with a raised eyebrow. "My orders are to protect our forces first and kill vampires second, but I'll watch your back."

"Why?"

"I like the looks of it."

"You haven't seen it."

"I go on instinct."

"Christophe didn't tell you the Karnak vampires are holding Ric and he knows stuff they're almost dying to find out?"

"Shit. No. I'm sorry. Christophe's people didn't mention that. Cicereau wouldn't give a fang about an ex-FBI man."

"And you?"

"I told you. I like you and your back, sight unseen. If he's your main man and if vampires want him that bad, I'll watch his back if we find him too."

I raised an eyebrow. Maybe Sansouci could be an ally, after all. "You help save Ric and I'll"—I really couldn't offer him anything he'd want—"try to return the favor some day."

He nodded briskly. "Fair enough."

"You don't mind going after your . . . kind?"

"These creatures aren't my 'kind', vampire or not." Sansouci frowned at me. "I've never seen even you so pale, baby pale. How'd you get Christophe to go to war?"

"My silver Irish tongue?" My knee-jerk, defensive quip had come too close to the truth. And Sansouci was no fool. I could feel my cheeks flaming as if I suddenly stood over a campfire.

"Huh. You paid his price, whatever it was, didn't you?"

"So did Cicereau, evidently."

Checkmate.

We turned to watch the Inferno forces and Cicereau's muscle men sling weapons over and torsos and every limbs. The echoes of the din were almost deafening.

Sansouci grinned. "Super-fine equipment. Never did cotton to mummies. The werewolves are only in human form right now, but they're fierce fighters even so, and needed some exercise." He eyed me again. "We going to run into those devil-dogs again?"

"Hyenas with eternal, supernatural strength."

"Good." Sansouci hefted his bandoliers tighter over his wide shoulders. "Thanks for the mission."

I stood alone. I felt as edged as a weapon, ready to turn my shame and fury against whoever opposed us. When Grizelle strode over, weapon-hung and holding a sword belt for me, I tightened with dislike.

"I'm your partner. I've got the flame-thrower, you've got the sword. Slash and burn is our game. Vamps are super-fast and super-powerful. No mercy is the only way to deal with them. You ready?"

I nodded. I was ultra-ready to show no mercy to someone. "What about . . . your boss?"

"What about him?"

"Who's his partner if you're with me?"

"Like you'd worry?" Her white smile showed the teeth of the tiger. She nodded to the dark river's edge.

I saw a tongue of stone pier thrusting out into the dark water where the river had widened into a lake as far as was visible in this dim underworld. A lone black figure stood at the end of the pier, one dead-white, ungauntleted hand throwing a veil of what appeared to be gray powder into the water.

He spoke, intoned, words that echoed off the stones.

"In the names of the murderers and the maidens and time immemorial, I command your ashes to congeal. I command you, La Gargouille, to rise."

Shivers coursed under my leather wetsuit as I remembered Caressa Teagarden's tales of her ancestor, the gargoyle carver of Nôtre Dame. This was not a mere gargoyle that Snow was summoning. This was the dragon of the Seine itself, supposedly burned to ashes by a holy cardinal.

Who was Snow that he could cast ashes on the water to rise as serpentine flesh and scale? What was he? Devil or angel . . . or something even more or less, using powers holy or hellish?

But that was then, the legend of the water dragon, in Medieval France, and this was now in Middle-evil Earth, and it was becoming reality.

The dark river water boiled like a vast pot of oil. Then a huge, pale-scaled form came rising, dripping gouts black as old blood, folding its webbed wings against its massive curved sides.

Only one head crowned its long, serpent-supple neck, but it bowed to Snow who leaped upon it. Up he rose to the cavern apex on that thorny, massive brow.

"This is a rescue mission, a raid," Snow's rock-concert voice boomed off the rock walls and water. "We will stop all opposition forces encountered with whatever means suits their breed and any mortal and immortal allies they may have.

"My mount's fiery breath will sear our foes dead, until they number few enough to get past. At that point we'll be hand-to-hand. Grizelle and I will lead, along with Sansouci of the Cicereau syndicate. Each fighter must be on the alert for a mortal prisoner, a Latino man of great value to the vampires—and a prize for our party. He'll be hidden and well-guarded."

The dragon began stalking, its huge body as hidden as the bulk of an iceberg, down the shallow river, towing an armada of empty shallow-bottomed barges. Its cave-entrance-size nostrils snorted mists of steam.

The armed forces shouted in triumph at the size and power of their leading edge, and waded to the thigh-tops into the fearsome dark shallows to scramble aboard the barges.

"Where are they going?" I asked Grizelle

She picked me up like a doll.

"Where we are. Along the doom-driven river Styx to the sacred river of the Egyptian dead and the temple of Karnak. I'm here on orders that you don't get your feet wet in Hell or in the river of blood that will soon flow under the Karnak."

Chapter Thirty-three

THE DOZEN or so barges were shaped like long-necked Viking craft with dragon figureheads.

Gliding along without the aid of oars in the deeper middle of the river, they were as silent in motion as ghost ships.

Armed warriors lined their sides. One thought of shields when envisioning Vikings, but these fighters wore their shields. I would bet the steel-studded wetsuits were fashioned of some impervious blend of materials that made them as supple as second skins and tougher than crocodile hide, chain mail or Kevlar.

The dragon's rear was a dinosaur-size mountain blocking everything ahead, a beaten metal wall of gorgeous scales. Every so often its submerged tail would twitch out of the oily water, splashing the fighters and making their Viking ships wallow wildly.

No wonder this uniform I wore was based on a modern wetsuit. Inside my own impervious body armor, I felt empty and anxious.

I couldn't believe I'd set this awesome force in motion.

I couldn't believe Snow as a dragon-rider, despite his stage shtick, much less as a dragon-raiser.

Some entrepreneur had imported the historical London Bridge to the Arizona desert as a tourist attraction back in the last century, making it a bridge over untroubled sand. The dragon, La Gargouille, though, had been called up from its own ashes. Why was Snow the custodian of such a legendary creature and how could he raise the dead beast?

I shuddered inside my taut leather and steel second skin, wishing I could have worn it for the Brimstone Kiss. Wishing I could slough my real skin like a snake and disown my Brimstone Kiss moments.

Yet, perhaps some events were foreordained.

If I hadn't unknowingly followed Caressa to Las Vegas and finally fulfilled the canceled Kansas interview, I'd never have known about the dragon. According to the legend, a saint had interred the creature's ashes. Was one required to raise it?

That would make Snow a good guy and my crawling skin wasn't about to concede that. The Devil, maybe, had called the monster home after its death in the mortal world and held it in waiting in this New Hell on earth of post-Millennium Revelation Las Vegas.

Snow's true nature didn't matter now, though, only that my conclusions were right: Kephron and Kepherati, the twisted soul sister and brother, held Ric captive and he needed to be rescued as soon as possible. If he was still alive to save.

The silver familiar had quit pretending to be subtle, changing into a scale-armored metal serpent as thick around as a cane. It sped over my body taking the positions of a scout. Once it wrapped itself around my forehead and assumed the position of the Egyptian Uraeus. It seemed to be straining to see ahead.

Grizelle, still in human form, hissed at it like a big cat. "I don't like snakes. Where did *you* get that bizarre familiar?"

"Why?"

"It creeps me out."

I was almost tempted to tell her the talisman was the spawn of her own master's long white albino locks, but resisted.

Lanky Grizelle looked pretty serpentine herself in the form-fitting black wetsuit with the hood almost matching the rich ebony color of her face. None of her white dreadlocks showed, but they bulked out the back of her skull. The effect reminded me a bit too much of the head of that classic bitch-monster, the creature from the *Alien* film franchise. She turned that formidable head to glare at me. The serpent swiftly slipped down to coil around my neck and hiss at her.

It had never made a sound before. I stiffened with alarm as much as Grizelle did.

"Does it bite?" she asked.

"I don't know. If it does, it would be better if the bite was venomous. The Egyptians have cobras to command."

"Do they swim?"

"Not that I know of."

Grizelle grinned at the dark oily water pooling around the sides of our craft, which were not wood, but scales, I noticed. Dragon hide?

She tapped one side with a cat-long claw. "Man-made. Metal."

"Did you read my mind just now?"

"No. What would I find there?" Her smile was sharper than her tiger claws. "Some human stew of unpleasant emotions, no doubt. My master is adept at drawing those out."

"Why?"

"His business. As this expedition is not." Disapproval dripped from her tone.

"I'm paying for it."

"Paid," she corrected me. Her green eyes studied mine. "I can't say I understand these human bargains. Unhuman bargains are sealed with blood, not a kiss."

"Then Snow isn't unhuman," I pounced.

"It was *your* bargain, not his." She was just as quick on the draw as I was at implications. "I don't understand why he'd mount such an aggressive underground force on your say-so."

"Ric—" I began.

"Why should anyone care about him besides you?"

She'd shocked me into silence. At Our Lady of the Lake, we were taught that every human soul was precious.

So was every life. Yet, what would still count in these post-Millennium Revelation days?

"Maybe what I want is more important than you think," I told her, lifting my head, and the silver serpent rising to strike in tandem.

She shrugged metal-glinted broad shoulders. What would happen to her wetsuit when she shifted to her white tiger form, I wondered? Her use of the suit implied her human form was vulnerable and so was the tiger, I guessed.

Vulnerable to injury, I reminded myself, not necessarily vulnerable to feeling.

We spoke no more, because the scenery was changing.

The rock walls were lightening to sandstone color and the water, reflecting them, looked muddy brown instead of deepest green-black.

Our river-borne war party was floating into the River Nile and Egypt land beneath the Las Vegas Strip.

THE HUSH that fell over the company as we floated past larger-than-life-size friezes of ancient Egyptian scenes made me release a relieved breath. The extent of the Karnak's hidden empire was living up to my advance warnings.

Heaving flames from wall-mounted torches along the route made the figures almost seem more real than painted, which made the armed invaders jumpy. I heard the creak of leather bandoliers, the scrape of metal being shifted, the click of firearms being taken off safety settings.

And La Gargouille began unfolding and flexing its huge leathery wings, adding to the thunderous echoes.

After a while, it occurred to me that not all the sounds of forthcoming battle might be coming from our forces.

Somehow Snow slewed the dragon's great head around. "Down!" he shouted in voice that reverberated as if electronically amplified. We all bent our knees and heads, just as the dragon released a fire-hose force of flames that raked the walls on both sides.

The exquisite art melted like crayons, but so did armed and armored Egyptian warriors. Unfortunately, more leaped into life from behind them on the walls.

La Gargouille slowly swung its huge haunches left and then right, driving the ships into the landings on either side so the riders could scramble onto the stones and engage the Egyptians hand-to-hand, spear-to-sword. The swords didn't stop them, and the spraying bullets just jolted the brown bodies pouring out from the walls like fire ants.

The dragon's hot breath was too broad to use with our own forces thick in the fray. It paused as Snow slid down the rough terrain of its scales to stand and fight.

Now the "little dragons" some fighters carried came into play, flame-throwers that fried the ancient figures like insects in a campfire.

The sizzling crackling sound was icky, but I saw a werewolf's hood being ripped away by one set of dark hands even as another drove a spear though the opening. Both Egyptians sank their fangs into either side of his neck as he fell, gulping a swallow of life's blood even as it surged away, and turning to head for me.

I'd jumped to the stones with the rest of my ship's riders. I took the sword Grizelle had given me two-handed and swung it horizontally from one man's broad shoulders to the other's.

Vampires they were, but also the result of unknown ancient Egyptian funerary rites. My blow was as strong as desperation could make it. I wielded my sword like a scythe and reaped two bloody-mouthed heads on the stones at my booted feet.

I don't know whether I was more horrified at destroying what might be ancient historical artifacts or finding it so easy to decapitate vampires.

It didn't matter. Other bodies were pressing against me, pushing me forward, running toward me.

It seemed unfair that our enemies were half-naked and we were swathed from head to toe in modern defensive measures, but seeing some wetsuited figures lying still on the stones with limbs and heads lying nearby in puddles of bright blood cured me of any second thoughts.

So I hacked and charged with the crude weapon I'd been given, my cheeks burning from the nearness of the flame-throwers.

And Ric.

How would we even find Ric in the mass slaughter?

I slipped on a pool of blood and went down, my whole body thudding with the impact. A helmeted Egyptian warrior was near enough for me to see the triumph on his face, in his kohl-lined eyes.

I struggled to get my long blade pointed up and braced to spear him as he dove down to slit my face downward with an axe.

A huge gray shadow slipped between him and me, and brought him down with his throat gushing blood as if a vampire chainsaw had been at him.

"Quicksilver!"

My dog was gone in a flash of fur, werewolf fast and strong, growling and snarling like the pack at Starlight Lodge, chasing his own pack: a trio of the powerful-jawed hyenas. The blood and fur that flew as he overtook the last one convinced me that only death would banish these creatures on their own ground.

I struggled upright just in time to slice off a mummy's wrapped arm. It felt like attacking the halt and the lame. These creatures were dry and sere, as easy to maim as the morning paper. Yet they kept coming, diverting us from the more dangerous vampire warriors.

In time, I only heard the ring of steel on steel, the thud of steel on flesh and bone, I only saw the contrails of blood catching the torchlight as they lashed the stone walls with a fresh wet embroidery of spatter.

The din, the heat, the motion . . . it was impossible to tell who was friend or foe, but I sensed Grizelle behind me, her long, lithe reach keeping enemies from reaching me even as I slashed and kicked and screamed my way forward, looking for Ric in this dungeon of chaos.

"Why? How? Quicksilver here?" I managed to shout.

She shrugged and elbowed an advancing mummy, then took it apart like a chicken dinner.

"He was on the boss's list."

Snow had somehow brought Quicksilver into this slaughter? As if it didn't matter if I lost my beloved dog too?

My weary sword arm lifted to cut down a pair of warriors, whose fallen forms erupted instantly in sizzling flames from the Inferno fighter bearing a flame-thrower behind me.

These creatures are not alive, I reminded myself again and again. These are undead predators and their zombic flunkies, no more than movie extras. These deaths aren't real, because the victims aren't alive.

But we are.

But maybe Ric still is.

Chapter Thirty-four

B Y NOW EVERYTHING was happening in slow motion and my senses finally understood that the battle was winding down.

Apparently, as many Egyptian soldier vampires had been decapitated as possible, as many zombie mummies had been minced to papery remnants. Who could tell?

Whether Snow stood, or any of his allies beyond Grizelle I didn't know. Or care.

Where was Ric?

We'd fought our way into the absolute deepest, darkest depths of the Egyptian tomb maze beyond the river, the master vampire lair. I'd seen not a glimpse of Kephron and Kepherati, too noble to join the fight, probably.

And no Ric. And no Ric? Was he dead and buried already?

No. That made no sense. They'd want him in one form or the other, alive or dead. Perhaps they might use him better dead. Newly undead to raise the dead. Were we too late?

No!

But we were up against the far wall of the current dungeon.

I couldn't beat my way forward past a stone wall.

I stopped, straightened and lowered my sword point.

The dragon's roars were distant. There didn't seem to be anyone left to skewer, slash, burn, or make doubly dead.

Behind me, Grizelle growled softly. Hearing a woman growl like a tiger is unnerving. I knew she'd shifted to tiger form earlier, but back to woman as the battle waned.

I knew she'd protected me on Snow's orders, and resented and begrudged Snow for that, but not for Ric's sake. He'd need me now as he never had before.

I felt Grizelle's heavy hand on my shoulder. She didn't much like me. Snow was her boss, her reason for being. He was too involved with me for her liking. But no six-inch-long tiger claws bit into my flesh, only inch-long supermodel fingernails.

And then I looked harder at the last wall.

Fallen bodies of all kinds mortal and immortal lay around us like effluvia coating a flooded floor.

Grizelle hissed behind me, an eerily human/feline sound. I heard Snow approach us. "Grizelle," he said without expression, sounding winded and weary. Snow weary? "What is it?"

There was silence. I felt I stood alone on an island.

And then the scene before my eyes took rational shape after the irrational jumble of battle when limbs flew and heads rolled and bizarre appendages twisted and broke off.

I viewed a mass of pale and dark shifting motion, of refuse and vermin devouring refuse. I saw a Dumpster from Hell disgorging its contents, leaving a swatch on the stone floor, and remembered the dead groupie behind the Inferno.

I took in iron cuffs bolted two feet from the floor. Empty.

I saw the verminous, devouring, shifting black blanket of bugs and the cloud of buzzing darting insects massing above them.

I discerned the barely visible oases of human flesh.

I roared like the tiger Grizelle was. The silver familiar melted from a breastplate into a thick chain in my hand that I wielded like a whip at the fist-size hovering insects.

They had bug-eyed evil faces with hypodermic-long stingers for nose and mouth. My whirling chain caught them in the pixie-size bodies and hurled them against the stone wall. They left fat trails of blood as their bloated forms disintegrated into cinders. Again and again they hit, smack, spilling blood.

Ric's blood.

Ric's lifeblood.

The roaring in my ears was stupefying, but vampire tsetse fly after vampire tsetse fly hit the wall. I hauled back until my arm would hardly lift again, until my bloody chain wrapped around an object behind me so solid it almost jerked me off my feet.

I looked behind, snarling like Grizelle. I saw Snow's black-leather forearm covered in a bloody spiral of metal. For a confused moment I thought the silver familiar had jumped over to him again.

Out of the corner of my eye I saw Grizelle bend and spray a shower of white over the festering floor.

I lunged to stop her, but Snow took my neck in one hand. "It's the salt they kept here, for the leeches. Let her use it."

Leeches?

I watched. And saw. Ric's naked lower body was alive with shiny black slugs, massed over his genitals, twining his legs, his arms, while his bare upper body was a smallpox field of the vampire bugs still biting.

Salt crystals fell like snow on this horrific human landscape of torture and literal eating alive.

Grizelle's human face was cast-iron with fury, her teeth bared to reveal the tiger's formidable fangs. She'd been frozen in mid-shift, unable to release either side of her nature in the face of this travesty. The beast part would run ravening to tear apart the perpetrators, the human part had to undo the obscenity as much as possible.

I felt the same conflict. Kill and rend and revenge. Save and succor and mourn.

The leeches were falling aside, Ric's naked human form revealing the horror of every inch invaded and bloodied.

I released the chain, feeling it lighten and armor my wrist, and fell forward, upon him. His face was sagged to the right, revealing the site of the vampire bat bite of his long-distant Mexican desert boyhood. My imitating that moment had become an exciting but natural part of our sex play. With my nil experience, it seemed harmless.

Now the place was a gaping, ragged wound where vampire after vampire had suckled. A mortal wound. A day of this and I hadn't known.

I Could. Not. Accept. This.

I Would. Not. Accept. This.

I Would . . .

The Kiss of Life. The instructive film from WTCH-TV. Two kisses of life, breathing into the mouth and throat and lungs, nostrils pinched shut, then deep pressure on the breastbone in rhythm. Two more kisses of life, deep pressure on the breastbone.

"Delilah, he's dead," came Snow's voice as if over a public address system, thin and echoing. "There are options," he said, "not ideal, but—"

I let his voice drift away. The body was cool, not cold. The blood was probably almost all drained. His skin was as white as mine where it wasn't pocked purple and red from the assault of thousands of bites over hours and hours.

Ric dead? No! Vampires *are dead in this town.*

Panting, I resumed my CPR rhythm.

Two kisses of life, ten fist pounds of life.

I'll eradicate every bloodsucker in Las Vegas.

Two kisses of life, ten fist pounds of life.

"Delilah, this is mad."

If Snow was one, he was history, despite his help today.

Two kisses of life, ten fist pounds of life.

Hands on my upper arms, one set of them tiger-clawed, trying to pry me from my task.

I shrugged them off with no trouble.

Two kisses of life, ten fist-pounds of life.

Sansouci too.

Two kisses of life, ten fist-pounds of life.

And Cicereau. Anything supernatural, even Lilith, if she qualifies, goddamn her for tempting me here to meet Ric and lose him like this . . .

I was sobbing through my fury, tears salting my face and Ric's wounds despite myself. I was so wrenched by surfeits of love and hate I thought I would explode like a blood-bloated vampire tsetse fly.

And still two kisses of life, ten fist pounds of life.

Nothing. I was tenderizing steak, breathing into the face of death itself.

My attempts to reanimate Ric were a travesty to his already ravaged body. I was finally exhausted enough that I couldn't press his breastbone with any force or do more than sigh into his cold, slack mouth.

I stopped, sensing everything still alive in that death chamber watching me with held breaths.

I put my hands to the side of his face and bent down one last time.

And I kissed him goodbye, with all my heart and breath and loss.

Long, a long time to kiss the dead goodbye. My tears washed his bitten skin.

No one stopped me. No one dared intervene.

Until I felt hands grasp my upper arms again.

Again, I fought being torn from his body, weaker now.

But the hands held me down.

His hands.

And the kiss took on a life of its own, probed and poured back into me my love and my despair and my last remnants of hope and desire.

And between my legs I felt the rise of blood between his legs.

I lost myself in lying with my lover, everything else forgotten.

And no one tried to stop us anymore.

————————

FINALLY, other hands grasped my arms and lifted me upright.

Love had weakened me where hate had not.

"He needs tending other than yours," Snow said, nodding at Grizelle.

She pulled free the blanket-sized linen cloth out from under the piled salt used to remove the leeches and wrapped it around Ric before lifting him in her powerful arms. Ric's eyes were shut. His skin was whiter than mine, but his lips were the faintest pink. Some tinge of blood, color, was returning to his skin.

All my muscles and bones were water. Snow held me upright only by my arms.

"Delilah, what have you done?"

"I don't know. Will he live?"

"I don't know. He'll exist." I could feel Snow sigh behind me. "He'd been bitten often enough and drained deeply enough to be revived as a vampire. If you'd waited—"

"Ric would never have accepted the half-life of vampire."

"And what half-life does he have now? Do you know, Delilah?"

"Why do you sound so accusing? I only did all I could to save him, more than anyone else was willing to do."

"What did you do, Delilah?"

"I gave him the Kiss of Life."

Snow slowly released me. I swayed on my feet but stabilized, and turned to face him. It was hard to forget how much I'd hated him moments before.

He nodded slowly. I sensed a heavy load on his what . . . soul, conscience?

"It's our deep connection," I told him, "our love. There was some small spark of life still there. I got through. Are you so lost you can't believe in the power of love even when you see it with your own eyes?"

He shook his head. "He was dead, Delilah. There are ways to get around that. Now, it's going to be your way and I don't know what that is, only that you could never have revived him unless you had first received the Brimstone Kiss."

"You're taking *credit* for this?"

"No. Responsibility. You've defied even supernatural laws, not to mention natural ones. This can't be good. For any of us."

"Say you. But it's not all about you and your fiendish kiss. It's about life."

I was rocked back on whatever strength I had left. I had recently taken the Brimstone Kiss and, within hours, revived Ric with what was left of it on my lips and in my soul. What I had humiliated myself to take from Snow, I had passed on to Ric and revived him.

Had I not submitted in desperation and self-disgust to Snow, I would have never been able to give Ric what I undoubtedly had.

The Resurrection Kiss.

Odd how a traitorous act, a Judas kiss, can spawn an act of love and redemption.

But I guess that was the whole point of the New Testament.

Chapter Thirty-five

TRUST SNOW's eternal, twisted sense of irony to give Ric and me the Inferno's bridal suite.

Of course, we needed the lavish extra bedrooms not for the reception celebration, but for the around-the-clock nurses.

Ric was still on blood transfusions. Not mine. Having infused breath into him, I was ready to contribute blood, but my type wasn't compatible, they said.

In fact, they said I should never be a blood donor. This was bitter news, now and for the future. They said my blood had an unknown trace element that might be lethal to others. Could have been from a childhood illness. So, if the vamp boys in the group homes had succeeded in biting me, would they have gotten a case of whatever my unorthodox anonymous blood could pass on? And what about Undead Ted, the vampire newscaster whose blood had poisoned my dog, Achilles? He'd sucked down a drop of my tainted blood. Had he paid a price?

Someone had notified Hector Nightwine that Quicksilver and I were necessary guests for now. A messenger had brought over Quicksilver's dishes and food and my laptop. There was a suitcase of comfortable clothes that even matched. I suspected Godfrey's fine CinSim hand had supervised the Enchanted Cottage staff for this task and felt strangely comforted by this care package from "home."

Quicksilver stayed by my side, by Ric's imported hospital bed. He'd lay his long nose on the hospital blanket near the foot for hours, and whine occasionally. He sensed my weariness, my despair at Ric's ordeal.

Those pale blue eyes would turn my way, a sickle of white along each pupil like a waning moon, under a worry-wrinkled sky of silver fur. Dog-loyal. Keeping watch with me.

I knew his problem. The constant coming-and-going of medical personnel kept Quick from using his healing lick therapy.

I was determined to spare Ric more scars to remind him of being helpless and tormented. When the nurses took a break or changed shifts, I pulled back the covers to let Quick swipe a lick or two over Ric's arms.

The myriad puffy red sores from the vampire tsetse fly bites were scabbing over, so this hit-and-run licking kept the nurses murmuring satisfaction that Ric "was healing nicely," without alerting them to the outside help.

The doctor had been relieved that Ric didn't test positive for being "infected" by "sleeping sickness" from the fly bites, unaware that these vampire tsetse flies didn't carry any parasites to infect his system.

Ric murmured awareness when Quicksilver braced his huge paws on the mattress edge to lave his face with warm, wet swipes. Quick's big tongue made an ideal canine washcloth.

Finally, one quiet hour when we were alone, I pulled the sheets down to Ric's hips and the usual green hospital gown up to his neck. Quicksilver immediately braced his paws on the mattress again to thoroughly lave the almost solid carapace of scabs forming on Ric's abdomen.

The leech marks on his groin and legs had already faded. I was relieved. I doubt Ric would have appreciated a crotch bath from Quicksilver, conscious or not.

Ric's neck was another matter and no job for Quick. The gauze bandage awkwardly taped to the spot leached Rorschach blots of blood and required changing hourly. The nurses wouldn't let me touch the dressing, nor Ric, who was drugged into a twilight state.

I watched each clean bandage slowly darken with leaking blood and studied the resulting blot like Caressa

Teagarden reading tea leaves. Once the image reminded me of the African continent. Once it looked like the profile of John Barrymore, no, Johnny Depp. Another time like a teapot. Another like a starfish. Then the wad of gauze would be changed and a fresh canvas was taped to his neck without my glimpsing the wound beneath.

Seeing it once had been enough. I'd eyed a huge, bloody hole, not a mere double-fang gash, but a gouge. I hated to think how many vampires had supped there.

I held my own hands as I leaned forward in the bedside chair after the nurse left, wringing them in an agony of guilt. Had the small sensual ritual of our love affair opened a road to an empire of vampires?

Had I, playing mock-vampire at that easily excited site, somehow extended an invitation to the unhuman? The ancient Egyptian vampires had used that small bruise, used the blood beneath the skin as a highway to Hell, playing on Ric's sleeping innocence, plundering his lifeblood bit by bit as torture, draining him to the brink of death. If I hadn't, if we hadn't, maybe . . . .

"Let him sleep and your conscience as well. You both need a long rest."

For a moment I thought it was Irma, back from going underground during the battle with the undead. I appreciated the lack of distraction.

No such luck. I turned to see Grizelle looming behind me in her imposing human form.

"What are you doing here?"

"I've returned from taking your dog out. He refuses to relieve himself here and spirit cannot conquer body forever."

I'd been so hypnotized watching Ric that I'd never noticed any comings and goings except as remote irritations.

"He is a valiant warrior," she went on matter-of-factly, "but even great warriors must piss."

"A valiant warrior?" I wasn't surprised because I'd seen Quicksilver at the attack, but I was amazed the great Grizelle would bestow any praise on me and mine.

"For a canine," she added with a wave of her ebony hand. The long lacquered fingernails for an instant seemed to lengthen into actual, awesome claws.

I glanced at Quick, worried. He was giving Grizelle that mischievous canine grin that said he reveled in her grudging respect.

I was so worried about everyone and every thing I loved now, maybe because I loved only two—and one lay like a sleeping prince in a forest of metal stands and snaking plastic tubing.

"I carried him naked from that dungeon," Grizelle continued a low whisper.

"I know. Thank you," I whispered back with that same sickroom intensity.

"I don't need your thanks. You need to understand what I know."

"What you know?"

"His wounds, except for the throat tear, were superficial, but his back is a maze of whip welt scars."

I tensed to realize that what Ric had fought to keep secret from me was casual knowledge to this bizarre unhuman shapeshifter and Snow flunky.

"I know, but he can't know that."

"Those are old, outer scars," she went on, "but they still sear his mind. He now has new, inner scars, and they have seared his soul. You have only revived him to feel them fully."

"So he should be dead, unfeeling, or undead, with no soul to feel anything instead?"

"You've no idea what you've done, have you?"

"I saved him, I hope, maybe at the cost of my own soul. I don't know yet what that demonic Brimstone Kiss did to me, and I don't care. I'll deal."

"I meant, what you've done to my master."

I embraced myself to contain a shiver. I didn't know which scared me more: this intimidating goddess of a woman-cat calling Snow her "master," or her hints and allegations about the state of Ric's and my mere human souls.

"What *I've* done to *him!* Your 'master' has forced me to taint everything I hold most dear just to slake his own ego."

Grizelle was silent for a long while. When she spoke, it was closer to a growl than a whisper.

"If you're strong enough to wrest this man back from the Land of the Wandering Dead, you're strong enough to undo the damage you've done. If you live long enough yourself."

I guess she meant that as a pep talk.

I HAD PLENTY of time to think, sitting there beside Ric's hospital-style bed. My discovery of the hidden vampire empire at the Karnak and its interest in raising truly "ancient" vamps would shake the city to its supernatural foundations.

Cesar Cicereau and his werewolf mob were the biggest losers. They'd won the werewolf-vampire war for the city decades ago, but a powerful vampire strain had been building secretly and subterraneously all along. The Karnak was far more than a new hotel-casino on the Strip. It was a visible announcement that the vamps were back, big-time: not assimilated vamps, or pseudo vamp wannabes, or even newly evolved "daylight" vamps like Sansouci. These were ruthless, Old World, blood-thirsty, power-hungry vamps with ambition and access to new Millennium Revelation methods of blended science and magic to raise more of their kind.

By sending Sansouci and support forces to Snow, Cicereau admitted the times were changing. I could see a lot of new alliances, and contentions, arising between everyone from Snow and Cicereau to Hector Nightwine and the CinSims to Howard Hughes and everyone else.

And Snow? If I could get my head around our personal wrangle, I'd admit he'd probably been the most up-and-coming force in pre-Karnak Vegas. In some ways he struck me as a kind of guardian, but one whose hands were tied. He hadn't played Brimstone Kiss with me as simply a sexual game, which was some comfort. It was a "job interview" of sorts. He was searching for a woman unsusceptible to the orgasmic kiss. I, with my virginal and murky non-sexual background, must have seemed a darned good candidate for resisting the Kiss. Which I had, but not enough to suit him, and not enough to avoid passing it on as a life-restoring force.

Lucky for Ric you agreed to the smooch, Irma said softly in the back of my mind, *but we didn't totally resist the ecstasy, sister. My toes are still curling.*

Shut up, I told her. I'm thinking.

As soon as Ric is recovered, I had a lot of things to do, like settle what's happening with the CinSims, who violated their set boundaries to help me. And I must find Lilith. Is she a Snow kissee who failed the test too? They knew each other before I hit town. Does she know about me? Or care?

And now Snow thinks I've perverted the Kiss to a function it should never have had. Can I kiss just anyone back from the dead? Kinda doubt it. The emotional mojo I poured into Ric was love and desperation-driven. It came from the connection we formed inadvertently dowsing for the dead together in Sunset Park. Is Snow right? I have I doomed Ric to become some quasi-alive zombie monster?

No, honey. Irma broke into my thoughts again. *Even the mighty Snow can't know that for sure. How do you think he got all that long white hair? Dude's obviously a worrywart.*

She made me laugh at last. Why borrow trouble? Ric and I would cope with whatever this second chance at life and love offered.

"Tomorrow," I told myself firmly in the immortal words of Scarlett O'Hara, "is another day."

"HE WON'T BE fully conscious for another day or two," said someone behind me what may have been minutes or hours later.

I felt my shoulders tighten even more at the sound of Snow's vibrant stage-seasoned voice.

"We won't know what you've made of him until then," he added.

I lashed myself around in the bedside chair. "And what about what *you*'ve made of me?"

Snow wore a black velour jogging suit. He'd had the forethought not to appear in the costume that would forever remind me of my humiliation.

"You're not dead," he pointed out.

"And he is? They take his blood pressure every hour. It's low, but steady."

"There are many ways to be dead and undead these Millennium Revelation days, Delilah. You may have invented a new one."

"What? Me? Only me? It was your supposedly potent Brimstone Kiss I may have passed on. Maybe that was all you, and nothing to do with me."

"And you'd like to think 'love' revived him? That's why you're so angry with me?"

"That's as likely as a proxy kiss from . . . whatever you are. Besides, I thought you didn't do men."

A small smile touched those pale lips. "You don't know who or what I do. I just came up to see if you needed anything."

"Less of you. If it didn't make sense to treat Ric here, I'd have him out of the Inferno in no time."

"This suite has been donated to him, not for your sake. I only came to warn you that you'll need to be prepared. We have no idea what's come back in Ricardo Montoya's body. Not even Grizelle."

"I do. Ric Montoya. He'll need time to mend, and more time to come to terms with that vicious torture, but I can tell you he never cracked. He never conceded anything, not his services in raising the dead, not a clue to how he did it. Nothing. *Nada*."

Snow moved forward to put a hand on Quicksilver's head. The dog growled softly but never took his eyes off Ric, with rapid sideways glances to myself. If I gave the word, he'd tear Snow's hand off.

It was his guitar slashing right hand, too. I was tempted. I deserved something back for my useless exercise in self-humiliation.

"This one probably knows better than we do what he'll be like," Snow said, not moving his hand. "But he can't speak."

Quick gave a short, sharp bark. Snow removed his right hand and lifted his left.

A small blindingly iridescent object was in it. A computer flash drive. He handed it to me. A peace offering? As if ever!

"You might want to stop publicly insisting on tracking down the killer of my groupie after you see that."

"Why?"

"Just look at the recording, Delilah."

"It's the hotel security record of the night of the murder?" I guessed, curious at last. "From the Dumpster area where the body was left? You kept it secret?"

"It's my hotel, my Dumpster, my security recording, my groupie. I didn't think the police needed to see it."

"You are so bad." I took the thumb drive, eagerly. This could exonerate me.

By the time I'd opened up and turned on my laptop computer on a nearby table, Snow had left as silently as he'd come. He wasn't nicknamed Snow for nothing. For soft and silent snow.

It took me a couple minutes to move my mind from Ric to tasks like operating a computer, but I finally clicked the drive into the proper port.

The first image spotlighted the empty delivery area and the Dumpster. I fast-forwarded until I spotted a person in the

frame. Two persons. I recognized my groupie, even in the dim
black and white light of night. She was facing the security
camera and mauling someone whose back was to me.

The groupie was pleading, grabbing, begging. Her
hands were reaching for the other person's neck, almost
as if to tear off the face, pull out the hair.

I got the shivers, remembering her clinging assault
inside the Inferno after Snow had left me that evening.
That crazy woman was like glue, invading my space. I
saw the object of her obsession lift an arm and bat her
away. The elbow caught the groupie in the forehead.

She fell hard and crashed the back of her head into a
metal dolly leaning against the Dumpster side.

The other person turned to leave, face caught by the
camera.

Myself, reaching up to pin my disheveled hair back
into a French twist.

I stood up.

Lilith!

Then she really wasn't dead!

But we are, honey, Irma said, emerging again. *At least
legally.*

And how! Lilith was a murderer?

*That babe's gotta be taken for you, unless you can
find and produce Lilith to clear yourself. You'd turn her
over to Homicide to face the gas chamber after going to
all that trouble to find her? No way.*

I slapped my palms hard on the desktop, until they
stung, trying to feel something. Snow had admitted he
kept a lot of things from me. Now I knew he kept them
from the police as well.

Something about the recording bothered me, but I was
too exhausted to name it.

Was this a bone thrown to a woman who'd failed the
Brimstone Kiss test and had almost lost her lover? Or
something to hold over her head? Because, surely, he had
kept the original.

I glanced to the bed and Ric, my sleeping prince.

The doctor had assured me the coma would lift soon. "He's young, vigorous. It's best he 'sleep' while he's recovering from nearly total exsanguination."

Perhaps a kiss—my newly empowered kiss—would awaken him. First, I needed to mentally purify my lips and mind and emotions.

I went over, knelt, put my hand on his cool, pale one.

I felt a chill circling my ankle. I hadn't even noticed where the silver familiar had ebbed during all the tumult. It now slithered softly up my leg and then my side and finally down my arm to become a simple braided-chain bracelet on my wrist.

Ric always loved me wearing silver.

Quicksilver, whimpering, laid the soft furred length of his muzzle on my hand.

I leaned, leaned, leaned slowly inward, until I could kiss Ric's cool, pale cheek. The dark lashes fluttered on his skin, then lifted slightly like a curtain of black snow.

"Del." The word was a croak, but even with his eyes closed he knew me, knew I was there.

The joy was overwhelming.

His face turned at last toward mine, eyelids struggling open.

How I thirsted for the glimpse of recognition and recovery in those dark Spanish eyes that I loved . . .

And I got it, my heart thumping with triumph . . .

Except . . .

I slowly realized that one dark iris had turned bright reflective silver, like a mirror.

Actors, Roles, Films and TV Series

Adventures of Sherlock Holmes, The (1939)
http://www.hollywoodgothique.com/adventuresofsherlock.html

Adventures of Sherlock Holmes, The (TV Series)
http://en.wikipedia.org/wiki/The_Adventures_of_Sherlock_Holmes_(TV_series)

Asta
(see *The Thin Man*)

Mary Astor
http://www.tcm.com/thismonth/article/?cid=161347

Gene Autry
http://www.geneautry.com/home.php

John Barrymore
http://findarticles.com/p/articles/mi_g1epc/is_bio/ai_2419200076

Ingrid Bergman
http://www.ingridbergman.com/

Blue Fairy, The
http://disney.wikia.com/wiki/The_Blue_Fairy

Rick Blaine
(see *Casablanca*, Humphrey Bogart)

Humphrey Bogart
http://www.humphreybogart.com/

James Bond (as portrayed by Sean Connery)
http://www.007.info/Sean_Connery.asp

Betty Boop
http://www.brightlightsfilm.com/16/betty.html

Borg
http://memory-alpha.org/en/wiki/Borg

Jeremy Brett
http://www.brettish.com/

Billie Burke (as Glinda)
http://www.kansasoz.com/infogoodwitch.htm

Actors, Roles, Films and TV Series (Continued)

Joel Cairo
(see *Casablanca*, Peter Lorre)

Casablanca (1944)
http://www.vincasa.com

Nick and Nora Charles
(see *The Thin Man*, William Powell, Myrna Loy)

Cigarette-smoking Man
http://www.bbc.co.uk/cult/xfiles/personnel/csm.shtml

Cecil B. DeMille
http://www.cecilbdemille.com/bio.html

Johnny Depp
http://www.johnnydepp.com/

Norma Desmond (played by Gloria Swanson)
http://www.youtube.com/watch?v=-RjyozCNNPo
(see also, *Sunset Boulevard*)

Dracula
http://en.wikipedia.org/wiki/Dracula

Dracula (1931)
http://www.bmoviecentral.com/bmc/reviews/34-duanes-reviews/64-dracula-1931-75-minutes.html

Enchanted Cottage, The (1945)
http://movies.nytimes.com/movie/15781/The-Enchanted-Cottage/overview

Fantasy Island (TV Series)
http://www.tv.com/fantasy-island/show/679/summary.html

Film montage of female Hollywood star faces
http://gibbscadiz.blogspot.com/2007/07/they-had-faces-then.html

Fiesta (1947)
http://www.youtube.com/watch?v=opi78lWMz94
http://www.youtube.com/watch?v=ykivlKJQHWE

Errol Flynn
http://www.errolflynn.net/

Clark Gable
http://www.clarkgable.com/

Dorothy Gale (played by Judy Garland)
http://oz.wikia.com/wiki/Dorothy_Gale

Godzilla (1954)
http://godzilla.monstrous.com/index.htm

Cary Grant
http://www.carygrant.net/

(Dr.) Jack Griffin
(see *The Invisible Man*, Claude Rains)

Jean Harlow
http://www.jeanharlow.com/

Hawaii Five-O (TV Series)
http://www.mjq.net/fiveo/

Katharine Hepburn
http://katehepburn.tripod.com/

Sherlock Holmes
http://www.sherlockian.net/

Howard Hughes
http://www.1st100.com/part3/hughes.html

Invisible Man, The (1933)
http://www.geocities.com/Hollywood/Hills/4337/invman.htm

Khan
(see Ricardo Montalbán, *Star Trek II: Wrath of Khan*)

Boris Karloff
http://www.allmovie.com/cg/avg.dll?p=avg&sql=B36942

Frank Langella
http://en.wikipedia.org/wiki/Frank_Langella

Ilsa and Victor Lazlo (played by Paul Henreid)
(see Casblanca entry, Ingrid Bergman)

Janet Leigh
http://www.imdb.com/name/nm0001463/bio

Vivien Leigh
http://www.vivien-leigh.com/

Lollipop League
(see *The Wizard of Oz* entry)

Lord of the Rings, The
http://en.wikipedia.org/wiki/The_Lord_of_the_Rings

Peter Lorre
http://www.reelclassics.com/Actors/Lorre/lorre.htm

Myrna Loy
http://en.wikipedia.org/wiki/Myrna_Loy

Bela Lugosi
http://www.belalugosi.com/lugosihomepage.html

Dorothy McGuire
http://www.imdb.com/name/nm0570192/

Patrick McGoohan
http://www.the-prisoner-6.freeserve.co.uk/pmg_info.htm

Maltese Falcon, The (1941)
http://www.filmsite.org/malt.html

Perry Mason (played by Raymond Burr)
http://www.perrymasontvshowbook.com

Meet Me in St. Louis (1944)
http://www.filmsite.org/meetm.html

Mogambo (1935)
http://en.wikipedia.org/wiki/Mogambo

Ricardo Montalbán
http://www.nndb.com/people/748/000022682/

Mothra
http://godzilla.monstrous.com/mothra.htm

Fox Muldar (played by David Duchovny)
http://x-files.redbrick.dcu.ie/Fox.html

My Man Godfrey (1936)
http://www.filmsite.org/myman.html

Neptune's Daughter (1949)
http://www.youtube.com/watch?v=nRqIb1Nj1

Nosferatu (1922)
http://video.google.com/videoplay?docid=-6185283610506001721

Notorious (1946)
http://www.filmsite.org/noto.html

Scarlett O'Hara (played by Vivien Leigh)
http://en.wikipedia.org/wiki/Scarlett_O'Hara

Bridget O'Shaughnessy
(see *The Maltese Falcon*, Mary Astor)

Phantom Empire, The (1935)
http://www.archiveclassicmovies.com/watch.html (scroll down)

Pinocchio
http://en.wikipedia.org/wiki/Pinocchio_(1940_film)

William Powell
http://themave.com/Powell/

Prisoner, The (TV Series)
http://theprisoneronline.com/

Psycho (1960)
http://en.wikipedia.org/wiki/Psycho_(1960_film)

Pulp Fiction (1994)
http://www.imdb.com/title/tt0110912/

Claude Rains
http://www.meredy.com/clauderains/

Basil Rathbone
http://www.basilrathbone.net/biography/

(Captain) Louis Renault
(see *Casablanca*, Claude Rains)

Rin Tin Tin
http://www.rintintin.com/

(Mr.) Roarke
(see *Fantasy Island* and Ricardo Montalbán)

Jane Russell
http://www.lovegoddess.info/Jane.htm

Scarecrow
http://en.wikipedia.org/wiki/Scarecrow_%28Oz%29

Snow White
http://en.wikipedia.org/wiki/Snow_White

Snow White and the Seven Dwarfs (1937)
http://disney.go.com/vault/archives/movies/snow/snow.html

Sam Spade
(see *The Maltese Falcon*, Humphrey Bogart)

Jack Sparrow
http://jacksparrow.moonfruit.com/

(Mr.) Spock
http://en.wikipedia.org/wiki/Spock

Star Trek
http://www.startrek.com/startrek/view/index.html

Star Trek II: Wrath of Khan (1982)
http://www.youtube.com/watch?v=UJTi7KJPx_E

Star Wars
http://en.wikipedia.org/wiki/Star_Wars

Sharon Stone
http://www.sharonstone.net

Della Street (played by Barbara Hale)
http://www.perrymasontvshowbook.com/pmb_c400.htm

Streetcar Named Desire, A (1951)
http://www.filmsite.org/stre.html

Sunset Boulevard (1950)
http://www.greatestfilms.org/suns.html

Thin Man, The (1934)
http://themave.com/Powell/powloy/films/thman/ThinMan.htm

Tin Man
http://en.wikipedia.org/wiki/Tin_Woodman

Actors, Roles, Films and TV Series (Continued)

Ugarte
(see *Casablanca*, Peter Lorre)

Rudolph Valentino
http://www.rudolph-valentino.com/

Wicked Witch of the West
http://oz.wikia.com/wiki/Wicked_Witch_of_the_West

Esther Williams
http://www.lovegoddess.info/Esther.htm

Wizard of Oz, The (1939)
http://www.imdb.com/title/tt0032138/

X-Files, The (TV Series)
http://www.scifi.com/xfiles/

Robert Young
http://www.classicmovies.org/articles/aa072698.htm

Zorro
http://en.wikipedia.org/wiki/Zorro

Selected Web Sites on Ancient Egypt

American Journal of Neuroradiology: "The Skull and Cervical
Spine Radiographs of Tutankhamen: A Critical Appraisal." Richard
S. Boyer, Ernst A. Rodin, Todd C. Grey and R. C. Connolly
> http://www.ajnr.org/cgi/content/full/24/6/1142

Tour Egypt! (various articles)
> http://www.touregypt.net (various articles)

GuardianUK: "Press Release: Ct Scan/8 March, 2005"
> http://www.guardians.net/hawass/press_release_tutankhamun_
ct_scan_results.htm

The British Museum: Ancient Egypt
> http://www.ancientegypt.co.uk/

The Griffith Institute: "Tutankhamun: Anatomy of an
Excavation: The Howard Carter Archives, Photographs by
Harry Burton (Anubis emblem upon pole and stand)
> http://www.griffith.ox.ac.uk/gri/carter/202-p0673.html

Delilah's Darkside Inferno Bar Cocktail Menu

Albino Vampire Cocktail
Invented in *Dancing with Werewolves*

"A sweet, seductive girly drink, but with unsuspected kick."
>   —werewolf mob enforcer Sansouci, in *Brimstone Kiss*

1 jigger of white Crème de Cocoa
1 ½ jigger of vanilla Stolichnaya
1 jigger of Lady Godiva white chocolate liqueur
½ jigger Chambord raspberry liqueur
[Other brands may be substituted]

Pour vodka and liqueurs in a martini glass in this order: Crème de Cocoa, vanilla vodka, and finally the white chocolate liqueur. Stir gently. Drizzle in the raspberry liqueur. Don't mix or stir. The raspberry liqueur will slowly sink to the bottom, so the white cocktail has a blood-red base (which adds a nice taste sensation at the end).

Brimstone Kiss Cocktail
Invented in *Brimstone Kiss*

"Sounds like something you'd sip on all night long and I'd knock back in couple slugs."
>   – Rick Blaine/Humphrey Bogart CinSim in *Brimstone Kiss*

2 jiggers Inferno Pepper Pot vodka
1 jigger DeKuyper "Hot Damn!" Hot Cinnamon Schnapps,
2 jiggers Alizé Red Passion
jalapeño pepper slice (optional)
2 ounces Champagne (for second version)

Version 1: Pour all ingredients into a martini shaker with ice. Shake gently. Pour into a martini glass garnished with jalapeño pepper slice. A hell of a drink!

Version 2: Pour all ingredients into a tall footed glass filled with ice. Stir well. Top off with two ounces of your favorite Champagne. A perfect frothy but potent brunch libation that might lead to pleasant damnation.

Special Sneak Peak from Juno Books!

An Excerpt from
Personal Demons by *Stacia Kane*
mass market paperback · ISBN: 9780809572557 · $6.99
from Juno Books

"Is she sleeping?"

Smack. "Whad'ya think? *Is she sleeping,* 'e says. Don't she look like she's sleeping?"

"Yeh."

"That is a sleeping woman, if ever I saw a sleeping woman," the second voice continued.

Megan opened her eyes.

The three men standing next to her bed jumped back, their expressions ranging from terror to curiosity.

"She's awake!" said the one closest to her. She recognized his voice as the second speaker, the one with the strongest cockney accent.

"You just said she was sleepin', Lif," said the next one. He was the tallest, with a large nose and scarred, gin-blossomed skin.

They were all big, broad men with small eyes and stubbled chins. They were all dressed in hitman casual: black trousers, black turtlenecks, black rubber-soled shoes, black windbreakers, black knit caps. Gold rings and watches completed the look.

Megan caught only a glimpse of these things before she seized the lamp on her bedside table and held it over her head. The cord refused to come out of the wall. She yanked at it with her left hand, aware not only that she looked silly, but that the men in her room had ample time to attack her while she sorted out her weapon. Their restraint from doing so provided her some comfort, but her heart still pounded in her chest.

"Who are you?" she demanded. Her voice squeaked.

Stacia Kane

The men glanced at each other, chagrined. The tall one spoke. "M'lady, didn't—"

"Good morning, gentlemen." Greyson Dante entered the room, clad in a black suit with creases so sharp Megan imagined he could cut himself on them if he wasn't careful. He was freshly showered and shaved, and smelled like vanilla and smoke. "Good morning, Megan. Just barely. Doing a little redecorating?"

Megan glanced at the lamp in her hand, glared at him, then looked at the clock. It was 11:30. "Shit!" She set the lamp on the edge of the table and pushed the covers back, ready to leap out of bed.

"Sit down," Greyson said, holding out his hand. "I called Brian already to make sure you didn't have to be up for a while yet. The shoot's not until two."

"Who exactly are these men and what are they doing in my bedroom?"

"Ah." Greyson looked at the three, who stood a little straighter under his gaze. "Megan Chase, may I present your bodyguards: Malleus, Maleficarum, and Spud."

"My what?"

"Your bodyguards. The one on the left is Malleus, the tall one is Maleficarum, and that one is Spud. I've assigned them to you."

Megan glanced at the three men, still standing against the wall like they were in a police line-up. She got out of bed and grabbed Dante's arm. "I need to talk to you."

"Excuse us," Greyson said, as she led him out into the living room and closed the bedroom door.

"Who are they? What the hell do you mean, scaring me like that? How do you think I felt waking up with strange men in my room after last night?"

"I told you who they are. They're your bodyguards. You need someone with you at all times, and I can't do it." He leaned in a little closer. "They wouldn't have been in there watching you sleep if you'd let me stay, you know. Care to change your mind for the future?"

"No." Megan was suddenly aware that she only wore a T-shirt. He'd seen her in her bra last night, but somehow that was different. She grabbed the blanket from last night off the couch and wrapped it around her. It wasn't great, but it was better. "Look, Greyson, don't think I don't appreciate your help. I do. And I—I'd like it if you'd keep helping me, because I don't want to die. But those men . . . I can't have those men follow me around. They look like they're going to kill someone."

"Only if that someone tries to get in their way," Greyson said. "Or yours. Besides, they're not men. They're demons."

"Of course. I should have known."

"Yes, you should have. Painkillers getting to you? Come with me." Without waiting for an answer, he handed her a cup of coffee, then led her through the French doors to the patio. Her little black cast-iron table and chair set beckoned, the blue and white mosaic tile tabletop looking as peaceful and cheerful as ever. The patio was her favorite place.

The sun had warmed the seats and warmed her skin, too, as she sat down. She sighed, relaxing, but then she caught sight of the shed. Everything came back, the rotting faces, the smell, the screams . . . she set down her mug and pulled the blanket more tightly around her shoulders.

Dante was silent for a minute. "I thought you might be more comfortable out here. Would you rather go back in?"

"No. No, I'm all right." The coffee was hot and strong, almost burning her tongue, but she forced herself to drink deeply. The cobwebs in her head didn't want to go away, and she needed to be on her toes. Which still hurt.

"You're in a lot of pain?"

"No more than I expected." She lied, it was a lot more. On waking she'd thought it wasn't too bad, but as she moved around she realized how badly her muscles hurt, how tender her skin felt.

"I might be able to help you with that."

"Sensual massage?" The minute the words were out of her mouth she regretted them. She'd meant it as a joke, but it sounded like an invitation. The forced laugh made it even worse.

Dante didn't reply, but he stood up and came closer to her. She raised her hand. "I was kidding about the massage, okay? Bad joke, I know, but—"

"Hush." He stood behind her, close enough for her to feel the warmth of his body, but not touching. She sensed his hands in the air over her head. He started speaking, muttering something under his breath.

Energy flowed down through Megan's head into her body, rich and thick, soothing her aching shoulders and arms, relaxing the muscles of her back. She tried to lean away, but he pulled her back, holding her in place while his power washed over her. Her fingers tingled and flexed involuntarily as the energy kept pouring down, until every part of her body felt alight.

It only lasted for a couple of minutes at the most, but when he was done Megan felt better than she had in days. She raised her arms experimentally. No pain. "How did you do that?"

"Fire demons learn healing skills pretty early." He cleared his throat. "Is that better?"

"Yes."

"Good." He sat back down and picked up his mug with trembling hands. Catching her look, he said, "Sometimes it takes a bit out of me. I'll be fine. We have more important things to worry about."

Damn, she'd been feeling so much better too. A cool breeze swept across the patio, sending the first fallen leaves of the season skittering over the concrete. "I don't even want to think about it."

"Too bad. You have to think about it, Megan, or you—"

"Look," she said through gritted teeth, "I get it. I'll die. Will you stop saying it? You make me feel like you're looking forward to it."

He shrugged.

"Thanks. Thanks a lot."

"What am I supposed to say? No, I'm not? I think that should be obvious. I wouldn't be here giving you three of the best bodyguards my family—or rather, my company— has, if I wanted you to die." He slammed his coffee cup back down on the table. "Hell, Megan, I could have killed you myself quite a few times by now if that was what I wanted to do. This isn't a horror film. I'm not waiting for the planets to align or for you to sign your soul over to me. I'm helping you purely out of the goodness of my heart."

He looked sincere, but Megan didn't believe it for a second. He definitely wanted something. She just didn't know what.

At the moment it seemed he wanted an apology, so she gave him one. "Sorry."

He nodded. "As for the brothers, I think if you give them a chance you might like them."

"Do I have a choice?"

"No."

"Are they armed?"

"No. They don't need to be."

"But you do."

He shrugged. "I'm not a guard demon. They are."

For a minute Megan considered telling him to fuck off and leave her alone. To take his demon bodyguards and go, then run away herself. It was a sweet minute, full of promise.

But she couldn't deny the reality of the night before. She didn't want to trust him, but she didn't see she had a choice. If he was offering to help her in order to put her in danger later, there wasn't much she could do about it. If he was behind everything that had happened, he wasn't going to stop just because she told him she didn't trust him. This was her life, and she was going to keep it.

He took her silence as assent. "Good," he said. "I have to go."

"Wait a minute. You need to tell me the rest of what's going on. You never told me who the personal demons are, or what their plan is, or what your plan is, or anything I need to know."

"All you need to know right now is to stay with the boys. They'll keep you safe. Oh, and I've ordered them not to touch you or bother you. If they do, let me know."

"You had to tell them not to—"

"We'll talk more later."

He left without saying goodbye.

THE "BOYS" WERE still standing exactly where she'd left them.

"Ah, hi guys," she said. "How are you?" It was kind of a stupid thing to say, but what was she supposed to say? What did one say to one's demon bodyguards?

The tall one—Maleficarum?—bowed, scooping off his hat to reveal two small but unmistakable horns on his head. So some of them did have horns. "At your service, m'lady," he said. "I 'ope my brothers and I will please you."

The other two followed suit. Six tiny horns pointed to the ceiling from three shiny bald heads.

"Thank you." She didn't know whether to laugh or cry. "I appreciate you being here."

"No need to thank us, m'lady," Malleus said. "Mr. Dante told us we was needed, and here we are. Ready to guard you. With our lives, you know."

"Yeh," said Spud.

"Well, that's fine. But I wonder if you could go wait in the living room, please, while I shower and change?"

"Sorry," said Malleus. "But Mr. Dante said we was to guard you. Every minute, 'e said. So we can't let you out of our sight."

"I'm sure he didn't mean when I'm—" she didn't want to say "naked" in front of them, so she substituted "—undressed. I wouldn't feel comfortable with that. I'm sure you understand."

"Mr. Dante said every minute, and that's what we're gonna do."

"I don't think he wanted us to watch the lady when she's all undressed," Maleficarum said. "She don't want you starin' at her naked."

"'e said every minute, Lif." Malleus folded his arms across his beefy chest. "You wanna be the one wot tells him we didn't do what he said? You wanna tell 'im we let her get done over or somefing? 'Cos I don't. He'll 'ave our heads, he will."

"I think he'll be angrier if 'e finds out we been lookin' at her naked," Maleficarum said. "I think she's 'is."

That was enough for Megan. "I am not 'his'," she said, drawing herself up to her full five feet two inches, "and you are not watching me shower. You may inspect the bathroom before I enter it. That is all."

Maleficarum narrowed his eyes. "And you'll tell Mr. Dante you made us take our eyes off you?"

Megan nodded. "Yes."

Malleus turned to Maleficarum and whispered something in his ear. Maleficarum turned back to Megan. "Could you put that in writin', m'lady?"

She glared at him.

Malleus looked down. "C'mon, guys. Let's check the bog."

The three of them trooped off into her bathroom, presumably to look inside the toilet and down the drains. Megan had to admit, the three demons seemed dedicated to their jobs.

And to Greyson Dante. Who exactly was he?

They emerged while she was still thinking. "Sound as a pound," Malleus said, giving her what he obviously hoped was a reassuring smile. In his squat face it looked more like a leer. "You go ahead. We'll wait 'ere."

She sighed. "Fine."